T0162632

In Her Heart

A Romance Novel by

S. Marie

Order this book online at www.trafford.com
or email orders@trafford.com

Most Trafford titles are also available at major online book retailers.

© Copyright 2012 S. Marie.
All rights reserved. No part of this publication may be reproduced, stored in a retrieval
system, or transmitted, in any form or by any means, electronic, mechanical, photocopying,
recording, or otherwise, without the written prior permission of the author.

Printed in the United States of America.

ISBN: 978-1-4669-6146-3 (sc)
ISBN: 978-1-4669-6145-6 (hc)
ISBN: 978-1-4669-6144-9 (e)

Library of Congress Control Number: 2012918272

Trafford rev. 10/02/2012

 www.trafford.com

North America & international
toll-free: 1 888 232 4444 (USA & Canada)
phone: 250 383 6864 ♦ fax: 812 355 4082

In Her Heart

Chapter One

{Eighteen months ago}

She couldn't breathe. As the edges of the blackness she'd been lost in engulfed her again, strong hands reached for her. When her vision cleared, a man clutched her hand while people in white looked on in disbelief.

Had she been drinking tar?

With tremendous effort, she spoke. "My mouth tastes awful. May I please have some water?"

One of the nurses bustled over to pour water into a cup.

The doctor regained his senses. "Ms. Endy, how do you feel?"

Another nurse checked vitals. Nurse Katie moved the cup with a straw to Elsie's mouth.

After sipping, Elsie answered the doctor. "Like a wrung-out dishrag."

They laughed—all, except for the man grasping her hand as if his life depended upon it.

Her thoughts whirled. *Am I dead and gone to heaven?*

She stared into the unmistakably rugged face of Rusty Garnet— international movie star.

The doctor directed his words to the same man. "Mr. Garnet, please leave while we complete an exam."

It really is Rusty Garnet! The thought jumped up and down in her head while she watched his departing form.

The doctor's voice broke through. "Excuse me. I said I'm Dr. Gallagher. What is your name?"

"Elsie Endy," she replied.

This question was followed by other similar questions she answered easily. However, one caused consternation.

"Do you know what day it is?" Dr. Gallagher asked.

She had no idea. "I don't know."

"Let's try for year and month," the doctor suggested.

Without thinking, Elsie answered, "April 2002."

Dr. Gallagher swiftly shifted his gaze to the clipboard as he wrote.

Then he spoke softly. "Do you remember the accident that brought you here?"

"No, but from the way my body aches, I'd guess a car accident," she surmised.

"Actually, you were thrown from a horse. A nasty blow to the head has had you in a coma for several days." His tone was even as he explained.

"On a horse? I don't know how to ride." Elsie's lack of understanding was evident.

The doctor continued clarifying compassionately. "Mr. Garnet said you learned while in Montana last summer."

She was adamant. "I haven't been to Montana. I moved back to the East Coast last summer."

Dr. Gallagher glanced at the matronly nurse who had fetched a fresh gown and warm washcloth. The nurse remained silent. Instead, she went about her intended task by wiping blood and phlegm from her patient's face.

"It's not unusual in patients with head injuries for memory loss to occur. This can be temporary. We'll take another CT scan in the morning to see if there's anything we can do." The doctor took another approach.

"And you're telling me this because?" Elsie questioned pointedly.

Unable to discern a way other than saying it directly, Dr. Gallagher stated, "It's September of 2011."

Elsie looked at the nurse in hopes it was a joke.

"I'm sorry, dearie. Give yourself time to heal and all of those years could return in an instant." The nurse patted her hand.

Confused thoughts spun in Elsie's head. The doctor exited.

"Let's change your gown. Then I'll get that hunky man of yours," her soothing voice remarked suggestively.

It couldn't be true. "Mine? I don't know him other than from movies."

"Tomorrow I'll bring in pictures, which might jog your memory." The motherly woman completed tying the clean gown.

She walked to where Rusty stood in the doorway. They spoke a few quiet words before she left them alone in the room. The famous actor walked toward Elsie. She smiled at him. When he got to the side of the bed, she could see his eyes welling. Suddenly, he sank to his knees, burrowing his head in her chest. She ran her fingers gently through his hair. The wet from his tears soaked through the front of the hospital gown.

After a little while, she queried, "Rusty?"

As he lifted his head to look into her face, an affectionate smile formed. "No worries, mate. You're back from walkabout."

{Present}

Elsie couldn't push the memory of those warm hazel eyes to the recesses of her mind, with them watching her from across the room. Her escort, Sean McEwan, noticed too. His bright green eyes made contact with hers.

"Love, when is the last time you talked to him?" Sean asked, placing his hand on hers.

"During filming," she responded.

Sean gave her a knowing look. "He sent the tea and biscuit basket from Pastry Perfect to our suite."

"I'm sorry, Sean." She fidgeted with the cufflink on his sleeve.

"It's okay, m'love." He lifted her hand to his lips. "If I were in his knickers, I'd be the same way."

The lights dimmed to indicate it was time for the award ceremony to commence. During the first break, Rich and his wife Janie finally arrived at the table.

"Sorry for being late. Small emergency at home," Rich offered.

Elsie asked Janie, "Everyone all right?"

Janie smiled easily. "Yes."

Sean caught them up to what they had missed. Till the waiter had fetched their drinks, it was time for the next presentation. During breaks the other couple mingled. Sean remained within earshot as he chatted with nearby associates. Midway through the ceremonies, Janie motioned for Elsie to join her for a trip to the ladies' room. Thankfully, they had it all to themselves.

Standing in front of the mirror, checking their makeup, Elsie asked hesitantly, "When you and Rich went to visit with Rusty, I noticed him look in my direction while you were chatting. Anything I should know?"

"He's worried about you. And I can't really blame him." Janie pursed her lips with concern. "You've gotten terribly thin—too thin."

Elsie's hand shook as she put her lipstick into her purse.

Janie hurried to apologize. "I'm sorry, Elsie. It's not a criticism. We're all worried about you. When Rich spoke to Sean a few weeks ago, he mentioned that you might not be able to make it tonight but didn't say why."

"It's from the treatments," Elsie explained minimally.

"Are they helping?" Janie asked without prying.

"They're prepping me for surgery." Elsie tried to make light of it.

Her face dropped. "Oh, Elsie, why didn't you tell us things had gotten that bad?"

"Please don't tell anyone, particularly Rusty. I don't want him feeling guilty," Elsie pleaded.

Janie shook her head. "I won't. But if there's anything you need, you know you can call us."

"Thanks. I'm just incredibly grateful for Sean," she stated.

"Yes, he is definitely head over heels for you." Janie smiled to erase the tension.

Upon the ladies return to the table, Rich remarked, "Sean was about to form a search party."

A blush of embarrassment brightened Elsie's ashen cheeks.

Janie laughed. "You know how we girls lose track of time when we're talking."

Sean leaned close to Elsie. "Anything you need to tell me?"

She admitted to "a bit of a headache."

"I'll have Branson bring the limo to the front." Reaching into the chest pocket of his tuxedo, Sean retrieved his cell phone.

"We need to stay for Best Director and Best Film." She stopped the hand holding the phone.

Bright green eyes searched deep blue ones for a moment prior to Sean placing the cell phone back into his pocket.

Elsie smiled in appreciation. "Thank you."

On impulse, Sean gave her a quick hug. "You know I can't say no to you."

At the end of the evening, no one at their table had walked to the stage to receive an award. To add to this disappointment, Elsie's small headache had evolved into a migraine. Her standing with her hands clutching the table caused Sean's eyebrows to rise questioningly.

Peering at him through her eyelashes, she spoke sheepishly. "You were right. It was too soon."

But it wasn't in his nature to be condescending.

Instead, he spoke to the other couple. "Elsie isn't feeling well. Would you two be willing to cover us on the way out?"

Rich and Janie agreed without hesitation. As usual, Elsie's balance had been affected. Even though she'd had no alcohol, her unsteadiness could be mistaken for imbibing too much. Having experienced similar episodes, Sean held her tight against him as they worked their way outside. Unfortunately, the night air was humid and did little to ease her discomfort. Rusty couldn't have picked a worse time to approach.

Rich tried to dissuade the intrusion. "Ol' pal, why don't you join Janie and me for a drink?"

The actor didn't heed the meaning of the director's words as he pushed his way to the other couple. "Excuse me. I would like to speak to Elsie privately for a moment."

Sean replied with an unusual amount of severity. "Afraid not tonight, mate. Ring us in the morning to arrange a time."

"I'm not your mate!" The Aussie ground through gritted teeth. "If you don't mind, I'd like to talk to my . . ."

Elsie pulled away from Sean to intervene before Rusty started an altercation. In her current state, things spun around as if she were riding a Tilt-A-Whirl. Both men grabbed for her at the same time.

Rusty's disposition worsened. "She needs a doctor!"

The Scotsman kept his tone low. "We've been to many. We just have to ride it out."

"Ride it out?" Rusty hissed. "They were supposed to go away, not get worse!"

Rich and Janie attempted to defuse the situation. But it was too late. The argument had escalated to physical. In their testosterone surge, they forgot Elsie. She crumbled to the pavement.

Janie gasped as she knelt by her. "Oh my god! She's bleeding!"

The men ceased grappling. Sean was instantly at Elsie's side. Even though the Scotsman lacked the Aussie's brawn, he effortlessly swept Elsie's frail frame into his arms.

"Make a path!" he demanded.

Rich and Rusty shielded them from the press as Sean carried her along the carpeted walkway to the waiting limousines. Janie trailed behind to pick up the dropped purse. When Sean reached Branson, he realized there was no way to maneuver into traffic. The look of fear on both men's faces didn't go unnoticed. Rusty whipped out his cell phone to bark orders. Soon a stretch SUV pulled alongside the line of town cars.

"Out here!" He led the way.

Rusty climbed in then reached down to take Elsie. His rugged face swam into darkness above her blood-smeared one as Sean begrudgingly passed her limp form to him.

CHAPTER TWO

FEELING A COOL wet cloth on her face brought Elsie to consciousness. Opening eyes met worried bright green ones, with furrowed hazel ones hovering over his shoulder. Attempting to sit made them spin like multicolored balls on a roulette wheel.

"Stay put!" echoed in stereo.

Not having the energy to move, let alone oppose anything, she remained lying across the seat. A pair of gentle hands lifted her head and shoulders onto a lap. As anticipated, Sean's fingers tenderly played with her curls. His brogue in soft tones soothed her to find a tolerable corner in her mind. In time, burly arms lifted her. Burying her face in a well-muscled chest, she inhaled deeply. As the waves of blackness sucked her under, she focused on that wonderfully familiar male scent.

{Eighteen months ago}

After spending another week in the hospital in Sydney, Rusty had taken Elsie to the family ranch. She felt uncomfortable since she still hadn't remembered knowing him. Matter of fact, she hadn't remembered anything new at all. The doctors insisted the memories were in her mind somewhere. The blow to the head and subsequent blood clots had damaged the neural pathways to where they were stored. It would take time for these to heal and certain triggers to access them. Because of the nature of the injury, she was grounded for at least six weeks. This prevented her from familiar surroundings and people that could aid in her overall recovery.

Rusty had been exceptionally solicitous. She wasn't allowed to be alone. He personally provided for her every need twenty-four hours, seven days a week. It made for some embarrassing moments, especially since dizziness was an ongoing condition. He sat in the bathroom while she showered and didn't leave her side until she was seated on the bed to dress. Understanding her modesty, he'd close his eyes to prevent seeing her naked. However, there was no way to hide her shapely curves from his hands those times he had to save her from falling. Plus, he insisted she sleep in his bed. The lounge chair he moved into the room served him. Some nights when they chatted, he stretched next to her. If he fell asleep on the bed, they would wake in the morning curled together. She began to enjoy those nights.

At the end of seven weeks, Dr. Gallagher approved her for flying, with the insistence they didn't stress her and no physical exertion. Rusty's assistant Sherry made the travel arrangements. Living on the East Coast of the U.S. made for an extremely long trip. To her delight, the layover in Hawaii was three days on Oahu. They took long walks along the beach holding hands. Even though she hadn't remembered anything of their previous relationship, Elsie began to have feelings for Rusty. Sadly, certain emotional healing from things in her past had not yet occurred. Therefore, she lacked the ability to believe in Rusty's feelings for her. She couldn't see beyond the hunky international star that could have any woman he wanted. So why would he want her?

They spent the same amount of time on the stopover in California. Here Elsie had an appointment with a specialist. They took another MRI. These were compared to the previous results, with no significant changes. After the appointment, they dined with Rusty's assistant. It was a bit disconcerting meeting Sherry and her husband Harris.

Sherry made a reference, which was lost on Elsie. "I tried to get you a reservation in the same hotel we all stayed in on Maui. They were completely booked."

While she and Rusty reviewed his schedule, Harris spoke with her on current finances. The numbers he shared shocked her beyond belief. He diligently explained that his job was to protect her financial interests along with providing any contractual counsel required. Upon their return to the hotel room, Rusty sat Elsie in front of a laptop. Reaching over her, he typed her name in the search field. To her shock, the search engine had numerous hits. He selected the site indicated as her main Web page, then stepped away. Instinctually, she grabbed his hand to keep him close.

As she read about the success of her books, she asked with awe, "Is this really me?"

"Aye, mate." He placed a kiss on the top of her head.

"But I didn't . . . I mean, I couldn't have done all of this, could I?" This time she turned to look up at him with eyes wide open.

"Love, you've proven you can do anything you have a passion for." His look was intense.

For a moment, Elsie had the oddest sensation. Her mind began to race. Blurred images sped by uncontrollably. Without warning, everything went black.

When she regained consciousness, Rusty was holding her tight against his chest. "Elsie! God, Elsie, please wake up!"

His scent reminded her of something. But each time she tried to identify it, the blackness lurking at the edges would encroach. Blinking rapidly, she forced it away. He went completely still watching her.

Softly he said, "Elsie?"

"That was weird," she replied as she sat up.

"Maybe you should stay there," he suggested, placing his hands on her upper arms to assist.

The room did a slow spin.

"Maybe you're right," she stated, leaning back again.

Reaching for the extra pillow, he placed it behind her to keep her semiprone. "Do you want me to call the doctor?"

"Don't be silly. It will pass." She brushed it away as inconsequential.

Sitting next to her, he argued, "This wasn't like any of the other dizzy spells."

"It's probably from flying." The last thing she wanted was to put him through a night at the hospital.

Grunting in resignation, he stood to turn off the computer. He returned to the space next to her on the bed. Tugging her to rest on his well-muscled chest, she breathed in that mysteriously familiar scent all night.

The next day they drove to director Rich Taylor's home. He and his wife Janie greeted them with exuberant hugs.

"I know you don't remember us, but we can't help it! We are so happy you are okay!" Janie explained at seeing the overwhelmed look on Elsie's face.

Unable to think of a funny quip, Elsie merely smiled.

"Since you don't remember seeing the house, I'll give you the tour," Janie said, taking her arm in sisterhood.

As they walked through the house, Janie chattered nonstop. In the study, a picture on Rich's desk caused Elsie to pause. Rich had his arm around her, standing at a podium. Both of them held an Oscar. A deafening roar filled her ears. Her legs wobbled. She clutched the edge of the desk. Janie's mouth was moving, but the words made no sense. As if she'd forgotten how to breathe, Elsie inhaled deeply, jolting herself out of the trance.

"Elsie, are you okay?" the homeowner asked with concern.

Taking a couple of normal breaths, Elsie finally replied, "Um, yes, it must be past snack time."

"Why didn't that hu-hunky man of yours say anything?" the hostess said, clearly annoyed with Rusty.

Again, Janie took Elsie's arm, which kept any weaving to a minimum. They went directly to the kitchen. Janie placed stuffed mushrooms and apricots wrapped in bacon on a cooking sheet.

"Those are my favorite!" Elsie said with delight.

The hostess smiled knowingly. "That's why I chose to make them."

Without thinking, Elsie opened the refrigerator to fetch a container of dip. After setting it on the counter, she went to a cupboard where the crackers were kept. It wasn't until after she'd sat down that she realized what she'd done.

Filled with embarrassment, she stated, "I'm so sorry! I can't believe I just did that."

"Apparently, part of that brain of yours is remembering something. Whenever you and Rusty visit, we nibble on dip while I prepare the other food," Janie happily explained. "Then I usually pour us wine. Are you allowed?"

"A glass or two won't hurt anything," Elsie replied.

Rich and Rusty joined the women in the kitchen. When the oven buzzed, they carried everything outside to eat on the patio. They talked and laughed. Unfortunately, none of it triggered Elsie's conscious memory.

On the drive to his condominium, Rusty shared his disappointment. "I can't believe nothing caused even a spark of a memory."

"'Fraid not. But if it matters, I had a wonderful time." Elsie gave him her cheeriest voice.

Putting her palm to his lips, Rusty said in a softer tone, "Of course it matters. I'm glad you enjoyed yourself."

CHAPTER THREE

{Present}

HEARING SEAN'S ACCENT thickened with emotion, Elsie listened intently. "I appreciate your help, but it's time you left. I need to take care of Elsie."

Rusty's tone sounded angry. "I'm not impressed with the job you've been doing."

"Well, that's not up to you!" Sean gave territorial warning. "Elsie is with me. If you know her as well as you think you do, she's where she wants to be."

Silence ensued. Then a door slammed shut.

"Wanker!" Sean muttered.

Elsie opened her eyes to discern what happened. "Sean?"

He leaned in close. "It's just us. I'll get your pills."

This episode was no different than any of the others they'd gone through recently. First, her pills took her numerous attempts to swallow, usually with water dribbling down her chin. Sean would assist her into loose-fitting pajamas. Then he would go around muting everything—telephone, cell phones, doorbell, and television. All lights would be turned off. Finally, he would carefully climb into bed to hold her. Feathery kisses on her forehead intermingled with soft singing. Every time she woke, he'd be right there beside her—just like he'd been from the first time she'd encountered him since the accident.

{A year ago}

Several months after her return to the States, Rich Taylor and Elsie had a meeting to discuss an upcoming project. Because he was trying to finalize his current film, they met in his studio.

"It's good to see you, Elsie!" Rich greeted her at the door with a hug. "Sorry about this. We needed a few voiceovers to get this one done."

"Not like I remember any of our previous meetings to know the difference." she quipped.

On the way to his office, he asked, "Have you heard from Rusty?"

"A couple of weeks ago, he called about a part he was doing. Hopefully, it will keep him out of trouble for the next few months," she answered, uncensored.

"Yeah, he's been on the front page of the tabloids too much recently," he replied with disappointment. "He misses you."

Arriving at his office, she accepted the offered bottle of water before responding. "He needs to see a psychologist, not a bartender. Plus, guilt-fed anxiety isn't going to aid my memory returning."

"It's been six months since the accident. Anything?" he asked, his caring mixed with curiosity.

"Up to when *Sifting through the Ashes* got published," she shared. "At least I remember being an author."

"I have to tell you, I was pleasantly surprised by your suggestions," he stated, tossing his recommendations for the cast onto the edge of the desk.

The compliment made her fidget. "It was a bit weird since in my mind I had only just started writing the book."

"I have to tell you how nervous I was having my own son work on the screenplay," he admitted amidst fatherly pride.

"Harry definitely captured the undercurrent throughout the story." She saw no reason to guard her answers with Rich. "Now it's for you and the cast to make it work. Doesn't Andie graduate this year? Bet she'd love to join you on this one."

He chuckled. "As an independent study project, she's already been helping me with the setup."

"Does that mean she's going to get directorial credit?" Elsie saw a lot of potential in Rich's daughter.

They were interrupted by his presence needed in the sound studio. She tagged along. One of the actors with the microphones in the room was Sean McEwan. She remembered when he'd been one of the prime candidates for James Bond a decade ago. He was also on the top of Rich's list of actors for *Sins of the Fathers*. While she waited for Rich to finish giving direction, she swore Sean kept staring at her. Feeling uncomfortable, she exited the soundproof booth to use the ladies' room. Inspecting herself in the mirror, she didn't find any issues with her appearance. After reapplying her lipstick, she went to rejoin Rich. In the hall, a dizzy spell hit. Firm arms prevented her from smacking into the wall.

"Are you okay?" a Scottish brogue asked softly in her ear.

Before she could answer, fast falling footsteps accompanied Rich's voice of urgency. "Dear God! Carla, call an ambulance."

"No, no. It will pass," Elsie opposed while still leaning against Sean.

Rich eyed her suspiciously. "Care to explain?"

"Flying, and I don't agree anymore." Her tone made it clear it wasn't for debate.

Rich's expression denoted his displeasure.

Facing the man who held onto her, Rich formally introduced them. "Sean, this is Elsie Endy. Elsie, Sean McEwan. Sean, would you please escort Elsie to my office? I should be there shortly."

The world had stopped spinning sufficiently for her to straighten.

As they began walking, she said remorsefully, "Sorry to be such a bother."

He replied cheerfully, "You're not. But it was an interesting way to get you alone."

Figuring he was naturally congenial, she didn't read anything into his flirtatious remark.

In the office, she attempted to dismiss him. "It was nice meeting you, Sean. Thanks for showing that chivalry still exists."

"You're the kind of woman that makes men want to be chivalrous." His flirting continued.

"Have we met before that I'm missing some underlying context to this banter?" Her bluntness had become a necessity with parts of her memory inaccessible.

In the cutest manner, he cocked his head to one side while he searched her face.

After a few moments, he answered in a serious tone. "We've never been formally introduced, but we've been to similar events where we've chatted. And you were absolutely adorable last year when Rich insisted on giving you his Oscar."

She turned red at the obvious compliment. "Thank you."

"Are the stories in the tabloids true that you dumped Rusty because he lost his temper and put you in the hospital?" he queried boldly.

"Are the stories in the tabloids true that your wife divorced you because she caught you in bed with a man?" she parried.

"Touché," he replied with a quirky half-smile.

Not having anything witty to prolong the conversation, she scanned the immediate vicinity for Rich's recommendations.

Sean picked the packet up from the edge of Rich's desk. "Is this what you're looking for?"

"Yes, thank you," she replied politely.

He read the title as he handed it to her. "Rich has been talking about this quite a bit. My daughter Eilish loves your books. Since she was fifteen when they first became popular, Kaitlyn and I read them first."

"And what does her father think?" Elsie responded coyly.

His eyebrows rose at her playfulness. "They start unassuming then pull the reader in with a surprising depth and wit—much like the author."

She didn't know what to say in response to his thoughtful compliment.

To her relief, Rich entered the office. "Are you better?"

Elsie nodded. "Yep."

"Let's finish so you can get some rest before tonight's dinner," he stated, sitting at his desk.

Taking the cue, Sean headed for the door. The two men nodded to each other.

From the doorway, the Scot made eye contact with Elsie. "I'm in town for the rest of the week. Maybe we could have dinner and share the truth behind those stories?"

After the door had closed, she turned toward Rich with an expression of disbelief. "Did I just get asked out?"

He couldn't help being amused by her reaction. "Why do you find that such a surprise?"

"Somebody like him with somebody like me—yeah right!" she stated sarcastically.

"Is that why you sent Rusty packing?" he asked in all seriousness.

She fidgeted uncomfortably with this particular question. "Not the only reason, but you know his reputation. Bad boy goes good for plain-Jane author. Without whatever supposedly transpired between us to prove that wrong, I'd constantly wonder why he was with me."

"You have some deep-seated psychoses, lady," he remarked.

"And yet you still insist putting my stories spun from that psychosis on the big screen." Her flip rejoinder contained a sharp edge.

Rubbing his long hands down his face, he sighed in surrender. "I didn't invite you here to argue. You and Rusty are both dear friends, making this situation difficult at best."

She had to agree. "I don't want this to affect our friendship either. How about we steer clear of topics regarding Rusty?"

"Rusty who?" he said convincingly.

They shared a smile of relief. With tension eased, they got to work and wrapped up by lunch.

The second she stepped through the door of her suite, she kicked off her shoes to wiggle her toes in freedom. She missed home already, but being here had its bonuses. Fetching the phonebook, she plunked onto the sofa. There were a number of top restaurants that did delivery. Selecting Chinese, she called to place her order. While she waited for it, she worked on edits to her current novel.

CHAPTER FOUR

A KNOCK ON the door indicated the food had arrived. Her stomach growled in anticipation. However, opening the door did not reveal a delivery boy. Peeking from behind the big bag with the Chinese restaurant's logo was none other than Sean McEwan.

Using an exaggerated Oriental accent, he said, "Derivery for Rady Endy."

"What on earth are you doing here?" she asked, motioning him into the room.

"Delivering your lunch," he stated obviously.

"You know perfectly well that's not what I meant." Her response lacked any level of amusement.

Sean merely smiled wider while removing her food from the large bag.

"Did you eat lunch already or am I sharing?" She reworded the question.

"I was returning from lunch when I heard the delivery chap confirming your room number with the front desk. A healthy tip and the bag was mine," he replied with a cocky grin. "But this is an extraordinarily large amount of food for one person."

"Should've guessed Carla would put us in the same hotel," Elsie mumbled before responding to his comment. "The room has a refrigerator and microwave. I'm going to be here a few days. If I get into writing, I tend to forget meals. Then when I do remember, I need to eat right away, not a half hour later."

She grabbed one of the takeout containers and pack of chopsticks. Sitting on the sofa by her laptop, she attempted to ignore him.

He followed. "Even though we're technically not sharing a meal, we could still share those stories."

Agreeing due to curiosity, she said, "Okay, go ahead."

She put more food in her mouth to force him first.

Taking the hint, he relaxed in the chair as he talked. "My wife and I were married shortly after I started acting. The only time I was home was between jobs. This worked great when we were young. Over time, this schedule wore on our relationship. The last five years we rarely shared intimacy. And when we did, we were going through the motions. Somewhere along the way, Kaitlyn fell in love with someone else. He makes her happy. We separated two years ago. When I visit the kids, I stay at their house."

"Why did it take such a long time to divorce? And why the story you were the one with another man?" she asked between bites.

"Eighteen years of assets took a while to divide. When we eventually filed, it didn't take long to finalize. That's when the tabloids found out." He explained further: "At the time, I had been bunking with a bloke to make things easier. He happened to be gay."

She nodded in understanding. "They certainly have a way to twist the facts into something to sell papers."

Shifting slightly, he prompted, "Your turn."

She closed the takeout box to place in the small refrigerator along with the unopened containers.

Perching on the arm of the sofa, she told her story. "My trip to the hospital in Sydney was because a snake spooked the horse I was on. Being a novice rider, I flew off and landed on a fallen tree. I spent several days in a coma. When I woke, my memories from the last decade were gone."

Sean leaned forward with an odd expression.

She continued. "After four months, nothing of significance returned. My comfort level with Rusty never got to where I believed we were romantically involved. Because things in my past were not so far away anymore, I had a lot of trust issues that doomed the relationship. Without those healing memories, I couldn't even reconcile who I'd become. And the tension of constantly trying to remember caused terrible migraines."

"You haven't remembered anything?" he queried.

"One morning I woke with eight years reloaded. The doctors believe the pathway opened because I'd gotten back into my routine along with not trying to remember," she repeated the usual answer.

"Why only a portion? Why not all of it?" he asked, his fascination unconcealed.

"They believe it's linked to when I began traveling to promote my books." She limited her reply.

His confusion showed plainly. "Why would that be a block?"

This had been a tough thing to understand. "My friend Sara filled me in on this timeframe. She said I was excited but fretted over being away from the kids. When I would return from book signings, I would become more of a hermit than usual. I hired my other close friend Trish to be my assistant. According to her, I wouldn't leave the house at all. She would get groceries and run errands. The doctors think because it was such a drastic change in lifestyle, my brain stored those memories differently."

"Back up. I didn't read anywhere that you have kids," he questioned.

"Reading up on me, huh?" she teased playfully. "Four-footed kids. When I first returned home, I didn't remember my current kids—Sophie and Tycho. With the reload, I remembered Sophie as a puppy. Poor Tycho . . . some days I think he's extra cuddly because he knows I don't remember his first two years. But I don't love him any less."

"Oh, that's right, show dogs," Sean remarked.

A large yawn forced her to cover her mouth. "Excuse me. Chinese food always makes me sleepy."

"Don't mind me if you want to take a nap," he offered.

"Yes, I want to take a nap. But you are leaving," she stated firmly, standing to escort him to the door.

He took the hint. "If you insist."

At the door, she said in a softer tone. "Thank you for stopping in and sharing the true story."

"The pleasure was all mine, m'lady," he replied with a theatrical bow.

His ridiculous behavior prompted a giggle from her. A large grin of delight filled his face as he departed.

Locking the door, another yawn reminded her that she needed to rest. It didn't take long to doze after she stretched across the king-size bed.

Hours later, the alarm announced it's time to get ready for dinner. She hoped the nap would ward away jetlag. Instead, it made it worse. With an hour till the car would arrive, she showered. This battled the lethargy. A simple summer dress with splashes of colors in impressionistic flower shapes had been packed specifically for this evening's dinner. Even though it was sleeveless, a light cashmere sweater would hide the bruising along the length of her left arm. Fluffing her short curls, she made sure the shaved sections stayed concealed. Granted, only two quarter-size circles had been removed, but she felt incredibly self-conscious. Trish told her repeatedly that with as thick as her hair was, no one would ever see them. Double-checking the clock, she finished with plum lips. She tossed the lipstick into her purse as she collected it upon her exit. During the descent in the elevator, her cell phone rang.

Seeing who was calling, she had to answer. "Hello, Sara. How are the kids?"

"Tycho chased down another groundhog, but Tom got him to give it up," her friend commented. "How are you feeling?"

"My meeting went well. And I'm on my way to dinner," she answered without details.

"That's not what I'm asking," Sara stated pointedly.

Sighing inwardly, Elsie replied, "As anticipated, the traveling has me tired. But when Trish made my schedule, she kept the afternoons open for naps."

"All right, call later if you need to." Sara sounded satisfied for the moment. "Bye."

Stepping outside, Elsie saw her driver standing by the car. "Good evening, Branson."

"Good evening, Ms. Elsie. You look rested," he remarked, holding the door for her.

On the drive, Branson remained silently focused on traffic much like he had that morning. She supposed this was how most of his clients preferred it. Evidently from previous trips, she'd become a regular. If she were scheduled in town, he would pass on other riders to be at her disposal. This was most likely a contractual arrangement by either Trish or Harris. Nonetheless, in his company, she felt like royalty. A steaming vanilla latte had greeted her on the drive to Rich's office earlier, this time an aromatic orchid poked from a water bottle. At the restaurant, he escorted her to the table reserved for Rich. The other nine chairs surrounding it were empty.

"Did I get the time wrong?" she asked.

Branson replied smoothly, "No, I expected to hit traffic. We are ten minutes early."

"That makes me feel better. I'd rather be early than late, anyway," she remarked.

His knowing smile indicated this was nothing new to him. "Have a nice dinner."

After Branson had gone, the waiter rushed to the table. "Something to drink while you wait, ma'am?"

To keep her hands busy, she ordered. "A club soda with lime, please."

Shortly after the waiter returned with her drink, Rich arrived. Seeing him speaking to the dining room host, she noticed Sean and an unknown woman next to him. Rich headed across the room to her, while Sean remained standing by the woman.

Kissing her on the cheek, Rich remarked, "The nap looks like it helped."

"Thanks. Let's hope it's enough to get me through tonight's gauntlet," she kidded.

"And here I thought the party tomorrow night would be more daunting," he teased.

"One torture at a time." She smiled to hide her nervousness.

Used to her humor, he stated, "It's not that bad. They needed to see for themselves that you aren't sitting in a wheelchair staring and drooling."

Thankfully, one of the studio executives appeared behind Rich, preventing him from seeing how close his words had hit home. She quickly shoved those anxious thoughts into a tightly closed box in her mind. The rest of the individuals involved in funding the film arrived on time. To her shock, Sean followed them. As introductions were made, he was included. The woman he'd been speaking to was one of the financial backers. When they sat, Sean moved deftly to hold Elsie's chair and claim the one next to her.

Leaning in closely, he whispered, "Rich thought a friendly face might help."

As the evening progressed, his presence welcomingly deflected the focus of attention. Dinner lasted almost two hours. During dessert and coffee, she sent a text to Branson to be waiting for her in five minutes.

At the appropriate time, she excused herself. "My clock is still on Eastern Standard Time, so if you don't mind . . ."

Everyone chimed in with "Good to see you," "Look forward to working with you again," "Sleep well," while Sean assisted her exodus from the table.

However, he remained at the table as she exited the dining room. The car pulled to the curb when she stepped outside.

Branson asked, "You skipped dessert?"

"Yes," she answered. "I had enough and am in the mood to write."

"My girlfriend owns Pastry Perfect. We could stop for something. It's only a ten-minute detour," he suggested.

Listening to impulse, she agreed eagerly. "That's a terrific idea!"

Branson made a call to his girlfriend. Elsie increased the volume on the speakers in the backseat to give him privacy. When they were outside the bakery, she noticed the hours posted on the door. The establishment had closed at four o'clock. Guilt at asking her to reopen was quickly dispersed as Branson's girlfriend, Amelia, greeted her warmly.

"Elsie, you look wonderful! I'm so glad your accident Down Under wasn't serious," she chattered with familiarity.

Elsie suspected Branson had been made aware of her jumbled memory, but he hadn't burdened Amelia with the same information. It also gave her the impression this wasn't the first time they'd taken this detour.

Amelia's voice overrode Elsie's thoughts. "I don't have any whole cakes. But there are enough pieces to put together a sampler. Also a new chai flavor came in the afternoon deliveries."

"Yes, yes, and yes." Elsie got swept into Amelia's zeal.

They left the shop with the driver carrying a full bag.

At the hotel, she insisted she could carry it. "I can handle this. You are done for the night. And I won't need you till 10:30 tomorrow."

"Good night, Ms. Elsie." The driver nodded.

"Good night, Branson," she replied.

Up in her room, she switched into pajamas prior to raiding the contents of the bag. Chai cheesecake and Chinese food sustained her late-night writing surge. At 3:00 a.m., she finally put her laptop aside for sleep.

This made for a rough start the next morning. Branson called her cell phone when she wasn't on time.

"I'll be down in a couple of minutes," she answered.

The relief was heard in his baritone voice. "No problem, as long as you are okay."

He was waiting for her in the lobby. He took her briefcase. She didn't mind. Not having a full night of sleep, she needed both hands to hold on to for climbing into the car. Instead of coffee, a refreshing pomegranate slushy waited in the drink holder. It couldn't be more perfect. A coffee today would've made her jittery.

As they were driving, he handed her an envelope. "I almost forgot. This was at the front desk for you. They said they turned on your message light. I figure you didn't notice since you were running behind."

"Thank you. You are right—what a morning! But I was on a roll last night. Matter of fact, I'd rather be picking up where I left off than going to review these script and storyboards," she replied with exasperation.

Taking a sip of the slushy, she added cheerily, "This drink is superb!"

Tearing at the flap, she opened the envelope. Darting her eyes to the bottom, she saw it was from Sean.

> *Elsie,*
> *Rich mentioned the shindig you are attending this evening.*
> *If you are without an escort, I am happy to offer my services.*
> *Awaiting your wishes,*
> *Sean*
> *Room 402*

By the time they arrived at Rich's studio, she had given the offer proper consideration.

"Branson, please contact Sean McEwan. He's staying at the same hotel in room 402. He will be my escort for this evening's party. Please inform him of the time we will be leaving the hotel," she requested. "See you at two."

"Yes, Ms. Elsie. See you then," he replied as she took her briefcase from him.

CHAPTER FIVE

RICH AND ELSIE accomplished far more than anticipated; it was enough that they cancelled their meeting for the following day. Since it was only a day early, she hardly felt it warranted rescheduling her flight. Most people would take the time to sight-see. To avoid anything provoking a migraine, she planned to stay in her room writing. If she were home, she'd sit on the bench swing while Sophie and Tycho frolicked in the yard. Trish would review correspondences with her. And a few hours after, Trish would leave for the day and Sara would take the short path between their properties to check on Elsie. These thoughts of home filled her mind for the drive to the hotel. It also helped fuel her need to write. Heating a container of the Chinese takeout, she dove into her latest story. Before she realized, it was four o'clock. This only gave her a half hour to get ready.

There were numerous pretty dresses hanging in her closet at home from which she could've chosen. However, an ocean blue Japanese silk brocade dress had called to her. Plus, the three quarter-length sleeves would hide the needle marks without making her too warm. A pair of teardrop sapphires ordained her ears. Her curls framed her face softly after a sprits and fluff. A little mascara and eyeliner accentuated her big beautiful eyes.

At 4:28, Elsie stepped into the hallway and into Sean. He was wearing a crisp white dress shirt, flashy blue plaid vest, and dark blue Dockers. To her shock, he hadn't shaved. Not that she minded; she actually preferred it. A low whistle of appreciation came from his lips at taking in the full view of her from head to toe. With no words spoken, he placed her hand in the crook of his arm. As they approached the car, Branson whistled a similar tune.

Since it was a fairly long drive, she tried to ease her nervousness by asking about his children. Eilish, the oldest, wanted to be an actor like her father. Thad, scheduled for university at the end of holiday, resembled Sean but loved architecture. With Kaitlyn involved in home design, it had been an expected choice. Jack, on the verge of puberty, thought of nothing except video games. Each time they drifted into silence, she prompted with another question.

"Love, if you are uncomfortable with me, why did you agree?" he finally asked in a gentle tone.

She laughed. "Actually, your offer was quite welcome. I'm uneasy in crowds, particularly with a high probability of bumping into people I don't remember. It can be quite exhausting."

"Anything you need. This is supposed to be fun." He gave her a wink.

When they arrived at the pier hosting the party, she had the strangest feeling of déjà vu. He held her hand throughout the majority of the evening.

Anytime a conversation got iffy, he would say, "Excuse me, they're playing our song."

And then he would lead her to the dance area. Dancing with him was effortless.

At the end of one dance, he took her to a spot in the middle of the pier. "Please wait here."

He spoke to the guy working the music. As the current song rolled into the next, the disc jockey handed the microphone to Sean.

"I want you to want me, I need you to need me . . ." His perfect pitch crooned across the crowd.

His actions mimicked those of a seasoned rock-and-roller as he immersed himself in the song. The dancers ceased to watch his impromptu concert.

As the song reached its final frenzy, Sean dropped to his knees directly in front of Elsie to plead his case. "I want you to love me . . ."

Extreme flattery overruled any embarrassment at such a public display. Swept into his performance, she leaned down to award him a token kiss.

He lifted her off her feet with a powerful hug as he stood. Emotionally, she was on cloud nine. Unfortunately, the overall strain initiated tension creeping up the back of her neck. Most of the evening, the pain was kept at bay with an occasional glass of champagne. However, when she returned from a trip to the ladies' room, the pier was on a tilt. Unable to find Sean among the throng of partygoers, she had to go at it alone. Carefully navigating around the dance area, she made her way to the end of the pier to view the bay. Another strong surge of déjà vu swept over her. Her breathing came in gulps as the blackness tried to seize her. Watching the sea lions stretched lazily on the floating platforms was soothing. Soon an arm slid around her waist.

His breath tickled her ear—his brogue, her fancy—as he spoke directly into it. "I hope you are enjoying tonight as much as I am."

When she turned to see if Sean was serious, he took advantage by kissing her. With lips slightly parted, the slow erotic movements of his mouth made her tingle.

At the end of the kiss, he said, "It's almost midnight, Cinderella. One last dance?"

"Mm hmm," she agreed.

They moved as one to Joe Crocker's "You Are So Beautiful." Inwardly, she forced the swirling thoughts and feelings aside to enjoy the moment. At the end of the song, they held onto each other for an extra note. Their walk from the boards was completed in a delirious daze. Once inside the car, he pulled her onto his lap for more passionate kisses. When he lay across the backseat with her still on top of him, Branson closed the privacy partition. Their bodies pressed together—soft feminine curves molded to masculine firmness. He caressed the skin exposed by the dress slits at each thigh. One hand slid up her back and neck to tangle in her curls. His beard stubble sensually scratched her skin as he nuzzled his way along the open Mandarin collar to her bountiful bosom. A moan of dormant desire suddenly set free escaped from Elsie's lips. Sean's ardor rose in response.

Unexpectedly disrupting their fervor, he jerked up and exclaimed, "What the?"

His fingertips had encountered the marred spots on her scalp. He reached for the interior light, displacing her unceremoniously onto the carpeting.

"Love, I'm sorry." The pitch of his voice increased several octaves indicating his frantic state. "What are those on your head?"

As he assisted her onto the seat, she composed a reasonable response without revealing everything. His eyebrows raised as his hand touched her left arm. While they were getting to know each other better, her sleeves had scrunched, exposing the nasty needle marks. The bruises couldn't be explained away other than with the whole story. Otherwise, they'd be fodder for suspicion.

"When I told you about my head injury, I didn't tell you everything. Only those closest to me know everything," Elsie said quickly before she hid in silent protection mode. "When I started suffering from migraines and extended dizzy spells, the doctors took tons of tests. One of the MRIs showed a shadow. But it was inconsistent. It took some time till they discovered why. The treatments are borderline experimental—that's why the shaved spots on my head and marks on my arm."

His face shifted to confused concern. "Cancer caused by an injury?"

Now came the part difficult to describe without pictures. "Not cancer. A vein blisters then seeps gradually to release the pressure instead of throwing an embolism. Each time the blistering stretches the vein. That's why it took a while for it to appear on the MRIs. The treatments are to shrink the blister before it stretches too far and to strengthen the vein so it doesn't stretch. All while avoiding clots or hemorrhage."

"That sounds incredibly dangerous." He was trying to wrap his brain around what she was explaining.

"It is. But if left untreated, it will eventually cause a massive hemorrhage. If that doesn't kill me, I would most likely go into a permanent coma." There was no way to sugarcoat the prognosis.

"Can't they go in there to patch or replace the vein like they do with a heart bypass?" he asked, grasping for a fix.

Her response was as antiseptic as surgical instruments. "First, we have to do these treatments. Then they will drill three holes in my head to use a laser. If that fails, they'll open my skull to do the vein replacement."

"Why not do that right away if it's so dangerous to wait?" His tone clearly denoted that he wouldn't stop until she'd given full disclosure.

She fidgeted.

When she finally spoke, her voice cracked with emotion. "The natural pressure of the brain tissue around it is most likely keeping it in check. If they remove any of it, it could blow like a geyser. This allots an incredibly short amount of time to make the repair. If they take too long, the lack of blood flow and oxygen would cause irreversible brain damage. Plus, because of how I reacted from the initial injury, the permanent removal of any damaged tissue could cause major side effects."

As the totality of what she had described made full impact, his face fell in futility. His body slumped against the seat. She slid to the other corner. Slipping her shoes off, she pulled her legs tight against her torso. A shiver ripped through her from the drastic temperature change in the small compartment. Branson always kept a lap blanket on the window shelf. She tugged it down across her shoulder and legs. An isolating silence filled the dimly lit space. This abrupt atmospheric shift summoned the earlier migraine. Since the party was such a long drive from the hotel, she had placed her medication in her purse. She pushed the blanket aside long enough to get her pills and a bottle of water.

When she curled into the corner again, Branson spoke via the intercom. "Ms. Elsie, we may have a problem."

Sirens could be heard approaching from behind. The car slowed to a stop on the shoulder as she dropped the partition. The emergency vehicles whizzed by them. Red and blue flashing lights could be seen coming to a halt farther ahead on the highway. Branson switched on his emergency bandwidth scanner. Sean moved forward, sticking his head between the front seat headrests to listen. Trusting Branson to get them to the hotel safely, she closed her eyes, anxious for the medication to work.

Sometime later, Sean was shaking her roughly. "Elsie? Should we get you to hospital?"

"Migraine. Let me sleep," she grumbled.

Then she was floating through the hotel lobby. Finally, there were soft pillows to bury her head in for total silence. For a while, she shivered uncontrollably. But at some point, a pocket of warmth encircled her.

CHAPTER SIX

In the morning, Elsie woke unusually well rested after a migraine. She felt a weight around her midsection as her stomach growled in need of food. Stretching, she encountered hairy legs. Slowly opening her eyes, she peered into a pair of bright green ones.

"Good morning, love. Feeling better?" Sean asked softly.

In a small voice she replied, "Remarkably."

Placing a kiss on her cheek, he reached across for the phone. "What do you want for breakfast?"

Grasping to hold onto her composure, she requested, "Croissants, eggs over easy, bacon, fruit."

"Goodness, you are hungry!" he remarked while waiting for the other end of the line to answer.

As he placed their breakfast order, her mind went into overdrive, trying to determine why he was there.

When he ended the call, he gave her a quick peck on the lips. "Twenty minutes. Do you want to shower first?"

"No, go ahead," she answered, afraid to leave the safety of the blankets in her current state of undress—only the lace panties from last night.

Lacking any modesty or clothes, Sean rolled out of bed to stroll into the bathroom.

At the door jam, he turned to face her with a cheeky grin and full frontal display of his morning erection. "Feel free to join me."

Thankfully, he didn't wait for a response. Glancing around the room, she didn't see her dress or his clothing. She waited till she heard him singing in the shower to scurry to the dresser for a pair of pajamas. After donning them, she selected clothing to wear after bathing.

Pausing at the increased volume of Sean's singing—"So beautiful to me . . ."—she noticed the contents of her purse dumped across the dresser top.

Was he looking for a condom? she wondered as her mind raced to find a memory of what they did after returning to the hotel.

Perusing herself in the mirror gave no discerning indications of what activities may have occurred. Realizing the pointlessness of dwelling on it, she fluffed her curls to make herself presentable. Too soon, he emerged from the bathroom brushing his teeth. A towel hung haphazardly from his hips.

Where did he get the toothbrush? she asked herself as she went in to locate her own.

Hers was still in her toiletries bag. Grabbing it, she brushed her teeth while waiting for her opportunity to shower without an audience. When he returned to finish using the other sink, she saw his toiletry bag.

But how or when did it get there? Her thoughts rambled with confusion.

This time when he exited the bathroom, she shut the door behind him to rush through the shower.

When she emerged fully clothed, he poked his head in from the other room. "Breakfast."

He wore different clothing than from last evening's event. She had enough of this puzzle.

She blatantly asked, "Did we have sex last night?"

Sean choked on his juice.

After clearing his throat, he responded indignantly, "Do you think I would be that reckless with you? From what you said about your condition, I hardly considered it an option."

Bright pink infused her skin with embarrassment, but she pushed on. "Then why were you in my bed naked?"

"I sleep in the nude," he stated simply.

"Why were you in bed with me?" she asked, her tone clearly one of displeasure.

"You don't know?" he asked in amazement.

Sighing with frustration, she reined it in to speak in a solicitous manner. "At the risk of exposing myself further, I don't know what happens anytime I have one of those headaches. After taking the medication, I crawl into bed. I wake the next morning lying by the toilet, on the kitchen floor, and even on my patio. If you would please enlighten me on what does happen, it might help."

While he chewed his current mouthful, he studied her face. Not wanting him to see how vulnerable she felt, she focused on eating. The food at least quieted her stomach.

After what felt like an eternity, he finally answered. "We sat on the highway for almost an hour, so we didn't get here until after three. I tried waking you. You said you had a migraine and needed sleep. I carried you here. I set you on the bed then went through your purse to find what you took while we were in the car. When I turned around, your dress and bra were on the floor—you in bed, face first in the pillows. After hanging your dress, I left."

Pausing, he refilled her cup of tea, even adding the cream.

He resumed after another swallow of his juice. "I wasn't in my room long when you called making no sense. I grabbed a few things to come back. As luck would have it, I had slipped your keycard into my pocket. When I got here, you were in bed shivering uncontrollably and muttering in agitation. The best way to warm you was body heat. You calmed as soon as I put my arms around you."

It took a few moments to process what he'd explained.

"I can't believe you did all of that." Awe filled her voice. "Thank you."

The look on his face resembled pride. "Anytime, love."

Finishing breakfast, he stretched with sated hunger. "What would you like to do today?"

He caught her off-guard. "Excuse me?"

Sitting back so the chair teetered on two legs, he said matter-of-factly, "Rich said you two finished early. I presume you have today free. I do as well. Why not spend it together?"

"Um, well, I guess. That is yes," she replied positively.

"Grab your purse and let's go!" he stated enthusiastically as he sat forward with a bang.

She didn't move as quickly. She didn't want him to notice her lingering dizziness. In the bedroom, she scooped the items on the dresser into her everyday purse. Before it rolled in, she snatched the lipstick for a little color.

When she rejoined him, he offered his arm. "Your chariot awaits, m'lady."

To her surprise, Branson was, in fact, waiting at the curb for them.

"Where are we going?" she asked once in the car.

"Wait and see," Sean stated with secrecy.

The weather seemed to be the only allowable topic for discussion. She read highway signs as they went. A recognizable name was San Jose. They took an exit ramp twenty miles too early. At this point, she decided to wait for the surprise. After ten miles of twisty roads, the ocean came into view. Branson drove the car through a small town. They drove toward an amusement park. The last thing she needed was rides to mess with her already faulty equilibrium. Farther along the avenue, they turned onto a lone pier with shops.

They strolled hand-in-hand on the ocean-weathered boards. Nearing the far end, they heard a distinctive barking. People were clustered at a section of the railing. Joining them, they saw mounds of sea lions sunning on a floating platform. The crowd grew. People began eyeing Sean and her oddly. Still holding her hand, he led her to the emptier side of the pier. Here she leaned on the rail to stare at the ocean. Occasionally, a sea lion would pop to the water's surface with a resounding snort. A couple of pelicans waddled nearby.

He asked, "Are you having a good time?"

"Yes," she replied with a happy sigh. "Thank you for removing us from that crowd. Maybe it's the medication messing with me, but were they staring at us?"

"I noticed too," he replied with chagrin. "Our lunch will have to be somewhere else."

She nodded with understanding. On the return walk, he called Branson to inform him of the change in plans. After lunch at an alternate location, they walked barefoot on its adjoining beach. This tired her quicker than anticipated. Her lack of surefootedness did not go unnoticed. Sean steered them to the sidewalk. This was a fair distance from the parking lot. Unexpectedly, Branson appeared with the car. Sean helped Elsie into the backseat.

When the car began rolling, she yawned. "Excuse me."

"I'm sorry. I should've thought this much physical exertion would be too much," he stated sympathetically.

She couldn't let him take the blame. "It's my fault, not yours. I should've considered how much time we were spending in the sun. The day after a migraine, I'm exceptionally susceptible to side effects."

"Side effects from the medication or your condition?" he asked with concern.

"Both. Anything I take is essentially for the overall condition—tailored to a specific symptom. Of which, each has a plethora of side effects." She kept her tone light and cheery, but the bleakness of the words was plainly perceptible.

They were on the highway heading toward the hotel when Sean spoke again. "If you have so many restrictions, why take a trip alone?"

"I don't have any restrictions. The doctors figure my body will set its limitations," she tried to explain. "I spoke to my specialists about taking this trip. They hoped it might help revitalize my spirits."

"You hardly appear despondent," he remarked.

"When I cast aside Rusty, they felt I threw away any hopes of a future," she replied, devoid of emotion.

"I take it that isn't how you see your parting from the Aussie," he stated rather than asked.

She shook her head, refusing to make eye contact with him. "No, but they wouldn't understand."

Even though it was obvious he wanted to press her further, he took her signal not to pursue the topic. Instead, he became solicitous.

"Why don't you lie down? You can rest your head here," he offered, patting his thighs with both hands.

With no thoughts of anything other than closing her eyes, she willingly obliged. She was wearier than realized. Of course, the current conversation drained her already limited resources. Talking about Rusty always caused an uncontrollable tightness in her chest. It was the same feeling she suffered when she woke from nightmares of the dogs disappearing. Usually she could push the intense loss away as overemotional nonsense. However, with her inner strength already drained, she endured the discomfort until sleep stole her away.

CHAPTER SEVEN

ELSIE STIRRED AS they arrived at the hotel.

Still somewhat groggy, she physically felt better; emotionally, not so. "I'm sorry, Sean. I didn't realize how little I do at home."

His amiable boyish grin reached his eyes with a twinkle. "I find that hard to believe seeing how much you wrote in one night."

Prior to responding to this comment, she spoke to the driver. "Thank you, Branson. My flight is 7:00 a.m. I'll see you at five."

"Yes, ma'am. I'll call at a quarter till to give you enough time," he replied with a nod.

"How on earth do you know how much I wrote the other night?" Elsie queried Sean as they stepped onto the elevator.

"Wait . . . you were snooping this morning while I was in the shower," she accused him, unsure of why he would do such a thing.

"I was curious about your next book," he replied contritely. "Blame it on a father wanting to impress his daughter."

"Please, she can't be that enamored with my books," she remarked, reaching for her room keycard.

Again, his boyish grin could be seen on his downcast face as they entered her suite.

"It's not merely Eilish, but her father too—particularly with the author." His eyes darted upward to make momentary contact with hers.

"You are strangely persistent!" she blurted out.

His head snapped up to look her fully in the face.

Recognizing it could be misconstrued as an insult, she backpedaled. "Good heavens, that was rude! What I mean is . . ."

"What you mean is"—he stepped on her words—"we don't know each other."

"Exactly!" she replied, at a loss on how he could read her thoughts.

"To you, we've only just met. If I tell you how well we do know each other, you may throw me out." His tone indicated his hesitation.

"Maybe we should order a bottle or two of alcohol before you tell me," she suggested with equal apprehension.

"Is it wise for you to drink with how you feel?" he questioned critically.

Staring back defiantly, she picked up the phone. "Definitely."

An obvious frown formed from his brow to his mouth, but he didn't argue with her decision.

"A liter of your best vodka, four bottles of the cranberry-pomegranate juice, bucket of ice and . . .," she paused, staring at him for his order.

"Scotch and soda," he muttered in a way that sounded like a growl.

"A liter of scotch, soda water, and double order of fries." She completed the call.

His face softened slightly. "Thank you for not being completely irresponsible."

"You are a parent, aren't you?" she said, her cavalier attitude building with every remark he made.

He began playing the same game. "And that's a bad thing?"

"Depends. Do you still let loose?" She wondered if he would take the bait.

"Find out after room service gets here." Plopping into the armchair, he sidestepped the challenge.

The voice in her head screamed to tell him this wasn't her. It was due to the increased pressure on her brain. The migraine had been a warning. The onset of the approaching episode was scarier than she'd anticipated, particularly since she knew what was happening this time and there wasn't really anything to prevent it. How could that voice get to the surface to tell him?

Suddenly, she inhaled deeply, as if she'd been drowning. Sean was kneeling directly in front of her.

His hands held onto her arms, keeping her upright. "Elsie?"

Her eyes grew wide; she knew she had a seizure. It was merely the kind where she stared, not of the grand mal ilk. She forced her focus on his worried face. When she tried to talk, the words were gibberish.

His eyebrows jerked up severely, furrowing his brow with fear. "I'm calling for ambulance."

"No!" It shot out of her as she clutched at his arms.

He bit his lip in consternation. "What can I do to help?"

She slowly and carefully enunciated her words. "Stay . . . please."

Something in his demeanor changed with her request. He pulled her into a hug. His firm hold of her had a surprising strength for his unassumingly lean frame. Concentrating on his breathing helped regulate hers. Several minutes passed and her muscles relaxed in unison punctuated by an involuntary sigh.

A few more seconds ticked by till he asked, "Over?"

Pushing herself away from his body to sit without assistance, she replied quietly, "For now."

Before he could continue questioning, the doorbell rang. "Room service."

"Don't move! I will take care of this." He stood to answer the door.

He didn't allow the server beyond the doorway. After signing the bill and tipping the man in hotel uniform, he wheeled the tray next to the sofa.

Instead of doling the food and drinks, he sat next to her. "What happens next?"

"I understand if you want to leave before this gets worse," she said, trying to erect walls.

"I'm not going anywhere. Now talk!" he demanded.

She attempted a different method of deflection. "Hmm, forceful, stubborn, but wrong accent."

"It's not going to work, love," he stated steadfastly. "You are stuck with me the rest of the night."

"Then strap yourself in for a fun ride." she snapped sarcastically.

"Are erratic mood swings an indicator you're going to have another seizure?" he asked while standing with her to help her teeter toward the tray.

"Yes," she hissed, resenting his easy manner.

At this point, a drink might improve her cantankerous disposition. It's not like it could really make matters worse.

"Hmm, I wonder if that might chase Sir Galahad away?"

Reaching for the vodka, she couldn't budge the lid on the bottle. To her surprise, he took it from her to crack the seal. He grabbed the tallest glass in which to pour the clear liquid. A couple of ice cubes and a splash of juice later, he led her to the sofa prior to handing her the full glass. She watched as he prepared his scotch and soda. After taking a long swallow from it, he topped the glass with only amber liquid—another thing he had in common with Rusty. He served the food. The fries steamed when he removed the lid.

"Ketchup or vinegar?" he asked.

"Both," she replied.

He administered the condiments to the fries. The coffee table was large enough to include the ingredients of their drinks. She nibbled fries while watching him move everything to within reach.

When he finally sat, she questioned, "How did you know it was a seizure?"

"I did a movie a few years back where the main character suffered from a brain tumor. I research parts thoroughly." Shoving fries into his mouth, he didn't bother to hide his smugness.

As they ate, the silence in the room bothered her. She turned on the television as a distraction from dwelling on when the next seizure would occur. Each time her glass came close to bottom, he refilled it. Clicking through the channels, she happened across one of Rusty's movies. That wouldn't help her mood. But then she found an early film of Sean's.

Unfortunately, it didn't have the effect for which she'd hoped.

He merely made fun of himself. "Look at that foppish Scotsman. His leading lady said he kissed like a fish."

Elsie stated sweetly, "I found his kisses quite enjoyable."

His face twisted in confusion at her statement. "Pandering to my ego or do we have a seizure coming on?"

"Allowing the alcohol to abscond with my accountability," she said with slightly slurred speech.

"An author with alliteration abilities," he parried.

Even though it really wasn't that funny, she laughed. This prompted his mirth too. The lightheartedness from the alcohol was welcome compared to her earlier surliness. With their laughter spent, she resumed watching the movie. He poured the last of the alcohol into their glasses for a final drink. Not unexpected, they had juice and soda leftover. These he put in the refrigerator with the last piece of cheesecake. He continued clearing the coffee table. She scarfed down the last of the fries as he removed the plate.

Sitting down again, he remarked, "How long are you going to torture me with this movie?"

"If you want, I can switch to *Warrior from Camelot*." Her voice sounded innocent enough.

His tone indicated he didn't buy it. "Watching your ex flex his well-muscled bare chest would make a lesser man feel impotent."

"Okay." And she changed the channels.

The timing couldn't have been better. In the current scene, Rusty was stripped naked then waded into the river to wash the enemy's blood from his perfect south-of-the-equator tanned skin.

"You win! I'm a lesser man!" he exclaimed. "I can endure my own movie with less threat to my masculinity."

When she switched back, she feared he'd spoken too soon. A particularly graphic love scene was playing. To her surprise, the tips of his ears turned red; but his face remained unchanged—unlike her own face, which became overly warm as she wondered what it would be like to share similar activities with him.

Suddenly, he became serious. "I'm curious about something you said this morning."

"What would that be?" She couldn't correlate what had instigated his comment.

"Us having sex—does that mean it *is* a possibility?" he asked matter-of-factly.

Trying to conceal her own thoughts on this matter, she answered in a stilted manner. "I'm not sure . . . I haven't since before the accident."

"Sod off. You and Rusty were still together. He agreed to separate beds?" he said with incredulity.

"Didn't you point out earlier that people can share the same bed and not have sex?" She didn't want to expose anything that might hurt Rusty. "The first couple of months I had severe limitations. When those lifted, other things got in the way."

"You said before it was because you couldn't believe he cared. I guess I don't understand why that prevented a physical relationship." Again, his voice lacked belief.

"There were other key things that had occurred in my life the years prior to meeting Rusty, which had been lost. These gave me confidence and comfort with who I am—personal issues with which I'd come to terms. With those wounds fresh in my mind, thanks to the accident, I hadn't yet found resolution. Rusty knew what those were and, well, respected my boundaries." She kept her narrative as vague as possible.

The next question from him was not the one she expected. "But you said you regained some of those memories. If Rusty said he wanted you back now, would you?"

Letting it cross her mind for a few seconds, she replied with a feeling of melancholy. "No, I wouldn't."

"Is that answer for anyone who might be interested?" He leaned nearer as he inquired sensitively.

"And who would want me in this condition?" she remarked realistically.

He responded without words. Instead, he closed the space between them to place his lips on hers for a tender kiss.

When their lips released, he whispered. "I have a confession to make."

She blinked expectantly.

"I didn't just happen on you in the hallway earlier this week. I was waiting for you." He explained further: "You fascinate me. When I saw the way you demurely accepted Taylor's Oscar, I have to admit, I had a crush on you. Each time we bumped into each other, it grew. I found out everything I could with hopes of wooing you. Unfortunately, there was no point when I heard that you and the Aussie were a couple. That is, until now."

Her mind whirled. There was a man sitting next to her who wanted to date her, not merely fill a lustful need. And he was aware of her dim prognosis. Had she shortchanged Rusty by not telling him the truth? However, this man wasn't Rusty Garnet, wanted by every heterosexual woman on the planet. Not that Sean McEwan was a slouch in the industry. But Rusty had a raw animal magnetism that Sean lacked. Sean had an unassuming and relaxed way to his personality. Rusty was more likely to get in your face than wait it out—whatever it happened to be. He'd tried so hard to convince her he loved her. If only she could remember what they had together.

A gasping breath broke her involuntary reverie. Sean held her, rocking gently. The smooth and steady motion eased the muscle tension related to the seizure. He leaned away to gaze at her.

In all seriousness, he asked, "Did I cause that?"

Her lips quivered as she smiled in reassurance. "No."

"But the literature says emotional swings can provoke a seizure," he said with anxiety.

"Yelling, em-m-motional p-pain, not happ-pp-pp-y." The stuttering and disjointed sentence signified things were worsening.

Even though it was early evening, time had come for pajamas and bed. Plus, she needed to pack. Standing to begin preparations for the trip home caused a severe dizzy spell.

He grabbed her before she went face first into the glass coffee table. "Where are you going?"

Pushing his hands away, she mumbled, "P-pack."

Swallowing hard in an attempt to equalize the pressure in her head, she stood slower. The world only tilted slightly. She made it safely to the bedroom by grabbing onto things along the way.

He followed on her heels. "I'll pack. You sit on the bed and point."

She had already separated her travel clothes; thus, making it easy. Each time she tried to help, he set her back onto the bed. He even packed the dresses in a manner to prevent creases.

When he got to her pajamas, she reached for them. Without saying a word, he left the room to give her privacy. It took longer than usual with fumble fingers. As it was, she'd been unable to unhook her bra.

"Hey, what do you want done with your laptop?" he called from the living room.

"Shoulder b-bag," she replied as he reentered the room.

Locating the travel bag, he unzipped the compartment for the laptop. In doing this, he came across her flight information. He relocated it to an easily accessible pouch in front then dumped the contents of her purse into the adjacent zipper pocket. Her medications were placed in Ziploc baggies in preparation for security. The suitcase and travel bag remained on top of the dresser, awaiting her toiletries and pajamas in the morning. He paced into the living room several times, ensuring all of her things had been accounted.

When he paused, she smiled in appreciation. "Thank you."

"You're welcome." He glanced around with uncertainty for a few moments. "I need to go to my room for a bit. Will you be okay?"

"Yes, go!" she replied.

Before leaving her alone, he made sure she had a glass of ice water and the remote control to the television.

"Don't do anything." His voice held an edge of warning.

She nodded in acquiescence.

Hearing the door leading to the hallway close, she lay against the pillows as she selected the channel playing *Warrior from Camelot*. Only fifteen minutes remained. Watching Rusty's character reunited with the woman he loved filled Elsie with melancholy. The onscreen kiss warmed her face with recollection of the kisses they'd shared after she'd woken from the coma.

She didn't remember seeing the credits roll across the screen. Apparently, another seizure ran its course, causing her to slide from the bed to the floor.

As she regained her sensibilities, a door shut. Struggling, she managed to climb onto the bed before Sean noticed.

Appearing in the doorway, he said, "Sorry, I took so long."

Glancing at the clock, she realized forty minutes had passed.

"No p-p-problem." She responded the best she could.

A chill formed goose bumps on her skin. She attempted to pull blankets up to get warm, but all she managed to do was clump them. He moved bedside to fix the problem.

As he did so, he remarked, "Wouldn't you be more comfortable without the bra?"

"Yes, help p-please!" The words sprang from her mouth as a run of indistinguishable syllables.

There was that boyish grin as he reached around to release the constraining piece of clothing. With gentlemanly manners, he faced the other direction to give her privacy while she removed it completely. In playfulness, she tossed the soft pink intimate garment over his shoulder. He glanced sideways at it. When he pulled it off, he read the size tag. On his way to put it with her travel clothing, she could see an expression of delightful surprise. Instead of the accompanying surge of warmth, another chill besieged her body with shivers. Without warning, he stripped to join her under the blankets. Initially, the proximity of his nakedness inundated her senses. However, the radiant heat he provided warmed her with a feeling of tranquility. Either that or another seizure removed her from any sensation of distress.

Chapter Eight

When Elsie regained coherency, the clock glowed 2:02 a.m. Sean still held her in his arms. Not caring if she disturbed him, she rolled to the edge of the bed. Sliding her legs till her feet touched the floor, she stood slowly. The nightstand served as a stabilizer.

"Love, where you off to?" he asked in his sleep.

"Have to pee," she replied, not really expecting him to hear.

When she habitually turned on the light in the tiled room, it glared brightly. She hurriedly flicked the switch down. After emptying her bladder, she washed the drool crust from her face. Returning to the bed, she drank the entire glass of warm water to ease her parched throat. It helped, but it also reminded her she hadn't eaten anything in eight hours. For some reason, these episodes would spike her metabolism, causing her to burn excessive calories. On the positive side, she had gone from a size 12 to size 6 in less than three months without dieting. The doctors felt this was too thin for her frame. According to their orders, Trish supplied the kitchen with foods that were usually at the top of diet taboo lists: pastries, pastas, and native Pennsylvania Dutch dishes. She needed to gain for an end goal of a size 9/10.

Working her way to the refrigerator, she thanked God for the cheesecake. Refilling her glass with juice and soda water, she moved to the sofa. She turned on the television to provide ambient lighting. It didn't take long for her to have company. For her modesty, he donned pants. Sitting with her, he opened his mouth for her to share the fare. Shaky hands made this difficult. He assisted by grasping her hand in his to direct the food without wearing it.

When the plate emptied, he finally spoke. "Are we through the worst of it?"

With her speech normal, she answered without effort. "Based on other episodes, I think so."

"That wasn't too bad," he remarked.

"Try being on this end!" she quipped sarcastically. "Lest we forget, we have nothing concrete to define when it might be killing me and I should be taken to the hospital."

"Are you always this dismally pessimistic?" he questioned while leading her back to bed.

A yawn muffled her response. "Depends."

As he pulled her into the warmth of his arms, he said, "I'll take that as a yes."

"Sean?" Doubts began forming in her overactive imagination.

"Not complaining, just getting bearings on you." He placed a reassuring kiss on her lips. "The alarm will wake us in less than two hours."

An hour later, neither of them had fallen asleep. And he had become aroused, which he tried to conceal from her. Every time she shifted, she bumped into or rubbed against his groin. All of the contact had not been unintentional. It was empowering. Here she was a medical ticking time bomb, yet his body gave away how attracted he was to her. According to the gossip newspapers, he'd dated very beautiful women. She doubted he had been barred from their beds. The feel of his hard masculinity against her soft feminine form spurned fantasies in her mind. This only fed her restlessness.

Unable to endure it any longer, he flung the covers aside to spring out of bed. "Bloody hell, woman! I can't do this anymore without making love to you!"

"I'm sor—," she began apologizing

He held up his hand, stopping her midword.

"It's not your fault!" he stated harshly. "I'm going into the bathroom to take care of this and shower. Unless you want to be ravaged, you will stay there and not say a word."

Her expression—wide eyes, hot cheeks, parted lips—had to give away she wanted him to do exactly that. But they both knew with the night she had, it could be detrimental to her current state of health. The bathroom door slammed shut behind him. Hearing water running, she climbed from bed to double-check that everything had been packed properly. Their earlier snack emptied the refrigerator, leaving nothing else for her to do until the bathroom became available. The impish side of her nature wanted to go in to see what he would actually do. That wouldn't be fair to him, especially after he'd been extremely patient with her seizures last night.

Standing in the middle of the room, deciding what to do next, she swore he called her name. She opened the door to the bathroom a few inches. Before she had a chance to ask what he needed, he groaned. Via the partially steamed mirror, she could see behind the shower curtain. Well, he did say he would take care of his tense situation. With a smirk, she pulled the door quietly shut. She climbed onto the bed feeling elated with the fact that she had that kind of effect on a man. Rusty would get similarly tense at times but never needed to "take care of it." Or if he did, it wasn't as urgent. She'd been comparing Sean to Rusty—but why? The only memories of Rusty were since the accident. Irritated with her train of thought, she needed to do something. She went into the bathroom to brush her teeth.

"Elsie?" Sean's voice jumped several octaves.

Of course, he couldn't follow through with his threat now. But he didn't know she was aware that he'd already shot his load. She began brushing her teeth. The look of shock on his face as he poked his head from behind the shower curtain almost made her choke on the toothpaste. Clearly, she'd thrown him a curve. Gleefulness sated the imp inside. He ducked under the water spray to complete his shower. Hearing the water cease, she went into the bedroom under the guise of spreading her clothes on the bed. When he emerged naked, she headed in to bathe. He walked in and out of the bathroom several times. She ensured the shower curtain concealed her sufficiently. As she dried, the alarm clock announced it was time to wake up. Expecting him to reset it, she didn't rush. By the time she entered the bedroom to complete dressing, the clock still blared. Glancing around the suite, Sean appeared to be nowhere. With her toiletries packed, she had nothing else to do. Oddly, her cell phone chimed an incoming text message. It was from Branson stating he would arrive in five minutes. This was a half hour ahead of schedule. Collecting her suitcase and shoulder bag, she departed the suite.

As she dropped her keycard at the front desk, she pondered why Sean left without saying good-bye. She didn't need to wonder long.

The lobby elevator opened to reveal him with his suitcase. "There you are!"

"Where else would I be?" she asked flippantly.

"Your room, getting ready," he commented flatly.

"Excuse me for being low maintenance." Her tone switched to sarcasm at his presumption.

The serious look on his face cracked open with a laugh. "You consider taking barbs during one of your erratic mood swings low maintenance!"

"You could've left," she remarked, testing him.

"And been an award-class prick," he said seriously.

She shrugged. "No, merely average like the others."

Branson appeared through the lobby entrance.

Nodding with a "Good morning," he took both suitcases.

Sean put his hand on her elbow to steer her outside. After assisting her into the car, he joined her on the backseat.

"Your flight leaves this morning?" she asked.

"Yes," he stated, not offering any further information.

Noticing two cups and a bag from Pastry Perfect, Elsie helped herself. Sean eagerly accepted her offer of the open bag. Only crumbs existed by the time they reached the airport. Branson hugged Elsie after retrieving her suitcase from the trunk. Sean lifted his own bag. The two men shook hands. Inside the terminal, Sean led her to the check-in counter. They split long enough to retrieve their boarding passes and check their bags. At security, he put her items into plastic bins for x-ray. After passing through without incident, he repacked her shoulder bag.

When she tried to take it from him, he tossed it over his shoulder. "I got it."

"I'm not an invalid!" she groused.

He smiled indulgently as he continued en route to the departure gates.

When they arrived at her gate, she attempted to dismiss him. "Thank you for everything."

"You're welcome," he replied.

Instead of walking away, he sat in the seat next to the one she chose.

"Don't you have a flight to catch?" she asked.

Taking her hand in his, he replied, "Yes, this one."

"What?" flew from her mouth.

"I rearranged my plans to fly east with you," he clarified.

"Why would you do that?" Her confused emotions blocked her mind's comprehension of the lengths and expense to which he'd gone.

"I didn't think it wise for you to travel alone," he remarked calmly. "I took your phone with me last night to call Trish. She agreed. Then I switched my flights."

She didn't know whether to be indignant or flattered.

All she could manage was an "Oh."

CHAPTER NINE

HAVING AN HOUR till boarding, Elsie retrieved her laptop to work. Sean casually placed his arm across her shoulders while he read the updated script for *Sins of the Fathers*.

They didn't speak again until the announcement "Ten minutes to boarding."

Putting away her laptop, she stated, "I'm going to the ladies' room."

"I'll walk with you," he replied.

For a moment, she thought he'd follow her into the restroom.

As she finished in the stall, another woman said, "That guy looks like the Irish actor Mc something. Oh, what's his name?"

A voice full of teenage disdain answered. "Oh, Mom, I think you have Sean McEwan on the brain. I can't believe you made us late for dinner last night to watch that movie. And he's Scottish, not Irish."

The conversation ended. Elsie hurried to wash and dry her hands.

Before she could say anything to Sean, he said, "My turn" as he handed her their things.

Forcing her impatience to the back of her mind, she mentally listed what she needed to do when she got home. It didn't take him long to reappear. As they returned to the departure gate, she glanced around nervously, hoping no one else would recognize him. They received a few looks, but thankfully no one approached.

At the waiting area, the attendant announced, "First class may now board."

That was them. Sean handled their boarding passes. Elsie noted they had seats next to each other. He must've arranged that too. Once on the airplane, she situated herself in the seat by the window. To find her seatbelt, she had to lift the metal arm between them. When Sean sat, he didn't bother pulling it into place. She was eager to turn on her laptop after takeoff. Her companion resumed reading his script. For the majority of the time, she lost herself in writing. Late in the flight, she noticed him placing his hand on her leg or arm whenever the flight attendant would talk to him. This began to distract the story flow in her mind.

When he leaned in to put a peck on her cheek with a "Do you need anything, love?" her concentration was completely gone.

Closing the lid to the laptop with unintended force, he gave her a sidewise glance.

"Is everything all right?" he asked.

Not wanting to be peevish, she replied, "Too many distractions."

Shifting closer, he spoke in low tones. "I know. The stewardess won't leave us alone."

"Flight attendant," she corrected. "And she's flirting with you."

He rolled his eyes. "Bugger! What's with some people? I've done everything allowed in public to indicate we're together."

"Reeeally?" she questioned exaggeratedly.

"Short of shagging you right here, I've run out of ideas," he remarked wryly.

"That's not what I was referring to!" she said. "I meant the 'we're together' thing."

He looked at her in bemusement. "Didn't I make it clear last night?"

"Not to beat a dead horse, but again we've only known each other a couple of days." Her patience with this topic wore thin.

"As I've said, we have chatted on several occasions. Each time I found you more enchanting than the time before," he stated unwaveringly. "And this time was no different."

In a bewildered whisper, she said, "You've seen firsthand that I'm damaged in more ways than one."

He smiled easily. "All the more reason to not let you get away this time."

Unable to find anything to dissuade him, she fidgeted in her seat. Then to her complete shock, in one easy motion, he released her seatbelt to haul her onto his lap for a kiss, a kiss that made her tingly from her lips to her toes. His maneuver also made his growing sexual attraction impossible to hide.

"Oh, excuse me!" The overly attentive flight attendant interrupted. "The captain has the seatbelt sign lit. We are encountering turbulence."

The woman's comment was both timely and appropriate. Elsie couldn't help giggling. However, she didn't want it to appear she was openly mocking the stewardess. As she carefully slid off his lap onto the other seat, she muffled her mirth against his shoulder. None of this went unnoticed by him. His responsive chuckle reverberated in her ear.

Seatbelts remained on for the last half hour of the flight. When the flight attendant passed by to collect trash, she slid a piece of paper into the script on his tray table.

He glanced at Elsie uncomfortably. "Should I?"

"Might as well," she replied, shrugging, even though she already suspected what was written on the small slip.

Unfolding it revealed as expected: "Call me" with a phone number.

"Bloody hell!" The look on his face displayed displeasure.

"Apparently, she doesn't think I'm competition," Elsie remarked.

Through landing his sour puss didn't relax; his demeanor with her continued in a gentlemanly manner. At the gangway, he paused. She slowed her egress to turn her head to determine why.

In a terse tone, he said to the stewardess, "I don't cheat."

Then he tossed the piece of paper in the trash container by the exit.

As he caught up with Elsie, he grasped her hand. She smiled as they continued along the gangway.

To her surprise, he exited the gate area with her. Approaching luggage claim, Trish came into view. Instead of the usual jeans and flannel shirt, she wore a skirt, body-hugging scoop neck sweater, and heels. Apparently, she knew Sean was Sean McEwan. When she saw Elsie, she began waving vigorously. Elsie returned the wave. Rather than hurry her pace, she slowed.

Sean noticed. "Is something wrong?"

She hesitated a moment prior to answering. "Not ready for the bubble to pop."

"Wait! What?" He stopped their progress to stare at her incredulously.

"You heard me!" she squeaked, pushing at him to move again.

He bent his head to kiss her cheek as they resumed walking. He wore a big grin the last few steps to Trish.

Elsie made introductions. "Trish, Sean. Sean, Trish."

"It's so nice to meet you!" Trish gushed with excitement. "The spare room is ready for you."

Sean greeted Trish with a relaxed hug. "Thank you for making the last-minute arrangements."

His enthusiastic response to Trish's effervescent personality triggered Elsie's insecurities. The new acquaintances chatted about the spring weather. Elsie said nothing. Finally, the carousel produced luggage from their flight. He fetched their bags. Trish led the way to the truck. Since he handled their suitcases, he didn't have a spare hand to hold Elsie's. At the truck, he stowed everything in the bed under the cover. Elsie climbed into the backseat of the cab; Sean, passenger seat. During the drive, Trish rarely stopped talking long enough for anyone else to speak more than a word or two.

CHAPTER TEN

ARRIVING HOME, ELSIE heard Sophie and Tycho howling from the backyard. She stumbled from the truck in her rush to go see them. Sean put his arm out to steady her.

A meek "Thank you" emitted before she hurried to the front door.

The jumbled mess in the bottom of her shoulder bag made it extremely difficult to locate keys. By the time she found them tangled with headphones, Trish stepped onto the porch.

While unlocking the door, Trish asked with concern, "Are you all right?"

"I wish everyone would stop asking me that!" Elsie's temper flared as she pushed past her assistant to go through the doorway.

Dropping her bag onto the nearest chair, Elsie strode to the French doors leading to the backyard. Stepping outside, the duet increased in volume and ardor.

Releasing them from their 12 x 20 kennels, she exclaimed, "Babies!"

She invited them to greet her fully by lifting her arms wide. As they sprang up, she hugged them exuberantly. Both dogs kept the force of their weight on their back legs, not their front legs, which rested on her torso. They snuffled and gently licked the air around her face all the while grumbling territorially at each other. Most people would find two dogs of their breed and size unwelcome at such proximity. For those who understood their true temperament, it was actually an endearing pack ritual. After Sophie and Tycho were done bonding, they dropped onto all fours to trot away. The dogs didn't stay away long. Soon they both turned with ears high on alert. This notified her that Sean had stepped into the yard from the house. Had it been Trish, the dogs would've merely flicked their ears in acknowledgement. Racing to their pack leader, they paused to tautly straighten their postures to full height. The two furred sentinels tightly circled her.

"Elsie?" Sean queried unsurely.

She didn't bother to look at him. Instead, she bent toward the dogs.

Rubbing their ears, she said in an easy tone. "It's okay. Go say hello."

With her reassurance, they jogged to Sean. From behind her, she heard him chuckle as the dogs introduced themselves. Evidently, he passed inspection since pluming tails swished by her on their way to the far fence. Warm hands slid down her arms to meet at her midsection.

His brogue rumbled against her ear. "It's getting chilly."

The couple stood in silence, watching the sunset.

With the final pink and gold rays in the sky, she whistled. "Come on!"

The dogs ran toward them at full speed. He released her for the walk into the house. The table had been set for three.

"Elsie, I hope you don't mind. It's one of your homemade lasagnas from the freezer," Trish said in an unusually subdued manner.

Raising an eyebrow in Spock-like fashion, Elsie eyed her inquisitively.

The other woman merely stated, "Since you'll be otherwise occupied for the next couple of days, we need to review a few things before I leave. The editor sent requests for revision on *Ashes to Wildflowers* along with the proposed book signing schedule. She expects it to be finalized when we meet. There's also a substantial stack of mail. It includes a few invitations that you'll want to send personal responses to along with your regrets."

It was Sean's turn to raise his eyebrows. His questioning expression was meant for Elsie. Rather than respond to him, she handed him the bottle of wine and corkscrew.

Addressing her assistant, she said, "Please get me the invitations."

He poured wine for everyone while Trish fetched the envelopes. With everyone seated, the dogs flattened on the vinyl flooring.

"You made this?" he asked. "It's delicious!"

Elsie glanced over the edge of the invitation she'd been reading. "Don't sound so surprised. You should be here when I'm in the mood to bake."

Trish chimed in. "It's true. When she gets that way, we both usually gain ten pounds each."

"I wouldn't mind being here for that," he remarked truthfully.

"Exactly how long are we graced with your presence?" Elsie asked, not bothering to move her eyes from the paper she read.

"Trish mentioned you have an appointment in New York on Monday with your editor. My flight home is Tuesday from LaGuardia." He finally explained his travel arrangements.

"Hmmm" was her only acknowledgement.

"When she gets involved in something, Elsie gives it her whole focus." Trish filled the silence. "If I hadn't already made plans with my daughter, Cassie, I'd gladly come by every day to take care of meals or drive you anywhere you want to go during your stay."

"Nonsense, enjoy time with your daughter. We'll manage," he stated between mouthfuls.

Elsie didn't appreciate being talked about as if she weren't in the room. However, it did amuse her that they failed to realize she hadn't blocked their conversation from registering. To keep them ignorant of this deception, she fetched a pen from the desk in the living room. Returning, she made no indication she noticed them watching her movements. She made notations on each invitation. Till she emptied her plate once, he had two helpings and debated a third. With the last of the wine in her glass, she moved to the living room. She sat in her usual spot in the oversized paisley chair. When Trish finished clearing the table, she took her seat in the cream brocade Queen Anne chair. Sean excused himself to the spare bedroom to unpack his bag. With the invitations completed, Trish set those aside to type the responses from home.

Elsie reviewed the schedule. "I agree with the corrections you've made."

When Sean emerged, he flipped through the stack of invitations.

"Do you ever go to these?" he asked.

"No, too much stress," both women responded in unison.

"Does that mean I shouldn't invite you to my upcoming premiere in New York?" His tone held hope, which his words lacked.

Trish replied first. "When is it?"

"June 8." His eyes remained on Elsie.

Her assistant flipped forward in the planner. Then she turned the book for Elsie to view the timeframe before and after. His eyes flicked to the page too. Elsie wondered if he'd seen the MRI scheduled earlier that week. Otherwise, there was nothing else planned. The book signings were April and May.

"Please give exact details to Trish so I am properly prepared. Trish, see if we can get an appointment with any dress designers while we are in New York. If we have to extend our stay an extra day, please do." Elsie gave directions in reference to the event rather than openly saying yes.

The dogs at the door wanting to go outside gave her a reprieve from dealing further with it. The last thing she needed was to get sucked into the drama of unreasonable relationship expectations. When she returned to the living room, Trish closed the planner.

"I should be going. As soon as I have those appointments scheduled, I'll put them in the book," she spoke while standing. "Elsie, would you please walk to the truck with me?"

"Excuse me," Elsie said to Sean as she followed Trish outside.

Trish didn't speak again till she opened the truck door. "He seems to really like you. Give him a chance."

"How am I not?" she parried. "I'm letting him stay in my home and going to his premiere."

"I know you are being you, but sometimes it can put people off," her friend remarked gently. "Let him see your sweet and caring nature."

"It's not particularly easy when one of my best friends flaunts her vivacious personality and sexy body at him." Elsie shared her own frustration.

Trish responded with sincerity. "I didn't know he was interested in you that way until he shared some specifics from last night's episode. Were you even going to tell me?"

"Yes, when I believed it myself." It was Elsie's turn to be contrite.

A devilish grin formed on the other woman's face. "And details of your latest conquest of an international actor?"

Elsie quipped, "If anyone is doing any conquering, it would be him."

"Really?" Trish's pitch increased with intense interest.

Blood rushed to Elsie's face. "Stop!"

Trish hugged her dear friend then climbed into her truck.

The rest of Sean's stay, the couple merely spent the time getting to know each other. There were occasional demonstrations of Sean's affection, but he kept things tepid and didn't venture into her bedroom. The lack of passion put Elsie at ease. She'd even begun to think he'd decided to not pursue anything beyond friendship.

That was until his parting remark when they deposited him at the airport on Tuesday.

Sean made a request. "Perhaps you could bake over the next few weeks till the film premiere. I'd love for you to round out those gorgeous curves of yours."

"What?" Had she heard him correctly?

"I always admired your curves." For the first time, his face showed embarrassment at an admission. "I'm already smitten with you. But imagine how completely besotted I'd be then."

Chapter Eleven

{Present}

A BANGING ON the suite door disturbed them.

"Bugger!" Sean muttered in Elsie's hair.

As he disentangled from her, she stated, "It's Rusty."

"The bloke doesn't give up. Are you ready to talk to him?" he asked.

"Not really, but I don't think he'll leave us alone till he makes sure you haven't disposed of my body," she quipped.

The return of her sense of humor eased the lines on his expressive face. Another door-pounding sent Sean reaching for pants.

He hollered, "Coming!"

Sean managed to get his jeans on, but not fully buttoned.

Yanking the door open, he said sarcastically, "Hope you brought breakfast. We're starving after last night."

Rusty stormed into the suite. "I've been calling for the last hour. How is she?"

Drying her face with a hand towel as she stepped from the bedroom, she responded, "Like Sean said—starving."

Her light tone and relaxed smile halted Rusty's tirade. The furrowing of his brow in irritation and worry quickly altered to face-dropping revelation. He glanced at Sean, only partially attired, then again at Elsie; his face went red with resentful embarrassment.

On his way from the room, he grumbled, "That was a quick recovery."

Sean closed the door behind Rusty's dejected exit. Unable to contain his mirth any longer, he chuckled for the length of the walk to where she stood.

"What just happened?" Her tone denoted her bewilderment.

"Did you even look in the mirror when you washed your face?" he asked with amusement.

"I didn't see a point to it," she replied sarcastically. "Why?"

"Come with me," he stated, steering her toward the nearest mirror.

Seeing her reflection, she gasped. Most of the buttons on her nightshirt were undone, and the few that were buttoned were in the wrong holes; thus, leaving a fair amount of breast and thigh revealed. Sean's grin validated what Rusty had surmised from their disheveled appearances. She rolled her eyes exaggeratedly at Sean's image.

Sliding his hand along her exposed thigh, he stated in a husky voice, "I wish we could."

His lips trailed along her nape and around to playfully nibble her ear. The delicious tingles it provoked had her in total agreement.

Sighing, she leaned against him. "I wish we could too."

Sean hugged her tight. "Before that overactive imagination of yours contorts that statement into my having a clandestine affair with anyone other than you, I'm not going anywhere. We'll get through this together."

"Um, Sean, clandestine means ill-fated." She faced him somberly.

It was his turn to roll his eyes. "Who would've ever guessed I'd fall in love with a lassie like you?"

"Or I'd love a sodding Scotsman?" she teased.

"Okay, that does it! I'm calling that wanker back to deal with you," he stated with false conviction.

"Where's my phone?" She broke free of his arms to find the device.

"Woman!" he exclaimed in exasperation at having no other rejoinder.

Instead, he picked up the hotel phone to place an order for room service. The search for her cell was short lived since he didn't take the bait. She went into the bathroom to shower. The hurt look on Rusty's face floated around her mind. For some reason, she wanted to cry. She took a deep breath to fight the tightening in her chest. It didn't stop the tears from forming. She stuck her face under the water spray to hide the telltale droplets. As she was rinsing the shampoo from her hair, a hand landed on her hip to slide forward across her midriff.

She shrieked, "Aaiiee!" and lost her balance.

Thankfully, Sean's quick reflexes caught her against his naked form. "Are you all right, love?"

Catching her breath, she said, "You startled me."

"Didn't you hear me tell you breakfast will be here in fifteen minutes?" he asked with concern.

"I must've been rinsing the shampoo from my hair," she remarked.

"I also told you Rich and Janie called to check on you," he stated, releasing her.

She shrugged, not knowing what to say. Moving away from him, she stepped out of the tub. After drying, she realized he wasn't singing. Had Rusty's appearance this morning rattled him more than he let on—much like it had her? Following each time she spoke to Rusty, she had weird dreams and migraines for weeks, which would be quelled by Sean's presence.

{Ten months ago}

The book signing tour went successfully uneventful until they reached Los Angeles. The last evening on the West Coast, Elsie had an appointment with Harris. Trish scheduled it for dinner. Naturally, his wife, Sherry, had been invited too. The two assistants discussed software packages and fashion; Harris and Elsie, finances.

While waiting for dessert, Trish broached a taboo subject. "Where's Rusty these days?"

Sherry responded in a manner that didn't belie any confidentiality. "He's actually flying into LAX at 8:40. But don't worry, I didn't mention anything about you being in town. Plus, you're going to Vegas and Tulsa. He's heading north to Montana."

Images of a ranch backdropped by an unending blue sky horizon materialized in Elsie's mind. Further related memories remained beyond reach. They still had another week traveling. Wanting to avoid an episode, she pushed it aside. Dessert arrived, preventing anyone from noticing her momentary distraction. It also transferred the conversation to a sweeter topic.

Upon returning to their suite, Elsie packed prior to climbing into bed. Two hours into sleep, the phone on the nightstand rang.

"Hello?" she answered groggily.

The only sound on the other end was a click of someone disconnecting the line. Probably a wrong number, so she replaced the phone receiver. Since she was awake, she went into the main part of the suite to fetch a drink. As she took a long swallow from a bottle of water, there was a banging on the door.

Who on earth could that be? She groused at the emptiness on the way across the room.

Peering through the peep hole, she exclaimed, "Hells bells!" at recognizing Rusty.

His oxford shirt was only partially buttoned, its tails wrinkled from having been tucked in for an extended period. When she opened the door, he grabbed her into his arms. Even if he hadn't hugged her close, the overwhelming stench of alcohol would've been pungent.

Fighting for a breath of clean air, she said, "Rusty, please! You're suffocating me."

After he released her, she asked pointedly, "Why are you here?"

"Heardjouwer in town!" he stated loudly with slurred speech.

"Ssshh! You'll wake Trish, and she'll have you forcibly removed," Elsie stated frantically.

She guided him toward her room. "In here so we can talk."

Rusty weaved and bobbed. She turned to shut the door. Without her continued assistance, he stumbled to fall onto the bed. Grunting, he crawled across the king-size mattress to the pillows. He buried his face into the one she'd been using.

She sat on the edge of the bed to place her hand sympathetically on his back. "Rusty, why are you here?"

Rolling onto his back, he opened his empty arms. The lost look on his face squeezed her heart. She moved to lie against his chest. His muscular arms wrapped around her. He held her firmly, but not where she felt threatened. His whole body relaxed, causing a huge sigh to expel from his lips.

He muttered, "Mishjou, mate."

She realized he wasn't there for any specific reason other than needing her. It had been four months since they'd seen each other, when she'd pleaded for him to go on with his life without her.

"What do you need to get through this?" she asked, full of compassion.

His snores answered for him. Knowing he wouldn't do anything other than sleep off his drunk, she slumbered in his arms.

She woke in the morning to a knock on her door, followed by Trish saying, "Wake up, sleepyhead!"

During the night, Elsie and Rusty had switched positions. Now she was lying face up with his head nestled between her breasts.

Trish spoke while taking a step into the room. "What do you want for breakfast?"

The darkness and blankets concealed Rusty's presence from her.

Elsie answered quickly to send her assistant away. "I'm really hungry—toast, scrambled eggs with sausage, and a waffle with fruit."

"Oh my, you are hungry. But the extra calories will do you good," Trish replied.

When the door shut, Rusty stirred. He stretched and rubbed his face between her breasts. His beard rasped enticingly against her skin. Suddenly he froze. He must've been trying to determine whose bed he was on.

She didn't give him time to wonder long. "Good morning, Rusty."

His tension eased only slightly. "How did I get here?"

"You were pounding on the door around midnight. I couldn't very well ignore you." She kept her voice low in case Trish hadn't gone to her own room.

"So . . . you invited me into your bed." His tone contained cockiness, followed by his lips partaking of her exposed cleavage.

"Not exactly," she said, pushing away from him. "I didn't need you waking Trish. We came in here to talk."

She turned on the light as she got out of bed. He groaned at the pain it caused in his head.

"I ordered you eggs and toast," she stated on her way to the bathroom. "I'm going to take my shower. You might want to consider taking one too. You reek!"

In case he attempted to join her under the hot spray, she didn't dawdle. Shortly after turning the water off, he staggered into the tiled room minus clothing. The brightness caused him to close his eyes long enough for Elsie to cover her own nakedness with a towel. As she hurried by him, he slid a callous hand across her bare butt. She wasn't worried he'd follow her for more. He had the look of befuddlement he always got after a night of extreme inebriation. Most of his showers would be spent trying to remember what he'd done or not done.

"Wait! How do I know that?" she questioned herself aloud. "Had he drunk a lot during our relationship?"

Wracking her mind for memories locked in an unbreakable vault would only give her a headache. Instead, she called the front desk for assistance regarding clothing for him.

After dressing in a peach-colored peasant blouse and jeans, she sought Trish. She was still in her room.

Elsie knocked and opened the door a crack. "Trish, can I come in?"

"Sure," her friend replied.

"I'm going to tell you something, and I need you to not flip out or think the worst," she said with uneasiness.

"What's wrong?" Trish put her hand on Elsie's arm with concern.

"Nothing is wrong, but you won't be happy." A grimace formed with her statement.

"Spit it out and we'll figure it out." Her friend used one of Elsie's own phrases.

Taking a deep breath, she blurted, "Rusty is in my room showering."

Seeing the fury form on her friend's face, Elsie rushed to explain. "He showed up drunk and in a state. If I didn't let him in, he would've just gotten himself into a situation to be splashed across the tabloids. Nothing happened. He passed out seconds after falling onto the bed."

Trish reined in her ire. "As long as he behaves himself, I will not allow him to upset you."

Again, Elsie had the sense of knowing that he only wanted to spend time with her.

It gave confidence to her next statement: "I can handle him."

"Okay." Trish nodded. "Breakfast should be here any minute."

Elsie returned to her own room. After collecting his clothes, she placed the smelly garments into one of the hotel's plastic laundry bags. A cloud of steam billowed with Rusty as he emerged from the bathroom. She pulled her oversized worn flannel robe from the suitcase.

Tossing it at him, she stated, "Put this on. Breakfast will arrive momentarily."

After donning the robe, he sat on the edge of the bed. "Elsie?"

Hearing the strangeness to his tone, she joined him.

But he couldn't seem to find the words to articulate his apparent apprehension. "Did we . . . or did I . . . ?"

She allayed his anxiety with the truth. "You made it to the bed and passed out."

Before he could say anything else, room service was at the main door.

She patted his leg. "Come on. A hot shower is only part of the cure."

When he didn't stand with her, she paused. "Rusty?"

He grasped her hand. "Why didn't you chase me away last night?"

Placing a hand on his face, she replied, "To save you from yet another embarrassing situation."

He tugged her onto his lap for a gentle embrace. "Thank you, mate."

Trish called from the main room. "Breakfast is getting cold."

This time when she stood, he followed. Seeing how the robe fit him perfectly made her wonder if it had been his.

Trish kept her word. "Good morning, Rusty. Did you sleep well?"

"G'day. According to Elsie, my snoring curled the wallpaper." He self-mocked to keep things light.

His words struck Elsie with the urge to laugh. She had said no such thing to him this morning. But she had a vivid memory of telling him exactly that at another time. If only she could remember the details. The smell of the food caused her stomach to grumble in anticipation.

Trish made an excuse to eat in her room. "I have to finish packing."

Rusty didn't notice the lameness of her statement. He merely dug into breakfast. Elsie relished the waffle with fruit and whipped cream.

Partway through the meal, he leaned toward her. "Whipped cream."

A light lick at the corner of her mouth turned into a kiss of wonder. Again, a similar scene flashed into her mind's eye for a moment. They were interrupted by a knock on the door. Relieved for the reprieve, she rushed to answer it. It was the order from the men's shop.

After tipping the delivery person, she held up the big bag. "Your clothing has arrived."

His brow furrowed with confusion. "You had someone go to my hotel?"

She stated, "That would be difficult since I don't know where you are staying."

"You could've called Sherry," he stated logically.

"Well, I didn't think of that. I called the shop next door." She dropped the bag dramatically at doing something that seemed incredibly stupid rather than benevolent, then went into her room.

Rusty must've recognized the meaning of her actions.

He soon followed with the bag. "You know, Sherry probably would've given me a rotten time about being here."

While Elsie finalized her packing in silence, he dressed. He folded the robe for her. When she zipped her suitcase closed, he lifted it from the dresser to the floor. He hadn't buttoned his shirt yet. Her eyes were fixated on his muscular chest. Images of painted fingernails sliding seductively across his chest had her wanting to do the same. Sapphires sparkled from a silver wedding band on the ring finger of the left hand. A matching band with smaller stones flashed from Rusty's hand holding reins. He struggled to keep his horse under control.

His voice boomed. "Elsie, hold on!"

She felt herself falling; then everything went black.

Trish's terse voice began registering. "Precisely why you shouldn't be here."

Taking a deep breath, Elsie glanced from Trish's concerned face to Rusty's frightened one. She was lying on the bed, not standing by the dresser.

Rusty helped her sit as she stated, "I'm okay. Sometimes I get lost in a labyrinth when I try to find the memory to something that pops into my head."

An expression of expectation etched his face.

"Snippets with no timeline or point of reference." She hated to disappoint him yet again.

It took all of his skills as an actor to conceal his misery. And then to further his Oscar-winning performance, he continued as if they'd only bumped into each other on the street.

In a breezy tone, he said, "It was, as always, an immense pleasure to see you, shag-worthy sheilas. But I must be off."

With a kiss on each of their cheeks, he sauntered from the suite without hesitation.

The two women looked at each other in shock.

Trish broke the silence. "Off his rocker!"

"I don't know whether to laugh or cry." Elsie shared her own feelings.

"Neither! He's not worth it," Trish stated vehemently. "We should be going. We don't want to be rushed at the airport."

Not necessarily agreeing with her assistant in regard to Rusty, Elsie merely pulled the handle on her suitcase to indicate her readiness.

CHAPTER TWELVE

By the end of the book tour, Elsie was exhausted from the last week of restless nights. Strange dreams plagued her slumber. There were headaches. Thankfully, none was migraine strength. The first night home she felt an overwhelming sense of loneliness. Even cuddling with Sophie and Tycho couldn't ease her mind. Calling Trish or Sara would only make her feel more of a burden on her friends than she already did. Unable to resolve this feeling, she baked: chicken, lasagna, cheesecake, cookies, and muffins.

When Trish arrived in the morning, she remarked, "I should've worn my fat pants."

"Ha ha ha," Elsie mimicked flatly.

"Take a seat. I'm going to get a cup of coffee and muffin. Then we will go through the stack of mail." Trish knew when to take charge.

As Trish sorted and opened mail, she came across a card that she slipped to the bottom of the pile. There was no point in asking why. She would share it eventually. Two muffins later, they had reached the end of the pile. Elsie was yawning uncontrollably.

"You get a reward for surviving the mail." Trish handed the card to Elsie.

It had an overseas postmark—Scotland. Her eyes went wide with a mixture of fear and excitement as she looked to Trish for reassurance.

The other woman smiled mischievously. "Go on. It won't bite."

Elsie slid the note card from the envelope. A scenic picture of wildflowers covered the front. Handwritten inside:

Dearest Elsie,

Should've never told Eilish I spent time with you.

She asks after you incessantly.

Anxious to see you in New York.

Hope you are well.

Still smitten,

Sean XO

Below which were flight numbers and times along with their hotel reservation.

Trish had arranged for her son-in-law to drive Elsie to the city the same day Sean's flight arrived. This gave the couple two full days to get reacquainted before parading in front of photographers. Happy thoughts played in Elsie's mind. An hour later, she woke to the smell of fresh coffee. When she entered the kitchen, she saw Trish standing on the patio. After pouring the steaming brew, Elsie joined Trish outside. The bright sun made her squint. Tycho and Sophie raced toward their beloved person.

"Hello, babies," she chirped at their approach.

Trish took Elsie's mug to allow her to schmooze with the dogs. Feeling loved, they trotted away to lie in the cool shade of the trees.

"Are you ready to tackle e-mails?" Trish asked.

"Yep." She accepted her cup.

As usual, Elsie worked on a storyline while they reviewed e-mails. She didn't reply to individuals. Instead, she would write a blog on her website incorporating their topics of interest. There weren't many so they created an outline to work from later. The doorbell interrupted.

Trish peered through the bay window. "FedEx."

"Hello, Jim. What do you have for us today?" she greeted upon opening the door.

The young man's deep timbre always made the women smile. "Why does Ms. Endy's publisher send express mail when they are the ones who send her out of town?"

Trish laughed as he handed her multiple envelopes. Before she could sign for any of it, Jim jogged to the side door of the vehicle. He reappeared with one small box sitting on two big boxes. Elsie watched Trish enjoying the young man's bulging biceps. Trish motioned for him to set the heavy items on the floor near Elsie. This gave Trish a great view of his firm buttocks.

"Thank you, Jim," Elsie stated with a straight face.

"You're welcome, Ms. Endy," he replied courteously to hurry onto his other deliveries.

Trish stopped him long enough to sign for everything.

Stepping inside, she remarked, "I agree with Jim. Why do they insist on sending royalty statements individually by the book instead of together?"

"You say that every month when they arrive. Dare say it might be a good thing I've forgotten the other one hundred times you've said it." Elsie poked fun at her dear friend.

"As long as Jim is our FedEx driver, I hope it continues," Trish kidded in response.

Opening the small box revealed the latest manuscript to go public midsummer. The large boxes contained books for signing. At least in these, the publisher shipped different titles together. Instructions were included in each plastic bag, separating the requests.

"Now we know what's on tomorrow's agenda," Elsie remarked at the large amount of books.

"Or we could stretch it across the week." Trish grinned with a glint in her eye.

She caught on to her friend's overt effort to see the hunky delivery man every day. "Or we could do that."

Elsie pressed "Save" prior to closing her laptop. "I am going to heat a muffin and read through this book."

"You don't want to save it for Tuesday?" Trish reminded her of the upcoming appointment at the hospital.

"Figured you'd want it since you are the one who sits and waits. I'm the one they are poking and prodding." Logic, as usual, pervaded Elsie's argument.

The next week sped by with a day at the hospital for tests and another day recovering.

Early the morning she was leaving for New York, Sean phoned. Hearing his voice gave Elsie a moment of girlish glee. This was quickly replaced with one of disappointment.

"Love, I'm terribly sorry, we're fogged in. My flight is grounded till it lifts." He stated the status of his flight.

"Okay, I'll cancel the hotel for tonight," she replied as Trish arrived.

"No, you won't!" resounded in stereo—from across the ocean and from her living room.

Trish's voice overrode Sean's. "You have an appointment for your dress. If you aren't there, Stan may never do one for you again."

Elsie stared at Trish when she spoke into the phone. "I'm sorry, Sean. Trish walked into the house. Now, what did you say?"

"You will go as scheduled. If I take off anytime in the next few hours, we could still have a late supper together," he replied optimistically.

"Okay, okay. You two win." Elsie agreed with their arguments.

"See you soon, love." Then he disconnected.

Trish waited for Elsie to explain. "Well?"

Her one-word response said it all. "Fog."

"Ah." Trish moved to the kitchen. "As soon as I get my coffee, we'll review your lists."

Having been friends for six years and her assistant the last three, Trish knew Elsie made lists for important things. Since the accident, the lists had become necessary for everything.

Suddenly, the dogs rushed to the back door with excitement.

"Good morning!" lilted cheerily through the screen of the slider.

"Good morning," Elsie replied as Sara slid the door open. "Oh, guys, let Sara inside."

The three women had coffee and cake prior to tackling Elsie's packing.

In the bedroom, Trish reviewed the list of things.

When she got to the clothing, she remarked with disbelief. "You wrote three outfits with no specific pieces."

"Let me see that!" Sara said with equal shock as she snatched the paper from Trish.

Elsie responded with uncertainty. "I was hoping you two would help me."

The two older women looked at each other and giggled like schoolgirls.

Sara spoke first. "I think someone is anxious to see a certain Scot."

Embarrassment infused Elsie's cheeks with the telltale color.

"And what exactly were you thinking about doing to, um, with the sexy Scot this weekend?" Trish asked suggestively.

"I don't know anything other than the premiere Saturday night," Elsie replied lamely.

"Then you are in good hands with us," Sara remarked. "Flirty and fun should do it. Don't you agree, Trish?"

"If I remember correctly, we bought extra outfits of that type for your trip to California. And since they aren't appropriate for book signings, they are still hanging in here unworn," Trish stated, stepping into the closet. "Plus, the weather this weekend is supposed to be in the fifties."

When she reappeared, she had items to fit the bill—a sundress, a trendy yellow blouse and blue plaid kilt-style skirt, capris and coordinating drape sweater.

Sara clapped excitedly. "Yes, yes, yes."

Elsie's face scrunched. "Do you really think that particular skirt is appropriate?"

"Of course, you look adorable in it," Trish stated adamantly.

"Adorable? I was hoping for sexy," Elsie retorted.

"Stick with cute. It softens your personality," Sara remarked.

"Thanks, I already feel sufficiently out of my element. Reminding me that I come across as harsh isn't helping." Elsie rubbed her forehead in consternation.

Sara immediately stood to hug her. "You know that we love you the way you are. We just want you to let someone else in to see and love the real you too."

Trish chimed in. "Two weeks ago you were perfectly confident about handling Garnet. Where did that woman go?"

"You saw Rusty?" Sara asked expectantly. "Why didn't you say anything?"

Elsie looked at Trish, then back at Sara. "Because you two have opposing opinions in regard to him. It didn't seem worth discussing an issue that would cause my two best friends to be at odds."

The two women referred to made eye contact.

Trish took the lead on the response. "We promised we wouldn't argue about it anymore. We only want you to be happy."

Sara completed the thought. "And we understand why you asked Rusty to leave."

"But you think it was unfair to oust him without full disclosure." Elsie's tone deflated at rehashing this topic.

"You knew him far better than we did. We trust your judgment," Trish stated forcefully.

"But if you ever change your mind, we'll support you," Sara challenged.

And there it was—dissension in the ranks. It was up to Elsie to smooth it over.

Or change the topic, no matter how blatant. "Did we remember the underwear and shoes for the dress?"

"Right here." Trish pointed to a specially marked bag.

Sara heard the terseness to her tone. "We've gotten everything on the list. Why don't you and I go outside while Trish packs the suitcase without your constant checking?"

"Sorry," Elsie remarked contritely.

Sara steered her from the room, along the hall, through the kitchen, and out the door.

While they walked the fenced perimeter, Sara returned to the previous topic. "Have you had any new memories about Rusty?"

"The usual disjointed ones. Remarks he made at breakfast felt like déjà vu. Plus, I saw a silver wedding ring with diamonds and sapphires." She relayed the same information she'd typed into her journal.

"Ah." Her friend sounded like a psychiatrist. "Then why not talk to him about it?"

"Because I can't handle seeing his eyes full of hope only to be transformed into loss and disappointment when the memory doesn't connect to anything." Elsie sighed at her own guilt. "Maybe if more things made sense . . ."

"Or if that leak in your brain was plugged to allow you to heal completely." The conversation ended the same as all of the others with this topic.

The two friends hugged at the side gate.

Sara gave her an extra squeeze. "I'm glad you're going this weekend. Don't overthink anything and have fun!"

"I will. Thanks for taking care of Sophie and Tycho," Elsie replied as Sara stepped onto the path leading to the gate into her own backyard.

The dog duo followed Elsie into the house. In the living room, she sat on the sofa to autograph the remaining stack of books. The suitcase waited ready by the door. Both dogs sniffed it. Tycho's tail dropped. Sophie moved to lie at Elsie's feet. Absently, she rubbed the gray girl's neck with her foot. Tycho paced. He even followed Trish too close on her way into the bathroom to get the door shut in his face.

Upon her reemergence, Trish requested, "Would you please hug him or something?"

"What? Oh, Mr. Mopey," Elsie responded. "I have two more books to sign, then I am all his."

As soon as she finished, she shifted to the middle of the sofa.

"Tycho. Sophie." She invited by patting the spots on either side of her.

Both dogs eagerly complied. They bonded until the dogs decided they had enough. This gave Elsie fifteen minutes to review everything one more time with Trish. Her son-in-law, Casey, drove in front of the house on schedule. After Elsie's bag had been loaded, the two women hugged.

"Don't do anything I wouldn't do," Trish recommended.

"That leaves things wide open," Elsie teased.

"Exactly!" her sexually adventurous friend responded emphatically.

CHAPTER THIRTEEN

ON THE NINETY-MINUTE drive to New York, Elsie allowed her excitement to percolate. Check-in went without a hitch. Entering the suite, she found a vase of exotic flowers from Sean. Also, the message waiting light flashed on the room phone. It was from Stan's assistant reminding her that they'd be arriving at 3:30. At 3:20 she donned the matching undergarments selected specifically to wear with the gown. When Stan and his entourage arrived, she answered the door wearing a robe. Her readiness pleased the designer. After slipping the dress on, she stepped into the shoes for full effect.

As the dresser zipped the emerald gown, Stan ordered, "Stop!"

With the gown held closed, he fussed with the bodice. Soon a seam ripper and threaded needle appeared. Elsie forced herself not to fidget as Stan reworked the delicate lace and chintz covering her breasts. Finally, he indicated for the garment to be zipped completely. To her surprise, it held her breasts securely without binding.

The designer clapped his hands together loudly once. "Now, my dear, walk away, then come back."

The skirt flowed smoothly as she obeyed his instructions. When she stopped in front of him, he ran his hands along the seams from top to bottom. Again, she had to keep from flinching at standard actions by a professional checking the lines of his design.

"Yes, yes. It will do quite nicely." The designer stated to his staff, "See how the fuller curves enhance the silhouette beautifully."

Snapshots were taken of the gown and its detailing. She didn't bother smiling since the camera lens never tilted upward to include her head in its frame. His assistant had warned her during their first appointment this would happen. The dresser assisted her out of the finished gown. One of the others held the robe for her to put on right away. It didn't take long to steam the garment. A total of thirty-five minutes passed from start to end with Stan and company.

Elsie had missed a call from Sean; still no estimated time of departure. Traveling in New York City alone after dark made her uncomfortable. Dressed again in tank top and jeans, she rode the elevator to the lobby. Even with the cashmere cardigan, her attire didn't meet the standards of the hotel restaurant. And the bar wouldn't be open for another hour. Not that she relished dining alone there. When she asked the concierge if any restaurants delivered, he handed her menus along with making recommendations. This helped ease some of her tension. On the ride to the suite, she realized she hadn't been totally on her own since the accident. Even at home, she was never completely alone, with Sara and Tom right next door. It wouldn't surprise her if Trish and Sara coordinated their schedules to ensure someone would always be nearby. Dwelling on being alone would only conjure unpleasant images. After ordering dinner, Elsie finished unpacking her suitcase. To her relief, Trish had organized everything into outfits. The inability to coordinate clothing successfully had nothing to do with her brain injury. It was rooted in constantly hearing during her teenage years that she was smart, not pretty. This warped her fashion sense. If you're not pretty, why bother caring what you wear. Thank goodness for friends like Trish and Sara. Sara had a flair for class. Trish wouldn't leave the house until jewelry, metal buttons, hardware on shoes, and purse all matched.

It was Elsie who would suggest throwing appropriateness to the wayside with, "Who cares what everyone else thinks? Be a fashion rebel."

To which they would respond: "There's a difference between a tasteful breach of fashion and outright mutiny."

To say the least, Elsie had walked the plank so often it had become second nature—thus, the reason she didn't make any important clothing decisions without one or both of her best friends there to save her from drowning in embarrassment. Amidst the outfits, she discovered a slinky lavender negligee. She wouldn't be shocked if Trish and Sara had conspired on this particular item. Shame, they hadn't included instructions on how to be a femme fatale too. The inner ramblings instigated the need for her laptop. Trish had argued with her not to pack it. While no one was watching, she'd slipped her travel notebook with its power cord into her shoulder bag. Several paragraphs later, dinner arrived. She fumbled a few minutes with her wallet till she had the right amount to pay the bill plus tip. The aroma of stuffed shells and garlic bread emanated from the bag. As she situated to eat and type, her cell phone rang. It was Sean.

"Hello!" she answered excitedly.

"—lo-uv." His words were choppy.

She wondered if he'd been drinking. "Any news?"

When he spoke again, it wasn't any clearer with intervals of static. "—after midnight—."

"I can't hear you. Send a text message. Okay?" she stated.

"—ay . . ." And the bad connection ended.

If his flight departed after midnight, he wouldn't arrive in New York until breakfast.

The whole night alone—she shrugged. Not like there was anything she could do to change the situation. It made her thankful she'd snuck the notebook. Elsie refocused on what she'd been typing. Hours later she had a strong start on a new book. No text message ever came from Sean. It was possible he hadn't felt it necessary. Uncontrollable yawning forced her to finally turn off the computer shortly before eleven. She stashed it in the drawer under her clothing. As she completed her nightly routine, she donned her usual flannel pants and camisole. The luxurious bed put her to sleep instantly.

A voice calling her name woke her some time later. Assuming it was a dream, she merely snuggled deeper into the pillow.

"Elsie love!" It sounded like Sean.

Since she hadn't fallen back to sleep, it must be real. Getting up to investigate, she flicked on lights as she went. The main door was open only as far as the security bar would permit.

Sean's voice came through the crack. "Elsie love. Thank goodness."

"Sean!" She, now fully coherent, pushed the door shut to remove the protection device.

Then she opened it to allow him entry. "I thought you weren't getting in till morning."

He burst through the door. "I was in line to board when I called."

Draping a garment bag across the closest chair, he turned to grab her into a fierce hug. "I am so glad to see you!"

His emotional state took her quite by surprise.

She waited till he released her to speak. "Did I miss something?"

"Hopefully me!" he remarked cheekily as he collected his things to move into the bedroom.

"I can't say as I actually missed you. But I did look forward to seeing you again," she stated candidly, following him.

He turned to peer at her aghast. "You didn't miss me?"

"I barely know you to have missed you! And it's not like we chatted on the phone since we last saw each other." Exasperation crept into her tone.

For a moment, he paused unpacking to stare at her intently. She fidgeted uncomfortably under his scrutiny. He resumed his task without saying anything. A chill in the room caused her to shiver.

He said softly, "Love, get under the blankets. I'll join you shortly."

As she willingly complied, he disappeared into the bathroom. She feigned sleep when his weight shifted the other side of the mattress. He wrapped an arm around her waist to pull her against him. Involuntarily, she tensed.

He whispered in her ear. "We're both tired. We'll discuss things in the morning. For now, sleep."

As he relaxed, she did too.

CHAPTER FOURTEEN

WHEN ELSIE WOKE, she turned to rub her face in the pillow. Instead, she encountered Sean's torso. His auburn chest hairs felt soft against her cheek.

The human pillow rumbled as he spoke in a thick voice. "Good morning, love."

"I'm sorry. I didn't mean to wake you," she replied, shifting away from him.

Halting her egress by tugging at her waist, she fell full against him.

"I don't mind," he said as his lips nuzzled her neck. "This is a very pleasant way to start our day."

His hands slid along her curves to pause at her firm derriere to explore her nether region.

"Don't!" she screeched and pushed to get away from him.

He stopped his advances to query. "Is something wrong?"

This time he didn't prevent her exodus.

She squirmed free from his loosened hold to stand by the bed. "You said we would 'discuss things in the morning.' It's morning."

He sat, propping pillows behind him for a comfortable position.

Stretching a hand toward her, he requested softly, "Please sit."

Filled with uncertainty, she hesitated.

"Please?" His tone pleaded.

She complied by sitting next to his legs, far enough from his hands. His displeasure with the distance could've been quickly concealed by the skilled thespian. However, his emotions remained exposed.

He started with an odd comment. "I thought you were comfortable with me."

"I am." She was perplexed. "I just found it strange how excited you were to see me, especially since you hadn't called over the last few weeks to get to know each other better."

"Isn't that what this weekend is for?" he remarked with a grin.

"It is. But, well, I don't know. Not hearing from you, I'm not sure what you want." She revealed her lack of understanding.

"Love, I thought I made it clear. I want to be with you. If I hadn't made plans with my children, I wouldn't have left." Clutching the blankets to keep his manly parts covered, he scooted across the bed to sit next to her. "If I had called, it would've made me miss you more and been a distraction from them."

Placing an arm across her shoulders, he continued. "I'm here now—and all yours."

"I just don't understand how you could miss me when you barely know me." Her past pain prompted pessimism.

"I've read all of your books. We've talked on numerous occasions over the last couple of years. Elsie m'love, I know you." His lips found the sensitive spot under her ear.

She shrugged away to stop him. "That's a me I don't know. How about you get to know this me?"

"You are the same you," he stated simply.

His claiming to know her better than she did herself put her on the defensive. "And you are suddenly the expert!"

Striding into the bathroom, she shut the door firmly for privacy.

A few minutes passed and there was a light knock on the door. "Elsie?"

Ignoring him, she turned on the shower. Under the pulsing hot water spray, she realized she'd been harsh. Closing her eyes, she drenched her hair, rinsing the shampoo from it. He had merely tried to clarify the situation.

Suddenly, he could be heard from the other side of the glass door. "Love, I'm coming in whether you like it or not."

"What?" she exclaimed in soprano rather than her usual alto.

Clearing the suds from her face, she opened her eyes in time to see him step into the stall with her. Not saying anything else, he reached around her for the soap. His manhood indicated he was affected by her nudity. But he did nothing about it; he merely washed. While she stood there full of shock at his audacity, she began to enjoy the unintentional show.

A subtle tingling sensation cascaded through her body. Firm hands soaped her curves. Bodies rubbed sensually. As his mouth covered hers in a deliciously wanting kiss, she clung to his muscular torso.

"Love?" Panic filled Sean's words.

She opened her eyes to see Sean's face above hers. Water dripped from his hair onto her cheek. A towel had been wrapped around her. Still naked, he sat on the tiled floor holding her securely.

"W-what happ-ppened?" she asked with bewilderment.

The breath he'd been holding released slowly with his response. "While I was rinsing, you put your arms around me. Your eyes were glazed like you were in a trance. When I asked what you wanted, you fainted."

Running through the minutes prior to passing out, she recognized it had been a memory of Rusty rather than Sean making a sexual advance. As with the other returning snippets, it had no point of reference.

Before Sean could pursue her thoughts, there was a knock on the door.

"Bugger! Room service. Will you be all right till I get back?" He carefully propped her against the shower stall.

"Yes, go," she answered, glad to have a few minutes to herself.

He donned a hotel robe on his way to the door. As she slowly moved into the bedroom, she wondered how his body felt as it tensed for release. That thought would make Trish proud. By the time he returned, Elsie wore underwear. Even though he'd just seen and held her naked, she blushed at his seeing her in this state of undress.

"You should've waited for me," he stated.

"It wasn't a seizure. Sometimes a memory flash causes a blackout." She explained what occurred. "Thank you for catching me before I got hurt."

While he selected clothes to wear, he remarked, "Any chance of you sharing the memory?"

It took a few moments to word an appropriate response to his request. "Not the specifics. But I will say that all of the flashes are triggered by the immediate situation."

As he processed the implication of what she meant, his forehead slowly furrowed into a look of annoyance.

Turning away from her, he carried his clothing into the sitting area. It didn't take long for her to dress in the plaid skirt and pale yellow blouse. She joined him for breakfast.

Sitting, she saw there was food for two. "I only ordered for me."

"When I picked up my room key, the front desk asked if I wanted breakfast. They added it to yours." His answer made sense.

Trying to lighten his brooding expression, she perpetuated the conversation between bites. "What did you have in mind for the day's activities?"

"Events thus far have curtailed indoor activities," he stated flatly.

"That can't be the only thing you expected?" Her tone was laced with reproach.

"Not expected, but hoped you might be so inclined." His words rang with regret.

This did not sit well. Forcing herself to swallow the food in her mouth, she couldn't find words to voice her own disillusionment. Internally, she berated herself for allowing the excitement to permeate.

Standing, she announced, "I have to stop by my publisher's. I should be back by lunch."

A look of surprise filled his face. "You haven't finished eating."

"Not that hungry," she replied, slinging her bag over her shoulder. "See you later."

"You shouldn't be wandering the city alone," he argued, pushing himself away from the wheeled table.

"Taking a cab to my destination is hardly wandering," she replied, her words drenched in sarcasm.

Striding toward the bedroom for shoes, he conceded. "I'll go with you."

Not heeding his remark, she exited the hotel room without him. The elevator doors opened immediately at pressing the down button. There was a couple disembarking from a taxi when she stepped from the lobby onto the sidewalk. The doorman waved to the driver to wait. As the vehicle drove away from the curb, Sean emerged from the hotel. Smug satisfaction eased Elsie's earlier irritation. It took another five minutes for her cell phone to play "The Scotsman." Answering it was not going to happen. However, curiosity retrieved the phone from her shoulder bag to listen to his message.

"Love, I am sorry I upset you. I want a relationship, not just sex. Please don't do anything reckless." Whether sincere or acting, the effort mattered.

The destination address was her responding text message.

Upon her arrival, she told the receptionist she was expecting someone. The rest of the staff flitted about her. They even provided a bottomless mocha latte. An hour later, Elsie finished her business. However, Sean had not appeared. Her cell phone didn't indicate any missed calls or text messages. Walking across the expansive lobby of the office building, she waffled on whether to return to the hotel or go shopping. A different decision was made for her when she stepped outside and into Sean. He hugged her with the same zeal as last evening's.

Catching her breath, she said, "You could've come to the office."

"I know," he replied, releasing her body to grasp her hand as they walked. "I only arrived minutes ago."

"It took you that long to decide to meet me here?" she asked before thinking.

"I had something to pick up, which took longer than I thought." His answer came easily. "Was there anywhere else you wanted to go?"

She shrugged. "Not really. Whenever I'm here I usually window-shop. Of course, it's always with Trish. It's our way of creating a wardrobe that I'm willing to wear yet fashionable."

"Your system appears to work since you look quite fetching." It was an earnest compliment to woo rather than seduce.

She responded with shy appreciation. "Thank you."

As they strolled aimlessly hand-in-hand, the earlier discomfort between them dissipated. Soon they came upon store windows to view. At the clothing displays, she would pause. Occasionally, she would take a picture to e-mail Trish. When they neared jewelry stores, it was Sean who would steer them toward the displays to gaze at the sparkly wares.

In one window, he quipped, "See anything you like, m'love?"

"These pieces are too much," she remarked. "Simply understated in silver is my style."

He smiled like he had a secret. She didn't pursue why.

Suddenly, his demeanor switched to serious. "Are you all right? I mean, is this walking tiring you?"

"Not at all, I'm enjoying it." Her answer chirped honestly.

This cleared his face immediately.

The rest of the day continued in an easygoing manner. They shared a relaxed intimacy with hugs, kisses, and personal touching. Again that night, the couple slept in a chaste embrace.

In preparation for the premiere, Sean spent the morning doing interviews. This gave Elsie plenty of time to write. It was a good way to keep her nervousness at bay. At noon, he appeared with sandwiches from her favorite deli per request. Stretched on the sofa together, they watched television and napped until her salon appointment. When she returned to the room, his low snores greeted her.

Kneeling by him, she whispered, "Sean, time to dress."

Shifting onto his side, he mumbled, "Come back to bed."

"You're on the couch and you need to get ready for the premiere." Her tone became stern.

He reached to grab her. In his muzzy state, she dodged his hands with ease.

As she walked toward the bedroom to dress, she stated loudly, "I bought sexy underwear for under the gown. No gown, no sexy underwear."

The mental image invigorated him. He rose from the sofa. His eyes forced wide as he moved by her into the bathroom. Reentering the bedroom in short order, he began stripping.

She asked bashfully, "Please, is it too much to ask for privacy?"

"Not at all, m'love," he chuckled as he collected his tuxedo and accessories.

"Thank you," she said sweetly, closing the door behind him on his way into the living room.

Ten minutes later, Elsie emerged to a patiently waiting Sean.

Seeing her, a low whistle emitted his approval. "You look lovely."

Before she could say anything, he continued, "But there's something missing."

She glanced down at her dress for fear that something hadn't fastened properly.

He removed a 4 x 4 velvet box from his tuxedo pocket. "The jeweler called yesterday right after your text message."

She watched in fascinated silence as he opened it to expose a two-karat heart-shaped ruby pendant on a delicate silver chain.

Making eye contact with him, she stumbled over the words. "It's beautiful. Thank you."

While he placed it around her neck, he stated, "I had several jewelers searching for this. It was a relief one of them came through before we left the city."

The fact that he had put such effort into a gift that fit her tastes intensified her already heightened attraction to him. Taking her hand, he slipped it into the crook of his arm on their way to the festivities. To her delight, she seemed invisible to the press. But to Sean, she was the center of attention, so much so his eyes continually found their way for long periods to where the ruby heart nestled.

"Stop staring at my décolletage!" she murmured in embarrassment.

He whispered in her ear, "I can't help myself."

The flattery fed her fervor for him. But they had a busy evening. Like at the party on the pier, he stayed by her side. The Taylors held a private party after the film. When the power couple saw Elsie with Sean, there was no look of shock.

Janie quickly confiscated Elsie for a trip to the ladies' room.

While they reapplied lipstick, Janie baited the hook. "You and Sean look cozy."

Unable to conceal her growing glee, Elsie's face broke into a wide grin. "I can hardly believe it!"

"Why? You are a wonderful person. And you know Rusty would follow you to the ends of the earth," Rich's wife remarked. "From what I've witnessed in this one, he's not too far from that either."

"You are as bad as Trish!" Elsie protested. "It's not like I have the kind of beauty that turns heads."

"Do you ever look in the mirror? You have natural curves and hair that women pay big bucks for." Janie couldn't hold her tongue. "There's just something about your face and eyes when you are talking to someone—they feel like they are the only person in the room."

"Sounds like you have a bigger crush on me than your husband," Elsie teased with a cheeky grin.

The married woman took no offense at the playful comment. "Now, that's the Elsie we all know and love!"

"Enough!" Elsie exclaimed in mock horror. "Rich and Sean will think we flushed ourselves if we don't get back soon."

Hours later, the two couples bid each other good night. As soon as the limousine began the drive to the hotel, Sean buried his face into Elsie's exposed cleavage.

His voice reverberated against her sternum. "I've waited all evening to do this."

The breath from his sigh of joy tickled nerve endings. After a few moments, his lips tasted the delicate skin cushioning his cheeks. He made a hot, moist trail from her bosom along her neck. Their mouths met in a kiss of ravenous desire. His hands greedily groped her curves; hers, his lean torso under the formal jacket.

When they broke for a gasp of air, she forced reason to the forefront. "Sean, can we please wait till we get to the room?"

Putting a small amount of empty seat between them, he replied thickly, "You're right."

The sexually charged silence made the remaining drive unbearably long. He thanked the driver as they disembarked at the hotel. His hand rested on the small of her back for the walk across the lobby. Other guests joined them in the elevator, which made for a tight space. With her slightly in front of him, their bodies pressed against each other. His hand shifted lower to boldly caress. She bit her lip to prevent a moan of pleasure escaping. As the elevator rose, so did part of his anatomy. The people around them were totally unaware.

As they neared their floor, one of the women remarked to another. "Did you hear? Rusty Garnet was on one of the late night shows. It's rumored this is the hotel he stays in when he's in New York."

The hand returned to its higher placement. When the doors opened, the other passengers parted for them to exit. Even after the doors closed and they were alone in the corridor leading to their room, his hand remained in its gentlemanly location. Upon entering the room, the anticipated seduction did not commence. Matter of fact, he put distance between them. The lid on the bottle of Jack Daniel's cracked under his firm grasp.

Unsure, she queried quietly, "Sean, I thought . . .?"

"Not tonight, love," he answered in a tone of defeat as he poured the amber liquid into a glass.

What Elsie couldn't understand was why the possibility of Rusty being in the hotel had doused Sean's ardor. Feeling dejected, she went into the bedroom to remove her gown. While it's on its hanger, she checked it for any damage. Satisfied there was none, she moved into the bathroom to scrub away the makeup. The teardrop ruby earrings were placed into a satin jewelry pouch. She wasn't ready to take off the heart necklace. As she dried her freshly washed face, she took in the whole reflection. In the foreground she stood wearing only the ruby necklace with an emerald green lace bra and panty set. In the background, Sean leaned against the doorframe still in his tuxedo.

Making eye contact with him in the mirror, she asked innocently, "Do you want something?"

Reversing into the bedroom, he didn't answer. She wondered how long he'd been watching. Done at the sink, she had no reason to linger. Donning a robe seemed silly since he'd already seen her in her underwear without motivation. As she emerged from the bathroom, he was hanging his tuxedo. The view of him in green plaid boxers and green socks made her giggle unexpectedly.

He looked up with a pained expression, which immediately muted her momentary merriment.

"Sod it!" He slammed the closet door. "Your memories of Garnet can bugger off! I'm here and I want you!"

With that forceful statement, Sean pulled Elsie roughly into an embrace. His mouth pillaged; his hands plundered. Her soft form molded willingly to his hardness. The sensations their caresses generated caused them both to emit guttural noises of wanting. He scooped her up to place on the bed. Before continuing his crusade, he hurriedly stripped their remaining undergarments. To her own astonishment, she tugged him down on top of her. Their limbs intertwined as their bodies rubbed against each other in sensitive places.

She didn't want to wait any longer. "Sean, please."

"Yes, m'love," he responded with equal urgency as he repositioned himself.

He waited till they made eye contact, then he was inside her. At joining, she didn't know whose moan was louder. As their bodies rocked in unison, fervor possessed her. When she asked for more, he gave with zeal.

Enjoyment echoed with his evident end emission. "Oh, Elsie m'love . . ."

This instigated her climax. Bright sparkles and images burst into her mind as the waves of pleasure surged through her body.

As she regained her senses, she relished the feel of him still in her. Gentle kisses feathered her neck and face.

Tightening his hold on her, he whispered in her ear, "M'love, please tell me it was that good?"

"Mm, when can we go again?" she purred with an atypical amount of confidence.

His head popped up to look at her face. "Really?"

"Mm hmm," she answered with a gyration of her hips.

A rumble of anticipation reverberated as his lips captured hers. The couple indulged in each other till the wee hours of the morning.

CHAPTER FIFTEEN

SHORTLY BEFORE NOON, Elsie woke. From the other side of the bed, Sean's breathing indicated a deep sleep. She carried clothing into the bathroom. Throughout her shower, her stomach grumbled incessantly. After which, she decided to run for the coffee and bagels she craved. Several notes were placed around the suite for Sean to find if he woke prior to her return.

Ten minutes later, Elsie quite literally bumped into Rusty. She was entering the bagel shop, he exiting.

"Krikey, mate?" he exclaimed, then hugged her unexpectedly.

Equally shocked, she smiled shyly. "Hello, Rusty. How did the talk show go?"

He answered while moving them along the sidewalk away from the door. "Smoothly. Visiting your publisher and making a weekend of it?"

Not comfortable sharing her new relationship, she answered with a partial truth. "Yes, just approved a final copy of the latest book."

Glancing around, he asked, "Trish let you out alone?"

"Occasionally, she lets me run free." Her playful response brought a grin to his tired face.

Her stomach growled in protest at smelling the food. "Excuse me."

Chuckling, he opened the door into the aromatic shop. "Sounds like you need food, mate."

He followed her. Ordering an assortment of bagels and two coffees didn't appear odd since he assumed Trish was along on the trip. He carried her fare and flagged a taxi, which he climbed into with her.

"The Ritz-Carlton Central Park," they said in unison to the driver.

Another big grin lit Rusty's scruffy face. Elsie couldn't help returning it with equal affection. This had not been a wise reaction. The brawny man read it as an invitation. He leaned in to kiss her—not a mere friendly peck, one of knowing and promise. It was familiar and intoxicating. For a few moments, she savored the feeling. The growing sensations caused by recent activities had her wanting to get lost in his touch. But that would only confuse the situation.

Breaking the lip-lock, she pleaded breathlessly, "Rusty, please don't."

"Why? You're enjoying it, aren't you?" he asked, his question rhetorical, as he pursued further intimate contact.

"I'm dating someone and he's waiting for me!" The words blurted out, lacking the compassion she'd have preferred.

The meaning of her words wiped away his happy expression. The taxi parked in front of the hotel. Closest to the curb, he exited to assist her.

As they walked onto the lift alone, he asked in a strained voice, "Is he good to you?"

Seeing the worry in his eyes, she replied truthfully, "Yes, the polar opposite of my first husband."

When the elevator doors opened at her floor, he delayed her exodus with a tentative hand on her arm. "Mate, if you ever need anything—and I mean anything—call me."

His earnest sentiment tightened her chest.

Stepping into the hallway, she said in a controlled tone, "Thank you."

The closing doors prevented the Australian actor from saying anything else. By the time she entered the suite, her tears overflowed.

"Hello, m'love. I was beginning to worry," the Scotsman said cheerily as he stood to greet her.

Kissing her cheek, his demeanor changed to anxiety. "What's wrong?"

She shook her head, unable to talk without making it worse. Sean placed the coffee and bagels on the table. Then he led her to the sofa.

They sat together, and he wiped away the salty droplets. "Did I do something?"

Again, she shook her head.

He asked another question. "Are you regretting last night?"

She managed to croak a "no".

Consternation filled his features. She didn't want to tell him but knew she should, particularly with her current emotional state. He removed the lids from the coffees.

Handing her the one with the extra cream, he ordered, "Drink."

She obeyed. Its enticing aroma had only been a precursor to the flavor. The distraction gathered her frayed emotions. He sipped from his cup of hot brew, watching her.

"I ran into Rusty." The reason spewed forth.

"And?" he prompted.

Taking another swallow of the coffee, she selected her words carefully. "We bumped into each other at the bagel shop then shared the same taxi."

His anger was restrained. "What did he say?"

Feeling the guilt creep into her neck and face, she muttered, "It wasn't what he said, he—"

Before she could complete the sentence, his ire exploded. "Sodding prick! What did he do to you?"

"It wasn't like that." With shaking hands on his flailing arms, she attempted to calm him. "He kissed me. And with everything else that happened, it was too much."

Sean stilled. It scared Elsie. She removed her hands.

In a guarded tone, he asked, "Are you having second thoughts about him and us?"

His suspicious question brought more tears. She fought to keep them in check.

But her voice revealed the renewed upset. "No! It's all just so unexpected."

His tension didn't dissipate. This distressed her further. Suddenly, from the agitation and lack of food, she hiccupped painfully.

This doused his anger. "You need to eat."

He opened the bag to prepare a bagel for her. No sooner had she taken a bite than they heard a muffled "Gypsies, Tramps & Thieves." Elsie dug through her purse to find the cell phone. This gave her enough time to finish chewing.

Swallowing, she answered, "Hello, Trish."

Her assistant replied, "Hi. Just giving you warning—Rusty is in New York. You might run into him."

"Too late," Elsie responded sardonically.

"That explains your tone. It didn't go well?" Trish asked fretfully.

"Not particularly," she replied, not sharing details.

Her friend could tell something wasn't right. "Sean's in the room and you can't talk about it."

"Yep," she answered minimally.

"Okay then, we will talk Tuesday." Trish disconnected the call.

Taking a second bite of the bagel, Elsie noticed Sean studying her actions. A knock on the door distracted his scrutiny. When the door opened to reveal room service with a pot of coffee, Elsie exhaled the breath she'd been unconsciously holding.

After the door closed, Sean carried the tray to the low table. "Your note said you went for bagels. So I ordered this."

"That's good. My cup is empty." It sounded stupid, but she had to say something.

He poured them both fresh cups. They ate in silence.

Finally, he spoke again. "Feel better?"

"Yes," she answered, cocking her head to one side.

Sliding across the sofa, he chastised gently, "If you hadn't gone without me, this could've been avoided."

"You were sleeping so soundly. It seemed wrong to wake you." Her tone was affectionately timid as she shared her reason. "Especially with how attentive you were all night. I wanted to show my appreciation, not run into the one person who bothers you."

Peering through her eyelashes at him caused the lids to flutter involuntarily.

"Waking up with you gone gave me a bit of a fright. Thank you for the notes. But I had rather looked forward to you beside me." It was his turn to clear things between them. "Garnet only bothers me because I'm afraid you will remember how close you two were and I'll be history."

His admission tugged at her heart. Words couldn't relay how his remark filled her with joy. Instead, she gave him a soft kiss on the lips.

His hand firmly held hers. "Rich called to see if we want to meet them for an early dinner."

"That would be nice," she agreed amiably. "But it needs to be someplace casual."

"I'll ring him back," he stated.

"Do you mind if I write till dinner?" she asked politely.

"Not at all," he answered with a peck on her cheek. "I'll ring him now to get specifics."

While she typed at her computer, he read through the script again in preparation for his next role. They hadn't discussed arrangements for that timeframe as of yet. Rich had finally convinced Sean to play the patriarch in *Sins of the Fathers*. Offering Sean's daughter, Eilish, the part of his daughter in the movie had sealed the deal.

This became the topic of conversation at dinner. Filming would start in a month in the UK. Ironically, it was also the opening scene. A few weeks would be spent taping in the studio, followed by autumn location shots in Pennsylvania in September and October. November and December would take them back to the studio. The movie was scheduled to be released next summer. Since Rich and Sean were deep in discussion, the women spoke quietly to each other.

Janie said, "We saw Rusty after you did."

A look of horror crossed Elsie's face.

The director's wife followed quickly with, "He didn't say anything other than you two had bumped into each other."

"Who I was seeing didn't come up?" She asked the question that concerned her most.

"Nope." Janie shook her head. "He didn't ask and we didn't offer."

Relief washed over her. "Thank goodness."

Full from dinner, both couples got dessert to go.

The city's early evening heat was stifling, which forced the couples to catch a cab. To make room, Elsie sat on Sean's lap. Till they arrived at the hotel, his desired plan for the remainder of the evening could hardly go unnoticed. Between that and the lack of air conditioning, sweat formed. The vehicle coming to a stop in front of the hotel had her anxious for a shower for two. The inevitable happened. They crossed paths with Rusty on the sidewalk, so much for keeping her lover's identity secret. Thankfully, he didn't stop to chitchat.

As he hurried to their abandoned taxi, he merely said "G-day" to the two couples.

She couldn't help wondering where he was going in such a rush. Perhaps a date? This annoyed her. Earlier she'd gotten upset because she thought she'd hurt him. Evidently, she wasn't as important to him as he'd led her to believe. When they entered the suite, she avoided Sean's anticipated advance.

However, he recognized the evasion. "What's wrong?"

"I feel grimy. I'm going to take a shower," she whined petulantly.

Her tone facilitated bathing in privacy. As she spread the sudsy bath gel across her skin, she thought of Sean's lips and hands on those same sensitive parts. She chastised herself for letting Rusty's actions affect her negatively. Sean deserved her undivided attention. After drying, she retrieved the lavender negligee hidden in the drawer. She stepped into the sitting area of the suite to locate Sean. The room was dark except for the television, his shirt draped on the nearby chair, the bottle of Jack sit prominently on the coffee table. A glass of the golden liquid made its way to his lips. At seeing her, he delayed his action. He watched as she walked across the room to him.

She asked with nervousness, "May I join you?"

Resuming his earlier action, he downed the contents of the tumbler. Tossing the empty glass onto the chair, he grabbed her. Pulling her onto his lap, he ravaged her lips and curves. When he attempted to remove the silky material, she stood abruptly. Lifting the hem far enough to expose her bare bum, she lured him toward the bedroom. Once there, she pushed him backward onto the bed. The rivet buttons of his fly undid with ease. His hard member sprang out uninhibited. Her fingers caressed this soft skin; he sighed with pleasure. When her lips replaced her fingers, he grunted in gratification.

It didn't take long for him to reach for her. "Elsie m'love, please . . . climb on."

As she straddled him, her moist, hot femininity welcomed his throbbing manhood. "Oh, Sean . . ."

His groans intensified as she moved to stimulate her own heightening enjoyment. He held on till her powerful orgasm engulfed them both.

Even after their breathing returned to normal, his arm's held her tightly on top of him.

"Before we fall asleep, I need you to promise me something," he said against her hair.

"Mm, what?" She didn't want to think.

"You will be here when I wake up," he stated.

Relieved it wasn't about Rusty, she readily agreed. "I promise."

After kissing her forehead, they drifted into blissful slumber.

Some time later, she jerked awake.

This disturbed Sean. "You okay?"

"Yeah, I must've been having a nightmare." She shrugged from ignorance.

Wrapping his arms around her again, he stated, "I'll protect you."

Curling tighter against him, she knew he would. This action woke another part of him. His hands slowly caressed her naked form. Her gentle nibbles on his chest informed him she wanted him to continue. Escalating his ministrations, they were quickly panting for more. This merging didn't disappoint either.

Checking the clock, she saw the alarm would blare shortly. She relished the intimate silence till it did.

"Bugger," he muttered, squeezing her close. "I'd rather spend the next two hours here with you."

"You're the one who agreed to join Rich for the morning interview. You can't renege now," she stated as she moved to exit their bed of decadence.

"Not yet!" He yanked her onto the bed and across his torso.

"Sean you have to—" Her giggles subsided into moans of pleasure.

Delivering her climax ended his delightful delaying deed. While he showered, she luxuriated in satiated sensuality.

Before he left to fulfill his professional obligation, he gave her a lingering kiss. "Stay put. I don't want any more encounters with Garnet."

"Jealous?" she teased.

"Immensely!" His tone was wounded as he replied with sincerity.

This unexpected response took a few moments to register in her sex-fogged brain. Till she realized they needed to discuss it, the suite door shut, denoting his departure.

To not miss his appearance on the morning show, she hurried through her routine. She ordered coffee from room service. Yesterday's leftover bagels served as a sufficient breakfast. With the television on in the bedroom, she packed their bags. The interview went well. However, to her horror, they also had Rusty on the show. Sean needn't have worried about her bumping into him. But Elsie was sure neither Sean nor Rusty had been all that happy to see each other.

When Sean returned, his disposition didn't indicate the two men had any kind of altercation. Since she had everything taken care of in the suite, they checked out.

On the drive home, she finally asked, "Were you and Rusty civil?"

"Yes, we were. It helped that Rich directed the conversation, or it may have gotten ugly," Sean answered without subterfuge.

"Rich is a very good director," she remarked wryly.

"That's why I agreed for Eilish to join the cast of *Sins of the Fathers*," he stated proudly.

Her face formed a pout. "And I thought it was because she begged you to let her be in one of my stories."

"That too." His chuckle filled the car.

Wanting to know where she fit in, she asked a related question. "When is your flight?"

"July 8," he answered, maneuvering around a car on the turnpike.

"Not to meet Eilish, to the West Coast," she clarified.

He glanced at her with an odd expression. "Carla won't make those arrangements until we see how filming is going."

She sighed in frustration. "Are you being obtuse for a reason? When are you leaving my place?"

"July 8," he replied the same way as previously but then added, "We have a month together. Didn't Trish tell you?"

Caught between anger at Trish and elation with Sean, it took a few moments to reply. "No, Trish didn't tell me. But I am very glad to have more time with you."

Grasping her hand, he lifted it to kiss. "Me too!"

Chapter Sixteen

{Present}

"ELSIE M'LOVE?" SEAN called her name from far away.

Opening her eyes, she saw him kneeling by her. His hair was damp, and a towel was knotted at his waist. He spoke again, but the words were garbled as if she was underwater. The words she tried to say echoed in her head as gibberish.

Picking up the phone, Sean requested, "Rus . . ."

Then she was in a tunnel, taking her away from consciousness. Each time she opened her eyes, disjointed events occurred like a scratched DVD skipping scenes. An unfamiliar doctor and nurse administered an injection into the IV attached to her hand. They spoke at seeing her eyes open. It was noise. Sean and Rusty argued in the hallway outside her room. Elsie yelled for them to stop. The words were barely a whisper. Rich and Janie intervened, separating the two men who loved her.

"Two men loved her" resounded in her mind as she sunk into the blackness.

Finally, Elsie regained full consciousness. The hospital room was dimly lit. The methodic beeping of the monitor by her bed was the only sound. Unsettled by the previous images, she pressed the call button. A young nurse ran into the room.

"Ms. Endy, you're awake!" Her words of excitement could be clearly heard.

Elsie rasped with effort. "May I have something to drink?"

"Of course. I will be right back." The nurse disappeared.

When she returned with a small plastic pitcher of crushed ice and an apple juice, she began chattering. "The doctor will be here soon to talk with you. I need to take your vitals before he gets here."

Elsie simply nodded while sipping at the juice-drenched ice.

The doctor appeared. Under his lab coat, he wore jeans, wrinkled lavender oxford, and loafers without socks. The collar of his white coat stood up on one side and smoothed down on the other. Elsie contained her mirth, but not the telltale smile.

"Aren't you chipper for spending the last sixteen hours in critical care?" he stated, lacking any bedside manner.

This only amused her further.

A little giggle escaped at the start of her scratchy response. "Other than a dry mouth and sore throat, I feel fine."

Reading the chart for the numbers the nurse had written, he seemed shocked. "Everything reads normal now. When you came in, we treated you for a stroke. You were having difficulty breathing so we intubated. After speaking to your doctor back east, we modified medication according to his recommendation for your ongoing condition. A couple hours ago, we removed the tube."

Watching her nod in recognition, the doctor continued. "We did an MRI. Your doctor from home is still studying the pictures to identify the cause of this atypical episode."

"When can I be released?" Staying in the hospital any longer than absolutely necessary was unacceptable.

Taken aback, the doctor answered in textbook form. "I'd like to run more tests and keep you under observation for a few days."

"No. I have been through every test and ones created just for my condition. The episode has passed." Her logic and determination had clearly been unaffected.

She put the doctor on the defensive. "It's 3:00 a.m. Let's see how you are at eight."

"That makes sense." Unable to argue this point, she shared her need for food. "Any chance of getting something to eat?"

"I'll see what we have in the lounge." The doctor exited after updating her chart.

The nurse reappeared ten minutes later with oatmeal, crackers, and another apple juice. After eating the little feast, Elsie dozed. At eight o'clock, she had met standard hospital requirements for release. The doctor phoned Sean to inform him she had woken and could be taken home. The nurse helped her dress in the clothing she'd been wearing yesterday.

Sean burst into her room less than fifteen minutes later. "Elsie m'love?"

"Yes, my sodding Scot." She openly teased his overdramatic entrance.

"Don't do that now." He hugged her frail form. "You frightened me."

"It has passed. May we please go?" she pleaded.

The doctor walked in at that moment. "Your release papers are signed. But if any other symptoms develop, please call. My number is on the paperwork."

"Thank you," the couple replied in unison.

Branson stood by the car as an orderly wheeled her to the curb.

Holding the door open, the driver remarked, "Good to see you are better."

She smiled. "Thanks."

Once seated, Sean handed over her cell phone. "Call Trish and Sara. Tell them you are all right and we are catching the next available flight home."

While she made her calls, he made some too. When they arrived at their suite, they were greeted by Rich and Janie.

"I'm sorry to have worried you all unnecessarily," she said contritely to the duo.

"We don't want to tire you. We just wanted to see you were all right," Janie spoke.

Janie hugged Elsie. Rich followed suit. As soon as Sean shut the door behind the couple, he opened her laptop.

"Sit," he ordered.

She obeyed. He prepared a cup of tea.

Handing her the cup, he stated, "I'm going to find us a flight home."

His focus on the computer screen didn't prevent him from watching her. She stood to select cookies from the gift basket.

Completing the snack, she stood to request: "I smell like the hospital. Do you mind if I shower?"

"Wait five minutes while I reserve our seats." His commanding tone sat her on the sofa again.

With a sigh of success, he closed the laptop. "Okay, m'love. Our flight leaves tomorrow at 6:00 a.m., with a transfer and short layover in Cincinnati. We should be home for dinner."

"Would you please text the specifics to Trish and Sara?" she requested on her way to bathe. "One of them will need to pick us up."

To do her bidding, he fetched her cell phone. Prior to completing his task, he assisted her into the tub. In case she had a problem, he stayed in the room while making the call.

After which, he met her with an open towel. "Tom will clear the driveway from last night's snow. He and Sara will meet us at the airport. Trish will get the house ready, including groceries. If there is anything specific you want, text her."

Elsie dressed in regular clothing rather than pajamas. "Can we have Chinese for dinner?"

"I'll run for it later," he stated firmly.

"There is one place I'd like to go to if you don't mind." She tested his tolerance.

Taking her hand, he responded, "Where would that be, m'love?"

Her words rushed with trepidation. "To talk to Rusty."

His body tensed, but his reply was compassionate. "If you need to, I understand."

"I don't need to. He wanted to talk to me about something. I'm curious as to what." She clarified her reason.

The tension drained away. "Your trip to hospital and our ensuing discussions covered it."

She didn't follow. "How?"

"Like everyone else who hasn't seen you for months, your appearance worried him. He wanted to make sure you were being cared for properly." He expounded his previous answer.

This only amplified her earlier guilt. "Oh."

But it did prompt another question from her. "How did he even get involved?"

"When you passed out the second time, I needed help. He was the obvious choice," Sean replied with a shrug.

She hugged him. "Thank you for tolerating him. I know it couldn't have been easy."

"When it comes to your wellbeing and happiness, I will do whatever it takes, including dealing with that wanker." His hands rubbed soothingly.

She sighed at the thought of how difficult it was for both men. Sean had suffered through her episodes, tests, and treatments without a single complaint. He respected her need to do it her way while still being there to catch her when things got shaky. He didn't deserve to deal with Rusty swooping in. Rusty now knew one of the main reasons she'd sent him away was because of her diagnosis and questionable prognosis. Adding insult to injury, she'd allowed another man in to basically usurp his role.

With this unusual seizure so quickly behind a regular episode, it signified her options had expired. She needed to finalize her affairs for the worst possible of outcomes.

Taking a lesson from Scarlett O'Hara, she said, "I'll think about that tomorrow."

In the meantime, she just wanted to be with Sean. Eventually, he moved her to the bed for a nap. Later when she stirred, he wasn't beside her.

His Scottish brogue floated from the living room. "No, I've got that covered with a Ghirardelli basket being delivered tomorrow. Anything else you can think of can't hurt."

It sounded like a conversation with Trish. Not wanting to spoil any other surprises, she busied herself with packing. Underneath her release papers, she discovered a folded 3 x 5 piece of paper. It was from a hotel notepad. It had the number 307 written on it. The way the 3 looped into the 0, she identified the handwriting as Rusty's. With her internal decision to set the date for surgery, she needed to talk to him. For however close their relationship had been, she owed him closure. Rebroaching the topic with Sean would not go well this time.

At her emergence, Sean's tired face transformed quickly into a smile. "Ready for dinner, m'love?"

Before she could utter a word, her stomach grumbled loudly.

"Okay then, I will be off," he chuckled. "Please order another pot of hot water for tea."

As soon as she ended the call with room service, Elsie hurried to room 307. Knocking on the door with determination, she willed herself not to flee.

The door flung open by a barely clad, intoxicated, and rumpled Rusty. "What the hell do you want?"

Not allowing his ire to forestall her intention, she spoke. "I, uh, wanted to thank you for your help the last couple of days. It couldn't have been easy, and I appreciate the depth of . . ."

Rusty's drunken swaying exposed a naked woman walking up behind him. The woman's hands slid over his shoulders to splay across his chest as she pressed her body against his. Elsie was stunned into silence. A similar image flashed in her head, causing her to grab for the doorframe. Rusty stepped away from the woman toward Elsie.

His tone sobered. "Mate, are you—?"

Collecting her shattered wits, she excused herself. "I'm sorry. I didn't mean to disturb anything."

Walking away quickly, she didn't want him seeing her distress. Reassessing her previous reasoning as faulty, she chastised her stupidity. Why shouldn't he be with other women? It's not like they were married! After all, she had replaced him. These thoughts raged. Somehow she managed to return to the suite safely. She fell across the sofa. Sobs ripped from the depths of her psyche.

Room service with the carafe of hot water disrupted her tear-fest. Realizing Sean would be back shortly, she had to bury this inexplicable sense of betrayal. She went into the bathroom to hide any signs of her frazzled state. To control her emotions, she started their packing. Upon his return, Sean poked his head into the bedroom.

Using an Oriental accent, he said, "Derivery for Rady Endy."

The reminiscent phrase made Elsie smile. To her surprise, the wafting aroma lured back her lost appetite. The food and tea sated her stomach. Unfortunately, nothing seemed to fill the emotional black hole that had formed from her destructive thoughts—earlier guilt for what she'd put Sean and her friends through, uncertainty of the outcome of surgery, fear that the dogs would feel abandoned, unresolved relationship with Rusty. Elsie leaned into Sean.

Feeling her mood shift, he queried, "M'love?"

Her tone conveyed crushing melancholy. "Everything I've put you through has been exceptionally difficult. And if the last forty-eight hours are any indication, it's only going to get worse."

With his voice full of compassion, he stated, "You're worth it."

She snuggled deeper into him. He planted a kiss on the side of her head.

"But there is something I need you to do for me." Rarely did he request anything she hadn't already given freely.

She gave him a questioning look.

"This episode wasn't like the others." His voice cracked with emotion as he pleaded, "When we return home, please schedule surgery."

"I will," she willingly surrendered.

He asked with skepticism, "No debate?"

"You're right, and I'm too tired to fight anymore." Her tone hadn't altered.

He studied her face before remarking, "Did we wait too long? You can't go into surgery without your chutzpah."

"I'm not giving up. For the time being, I need to stop struggling with how I feel about everything and just be." Her eyes welled without overflowing.

"I'll *just be* right here with you." Even though his words were a play on hers, they were heartfelt.

CHAPTER SEVENTEEN

SLEEP WAS ELUSIVE that night for Elsie. The black hole sucked her into overanalyzing prior encounters with Rusty.

{Six months ago}

Filming of *Sins of the Fathers* had been moved to Nesquehoning, Pennsylvania. The nearby extinct coalmine and neighborhoods with remnant period housing served as the perfect backdrop. The novel was a dramatization of her grandfathers' lives and how they had impacted her parents. It was a geographically appropriate location. It had been written as a love story reminiscent of *Romeo and Juliet*. Sean played Elsie's beloved yet devastatingly flawed Pappy, her paternal grandfather. This character perpetuated the story through five decades. Elsie believed with all of her heart that Sean's portrayal would finally recognize him for an Academy Award.

Reds and yellows painted the trees with vibrancy, which signified the exuberance of the immigrants finding a new home. As if on cue, a thunderstorm washed the trees bare to portray the harsh washing away of innocence and trust. With the approach of winter, the gray clouds and hibernating plants illustrated the continued hardship. Rich couldn't have created a better backdrop to accentuate the story's emotional progression. Eilish, Sean's daughter, played her role with youthful verve. Sean's overprotective nature forced Rich to send him to wardrobe or makeup as a distraction during certain scenes.

A week into these location shots, the actor who had accepted the role of Elsie's maternal grandfather was in a serious car accident. He would be unable to fulfill his contract. Rich sent Elsie an e-mail as soon as he heard. With only another week till this actor's first scene, Elsie had no qualms about Rich finding an acceptable resolution. The father of the second family in the storyline died in his forties of a heart attack. But the few scenes he would be in set the stage for revelations later in the movie. The same day the replacement appeared on set; Elsie did too. Trish and Sara had been anxious to see some of the filming. Elsie finally agreed on a day for them all to go watch.

Seeing Elsie's unexpected arrival, Sean commandeered her for a few private moments. Eilish played hostess to Trish and Sara. Needing to be smudged with coal grease for his next scene, Sean went to makeup. Eilish's bubbly personality explained the upcoming scene to the two other women. Remembering every passage of the script, Elsie moved closer to watch the take. She viewed the monitor over the director's shoulder. The man hired to play her maternal grandfather had his back toward the camera. There was something familiar about him.

Rich yelled cut to the actors. Then to Elsie he said, "I need to tell you—"

His words were interrupted by a voice saying, "G'day, mate."

She felt ambushed. "Rusty?"

Even the period bushy mustache couldn't conceal his cocky grin. She fought the urge to slap it off his face. In contrast, Rich's expression was thoroughly apologetic.

First, the director dealt with his actor. "Don't you need a wardrobe change for the next scene?"

Rusty strolled away still grinning.

Rich put his arm across her shoulders as he spoke in a consoling tone. "I'm really sorry. But Rusty was my original choice for this part. And knowing the story in intimate detail, he didn't need added time to step into character."

Sighing audibly, she acknowledged his logic. "You did what was best for the movie. Catering to my feelings won't get that done."

No sooner had they made amends than Sean appeared full of ire. "I just ran into Garnet. You cannot seriously tell me you hired that wanker?"

Elsie stepped away to let Rich handle his temper tantrum. Both Trish and Sara gave her questioning looks at noting Rusty's presence.

"I trust Rich's judgment. He needed an actor on short notice. Rusty was available." Her tone made it quite clear the subject was closed.

The trio watched intently as Rich did a brief placement run-through with the two experienced men. Usually, actors are given the opportunity for a rehearsal.

In this instance, as soon as Rich returned to his chair, he announced, "Action."

Onlookers witnessed two masters barely hold their personal conflict in check to deliver scene after scene with inspired perfection. It was a sparring of skills rather than fists as they subtly challenged each other. The underlying animosity between the two men transpired into their scenes together. Since their characters clashed in the story, Rich's decision could be considered relative to genius. Each time a take ended, the two would go to opposite corners to await further direction.

Watching this tensed display exhausted Elsie. As soon as her girl friends noticed the strain, they invented excuses to head home.

On the drive, Trish broached the obvious question. "Since we could practically feel the overcharged testosterone, I take it Sean didn't know Rusty would be there?"

"Rich probably only told Carla," Elsie remarked. "Even if part of what we felt translates to the screen, his strategy will pay off."

"What about you?" Sara pursued an equally tenuous tangent. "How do you feel about seeing him?"

She shrugged at her answer. "It took me by surprise. He's a good actor. He should do the part justice."

The other two women shared a look; then Sara asked, "And Sean?"

"Oh my god! I forgot to say good-bye to him," Elsie shrieked with sudden realization.

Digging through her purse, she retrieved her cell to send a text message to him. "Headache went home. XO."

Once home, Trish puttered about the house, doing odd tasks until dinner. During this time, Elsie worked on one of her novels. Writing allowed her to work through her unsettled emotions.

Sean called.

Lacking any formalities, he asked, "Are you all right? Do you need me?"

It took a moment for her to register what he referred to. "No, not that type of headache."

"I thought seeing Garnet would cause issues," he stated with concern.

"It was a bit disconcerting not having any warning. The tension between you two was too much to watch any longer." There wasn't any reason to hide the truth. "Rich certainly has a flare for finding a way to get the best from his actors."

"I hate to admit, but the takes he let us screen were incredible." He offhandedly shared his respect for both Rich and Rusty.

"Guess he'll be glad you approved of his choice," she replied sardonically.

"Cheeky, m'love, cheeky," he teased. "Call if you need anything."

"I will. Love you." Her words were sincere.

As usual, he stayed on the line till she disconnected.

Her sleep that night was plagued by disjointed images of Rusty and her together—holding hands, walking on a beach, hugging, laughing, and enjoying sex. A chill rippled through her body, waking her. As she stood, the sweat-soaked pajamas in the frigid room made her shiver uncontrollably. After quickly donning fresh flannel pajamas, she went to the living room to discover why the house had gotten cold. The embers in the woodstove barely glowed. Kindling reignited the fire so logs would burn successfully. The clock chimed 3:00 a.m. Sophie and Tycho stretched and yawned on their way to the kitchen. She pressed the "Start" button on the coffeemaker prior to letting the dogs outside. An extremely cold wind whipped inside at opening the door. Rushing to close it, she returned to the woodstove for warmth. The weather station on the nearby table indicated the outside temperature as 30 degrees. It hadn't dropped any lower than predicted. However, it was the first freeze for the season. She must've misjudged how much wood to load into the stove when she went to bed. Thinking hard, she couldn't remember if she had fueled the fire. As her dreams indicated, seeing Rusty had bothered her more than her conscious mind had permitted. Opening the laptop, she verified the chapters written last evening were in fact there. They were. Maybe it was merely her focus on the current book that distracted her. Her mind churned as she waited for the coffee to finish brewing.

Since Sean had begun filming, this was the first she'd seen him. The weeks prior, they'd spent every moment together, which had curtailed her writing. Once he'd not been a constant fixture, she'd thrown herself into a novel. The current book for the editor was almost complete along with two others. She wanted to have enough finished for when surgery became necessary. Not that she needed the income. She'd earned more than enough to date; she didn't have to type another key. Not to mention, she'd become one of Rich's primary investors, which brought substantial returns. An interest-bearing account already contained two decades of salary for Trish. Automatic payments were sent to her checking account on a weekly schedule. Several similar accounts existed to parse Elsie's money as needed for the next few decades. Harris suggested this strategy to assist Elsie in reaching each goal she'd set. Not only had she reached these, but she also substantially exceeded them. Writing had never been about making tons of money—merely making a comfortable living doing something she loved. She only ever wanted people to enjoy the books, and maybe learn something about human nature.

Sighing audibly, she added cream to a big mug of coffee. Moving to the living room, she settled in her chair. Before getting into the groove of the book from last night, she opened her journal to record her dreams. There were similar entries listed. None of them were sufficient to unlock her mind. They were like movie trailers—teasing her into wanting to seek the attached memories. Each time she'd follow the trail into the recesses of her mind, it became an unproductive spelunking expedition into the blackness. Such occurrences would upset Trish. The neurologists considered her ability to regain consciousness afterward extremely risky. Finished with the journal entry, she eagerly delved into completing the book at hand. Trish would be running errands—bank, butcher, bakery, supermarket—all morning. This meant she wouldn't appear until noon at the earliest.

At daybreak, Elsie took a respite to shower and dress. The weather channel had listed a high of forty-two for the day. This prompted her to select a pale purple long-sleeved tee and coordinating flannel shirt and jeans. Her short hair didn't take long to blow dry. Padding across the kitchen in yellow chenille slippers, she refilled her cup. Through the window, the dogs could be seen frolicking with abandon. The sound of a chainsaw echoed across the gulley from the Slater farmland behind her property. She grabbed the bag of shortbread from Eilish to nibble on while she worked.

Midmorning the dogs began pitching a fit in the yard. She went outside to investigate; the wind was blustery. Locating the dogs at the fence corner opposite Tom and Sara's property, she heard a vehicle coming from the same direction. It sounded like her old jeep that Tom would use to police the outlying parts of their properties. Knowing it was nothing to be concerned about, she stepped back into the house. In case Tom stopped in to share his findings, she prepared another pot of coffee. A few minutes later, the dogs' greeting frenzy increased. Tom must've entered the yard. Expecting him at the door momentarily, she pulled another mug from the cupboard. Oddly, the dogs' continued woos of excitement didn't move toward the patio. Before Elsie had a chance to invite Tom inside, her phone rang.

It was Trish checking on her. "How are you this morning?"

"Busy typing. Why?" Elsie questioned.

"With seeing Rusty yesterday, I was concerned you'd have nightmares." Trish had no qualms getting to the point.

"No nightmares." It was the truth. "I woke up early. Good thing too. The stove needed wood."

"I know! I had to scrape frost off my windshield." Her friend added, "I'll see you in a few hours."

The two women ended their call. Elsie resumed working. Some time had passed when she suddenly heard muffled cursing. Hurrying to see why, she didn't bother with a coat.

Stepping outside, she called, "Is everything okay?"

The face under the battered baseball hat that turned to respond was not Tom's.

It was Rusty's. "I'm sorry, mate! While I was stacking the wood, Tycho climbed on top, causing an avalanche."

For what felt like an eternity, she stood dumbfounded with her mouth agape.

"Mate?" he asked with uncertainty.

"What are you doing here?" The first thing that popped into her mind, popped out of her mouth.

"When you left without telling Rich or the Scot, I got worried. Figuring you wouldn't answer when you saw it was me, I called Sara. Then Tom asked if I had time to help him take care of a tree the storm had blown down," he explained in detail, giving her time to regain her senses.

"That still doesn't explain why you're loading wood onto my pile," she stated, still somewhat confused.

"It was an old walnut tree on the edge of the properties. There is more than enough for both houses." He resumed stacking the shifted logs. "And I owe Tom a new chain. It's a good thing we bought a spare one to go with that chainsaw when we bought it for him last Christmas."

She laughed. "I'm surprised he didn't have a second chainsaw."

"He offered to go buy one, but we wouldn't have gotten started till about now," he stated with an easy grin.

"What on earth time did you two start? What about filming?" Her curiosity overrode her suspicion.

Taking a smaller log from the red malamute's mouth, he answered, "Not in today's shots. Arrived at seven for a bowl of oatmeal and cup of coffee till daylight broke. It was a massive tree. I was glad it wasn't close to the fence or the house."

A gust of wind caused her to shiver noticeably.

"Krikey, mate! You are going to catch pneumonia. Get inside!" he hollered at her as he pushed her to the door. "As soon as I finish with this, I will come in to warm up."

He pulled the door closed before she had a chance to argue. To keep her overactive imagination from spinning unreasonable yarns, she prepared breakfast—eggs, fried potatoes, ham, and toast.

When Rusty entered the house, he inhaled deeply. "Mate, something smells delicious. Is that for me?"

Turning with a loaded plate of steaming food, she replied, "It's not like I ever eat this much."

"Oh, there are times you do," he chuckled while shucking his outdoor wear to hang on the hooks by the door.

She retreated to the counter to push the toaster lever. Suddenly, he grabbed her from behind.

Placing his cold face against the side of her neck, he mumbled, "Mmm, you smell enticing too, my tumbleweed."

His light kisses with the shaggy mustache tickled.

"Rusty!" She squirmed free of his embrace.

She fetched his coffee to cover her embarrassment. The chair creaked under his formidable frame. No sooner had she delivered his cup than the toaster popped—another reprieve to allow the crimson to fade.

"It tastes as good as it smells," he stated, then added, "Both."

So much for the color of her cheeks returning to normal.

"Aren't you eating?" he asked.

Before she could say she wasn't hungry, her stomach complained that the cookies from earlier had been insufficient. This forced her to scoop food onto a dish and join him at the table.

"When did Tycho start climbing on the woodpile?" Rusty made small talk.

"Don't know. Guess he was showing you who's boss," she remarked.

Between mouthfuls he quipped, "Or showing off to get my undivided attention?"

She conceded, "Or that."

He'd lived here with her for two months till they parted ways. The dogs loved him. Was it any wonder Tycho missed having a strong alpha male as his role model? With only a few bites eaten, she pushed the food around her plate. Rusty helped himself to another serving.

"Mate, I do miss your cooking among your other outstanding qualities." His voice cracked with unintentional emotion.

Finally! She wasn't the only one affected. "Thank you. But it would be better for both of us if you didn't say things like that."

It didn't seem to impede his appetite. However, when he cleared his plate for the second time, he placed it in the sink.

Patting his stomach, he moaned, "I won't need to eat for the rest of the day. Thank you."

"You're welcome, but I should be thanking you for cutting the tree and providing wood to keep me warm," she countered.

"It is the only wood I'm allowed to use to warm you with anymore." His eyes crinkled impishly.

She couldn't hide her mirthful smile at his sexual play on her innocent words. "Very cute, but . . ."

"But you are otherwise spoken for." His tone remained light. "You'd be disappointed if I didn't try."

"That may very well be true. It doesn't mean you need to act on it every time we see each other." Her statement bordered on harsh.

He ignored her testiness while he readied to depart. "Tom can handle the remaining section of the fallen tree on his own."

"So you won't be back again?" It sounded wistful even to her ears.

"Is that your way of saying you were glad to see me, mate?" He didn't wait to hear the answer before closing the door between them.

The man certainly had a knack for making her go addlebrained. From the safety of the laundry room window, she watched him interact playfully with Sophie and Tycho on his trek to the side gate. A wind gust tousled his hair. Hearing the jeep engine, she returned to the kitchen. Her mind chased in circles for the origin of the tumbleweed endearment. It derailed her train of thought from the story she'd been diligently trying to finish.

Chapter Eighteen

SHORTLY AFTER NOON, Trish arrived. Elsie said nothing in regard to her morning visitor. She eagerly assisted carrying the bags into the house. While Trish reviewed e-mails for anything requiring a response, Elsie put the groceries away. The productive afternoon with Trish enabled Elsie to not dwell on Rusty's visit. However, it resurfaced at 3:00 a.m. If nothing else, she completed the book by the time Trish clocked in the next morning. This spun rereads for continuity, loose ends, and standard corrections. At least, Elsie made good use of the persistent sleepless nights. Within a few days, an electronic copy of the manuscript was sent to the editor.

A week later, the morning of Elsie's birthday, Trish arrived with chocolate chip muffins. Numerous gifts—vase of African daisies from Sean, basket of assorted coffees and cookies from her editor, basket of Godiva chocolates from the Taylors, bouquet of white daisies from Rusty—were delivered. Since the baskets came via FedEx, Trish got to see the driver flex his muscles many times that day. Sara popped over to spend the morning with Elsie and Trish. Another very special delivery appeared in person midafternoon.

Close to 2:00 p.m., Trish received a text message. "Casey is upstate working a job. And the part Cassie's car needs won't be in until tomorrow."

"Go. Never let a pregnant woman wait." Elsie shooed Trish on her way. "Give her a hug for me."

Alone at last, Elsie shoved her face in the flowers. Not only did they smell good, but their soft petals also caressed her cheeks. A feeling of love filled her with overwhelming happiness.

There was a question she refused to ask herself: "Which bouquet made her feel loved the most?"

She curled into the comfortable corner of the couch for a nap. The dogs took her cue to find a spot to stretch across the floor for a midday snooze. The movie *Brigadoon* filled her dreams just prior to waking. Words of love murmured against her skin. Opening her eyes revealed it wasn't a mere dream.

She greeted with a sleepy smile. "Mm, Sean."

"Surprise," he responded in an equally subdued yet apparently pleased voice.

"Is this a birthday bootie call?" she asked seriously.

"Are you going to give me a hard time if I say yes?" he questioned cautiously.

"A very hard time if you let me," she said seductively as her hand rubbed his groin suggestively.

"Oh, don't stop," he moaned.

This prompted her to undo the rivet buttons on his jeans to slip her hand inside. Since the Scot didn't bother with underwear, her fingers encountered the soft skin of his growing manhood without impediment. Under her shirt, his hands massaged breasts and teased nipples.

"It's your birthday. I should be catering to your needs," he rasped with barely constrained passion.

Nibbling on his neck, she stated, "You are."

Her ministrations continued until he pleaded, "Please, m'love. I need to be in you."

"Yes, Sean!" she groaned.

Grasping her firmly, he shifted her to remove their pants. After verifying her moist readiness, his hard member thrust inside her with unrestrained ardor. Her hips arched against him with wanton desire. Their heady need for each other shot them to a finale of intense pleasure.

After catching his breath, he said, "Your present is on the table."

"I thought I just unwrapped it," she purred with satisfaction.

"As much as I thoroughly enjoyed this romp," he mumbled while kissing her exposed skin, "it wasn't exactly how I planned this."

"Aren't you the one always saying a plan is merely a means to an end and I should go with the flow till I get there?" she argued lightly.

His chuckle reverberated through his body and hers. "Aye, but with our short window of opportunity, I have a detailed plan."

"What could be that important?" she asked suspiciously.

"You, m'love." He rested his head on her chest between her breasts.

His words confused her. Instead of thinking about what it meant, she savored the feel of him.

"Elsie?" Hands grabbed her shoulders roughly.

"What?" she grumbled at the disruption. "I'm sleeping."

"Oh," Sean emitted with a relieved sigh.

The opening of the woodstove let her know he'd moved across the room. She sat up, pulling her clothes into place. Standing to get something to drink, she ran her fingers through her pillow-flattened hair. When he slammed shut the door of the iron hearth, it startled her.

"Did I miss something while I was asleep?" Redirecting her path, she placed her hand on his back.

"Garnet was here," he stated in a strange tone.

"Yes, last week. He helped Tom with a downed tree then loaded a portion of what they cut onto my woodpile," she replied truthfully.

He didn't accept her response as complete. "He came inside."

"It was cold. Out of thanks, I invited him in to get warm." With this answer, she dropped her hand.

"And exactly how did you warm the Aussie?" he growled through gritted teeth.

His comment irritated her. "Coffee. You are making an iceberg out of a snowflake."

He remained silent while she stomped into the kitchen to pour herself a glass of water. She stepped toward the door to check on the dogs. There was a worn baseball hat sporting "Mountain's Majesty" hanging from the far hook. How had she overlooked it all week? Evidently, Sean hadn't.

"If I had been trying to hide the fact Rusty was here, why wouldn't I have hidden the hat he forgot?" She used the incriminating evidence to turn the tables. "And when you return to the set, which may be any minute now, you can take it with you."

As she pivoted toward him, she realized he'd been watching her. Studying his face, she saw a myriad of emotions as he processed everything.

"He left yesterday. He's not scheduled for filming again till we tape interior shots at the studio," Sean explained in a normal voice.

Her haughty tone challenged him. "Well then, I guess it will remain here, on display, until which time it can be returned to him."

Sean caved.

His demeanor was penitent as he moved to her side. "Elsie m'love, I shouldn't have gotten angry. But it was rather disconcerting since you hadn't mentioned he was here. It worries me every time he appears that you'll suffer a setback."

Resting her hand on his chest, she replied, "Precisely why I didn't tell you. And yes, it has stirred things again. But as usual, nothing makes sense."

Sliding his arms around her, he spoke softly, "So you aren't sleeping well, are you?"

"Nope," she responded without further elaboration.

"It's dinnertime and I am starved. What do we have?" he prompted a change of subject.

"As if you didn't already know!" She accused him of blatant subterfuge. "You told Trish you were hungry for bangers and mash, didn't you?"

He smiled sheepishly. "I did mention it. But I had no idea she'd make sure you'd have the ingredients for tonight."

"You start peeling potatoes. I want there to be enough for you to take leftovers to Eilish," she ordered.

Hugging her tight, he teased, "If I decide to share."

"Selfish bastard!" she said with mock seriousness.

"When it comes to you, I most certainly am." He claimed this character flaw with pride.

Once the meal was cooking, Sean insisted Elsie open her present. The size and shape had her anticipating earrings. Even with the wrapping paper gone, the velvet jeweler's box gave it away. However, when she lifted the lid, it revealed a half-karat heart-shaped ruby ring.

Moving next to her, he took her hand in his. "I want to marry you but understand your misgivings."

Finding her voice, she said, "Thank you. It's lovely."

"Okay, I took you by surprise," he said, looking for reassurance.

"Um, yeah." She struggled with what to say. "Are you asking?"

"I love you in a way that won't ever change. Even when I get upset about Garnet, I still love you heart and soul." He stumbled over his strong emotions. "I am asking but not expecting an answer right away."

"I love you too," she answered with equal depth. "I just need more time."

He nodded in understanding as he slipped the ring onto her finger.

Her lack of an affirmative response didn't dampen their time together. When her 3:00 a.m. waking occurred, Sean made love to her, bringing her to multiple orgasms to his one. They nestled together till 5:00 a.m. He was expected on set by 7:00 a.m. A happy haze hung about her for hours. Trish took advantage of Elsie's mood by asking for a three-day weekend, like Elsie would've said no anyway. That night, she slept straight through till morning.

Unfortunately, the cure was short lived. During the day, something nagged at her. Unable to focus on writing, she organized her closet. She hoped the mundane task would allow whatever was stirring in her subconscious to surface. After she completed with the clothing, she moved to the flowered storage boxes on the overhead shelves. Most of these were marked with what was inside: tax returns, contracts, medical history, and photograph albums. There was one box missing a tag. A bit of dizziness reminded her she hadn't eaten lunch. Finished replacing the boxes, she went to the kitchen to microwave the leftover bangers and mash Sean had forgotten. It was still daylight, so she took a walk around the fence. The dogs tagged along. A cold wind sped her pace to reenter the house. Hanging her coat on the rack, she spied Rusty's cap. The elusive feeling from earlier resumed. It confirmed what she already suspected—it was something in regard to him. A glass or two of wine wouldn't fix it, but it couldn't hurt. A silly romantic movie rounded out this pattern of escapism. By the bottom of the bottle and the end of the movie, she stopped thinking altogether. Yawning uncontrollably sent her to bed. A few hours later, she woke in time to hear the clock in the living room chiming 3:00 a.m. Another day would not be wasted on useless folly. This resolve made for being productive. However, the insomnia continued.

CHAPTER NINETEEN

MIDWAY THROUGH THE following week, the insomnia took its toll by instigating a full-blown episode.

She woke in a hospital room. In the chair next to the bed, Sean slept in an extremely uncomfortable position.

"Sean?" she croaked.

He jerked upright groggily. "M'love?"

She searched for the control buttons among the wire leads and intravenous line to move the bed to a sitting position. This caused a monitor to signal an alarm. The floor nurse rushed into the room.

Resetting the blaring device, the female nurse questioned, "Ms. Endy, how are you feeling?"

"Thirsty and a little warm," Elsie replied as Sean grasped her hand.

The nurse checked Elsie's temperature while talking into the intercom to the floor station. "Please page Dr. Vilanger that Ms. Endy is conscious."

Sean dropped a kiss on Elsie's forehead. "Be back shortly. The girls went to the cafeteria for a snack."

With his departure, the nurse went through the standard questions to determine Elsie's level of coherency. Sara and Trish arrived before the doctor. The two women clucked and fussed.

"What happened?" she asked.

Sara shared the details. "Around 5:00 a.m., Tom heard the dogs howling. When ours took a breather, he heard Tycho's bordering on a screech. We called while we threw on sweats. Not getting an answer, we ran over. I grabbed the flashlight, Tom his 22. He was concerned the coyote had crawled under the fence into the yard. In the darkness, both Sophie and Tycho were lying on the patio, howling and whining. But neither ran to us. We were too far away for the flashlight to distinguish what they were guarding. It took till we were almost to the patio for the backlight to turn on to see it was you. By the way, Tom is going to adjust that motion detector."

Dr. Vilanger's entrance cut Sara's story short. "You can thank those hairy beasts of yours for saving you from a severe case of hypothermia."

Sean arrived a few steps behind with a cup of juice from the cafeteria.

"Hello, Josh." The unique nature of Elsie's condition had forged a personal bond between the young neurosurgeon and his patient.

"Hello, dear." He touched her hand affectionately as he perused her chart for current vitals.

Sean gave her the cup. Sipping at the straw, the cranberry juice slid soothingly down her throat.

The doctor nodded to Sean as he explained his findings. "Before you ask when you can go home, the answer is not for a few days. Last night's MRI concerns me. We need another one now that you are conscious. And there are some other tests I'd like to take to determine what is going on in that noggin of yours. Dr. Jace and Dr. Eisenberg have reviewed the pictures and agree it warrants further testing."

Elsie's face was the only one in the room not expressing distress at this news.

"Then let's get started. The sooner you have your test results, the sooner I can go home." Her pluck always brought a smile to the doctor's face.

Trish, Sara, and Sean all stayed in the room while Dr. Vilanger described each test, possible side effects, and expected results. Most of the tests were nothing new. Two of the tests were experimental, developed specifically for her condition. Because of the different contrasts needed, they couldn't be mixed. It would take eight to twelve hours for each chemical to be flushed from her system. This required at least three days as a patient, assuming everything went as planned. Not surprisingly, she remained in the hospital for another five days. During which, she insisted Sean return to filming. Upon her release, there was a major restriction to her daily diet—no caffeine. Plus, the specialists were finalizing the preparatory treatments for surgery.

Sean eked a couple of days from the movie schedule to spend with her prior to flying to the West Coast. She, on the other hand, was grounded for two weeks. Since Cassie was due to give birth prior to Christmas, Trish wasn't willing to be longer than an hour away from her. And the thought of spending a week traveling across country alone by train didn't appeal. Elsie would wait for doctor clearance. However, this meant her trip would coincide with Rusty's presence on set. The only way to avoid it would be if she didn't go altogether. Not really an option without disappointing numerous people.

The week after Thanksgiving, Elsie boarded an airplane to fly west. Branson and Eilish met her at luggage claim. The young actress chattered excitedly.

Elsie interrupted to make a request. "I haven't eaten since this morning. Can we pick up dinner on the way to the hotel?"

Eilish replied, "Father says you like Chinese. How does that sound?"

"Wonderful!" Elsie remarked.

The two women gave their choices to Branson for him to call in their order. He ended up missing Elsie's suitcase the first time around the carousel. Along with fetching dinner, they stopped at Pastry Perfect. Danish, croissants, muffins, caffeine-free herbal teas—assorted items would supply them for the next few days. Sadly, none of it contained chocolate. Instead of going to a hotel, the chauffeur drove them to an exclusive gated apartment complex. Eilish led the way to their flat.

After delivering everything inside, Branson bid good evening. "Ms. Elsie, I will come by at ten to take you to the studio."

"Thank you," she responded appreciatively.

Once alone, Eilish hugged Elsie exuberantly. "It is good to see you! Father has been terribly moody."

Elsie sighed tiredly. "When is he expected?"

"Probably not till seven or eight," the young woman chirped. "We have loads of time till then."

She commandeered the conversation throughout dinner. After which, she gave Elsie a tour of the accommodations. The two bedrooms were separated by adjacent bathrooms. This eased some of Elsie's discomfort as she wheeled her suitcase into Sean's room. While she unpacked, Eilish talked on her phone. They reconvened in the living room for tea and dessert. Seven o'clock came and went with no Sean. So did eight o'clock. By 8:30, Elsie couldn't stay awake.

No sooner had she relaxed under the blankets than Sean burst into the room. "M'love, please forgive me. We got hung up on a scene."

"Let me sleep and I'll forgive you," she mumbled, burying her face into the pillow.

He immediately knelt by the bed. "Are you all right?"

"Yes!" she replied exasperated. "To me it's almost midnight. And I'm exhausted."

"Do you mind company in there?" he asked.

"It's your bed," she answered glibly.

The door was closed and locked. Water ran for a few minutes. Finally, he joined her in bed.

"If it's okay with you, I'm going to ravage you in the morning," he said as he pulled her into his arms.

"I'd be disappointed if you didn't," she murmured, wiggling her butt against him.

"Don't tempt me, woman," he growled against her neck.

Instead of enticing passion, his gentle kisses facilitated her tranquility.

Come morning, he made good on his promise—twice. With father and daughter departing at 4:30 a.m., Elsie fell back to sleep. Another three hours passed before an empty stomach forced her from bed. A leisurely breakfast of tea and croissant prepared her mentally for the day ahead.

When she arrived at the studio, Rich greeted her with a warm embrace. "You look well, far better than I expected. How many days do we have you?"

"Eight, if you can stand me that long," she responded with equal congeniality.

Keeping his arm across her shoulders as they moved to the active set, he stated affectionately, "If I could have you with us all of the time, I would."

"Flatterer," she teased.

"To warn you, today we are taping the last scene." He settled her in the padded director's chair made specifically for her frame.

Giving him an odd look, she said, "Yeah, I saw the schedule. Why do I need a warning?"

"Because Sean will be sporting white hair for a few days while we shoot the other scenes with him aged," he expounded. "It might be a bit disconcerting."

"Or I could have some fun with it?" Her tone chirped impishly.

"Too much information, my dear. Too much information." His voice filled with mock mortification.

His attention refocused as they prepared for the next scene. This suited her fine. Most of the crew didn't take notice of her presence—another welcome blessing. However, her laptop remained in her bag. She wanted to watch the final scene. It had to be poignant. Sean didn't look for her when he arrived. Not only physically, but emotionally he was in character. He sat in the worn period chair. His white hair gleamed whiter as the crew situated the lighting. Off to the side was a little girl with bright blue eyes and strawberry blonde ringlets. She wore a flowered flannel nightgown. Her cuteness put Shirley Temple to shame. Rich had requested pictures of Elsie between the ages of three and five to assist in casting the part. To keep the story fictional, Elsie had written the paternal lineage as Scottish and English as opposed to her actual of Indian and English; thus, providing those characters coloring for redheads.

Rich called, "Action!"

Sean began filling his pipe with tobacco.

The little girl stepped into the frame to speak shyly. "Pappy? I can't sleep."

"Climb on my lap, Suzie-Q," Pappy said, Sean in character, patting his legs.

The little girl did as told. She snuggled into his thermal shirt-covered chest. After lighting the pipe, he began to rock the chair gently. From the sidelines, Elsie recognized the cherry tobacco. Rich definitely had a flair for details even though the audience wouldn't smell the sweet odor. For

Elsie, it transported her to those times she'd climbed into her Pappy's lap for refuge.

Through a fog, she heard Rich say, "Cut."

The little girl returned to her starting mark. The pipe was replaced in preparation for the second take. This occurred multiple times over the next hour till all angles and nuances were captured.

From behind Elsie, a warm hand landed reassuringly on hers. "Mate, you're ice cold."

Forcing her eyes to focus on the here and now, she registered Rusty standing next to her.

It took a few moments for her to think sensibly. "Hello, Rusty. The scene brought back memories from my childhood."

"But some of those memories are better left in the past, aren't they?" he queried with concern.

Grimacing, she nodded in agreement.

"Do you want me to get McEwan?" he said in a humbly accommodating manner.

"No, he needs to concentrate," she replied. "I'll just get a cup of herbal tea."

He assisted her as she struggled to get up from the chair. "Have you been ill?"

She answered on the way to the catering table in the next room. "Um, I spent a few days in the hospital a few weeks ago."

"Why?" His tone indicated his alarm, but his volume remained low to not disturb filming.

"Sara and Tom found me passed out on the patio." She shared enough pertinent information to explain the circumstance.

"Krikey, mate! What happened?" There was no one else in the buffet room to hear his raised voice other than her.

"A long bout of insomnia and too much coffee without food caused a dizzy spell." She shrugged to give the impression it wasn't serious. "However, the doctors have highly recommended I avoid caffeine altogether."

"No coffee, chocolate, or Coca-Cola. How are you surviving?" His tone relaxed as his words signified how well he knew her.

With an easy smile, she stated in a light tone, "Rather snarky at times."

He stated suggestively, "I can think of a few ways to remedy that."

"Behave!" she groused, tossing the used teabag into the trash.

"Is that a snark?" he teased.

"Stop baiting me." This time her words were emphasized by her exit from the small room.

At her chair, Sean greeted her. "Hello, m'love."

As she hugged him, she noted the redirection of Rusty's course from her toward Rich. The smell of the cherry tobacco clung to Sean.

"I'll be here till seven or eight again. You don't need to stay. Eilish only came in for a few promotional interviews with her costar. Go shopping or something with her this afternoon," Sean suggested.

"Are you trying to get rid of me?" she asked suspiciously.

He began to respond. "I saw you leave with Garnet."

She quickly interrupted. "He was merely concerned with my reaction to the scene."

"If you would let me finish . . ." He took a deep breath then spoke again. "I talked to him earlier and asked him to stop by while we did this scene. He was the only other person who would truly understand how today's scene could affect you."

Her mouth dropped open with shock.

Rich and Rusty reached them before she could speak sensibly.

"McEwan, take advantage of that. It's not often she is speechless," Rusty quipped as he departed.

Rich remained with the couple.

"He has a point, m'love," Sean stated.

"I can't believe you two were in cahoots!" she exclaimed indignantly.

The tips of Rich's ears turned bright red.

"You three?" Feeling betrayed, she stomped off to the ladies' room.

By the time she returned, her tea had cooled sufficiently to drink. Sean and Rich were occupied with a different scene.

Eilish appeared by her side. "Are you ready to go?"

"Just a few more minutes till your dad completes this scene," Elsie replied.

When Rich called "cut," Elsie waved to Sean.

He rushed over to hug and kiss her good-bye.

She dodged the kiss. "Not until the makeup is removed."

"Oh yeah, I forgot," he responded with a kiss on her cheek, then on his daughter's.

CHAPTER TWENTY

THE AFTERNOON SPED by with the numerous stores Eilish insisted upon shopping. She even had to buy an extra suitcase for the trip home. With the paycheck the girl was making, she was entitled to spend some of it. Poor Branson was the one who had to determine how to fit it all in the trunk. At four o'clock, stomachs demanded dinner.

"There's a great burger place nearby. It doesn't look like much, but the burgers are phenomenal," the driver suggested.

Both women eagerly agreed.

When they parked, Branson took off his jacket to join them. "The patrons can be a bit rough."

At the entrance, Elsie had an intense moment of déjà vu.

Branson stopped her from banging into the door. "Are you all right?"

"Yes, I just should've had a snack earlier." She brushed it off as low blood sugar.

He nodded to the bartender as he steered them to a table. "Maybe a beer isn't a good idea?"

"One will be okay," she stated, perusing the menu.

Branson held up three fingers for the bartender. They ordered their food upon the arrival of the trio of drafts. An hour later, they were stuffed. While Elsie paid the bill, she saw a familiar torso in the back of the room. It moved in a not so straight line toward her.

"Yew following me, mate?" Rusty slurred.

Ignoring his remark, she said to the bartender, "Throw his tab in too."

"No, no," he grumbled loudly.

Pulling his wallet from his pocket, he flipped it open forcefully. Credit cards, money, and a photograph—contents flew across the bar. Elsie helped fumble fingers retrieve the items. The lone photograph was of him holding her on a beach wearing leis. Rusty handed one of the cards to the bartender. The rest he shoved together into the bill section of his wallet. The bartender handed Elsie her bill, credit card, and Rusty's card. She signed the bill then shoved the cards and receipt into her purse. Grabbing Rusty's arm, she pulled him outside to where Branson and Eilish were waiting. He staggered alongside her.

Branson recovered from his shocked expression before Eilish. "I'll call one of the other drivers to get him from the apartment."

"He'll have to be carried by then, and we can't put him in a cab alone." Elsie thought logically for a moment. "After you get us a cab, deliver Eilish home safely."

Branson hesitated before agreeing. Thankfully, flagging a taxi went easier than anticipated. Branson loaded the drunken actor into the backseat and talked to the driver.

Elsie hugged an upset Eilish. "Don't worry. I'll be home shortly."

Rusty had more to drink than Elsie realized. His head rested on the window shelf, with his open mouth snoring. A half hour later, the taxi pulled in front of the hotel she stayed in the last time she visited Rich. Rusty stumbled from the car. She paid the driver quickly then followed Rusty's weaving form. The elevator doors opened at his approach. Several people disembarked. She had to hurry to join him as he stepped inside and pressed a button. He leaned against the wall. She didn't know what to do other than get him safely to his room. When the elevator stopped, she stayed by his side. At the door at the far end of the hallway, he pulled out his wallet. The contents dumped on the floor. He began muttering obscenities. Her cell phone playing punctuated his curse words.

"Hello?" she answered, seeing Branson's name in the window.

"Ms. Eilish is home safely. Are you at the hotel?" he asked with concern.

"Yes. We just got to the room," she answered, searching the floor for the keycard with Rusty.

"I'll be there shortly." The loyal driver disconnected the call before she could argue.

As she slid the phone into her purse, the receipt and credit card poked her hand. Since Rusty was still crawling on his hands and knees, she chose to put them in the correct place in her wallet. Unfolding the receipt to place with the bills, she encountered two cards. One was her credit card, the other Rusty's room key.

"Got it!" she exclaimed, slipping it into the card reader.

The light turned green. The door unlocked.

She nudged his shoulder with her leg. "Rusty."

With the dropped items clutched in his hand, he used the door frame to stand. She laid her purse on the coffee table before turning to assist him. He pushed by her for the bar.

"Haven't you had enough?" she remarked sarcastically.

"Like it matters!" he growled.

"It does." She watched him down a tumbler of scotch. "Why are you drinking so much?"

"Seeing yew, not being able tahold yew. Knowing he's loving yew." The alcohol fueled his cavalier attitude. "A man ken only take samuch!"

"Don't you think I would remember if I could?" she spoke, equally emotional.

Even in his drunken haze, her statement seemed to register. He slammed the glass down then strode shakily away from her to the bedroom. She trailed behind him. He'd gone through to the bathroom.

When she stepped into the tiled room, he swore. "Fuck, woman! Must yew watch me take a piss?"

Ignoring him, she searched his toiletries bag. What she was looking for, she wasn't sure. A strange smile formed on his lips. He stripped on his steps into the bedroom. Only faded blue boxers remained.

Still smiling, he lay on the bed. "Join me?"

She couldn't believe he asked that. As she viewed him lying on his side, she saw what looked like a paw print on the front of the boxers. The two of them dancing and wearing the same matching boxers flashed in her mind.

Whatever her face displayed, it caused Rusty to shoot upright. "Mate?"

In his current state, this was not a good idea. He immediately sat.

Before either one could say anything, the doorbell rang.

"That's Branson," she stated on her way to answer.

At the bedroom door, she hesitated. "Please don't screw your life up because of me."

She retrieved her purse. Branson's anxious face greeted her upon opening the outer door.

"Let's go," she said on her way into the hall.

He replied with relief. "Yes, ma'am."

When Sean arrived home, Elsie shared an abridged version of what happened. Telling him the details of Rusty inviting her into bed would only cause further friction between the two actors.

The next five days on set went without incident. Rusty's scenes were scheduled in the afternoons. By which time, Eilish had whisked her away. Since the scenes with the young actress had completed taping, she had far too much available free time. Branson definitely earned his money that week. It was a challenge for Elsie to keep her spending controlled with Eilish's energetic excess.

Much to Elsie's relief, Sean's hair was dyed to its natural color two nights prior to her departure.

Her last day proved to be less than relaxed. Rusty was in all of the scenes that day. In one in particular, he and Sean were to brawl. In several instances, Rich and some of the crew had to step in to break apart the two actors. Real blood replaced the fake blood makeup had prepared. This upset Elsie.

Unable to take it any longer, she approached Rich. "Please, can't you get them to stop?"

"Honey, I won't let them hurt each other too much. I specifically rescheduled it as their last scene together," the director clarified reassuringly.

"What about the cuts and bruises?" she countered.

"Makeup will conceal them," he explained confidently. "Now, let us get back to work."

She returned to her chair in reluctant acquiescence. There was no usual appearance of Eilish at eleven. Fifteen minutes later, Rich broke for lunch. Sean rushed to Elsie.

In a cheery voice, he said, "Give me ten minutes, then you have me all afternoon."

She asked in disbelief, "Really?"

"Yes, really," he stated with a quick kiss on her cheek.

After he disappeared, Rusty walked over, holding a bag of ice to his lip under his bushy mustache. "Mate?"

Seeing the back of his scarred hand bloodied, she reached out to touch it tenderly. An empathetic wince emitted. For an instant, they were suspended in time without distraction.

His voice broke the moment. "I wanted to apologize for the other day."

"It's all right," she stated breezily. "Hopefully, over time it won't be as difficult for either of us."

Before he could say anything else, Sean arrived. The cuts and bruises were visible on his face as well.

"Ready, m'love?" the Scot queried.

"Definitely!" she exclaimed a bit too cheerfully.

Quickly concealing his crestfallen expression, Rusty said with forced lightness, "Enjoy your afternoon."

"Thanks," the couple replied in unison on their exodus from the studio.

With Branson chauffeuring Eilish, Sean drove. They stopped for takeout on their way to the apartment. However, upon arriving home, Sean placed the food in the refrigerator. Then without warning, he emitted a primal grunt prior to throwing Elsie over his shoulder. She shrieked at his unexpected action. Carrying her into the bedroom, he dropped her dramatically across the bed. Grabbing him, she yanked him down with her. Their smiling lips met for a passionate kiss. They pulled at each other's clothing until they were both naked. With no words spoken, they merged with gusto. Sighs and gasps of pleasure and final fulfillment resonated from the room all afternoon. When they raided the refrigerator, they finished a climactic joining minutes before Eilish entered the apartment. The only hints of this were Sean's red ears and Elsie's inability to make eye contact with her lover's offspring. Thankfully, the young woman only came home long enough to change for dinner with members of the cast and crew. As soon as she left, Sean and Elsie resumed their coupling.

In the morning, Sean took her to the airport.

"I will see you again in two and a half weeks. And I will stay through your treatments," he stated as they neared the security checkpoint.

"Wouldn't you rather be with your family longer?" She fidgeted.

"Woman! Don't be so damned difficult," he said in an exasperated tone.

She knew he wasn't angry with her. His irritation was fed by them spending so little time together.

They hugged and kissed and said farewell words. "Love you."

As the line to the metal detectors advanced, she wondered if Rusty had reacted the same way each time they had parted.

Chapter Twenty-One

{Present}

By MORNING, ELSIE had an excruciating headache. This worried Sean as he prepared them to travel east. When they climbed into the car, they found the usual bag from Pastry Perfect. Eating and taking two of her pills lessened the intensity of the headache to bearable. Instead of dropping them at the terminal door, Branson parked to assist with the luggage. Sean had his hands full keeping her from getting lost in the crowd. The combination of the lack of sleep and medication slipped her into a pleasant state of unconsciousness prior to the airplane taking off. Five hours later, he woke her to switch flights. This leg they were only in the air for an hour. Elsie remained awake. As soon as they disembarked, she made a beeline for the restrooms. Along with emptying her bladder, she took another dose of pills to combat the impending episode. A two-hour layover and another flight finally delivered them to where Tom and Sara waited.

For the drive home from the airport, the women rode in the backseat. After filling Elsie in on the dogs, Sara asked, "What's the next step?"

"The doctors are reviewing the results of the latest tests and pictures," Elsie responded flatly. "Most likely, we'll schedule surgery."

The older woman's restrained tears could be heard. "Let us know what you need."

"At this point, Sophie and Tycho are my first concern." Elsie leaned her head back with her eyes closed. "Harris has had the paperwork prepared for some time. I just need to sign everything."

"Elsie, there's something we need to discuss," Sara said hesitantly.

"Can it wait for tomorrow?" she asked in a pleading voice.

"Of course," Sara replied, patting Elsie's hand.

When they arrived home, Tom helped Sean carry the luggage into the house. Sara helped Elsie change into pajamas. Being in her own home eased some of Elsie's tension.

Sean entered the bedroom holding her phone. "M'love, it's Dr. Vilanger."

Elsie accepted the phone. "Hello, Josh."

The neurologist spoke. "How are you feeling?"

"My head is foggy. Everything is an effort," she replied truthfully.

"I want you in my office tomorrow," the young doctor stated, along with a lot more that didn't register.

She interrupted. "Nothing is making sense. Tell, Sean."

Shoving the phone at Sean, she sat abruptly on the edge of the bed, almost missing it. Sean grabbed her to shift her into a safer position.

Then he took the phone to speak into it. "Doctor? Elsie is having a hard time focusing. What do you need us to do?"

Further conversation wasn't audible with Sean striding from the room. It didn't matter. Her pillow beckoned. Sara said something to Elsie, but it sounded like gibberish. Later, Sean's soothing singing could be heard.

Snuffling and rough tongues on her face brought Elsie to the present. Sophie was on the bed next to her, Tycho by the side of the bed—both vying for her response.

"Babies, please!" Elsie grumbled at them as she sat.

This prompted them to woo in adulation.

"Okay, guys, let me through," Sean stated in a commanding tone as he walked into the room.

Pushing his way past the furry beasts, he sat next to her. "How are you feeling, m'love?"

"Like I have the flu," she muttered, leaning against him.

"The traveling hasn't helped," he remarked. "We need to get you showered and dressed for your appointment with Vilanger."

"Okay." She nodded as he helped her stand.

Her legs felt like she was wearing forty-pound ankle weights. In the bathroom, he stepped into the shower with her. His hands soaped and shampooed. By the time he finished rinsing the suds away, the fog in her brain began to dissipate. He moved her to the bed then selected an outfit for her to wear. After he finished dressing, he left her alone in the room. It didn't take her long to dress in the jeans and oversized button-down shirt he'd selected. Padding out the hallway in her bare feet, she almost collided with him carrying a tray.

"I was bringing you breakfast," he stated superfluously.

"I see," she replied with awe. "I've spent enough time in bed and would like to sit in a chair."

Turning, he said, "Your wish is my command."

A half hour later, they were on their way to see the doctor. The day was filled with numerous tests—blood, memory, coordination, and another MRI. At lunch, Sean left to get her a Sloznik's sandwich.

He said, "I want to avoid inflicting hospital food on you until absolutely necessary."

Elsie suspected it was an excuse to escape from the drama for a while.

Late afternoon, Dr. Vilanger finally led them into his private office.

His tone indicated his own disappointment. "I'm sorry, Elsie. We've all reviewed the test results and agree. There is no further alternative therapy. Surgery is the only option remaining. The seizures have escalated to a level where we believe you may not recover from the next one."

He continued talking to the mirroring sullen faces across the desk from him. "The pictures from two days ago show a pool of seepage you hadn't displayed signs of previously. Today's shots indicate the pool has dissipated. Reviewing the trend of the occurrences, we gauge a four- to six-week window till another severe episode. But we suspect smaller ones will occur till then. Any questions?" The doctor finished delivering the bad news.

Not needing to ask questions that they'd heard the answers for numerous times prior, Elsie spoke. "I'll call you in a day or two to schedule everything."

It worked. Sean remained mute. When she stood, so did the men.

Her parting words were, "Thank you, Josh." Then she exited the room with Sean in tow.

When they stepped onto the elevator, Sean grasped her hand in a death grip. Elsie knew he wanted to embrace her but deferred to her hard expression. If he hugged her, she would fall to pieces. Humpty Dumpty needed to stay together until they reached the sanctuary of home.

Silence filled the car on the drive. Fear rattled in her mind—not of death, but of forgetting everything. If all went well, it could mean her missing memories would return along with the permanent cessation of the migraines. However, the much higher probability of losing herself or her current life scared her. She loved Sean and knew without a doubt he loved her, something she'd only ever felt with her dearest friends. Losing that would send her to the desolate wasteland of her life before him. She'd rather endure the migraines than revisit that place. But the inevitability of the next seizure putting her into a permanent coma could not be denied. Plus, she couldn't put her friends through this anymore. As soon as the couple stepped across the threshold of her home, Sean pulled Elsie into a tight embrace. Only tears were shared.

Chapter Twenty-Two

THE FOLLOWING DAY, Harris did not shirk his duties. Elsie signed, sealed, and faxed every possible document needed. After the first few, she began skimming the paperwork. Harris had no reason to cheat her. He had more than enough clients wealthier than her.

Throughout the morning, there were very few instances when Sean wasn't an appendage. In the afternoon, he and Tom policed the properties in preparation for an impending storm. A late March nor'easter had been predicted. It would begin dumping on the region overnight. This allowed her the opportunity to call Dr. Vilanger to discuss lifting certain restrictions and scheduling surgery. With all of the legal issues completed for any contingency, she could focus elsewhere. She cooked to ensure they had enough meals to heat on the woodstove should they lose electricity. When Trish returned from running errands, she boxed the latest stack of signed books.

Elsie spoke. "Please inform the publisher no more book deliveries until further notice."

"Okay. It's not like they weren't expecting it," Trish replied glibly to conceal her feelings in regard to the upcoming surgery. "Where's Sean?"

"He's with Tom, getting prepared for the storm. They drove to the Grimmel farm to fetch bales of straw," Elsie answered absently. "He should be back soon if you want to leave. Take some muffins too."

"That would be great. I wanted to stop for a few groceries," her assistant stated, going into the kitchen.

Following the other woman, Elsie asked perplexed, "Why didn't you get them while you were running my errands?"

Trish shrugged. "I was so concerned with accomplishing the items on the list it didn't cross my mind until now."

Elsie rolled her eyes then said lightly, "Well, let's get a goody bag together and you're on your way."

It wasn't long before Trish was donning her coat. Elsie pulled hers on to assist with the bags. At the truck, the women hugged.

"There's no reason for you to attempt the roads tomorrow. Start your weekend early," Elsie offered.

"Thanks. I can spend the time with Cassie and the baby while Casey clears parking lots," Trish said happily.

Elsie stood on the porch, waving as the truck moved down the driveway. Inhaling the crisp cold air felt refreshing. She went inside only to exit through the back door. Both dogs ran eagerly to her. After schmoozing with them, she strolled along the fenced-in perimeter. Soon the chugging and pinging of the jeep could be heard. The dogs ran to the gate at the corner of the house to greet Sean. She could hear his voice, but not the words, as he responded to their howling. They sniffed at the bale he carried across the yard. Tycho grabbed a mouthful of straw. The big red dog took off at full speed to the far side of the yard with his prize. Sophie laid chase for a few yards then returned to Sean. After the bedding was shoved into the first doghouse, Sophie forced her way in to make a comfortable nest. Even with the second doghouse filled, Tycho remained where he was rolling on his stolen portion. Sean didn't notice Elsie walking toward him until he'd exited the yard. He quickly retraced his steps. Reaching her, he grasped her hand as he leaned in for a kiss.

"You're frozen," he remarked with a frown.

"Maybe you could thaw me out." She smiled suggestively.

"Go inside, woman!" he ordered sternly.

He must've seen her smile fade since he quickly said in a softer tone, "Go in and make us Irish coffees."

"Okay," she agreed.

By the time he entered the house, she was spraying whipped cream on the hot beverages. After removing his winter wear, he made a beeline for her.

"I'll refill the wood box in a bit," he stated, accepting the mug.

Taking her hand, he led her to the sofa.

After getting snuggly, he asked. "Have you gotten everything completed?"

"Yes. I placed a call to Dr. Vilanger about surgery." She sipped at her coffee. "We went over possible dates. He didn't want to commit until he reviewed a few things. But he promised to call next week with a definite."

"Then I'll postpone my trip home," he stated evenly.

She sat forward to turn to face him. "No! We're talking not for another three weeks. He really wants Dr. Jace here for the surgery, and that's the earliest her schedule has an opening. You can still spend quality time with your children. And this might be your last chance for a while."

By his expression, she could tell he was giving merit to her imploring argument. When he reached for his empty mug, she handed him hers.

To explain, she remarked, "You're making me warm enough."

He chuckled as he hugged her tightly. "I'll leave as planned on Monday. But you call anytime you need me."

She sighed internally with relief at his concession.

"Before I get too comfortable here, what else needs to be done for this snowstorm?" he asked.

Stepping through the usual tasks in her mind, she replied, "Nothing else that I can think of."

Finishing the second mug of coffee, he shifted forward to stand. "It shouldn't take long."

"Uh-huh," she responded distractedly.

As soon as he disappeared outside, she headed to the bedroom. There it was, hanging in the closet amidst the summer dresses. The silky lavender negligee sliding on her skin heightened Elsie's need for Sean to make love to her. Because of the medical treatments, the last time they'd been able to share physical intimacy was January 2. Grabbing her flannel robe, she concealed the purple enticement. When she emerged, he'd gone back outside for another load. She busied herself with filling the dishwasher. Soon enough, he returned. After emptying his arms, he moved to the kitchen to remove his boots and hang his coat.

Watching with impatience, Elsie finally said, "I have another box for you to fill with wood."

He turned only his head to look in her direction. She dropped the robe to reveal her meaning.

His raised eyebrows prompted her to clarify. "This activity has been cleared by the doctor."

That was all he needed to hear. In two easy strides, he swept her into his arms to carry to the bedroom. Placing her on the bed, he stripped off his clothing before joining her. His body clearly indicated his want. He fought to control his ardor. Every time she pressed or brushed against his manhood, it throbbed in anticipation of release.

Feeling her own urgency, she told him, "Sean, please. It's been so long."

"I don't want to rush you," he replied with barely contained passion.

"Rush me," she moaned as she arched her moist femininity against him.

This was his undoing. Without further hesitancy, he slid inside her. Two months of pent frustration exploded in carnal pleasure. Hearing his groan of supreme satisfaction surged her senses to orgasm. Sean tightened his hold on her as he buried his face into her neck. She tenderly caressed his back. They lay like that for an extended time.

Finally, he shifted his head to speak. "M'love, when I return, would you please marry me?"

With unquestioning serenity, she answered yes.

He squeezed her tightly. "Thank you."

"Thank you for still wanting to marry me," she said quietly.

She could feel his smile as he kissed her cheek. He shifted to her side to drift into a content slumber. Sleep wasn't possible for her. Instead, she savored the moment. The wind began to blow outside. Knowing the dogs were still running the yard, she climbed from bed. Since her robe was on the kitchen floor, she reached for Sean's. The delicious aroma of the roast chicken in the oven wafted in the air. She picked up the robe. Peering through the window, the snow had begun falling. The dogs came running when she whistled for them from the laundry room door. They barreled through the opening, their coats caked with snowflakes. With towel in hand, she dried them prior to allowing them into the main part of the house. Their noses lifted to inhale the smell of food. They chattered at her delay in feeding them.

"All right! Give me a couple seconds here," she stated from the other room.

After hanging the damp towel on the drying rack, she scooped kibble from the dog food bin. The dogs rushed back into the tiny room.

From behind them, Sean asked, "Am I next for being fed?"

"I suppose," she replied.

"If you want more of what we just had, please feed me," he clarified.

The mock desperation on his face made her laugh. While he fueled the woodstove, she placed dinner and plates on the table. Done eating, the dogs danced at the door.

Leaving them outside again, Sean commented, "Wow, it's really coming down."

"It's a good thing your flight isn't till Monday," she remarked, fetching silverware.

Closing the door, he shivered. "Bugger, woman! It's colder here than on the highland moors."

"Maybe if you put on more than boxers . . .," she stated.

Hugging her close, he quipped, "Be glad I'm wearing anything."

"True. However, if you weren't, you would have frostbite on your bits and pieces." Her parry made him chuckle.

"I can think of a place that would warm them right up." Those same bits and pieces pressing firmly against her buttocks emphasized his words.

"I thought you were hungry," she reminded him.

"Always for you." He exposed her shoulder to take a playful nip. "But the meal you made smells delicious."

After dinner, the dogs were brought in for the night. Sean and Elsie relaxed in the toasty living room as the snow fell. When they went to bed, their lovemaking was unhurried.

CHAPTER TWENTY-THREE

MONDAY MORNING ELSIE and Sean hugged good-bye.

"Text me when you land safely," she requested.

"I will call you every day," he stated.

"No. You focus on time with your children." Her argument gently dissuaded him. "I'm going to be too involved with edits and finishing books."

One final loving hug and lingering kiss, then Sean stepped into the security line. Elsie, Tom, and Sara waited until he'd made it through the metal detector without incident. Silence filled the drive home. They stopped for breakfast at the diner at the bottom of the hill from home. Not particularly busy, the owner chatted about the recent snowstorm. By the time they left their extended stop, Sean had texted twice. First, he'd landed at LaGuardia. A few minutes ago, he was boarding the airplane for Edinburgh.

No sooner had she taken her coat off at home than her cell phone rang. It was Dr. Vilanger. Dr. Jace's schedule opened. She could travel Tuesday night to perform surgery Thursday morning. Elsie would need to be admitted Wednesday. She didn't think; she agreed immediately. When they completed making the arrangements, Elsie called Sara.

Sara answered the phone with a nervous, "Are you all right?"

"Yes. I wanted to let you know Dr. Vilanger just called." She relayed the latest. "Surgery is Thursday morning. I'll be admitted Wednesday."

"Oh my god! Did they find something new on the MRI?" The older woman's voice sounded on the verge of frantic.

"Nothing like that. Dr. Jace's schedule opened. Otherwise, it could be another month." Elsie hurried to clarify.

"What about Sean?" Sara asked her next item of concern.

"He's over the Atlantic. There's no point in telling him or he'll want to come back. By which time, I'd be in surgery. He needs to be with his kids," Elsie explained with no regret. "Besides, when he returns, we're getting married. So he'll only be momentarily miffed with me."

"Married?" Sara questioned. "When did that topic get reopened?"

"The night of the snowstorm." Her response held only a hint of her happiness.

There was a lengthy pause prior to Sara speaking. "Well, I guess we have a party to plan for in six weeks."

"I'll leave that to you and Trish since I'll be incapacitated," Elsie quipped.

"Consider it taken care of," Sara stated prior to ending the call.

The rest of the day Elsie and the dogs cuddled on the sofa. Late in the evening, the awaited text message from Sean was received.

The next morning when Trish arrived, Elsie updated her on the schedule change. Within the hour, all legal parties were notified. Sara popped over for coffee. She stayed all day. By noon, Elsie's bag for the hospital was packed. The trio laughed and cried throughout the day. Around 5:00 p.m., Tom appeared with dinner. However, he didn't stay; he returned home to give the ladies extended time together. Finally, a little before 9:00 p.m., Trish and Sara departed. Elsie couldn't sleep. She cuddled with Sophie and Tycho until they couldn't take it anymore. In case she didn't survive, she wrote letters to her friends reiterating how much they meant to her. These she placed in her underwear drawer. Here was where she knew they'd find them. Neither would allow her to be buried without sexy underwear. There was also a letter to Sean in her jewelry box. A feeling of guilt nagged at not having a letter for Rusty. However, after their most recent encounter, it lacked any suitable justification.

Sitting on the front porch, she watched what could be her last sunrise. Surgery would be underway tomorrow at this time. A long hot shower followed another round of excessive snuggling with the dogs. Unfortunately, neither combated her restlessness. With well over an hour till they left for the hospital, she took a walk in the crisp morning air. The dogs remained in the confines of the fence while she strolled to the outer edge of the property. Across the gulley at the acres of fallow farmland were visions of the green hills populated with cattle. Guernsey and Hereford—calves frolicked in her mind. A stiff gust made her shiver. She retraced her steps to the house. For whatever reason, she thought of Rusty as she hung her coat. Her hand rested for a moment on the hook where his hat had hung those few weeks last year. With Trish's entrance through the front door, Elsie moved toward the coffee pot. As Elsie poured a cup for Trish, she double-checked the bag for the hospital. Soon enough, Tom pulled in front of the house. Sara came inside to ensure everyone was ready. None of the women uttered a word. They'd said it all yesterday. Today they were standing at the precipice of an intense emotional chasm. To say anything would start a triple crying jag.

Elsie led the dogs outside to their kennels. She hugged each of them so tightly even Tycho squirmed. Before reentering the house, she wiped the droplets from her cheeks. If anyone of them showed weakness, the other two would fall apart. During the drive to the hospital, Tom kept switching the radio station to ensure only happy tunes filled the Saturn. Depositing the women at the entrance gave him a reprieve while he parked. As soon as Elsie said her name at admitting, they were asked to wait.

A few minutes later, a familiar male nurse approached them. "Hello, Ms. Endy. I don't know if you remember me—"

"Billy! You weren't here the last time I was admitted." Her interruption acknowledged him in a warm tone.

"Actually, I was the morning they brought you in with hypothermia. But my shift ended prior to you regaining consciousness. And I had family plans I couldn't skip to stay here," he explained as he led them to the elevator. "All of your paperwork is in your room. Dr. Vilanger had admissions take care of it yesterday to keep things as stress-free as possible. It just needs your signature while we get you settled and ready for your MRI."

As expected, the room was a private one. Numerous monitors were parked to the side awaiting use along with the crash cart. While Trish and Sara unpacked Elsie's bag and organized the side table, Nurse Billy reviewed the forms. When the numerous signatures were completed, he exited the room to allow her to change into pajamas. He didn't stay away long. Upon the nurse's reappearance, he had a tray with needles and tubes. Tom was a step behind him.

Turning to the other two women, Billy stated, "Ladies, I believe you have an appointment to give blood."

Tom spoke for them. "Yes, we should go do that while you turn Elsie into a pin cushion."

Sara and Trish didn't argue. Neither of them liked being in the room when needles were stuck into their best friend. After they exited, Billy started the IV lead. The IV bag wouldn't be attached to it until later. However, Elsie needed it for them to administer the valium during the MRI. He also drained several vials of blood for final levels. Then he left her alone. She turned on the television to drown the noise in her head. Not ready to fully relinquish control, she sat on top of the bed covers. The trio returned. Dr. Vilanger stopped in to go over the schedule for the afternoon and tomorrow morning's surgery. Every time someone walked by, Sara would strain to see who it was.

Eventually, the specialist moved on to visit another extreme case. There was a second female patient who suffered from long-term side effects of brain damage due to a car accident. They planned to do the same type of surgery on her. When Dr. Jace arranged to fly in for Elsie's surgery, Dr. Vilanger suggested they collaborate on the similar case. The other patient, also experiencing severe seizures, had eagerly agreed to travel to the East Coast. This gave Elsie a sense of peace that she wasn't the center of attention. To most people this would seem odd. For her, it meant all of this effort wasn't just for her. And whatever the outcome, it would help people in the future with similar injuries.

"... at five tomorrow morning." Elsie's thoughts had blocked what Trish had been saying.

"Okay," Elsie replied, not wanting them to know she hadn't been listening.

Glancing around the room, Elsie realized she wasn't the only one distracted. Sara repeatedly straightened the small photograph album and stack of puzzle books sitting on the side table. Tom stood by the television, watching the weather channel intently. Her friends needed to leave to deal with this in their own way. She toyed with the idea of pressing the button for a nurse.

Thankfully, Nurse Billy walked into the room, stating, "They're ready for your headshots if you are."

The trio quickly focused on Elsie for kisses prior to departing.

In an exaggerated theatrical tone, Elsie said, "I'm ready for my close-up, Mr. DeMille."

As the nurse wheeled her to the elevator, he asked, "What was that all about?"

After the doors closed, she voiced her opinion. "They feel helpless, making it harder on them than on me."

"It usually is," Billy remarked. "Will they be coming back this evening?"

"I'm not sure," she replied.

The doors opened for him to wheel her to the MRI waiting room. It didn't take long for one of the technicians to call them into the room with the imaging machine. Like the numerous times prior, goose bumps formed from the coldness of the room. Billy was already pulling blankets from the heated drawers in the wall. One of the technicians assisted her onto the platform. While Billy wrapped her legs with a warm blanket, the technician encased her head in the stabilizing basket. A different nurse administered the sedative. As the medication relaxed her, the platform moved into the imaging chamber. A sensation of being lifted and placed in a wheelchair barely registered.

Elsie woke feeling muzzy. She struggled to sit. Strong male arms assisted her. Without thinking, she buried her face into his neck.

A voice without an accent stated, "I'm not who you think I am."

Her eyes flew open as she jerked away to see who was talking. It was Nurse Billy Pfeisen.

"Billy?" she questioned.

He spoke with concern. "How do you feel?"

"Confused. Weren't you taking me for an MRI?" she replied.

"We finished that over two hours ago. Did you take anything yesterday or today?" he asked while taking her vitals.

"No. I figured if I started with a headache, you guys would pump me full of the really good stuff." she said, trying to ease the lines on his face.

"You missed lunch. Do you want me to get you something from the cafeteria?" His demeanor hadn't changed.

"A Coke and fries, please." She reached for her photo album.

When he started to leave, she called him back. "Wait."

"Was there something else?" His tone was conciliatory.

Pulling a twenty-dollar bill from behind the picture of Sophie and Tycho, she handed it to him. "Here, get yourself something to eat too."

A strange expression crossed his face. "Elsie . . ."

"Please, Billy. You sat here waiting for me to wake up." Even though he hadn't told her, she knew he'd been there.

Whether her logic swayed him or he didn't want to argue with her, he accepted the money. After he left, she used the bathroom with the IV pole's assistance. They'd hooked her to a bag while she was unconscious. Glancing in the mirror, she fluffed her hair. It would probably be the last time she'd do that for months to come. It took a bit to get settled in bed where the IV lead didn't get in her way. Her stomach rumbled. Maybe she should've ordered more than fries. Then again, they'd be delivering dinner soon. She hoped it would be something substantial. Hearing his voice conversing nearby, she anticipated the nurse's reappearance. Along with Nurse Billy, Dr. Josh Vilanger entered the room.

The doctor sat on the edge of the bed. "Elsie, I'm sorry about earlier. As you know, we had another patient flown in for similar surgery. Because the other patient has adverse reactions to valium, the nurse used the same muscle relaxant on you as on her. Even though the dose was titrated to your tolerance levels, it still knocked you out."

"Why mess with my usual cocktail the day before major surgery?" This irritated her.

Dr. Vilanger ran his hand through his hair, indicating his own frustration at the change. "Dr. Jace and I both spoke at length with the nurse explaining the error in judgment. And . . ."

He stopped for a moment to glance at Billy, who in turn completed the doctor's sentence. "And because of the mistake, your surgery has to be pushed to Friday. We need to be sure it is thoroughly flushed from your system to prevent any further side effects."

Here the doctor spoke again. "As luck would have it, when we reviewed today's pictures, we saw the other case has degraded dangerously. We'd have had to swap the surgeries, anyway."

"Oh, okay," she responded for lack of anything relevant to say.

The doctor and nurse shared eye contact. Then they both started chuckling.

"What?" she whined from not understanding the joke.

Dr. Vilanger sobered first. "Your understated response."

"What did you expect me to say?" she groused.

"I don't really know. But I'm so used to having to debate everything with you that this was uncharacteristic," Josh explained.

Their glee exasperated her. "Now that I've amused you two, may I have my fries?"

Billy opened the foil to reveal the fries. Elsie began to munch on them one at a time. A takeout box contained Billy's salad.

"I'll leave you two to eat. Dr. Jace and I will check on you in the morning," the doctor said on his way out.

Lettuce crunching under a fork was the only notable sound as she contemplated another day until surgery.

"Aren't the fries hitting the spot?" Billy asked between mouthfuls.

"Huh?" she replied before the question registered. "Oh no, they are perfect. Just trying to determine what I'm going to do tomorrow to keep myself from going insane."

"Hadn't considered that," he responded thoughtfully. "What games would you like?"

"Scrabble, Clue . . ." Suddenly, she remembered an idea they'd discussed previously. "Hey, I thought they were going to hook up a DVD player so I could watch movies?"

"Damn!" Little bits of green spewed with his exclamation. "I knew I was forgetting something."

She smiled. "No big deal. Just bring it along tomorrow. And lots of movies—funny movies."

"You got it." He resumed eating his meal.

With the fries gone, she focused on the television. The weather channel reiterated the facts on the winter storm hitting the Midwest. Airports such as O'Hare in Chicago shut down till morning. Interviews with passengers stuck until flights restarted were interspersed. Some flights had been rerouted when conditions at the destination airports deteriorated to hazardous. Evidently, the side effects of the drug were lingering since she felt increasingly sleepy. While she dozed, Rusty's image appeared on the television. His face swam in her dreams.

CHAPTER TWENTY-FOUR

A PERSISTENT SQUEAKING roused Elsie. It was the orderly delivering dinner. She waited till the noisy cart wheeled from the room to shift to a sitting position. Dinner—veal parmesan, rice, and yellow squash—didn't appeal.

Nurse Billy came into her room with a large cup. "Iced tea to drink with your meal."

She said thanks while pushing the food around.

"What movie would you like to watch while you eat?" he asked, moving toward the table directly below the wall-mounted television set.

"How'd that get here?" she exclaimed at seeing the DVD player.

"My roommate dropped it off for me," he replied, putting a disc into the slot. "How are you feeling after that nap?"

"Not as good as earlier." Her sluggish actions relayed her answer as much as her words.

He checked her vitals. "It'll take a bit for that drug to leave your system."

"Well?" she questioned.

"Your numbers are within standard parameters." He entered them into her file.

"No, are you going to press play?" She pushed the food away and pointed to the television.

He grinned sheepishly. "Oops."

"You know, that is not something anyone wants to hear in a hospital," she said, glowering at him.

Ignoring her jab, Nurse Billy stated, "Watch your movie. With your surgery being rescheduled, my shift is ending now."

"Have a good night, Billy." She accepted the remote from him.

"If you start feeling weird, you buzz for Nurse Shaner." His tone was extremely serious. "I'll see you in the morning."

Thankfully, he had a few classics in his collection. The movie he'd selected was *Some Like It Hot*.

Halfway through the film, Trish appeared laden with goods. "Nurse Pfeisen called to let us know your surgery had been pushed back a day."

As she emptied bags, she shared the afternoon she spent with her granddaughter. A stack of movies were placed on the table with the DVD player. A six-pack of ginger ale, cranberry juice, and family pack of Nutter Butter crackers remained in the bag.

From her shoulder bag, she removed Elsie's ledger book. She wanted to clarify amounts on a few line items before sending them to Harris. When that was completed, Elsie prompted Trish to continue talking about her granddaughter. After another hour, Tom and Sara appeared. They were also carrying bags. A delicious aroma emanated from one.

"This was cleared when we were here earlier," Sara explained as she opened the plastic container to reveal ham and candied yams. "Since you'll miss Easter dinner, we thought you'd like this."

Elsie forked a combination bite of ham and yam into her mouth. "Mmmm."

After swallowing, she said, "I've died and gone to heaven."

Suddenly, Sara burst into tears. "Don't say that! We love you!"

Tom placed reassuring arms around his wife.

Elsie started to say, "I didn't mean . . ."

At seeing Trish dabbing at her eyes, she asked, "Not you too?"

Her other friend nodded, trying to keep her emotions in check.

"Come here." Elsie pushed away the table to open her arms wide.

Accepting the embrace, Trish allowed her tears to flow unchecked. "We're supposed to be comforting you."

"You will both have your hands full taking care of me after surgery. I expect lots of doting and fulfillment of the slightest whim." The remark intended to lighten the atmosphere in the room.

It worked. Trish stood to wipe away her tears. Elsie resumed eating the special meal.

Sara managed to find her sense of humor. "I thought that's why you have Sean."

"Then I guess you two are off the hook. He should be back in the States about the time I'm released," Elsie parried good-naturedly.

"In the meantime, we will take exceptional care of you," Trish stated with a smile.

"You always do," Elsie remarked with sincerity.

Nodding in agreement, Sara pulled a pretty lap blanket from the second bag.

As Sara spread it across the patient's legs, Elsie exclaimed, "Daisies! I love daisies!"

"I figured it would last longer than flowers in a vase," the older woman stated.

Elsie stilled uncharacteristically.

The two other women noticed immediately. "Else?"

A moment passed for her to contain her emotions.

In as light a voice as she could muster, she replied, "When I was in the hospital in Sydney, Rusty gave me a robe with daisies on it. And he made the same remark about it lasting longer."

Trish said, "I know every piece of clothing in your wardrobe. I've never seen it."

"Huh . . . You're right. Guess that's a good thing since you're allergic to chenille. Wonder what happened to it?" Elsie asked, not expecting anyone to have an answer.

Sara suddenly seemed far too interested in folding the handle bag precisely by its creases.

It was obvious to Elsie that her friend knew something in relation to this. "Sara?"

"One of the times I phoned him during your recovery, he told me the same story." Guilt laced her response. "When I saw the blanket, I thought it was a good sign and had to buy it."

"Oh." With an odd sense of disappointment, the word fell from Elsie's lips.

She quickly covered with, "I thought maybe Tycho had hidden it in his doghouse like he did my sweatshirt right after I got home from Australia."

Trish remarked, "Didn't it take us three washings with bleach to clean that?"

"Bleach would've definitely ruined the chenille," Sara continued with the refocus of the conversation. "What did you choose to put in his doghouse for this hospital trip?"

Not wanting to cause any further emotional upheavals, Elsie didn't dissuade their subterfuge. "One of my flannel nightshirts was fraying thin in a few embarrassing spots."

"The one I've been trying to convince you to throw in the trash since last fall? You wouldn't let me because it was Sean's favorite," Trish pointed out.

The next comment from Tom surprised everyone. "Those spots were probably why it was his favorite."

Sara punched her husband in the arm while they all laughed.

Nurse Shaner promptly poked her head into the room. "Please keep it down. You are disturbing the other patients."

"Isn't she just a ray of sunshine?" Sarcasm saturated Trish's words after the nurse disappeared.

Even though Nurse Shaner would never win a Miss Congeniality award, she did her job very well. "What do you expect? Most of her usual patients are in comas. Besides, not everyone can be like Billy."

"Where is Billy? I thought he was supposed to be your personal nurse?" Sara questioned.

Before answering, Elsie swallowed the last bite from the food container. "With surgery pushed a day, they rescheduled his hours."

"But he'll be here tomorrow, right?" Again, Sara's demeanor seemed odd.

"Yes." This time Elsie didn't pursue why.

In the ensuing silence, they watched the progression of the winter storm hitting the Midwest.

Tom asked what they were all thinking. "Will they proceed with surgery if the storm doesn't dissipate till it gets here?"

"Depends on its timing. We'll see tomorrow afternoon." Elsie's response relayed the words the doctor used earlier at her duplicate question.

Promptly at eight o'clock, Nurse Shaner requested the visitors depart. No one argued. They were exhausted from the day. And they had to go through it again tomorrow. It didn't take long for Elsie to fall asleep. A soft glow came from the television with the Weather Channel airing on mute.

CHAPTER TWENTY-FIVE

WHEN ELSIE WOKE, the television no longer lit the room. The clock displayed 4:18. Getting from bed to use the bathroom, she noticed the IV catheter didn't have a line attached anymore. They must've felt enough fluids had been run to flush her system. Granted, another bag would be connected in preparation for surgery. Not contending with the cumbersome contraption made things easier. While in the little room, she washed her face, brushed her teeth, and fluffed her hair. In twenty-four hours, those reddish brown curls would be shaved off. Sighing audibly, she knew it didn't bother her. What bothered her was the same thing that woke her. It started last night when Sara mentioned Rusty. If he cared, he'd contact her. As she collected the water pitcher to fetch ice, she chastised herself. Here she was upset because Rusty hadn't called; and she's the one who hadn't informed her fiancée of the change in circumstances, particularly since it was such a high-risk procedure.

"What are you doing out of bed?" Nurse Shaner's strict tone questioned at seeing Elsie in the hallway.

"I just wanted some ice," Elsie explained.

Taking the plastic pitcher from her patient, Nurse Shaner commanded, "Get back into bed. I will get it."

Thinking it was not worth arguing, Elsie complied. Before climbing into bed, she retrieved a bottle of cranberry juice from the bag of supplies in the bottom of the closet. The nurse entered the room as Elsie pulled the blankets across her legs.

After placing the ice on the tray table, Nurse Shaner checked vitals. "How are you feeling this morning?"

"Okay. I didn't realize how much that other medication bothered me until now," Elsie replied truthfully.

The nurse asked another question: "Any discomfort or headache?"

"Nope. I almost feel like a fraud taking up a hospital bed." Her hands worked on pouring ice followed by juice into the empty iced tea cup.

"At six, I'll return to assist with bathing." Nurse Shaner's statement didn't require acknowledgment.

"I'll be ready with bells on," she said to the nurse's back.

Her cheerfulness hadn't altered the nurse's no-nonsense demeanor one iota. Elsie selected a cute pair of pajamas for the day. In the following days, her only clothing would be a hospital gown.

"Elsie?" a male voice called to her.

"Good morning, Josh." She stepped from behind the bathroom door to see Josh and an attractive female doctor. "Er, Dr. Vilanger."

"Elsie, this is Dr. Anya Jace. Anya, this is Elsie Endy." Josh introduced patient and doctor.

The two women said hello in unison as they shook hands.

The female doctor's hands were small but strong.

Elsie returned to bed as Josh continued talking. "You look livelier than you did yesterday. And Nurse Shaner says your numbers are good. I must say, I'm not particularly surprised to see you awake with everything going on this morning."

"Thanks. I do feel better," she responded.

"We just wanted to stop in to see you before we head to surgery." Dr. Vilanger patted her blanketed foot. "We'll stop in later."

"Good luck," she stated with a sincere smile for both of them.

He nodded and returned the smile.

"Nice meeting you in person," Dr. Jace stated prior to the neurology duo exiting the room.

Dr. Vilanger's tall athletic form waited gentlemanly for the much shorter feminine form to precede him through the doorframe. Josh had always been respectful of women. There was something different in his demeanor with Dr. Anya Jace. Even when they weren't talking, his attentiveness remained highly focused. This boded positively for surgery.

A few minutes before morning visiting hours started, Nurse Billy entered the room carrying a stack of magazines. She sat Indian style on the bed watching television.

"Good morning, Elsie. While I was at my parents' for dinner last night, my mom insisted I take these for the waiting room. I thought you'd like first dibs," he suggested, placing the periodicals at the foot of her bed.

"Thanks. Any word on how the other surgery is going?" she asked pensively.

"Nothing as of yet, but they aren't expected to finish for another couple hours," he replied while doing his usual duties.

"I know. I just thought maybe . . ." She fidgeted with the hem of her pajama pants.

"Stop thinking and relax," Billy directed amiably. "Your friends should be here soon."

No sooner had he finished saying it than Trish burst into the room. "Good morning!"

"Good morning," Elsie replied with equal enthusiasm.

"You wouldn't believe what I went through this morning to get your decaf coffee with extra cream and crullers from Dunkin' Donuts." Her friend set the mentioned items on the tray table then flung herself dramatically into one of the chairs.

"Do tell!" Elsie prompted as she opened the bag.

"Everyone is crazy with this approaching winter storm. It didn't help that I got a late start. I even had to wait in line to fill the truck with gas." Trish's frustration finally vented. "I'm glad I got groceries yesterday on the way to Cassie's. I can't imagine what it's like inside a supermarket after the crowd in Dunkin' Donuts."

Her voice slightly muffled from the doughnut in her mouth, Elsie said, "Well, I appreciate this. Breakfast was eggs rather than oatmeal and fruit."

Trish sat forward to remove her coat to drape across the footboard of the bed. "What are these?"

"Billy's mom sent them for the waiting room. He left them here so I could select a few to read," she explained. "With the snow starting this afternoon, everyone should stay home."

"We discussed that yesterday on the way down in the elevator. I'll be here till twelve. Sara will be here from twelve to two." Trish shared their arrangements.

"That works." She nodded in favor of their agreement.

The next two hours zipped by with Trish. She left before Sara arrived. It was another fifteen minutes till Sara appeared.

She carried a small tote containing another helping of Easter dinner. "Hi! Sorry, I'm late. Traffic was atrocious."

"Trish said the same thing," Elsie responded.

"Just me and Trish today?" Sara asked.

"Dr. Vilanger and Dr. Jace popped in this morning before surgery," she answered. "Should I be expecting someone else?"

Sara finally admitted, "I hoped Rusty would come."

"After the last time I saw him, it's obvious he has moved on." Elsie hid her own disappointment. "And why shouldn't he? Sean and I are getting married."

"I know you love Sean. But I also know how much in love you and Rusty were." Sara couldn't hold her tongue any longer. "What if the operation is a complete success and your memory returns?"

It was Elsie's turn to reveal her own secret. "The only thing I hope for is that they fix the damage so I can live a normal life. Do I have regrets and feelings in regard to Rusty? Yes. But life moves on. I can't unlock the past."

Sara wiped the tears from her cheeks. "You've been holding too many things close. You know that you can share without judgment."

Elsie grasped her friend's hand. "I know. But I've put you all through so much already."

The two women hugged.

Gently stroking Elsie's hair, Sara said, "I needed to be sure you are listening to your heart, not just your head."

"Sean wouldn't be in my life if I hadn't," she shared with the older woman.

Releasing her, Sara opened the food containers. "I guess you earned this."

"Gee, thanks." Elsie smirked.

The meal was as delicious as the day before.

"There's more in the nurse's refrigerator for dinner. I also included some for Billy," Sara stated.

"That's wonderful—thank you. He'll be missing Easter Sunday with his family too," Elsie commented.

"You know, it really surprised me they schedule these surgeries going into a holiday weekend," the older woman remarked.

"It did me too. But it was their decision." As she thought about it, she commented, "It isn't really a holiday known for accidents. Maybe they thought it would be quiet. Of course, the impending storm is changing factors."

"Now I'm sorry I mentioned it. Any chance we can request they rewire part of your brain while they're in there so you don't overanalyze everything," Sara teased with affection.

Elsie parried with, "I'm sure Dr. Vilanger would if he could."

The humor relaxed the tension that the discussion in regard to Rusty had generated. Spying the tabloids, Sara began sifting through them. As she did, Elsie made selections. They stopped suddenly. There was a picture of Sean and Rusty grappling in tuxedos on the front cover dated last week. Both women grabbed for it.

"It might not be a good idea reading this," Sara suggested sternly, not releasing her grasp.

"I take it you and Trish were in cahoots that I didn't get a copy last week," Elsie accused.

"It was Sean's idea to keep it from you. We were merely trying to prevent you from getting upset," Sara argued their reasoning.

"I know about it now. You might as well let me read it," Elsie countered with the obvious.

Sara relinquished her hold. "True. You will dwell on it either way. Maybe it's not that bad."

Near the bottom of the pile was another one with the same picture and the headline: "Garnet vs. McEwan Tarnish the Golden Globes."

Neither woman said anything as Elsie added it to her small stack. Sara put the two she'd selected with Elsie's. It would give her something to read tomorrow morning during surgery.

Breaking the silence, Elsie asked, "How are the dogs?"

"Tycho won't let Sophie anywhere near his doghouse. We suspect he is guarding your nightshirt," Sara shared. "I was going to grab a used towel to place in Sophie's box, but Tom thinks Tycho will want that too. At which point, Sophie won't allow it and we'll have a fight on our hands. Since she isn't pushing the issue with his kennel, we'll leave things status quo."

"If he's getting that way already, you may really have to watch him during house time." Her tone indicated her worry.

The two women discussed dogs, specifically things related to Tycho, for the remainder of the visit.

From all that Sara and Trish had filled Elsie in about Tycho's puppyhood, she could tell he was a mama's boy. Overall, he was an extremely well-tempered dog that didn't fuss when bathed or groomed. Even when he'd gotten burrs imbedded in his eyelid, he allowed the veterinarian to remove them without a sedative. This filled Sara with pride. It was the one trait he inherited from his grandmother, Molly. Sophie and Deedles had all of their mother's physical characteristics. Deedles had Molly's temperament; Sophie, their great aunt's temperament. It wasn't a bad temperament. However, if there was a rule to be tested, she would do it. It amazed Sara and Elsie how sisters who looked like twins would exhibit such diverse personalities. As a result, Sophie had been bred to a very docile male. The dog was bland for showing but had good structure. It didn't appear the breeding had taken. That's apparently when Elsie agreed to go to Australia with Rusty. The horse riding accident occurred prior to anyone realizing Sophie had gotten pregnant. Sara lived at Elsie's home for the seven weeks. Sophie gave birth not long after Elsie had been released from the hospital in Sydney. By the time Elsie made it home, the only puppy had bonded with Tom and Sara and vice versa. It struck them all as karmic justice. Deedles had required emergency spaying the spring prior due to a case of pyometra. There was really no choice to be made. The little black-and-white female moved next door. Her call name was Oreo with a registered name of "WindyAcres' Love N Magic." Both women planned to bring the line together with Tycho and Oreo. There was good chance for a puppy to challenge Molly's record. Tom had already come up with that puppy's name: "WindyAcres' DoubleStuff."

Not long after Sara left, it began to snow. To occupy her thoughts, Elsie checked the DVDs. It was easy to determine who brought which ones. Sean's movies were from Trish. A separate pile starring Rusty had been chosen by Sara. Selecting one, she put it in the DVD player. The movie played unnoticed as Elsie finally opened the gossip paper. She didn't flip to the article right away. A page at a time was read as a way of acclimating herself to what would come. It didn't prepare her for the picture of Sean carrying her limp form or the close-up of her bloodied face. The article inferred that one of the men had struck her during their physical altercation. It also insinuated that Elsie suffered from mental instability. This they substantiated with her numerous visits to a psychiatrist. In fact, she had been seeing one in an attempt to unlock her memories. But how did they know that? She wrote a note for Trish to inform Harris. Elsie's subsequent visit to the hospital a day later wasn't mentioned. Maybe it missed the printing deadline. Or if they snapped a shot of the two actors arguing there, it was probably held to sell more papers the following week. She buzzed the nurse's station. No voice came over the intercom.

Instead, Billy hurried into her room. "What's wrong?"

Recognizing she shouldn't have called for him, she thought of something viable. "A little lightheaded. Any chance for yogurt or fruit?"

"Let's take your blood sugar first. You and Sara seemed to have a good visit." The nurse filled in the thirty seconds with small talk. "I can't believe it started snowing already."

Elsie followed his lead. "Me too. I was relieved when she called to say she made it home safely."

The machine beeped.

"Yep, your sugar is low. Do you want anything else while I'm downstairs?" the nurse asked solicitously.

"Do they carry these in the gift shop?" she requested, holding up one of the other newspapers.

"I don't know. I can check," he commented. "Aren't you getting your fill with what Mom sent?"

"I read an article where the story is continued this week." It wasn't really a fib; she merely omitted that the story included her.

The paper with the other picture didn't include as many details or spin them with as much flair.

Returning from his errand, Billy only carried food. "The gift shop has a limited selection."

"No big deal." She accepted the yogurt and plastic spoon. "Before you leave, I take it surgery didn't go well. It's been hours since it was supposed to be done, and Josh hasn't stopped in."

"You know I can't talk about another patient. You will have to wait for the doctors to inform you of the outcome." The nurse averted his face as he exited the room.

Less than ten minutes later, Dr. Jace entered. "Nurse Pfeisin said you wanted to talk to Dr. Vilanger. He's gone for the day. Is there something I can do?"

"From this morning's conversation, I thought he would stop in for a final check." Elsie plucked at the daisies on the blanket.

"I can do that." The female doctor perched on a chair.

Dr. Jace outlined the preparatory steps then began reviewing the actual surgery.

"...will expose the ..." She stopped in midsentence.

Examining the delicate features of the doctor's face, Elsie noticed a momentary flash of uncertainty. Seeing this loss of composure was unexpected. Without hesitation, Elsie sat forward on the edge of the bed.

Placing her hand on Dr. Jace's, Elsie asked softly, "What happened?"

The other woman looked at Elsie with wide eyes pooled with angry frustration.

Elsie tried again. "She knew as well as I do that we ran out of options. And the probabilities were slim at best."

"The repair worked, but it took too long. The test results after surgery showed she was brain dead." The tempestuous tears spilled onto Anya's cheeks.

Keeping her voice quietly calm, Elsie asked, "What caused her to become brain dead?"

"The blood oxygen levels dropped too low for too long during surgery," the doctor answered clinically.

"What caused the levels to drop that low?" Elsie needed the doctor to expound on this.

"The amount of blood lost combined with the time to make the repair severely limited the oxygen flow to the rest of the brain. Far more than we anticipated." It was another controlled response from the capable physician.

Keeping her own fear contained, Elsie prodded lightly, "What didn't work that we can do differently for my surgery?"

"I don't know." The tear supply was renewed with her agitated answer. "As soon as cause of death was determined, Josh left—three hours ago. I've tried calling him, but he won't call me back."

Elsie said forcefully, "I need the two of you to resolve this or I won't let you operate. I'd rather risk Russian roulette with the seizures."

"But the next one will, in all probability, either kill you or put you in a permanent coma," Dr. Jace argued.

Elsie smiled mischievously. "And if Dr. Vilanger was made aware of my position . . ."

The tears ceased as the ploy registered.

Determination set into Dr. Jace's shoulders as she stood. "I do believe his service will be paging him."

CHAPTER TWENTY-SIX

TWENTY-FIVE MINUTES LATER, Dr. Vilanger strode into Elsie's hospital room in a less than amiable frame of mind. "What do you mean you aren't going through with surgery?"

He was disheveled, and a stench emanated from him—a smell Elsie recognized.

Instead of answering his question, she blurted, "You've been drinking!"

"Not that it's any business of yours! I had one drink and fell asleep. I knocked over the bottle when I reached for my pager," he growled with irritation.

"Shame a cop didn't pull you over," she struck with stinging sarcasm.

"What the hell is that supposed to mean?" His anger still blocked his rational thinking.

"You're the smart one, you tell me." She jabbed at his ego.

He ignored the remark to ask in a moderately less offensive tone. "Why are you refusing surgery?"

She didn't pull any punches. "Because you haven't done anything to resolve why the other patient died."

Josh threw his lanky form into the same chair Anya used earlier. "We did everything right. The procedure just took too damn long."

"So instead of finding a way to shorten the procedure, you went home to drink?" she asked pointedly.

In a humbling motion, he put his head into his skilled hands. "Even if we shortened the procedure, yours is deeper and will take longer to get to."

Getting out of bed, she rubbed the place between his shoulders. "Go take a shower. Then you and Dr. Jace come back here to discuss options."

The doctor agreed without further dispute.

Before Elsie could buzz the nurses' station, Billy entered. "What's this you are refusing surgery?"

She filled him in on the conversation with Dr. Jace and the most recent one with Dr. Vilanger.

"I want them in this room talking until they find the answer. Or I am leaving." Her mind was set.

"What can I do?" He obviously wanted to help.

"Third-party perspective," she said glibly.

"Why don't I get your dinner while you wait for the doctors?" he suggested.

She shook her head. "I'm too aggravated to eat."

"You need to calm down. Getting this upset is raising your blood pressure and could cause complications." Billy spoke with concern.

To prevent lashing at him with a bitter retort, she pushed the pitcher toward him. "Ice, please."

For the next eighteen minutes, Elsie repeatedly organized the stack of magazines and picked imaginary fuzz off the blanket. Nurse Billy watched with apprehension. Till the doctors arrived she was in a frenzied state. At seeing her current appearance, one doctor checked pulse; the other, blood pressure.

Before either doctor could remark, Elsie stated, "This isn't going to improve until you two find a solution."

The two doctors shared a look. Their patient was correct. They needed to evaluate the morning's surgery, or another patient they'd both become emotionally attached to would die.

Night began to fall along with the snow. They weren't any closer to an answer. The doctors broke for dinner. Meanwhile, the nurse took care of his patient. The Easter meal didn't taste as good. It was due to her mood, not the food. Nurse Billy left for a few minutes to get ice.

Unexpectedly, Nurse Shaner entered the room. "Good evening, Ms. Endy. How are you feeling?"

When the female nurse checked her pulse, Elsie remarked, "Goodness, your hands are freezing!"

"I'm terribly sorry. The sidewalk is icy and I fell into the bushes. Snow got up my sleeves and inside my coat." An involuntarily shiver rippled through her as she explained.

Nurse Pfeisin joined them in time to hear the story. His course to the tray table halted. The movements of his face indicated he was in deep contemplation.

Unexpectedly, he blurted, "That's it!"

He quickly placed the pitcher on the table, missing it. As he rushed from the room, plastic breaking from impact and ice skittering across the floor echoed. Elsie and Nurse Shaner stared at the empty doorway in confusion. However, the fastidious nurse didn't dawdle longer than a moment. She grabbed the spit pan and began picking up ice. Elsie joined her.

"Ms. Endy, you are a patient—return to bed. I am quite capable of clearing this," Nurse Shaner stated sternly.

"I'll make a deal with you." Elsie bartered, "You call me Elsie, I'll get back into bed."

After thinking a few seconds, the nurse accepted the offer. "Agreed . . . Elsie."

A smirk was quickly concealed as Elsie complied by climbing under the covers. She made an overt fuss of channel-surfing for something interesting to watch. Nurse Shaner completed the cleanup unassisted.

"I'll be back directly with a replacement towel and pitcher," the nurse said on her exit, bringing the towel used to wipe the floor dry with her.

It was then that Elsie realized that she now had two nurses specifically assigned to her. And Nurse Shaner's dedication was why she had come in a full shift early. She didn't want the winter storm preventing her from being at work when she was needed most, especially since her initial patient assignment didn't survive surgery. For the next twenty-four to forty-eight hours, Nurses Pfeisin and Shaner would be interchangeable.

By the time Nurse Shaner returned with a fresh pitcher of ice, the doctors and male nurse could be heard approaching. Nurse Shaner attempted to leave as soon as they filed into the room.

Dr. Vilanger spoke to the nurse to prevent her exodus. "Nurse Shaner, didn't you work in an ER near the Finger Lakes before coming here?"

"Yes, Doctor," she answered warily as she stepped back into the room.

"When we were selecting nurses for this surgery, you were chosen because you stayed with a patient's case until they were no longer in critical care," Dr. Jace stated with barely contained anticipation. "Your file also indicates you encountered a substantial amount of hypothermia cases."

"During the winter months, we'd see at least one a day—anything from falling through the ice, exposure to the elements, and children or aged due to the lack of sufficient heat in their homes," Nurse Shaner supplemented.

"Do I need to be here for this?" Elsie interjected.

Dr. Vilanger nodded to Nurse Pfeisin.

Billy sat on the edge of the bed. "Not that long ago, you were brought into emergency. You were found unconscious on your patio."

"Yes. The last thing I remember from that was a migraine. After taking my medication, I went to bed. Then I woke up here." Elsie filled in what little she knew.

Dr. Vilanger spoke. "From the shots of your brain, we deduced you were having a major episode. You were outside in the cold for an extended period, causing your body temperature to drop. And those beasts of yours kept you just warm enough so your body didn't shut down. We believe this incident of hypothermia slowed your system enough to allow the blister to dissipate slowly."

"What does that have to do with . . .?" Elsie began asking without allowing her brain to connect the dots.

Suddenly, their narrative made sense. "Oh. Oh!"

All five of them smiled in unison.

"May we continue with surgery as scheduled?" Dr. Vilanger verified.

"Yes," Elsie confirmed. "But does that mean you are going to stick me in a snow drift a couple hours before surgery?"

"No. However, the four of us need to adjourn to my office to determine the exact method and timing for putting you into a similar hypothermic state." The lead physician stated while motioning for the others to follow.

Almost two full hours passed prior to anyone's reappearance. Dr. Vilanger came alone. After explaining the plan for prepping her for surgery, he had another release form for her to sign. The quartet would be getting some sleep. Since they were remaining in the hospital, the overnight floor nurse would rouse them if needed. They both felt confident with this resolution as the doctor bid good night.

CHAPTER TWENTY-SEVEN

EVEN THOUGH THE hour was late, Elsie couldn't sleep. Whether she slept or not didn't matter. For a sense of comfort, she popped one of Sean's movies into the DVD player. It helped, but it didn't give her that secure feeling she needed. At midnight, the floor nurse checked in on her.

Elsie requested, "There's food and soda in the closet. Would you please put it in the lounge for anyone to take?"

"If you get thirsty, I can bring you a lozenger," the duty nurse offered as she removed the bag of groceries.

"Thanks," Elsie replied courteously while flipping through the photograph album.

What she wouldn't give to have Sophie and Tycho lying with her to rub faces. She pulled one of the pictures of the furry duo from its slot to hold to her face. It was a silly gesture, but she hoped they understood how much she loved them. She repeated this action with a few of the other pictures. With the last one she removed, something else came with it. It was a picture of her and Rusty gazing happily into each other's eyes. They were standing on a beach wearing leis. They were dressed similarly as the one in Rusty's wallet. She didn't remember it being taken, but she knew it was in the Island of Maui. When they'd flown to the States after the accident, their layover was on Oahu. Plus, Rusty had been extremely protective anytime he noticed someone with a camera. The date digitally stamped on the back of it was three weeks prior to the accident. Her throat choked with emotion—a sense of great loss. Tears sprang from her eyes. After the crying ceased ten minutes later, she blamed it on the overwhelming lack of control in regard to the outcome of surgery. The pictures were replaced into the album.

Water from sink could be used to rinse her mouth. However, phlegm hung in her throat. She buzzed for a lozenger. While she waited, she selected *Sifting through the Ashes* to play next. On one of the first days they'd arrived home from Australia, Rusty insisted they watch it. It had been the first time she suffered an episode, of which, she'd told no one until she experienced a second one a week later, which he witnessed. The nurse delivering the lozenger interrupted her reverie. Elsie dimmed the lights to watch this movie. By the time the credits rolled, a peaceful slumber embraced her.

She was gently nudged awake.

"Elsie, it is morning," his husky voice whispered.

Her eyes opened to focus on Nurse Billy. She smiled sleepily.

"I want to show you something." He urged while assisting her into robe and slippers.

He wheeled her to the door of the observation patio. In the dark of the early hour, she could see a path had been shoveled to the wall. The virgin snow glistened with the stars overhead. The stillness of the sleeping suburb swept Elsie with serenity. When she finished soaking it in, she squeezed Billy's hand. The silence stretched until they reached her room. Nurse Shaner was waiting for them with the supplies to prepare their patient for surgery. The phone on the nightstand rang. This did not deter the nurses from going about their task. It was Trish. As expected, she was snowed in. They shared loving sentiments then ended the call. The phone rang again. This time it was Sara. Tom had gotten up at 2:00 a.m. to clear the driveway by 4:00 a.m. He'd accomplished his task. Unfortunately, the state hadn't plowed the roads yet. Their attempt to make it to the hospital ended seconds from turning onto the road. They'd slid sideways down the hill. Tom steered them safely into the diner's parking lot. Words of affection closed this call too.

The doctors arrived to make a final check then headed to the operating room to confirm things were ready there. Nurse Shaner injected a sedative into the IV.

Next thing Elsie knew, she was on a gurney wheeling along a hallway. The drugs were taking affect. Fluorescent lights swirled a myriad of colors around her in tie-dye fashion. Out of nowhere, a scruffy face filled her frame of reference. A hand grasped hers. He spoke, but the words sounded foreign. They crammed into an elevator. When the elevator reached its destination, he was not permitted to exit. However, they did allow him a private moment with her. His free hand gently rubbed her shaved head.

Finally, words registered. "I love you."

In her head she responded. Whether or not the thought formed into anything other than gibberish, only he heard. A tender kiss touched her lips, and then his image dissolved. The magic carpet ride landed abruptly with the bright glare of the operating room. The doctors greeted her through their surgical masks. It was time to induce the hypothermic state.

Dr. Vilanger asked, "Are you ready?"

To ease everyone's apprehension, she teased, "Make me a popsicle."

Prior to the blackness enveloping her, Elsie saw the crinkles at the corner of Josh's eyes as he smiled.

Chapter Twenty-Eight

Unrecognizable sounds, flashes of light, sensation of falling, extreme cold, a fuzzy face rubbing hers, words of love—all darted the periphery of Elsie's mind. Each time she reached a semblance of consciousness, she would be mentally yanked to a place where time and space didn't exist.

After what seemed like an eternity of struggling, she opened her eyes. It appeared to be a hospital room. Someone's torso rested on the side of the bed, bent over from the chair. With extreme effort, she moved her fingers to brush them against the person's exposed neck. The head turned in her direction; but a strong male hand rubbed the face, blocking it from view. This time her finger brushed her visitor's fingers.

The hand dropped away as he quickly lifted his head in shock. "Elsie?"

Something prevented her from speaking. The familiar haggard-looking man pressed the call button. Whatever was said over the intercom was lost as her thoughts spun trying to identify him. People in medical garb rushed into the room. A man in a white lab coat spoke directly to her. His words were garbled. Exhaustion caused her eyelids to flutter shut. More strange dreams plagued her. The next time her eyes opened, a different man and a woman were gazing at her with anxiety. A parade of familiar faces appeared each time she woke. However, she never remained coherent long enough to recall their names or her relationship with them. The only thing that defined a new day was whether her visitors wore the same clothing. If she went by the number of times she woke, months had passed; by their clothing, only a few days.

Eventually when they spoke, she understood. The intubation still incapacitated any verbal response. Her means of communication was via squeezing a hand or blinking her eyes. It also required the right question asked. The husband-and-wife team caught on quicker than the others. During one of her conscious moments, the couple talked about Sophie and Tycho. At first, Elsie thought they were telling stories about their children. A story where the boy chased a coyote didn't make sense. The woman opened a book and pointed to a picture of two Alaskan malamutes. Immediately, Elsie knew Sophie was the gray bitch; Tycho, the red dog. Memories of other similar dogs flashed through her head. In the way the woman beamed at her, Elsie deduced the recognition had played across her face.

After a few days, the doctor determined the breathing tube could be removed. However, the severe soreness stymied speech. The nurses managed to get her into a stable sitting position. This prompted them to give her pen and paper. It took several tries for her fingers to function properly. Things she wrote weren't always legible. But it did give the doctor a place to start with her physical therapy. A ten-minute refresher course of the alphabet and a child's writing book opened the pathways in her brain for reading and writing.

She wrote a few simple questions: "What's your name?" and "How do we know each other?"

When she showed these to the couple, the woman began to cry. Her husband led her from the room.

Soon the doctor entered. "May I see what you wrote?"

Elsie nodded and handed the sheets of paper to him.

His response to these was, "I am Dr. Josh Vilanger. I have been the specialist on your case for the last year. Do you know why you are here?"

She shook her head negatively.

In a very calm voice, he answered, "You had brain surgery a week ago."

Her hand went immediately to her head. Her face was filled with alarm at feeling the bandage encasing it.

Seeing this, he hurried his explanation. "It's okay. We fixed it. As expected, you spent four days in a coma. However, you did experience a few minor strokes. Everyone is anxious to see how you've been affected."

Her eyebrows furrowed as she held up three fingers.

"Yes, it's been three days since your first regained consciousness." His face relaxed as he replied. "There's swelling in the brain, which appears to be preventing you from functioning normally. This isn't unusual. However, things have been rough. It's going to take time to heal. Any bumps we encounter from this point forward will be a walk in the park."

His confident statement allayed her fears. The doctor exited the room. Soon the couple returned.

The woman gave Elsie a bright smile. "I'm Sara, and this is my husband Tom. We've been best friends for two decades."

Elsie knew what Sara said was true. This had her face forming an equally cheery smile. Sara leaned in to give her a gentle hug. This seemed to ease the sorrow the other woman had been feeling. Maybe the doctor had given her friend the same pep talk. The male nurse joined them. He carried a cup with a straw.

"Elsie, Dr. Vilanger said you are having a hard time identifying us. I'm Nurse Billy Pfeisin. I've been with you for the last year too," he said with ease. "There's apple juice in the cup. We're going to give this a try. It may hurt on the way down, so only a sip."

She eagerly reached for the cup. Nurse Pfeisin kept his hands under it in case she couldn't keep hold. The cool, sweet liquid was welcomed by her dry mouth. The first sip did hurt a bit, but the overall quenching made it worthwhile. She tried another sip before placing the cup on the tray table.

Satisfied she wouldn't choke, the nurse said prior to leaving, "Nurse Shaner will be with you this evening. She's scary but very good."

Sara and Tom remained with her until her eyelids got droopy.

Elsie woke to see she had another visitor. The foreigner sat by the bed watching television. As she shifted, she realized he was holding her hand. Feeling her movement, he turned.

She mouthed hi with a sleepy grin and a squeeze to his hand.

"Hello, love," he said softly, dropping a kiss on her cheek.

With her free hand she reached for her two questions then handed them to him. His unshaven face sagged in disappointment. Rather unexpectedly, he dropped to his knees, burying his face against her stomach. His body shuddered with sobs. Even though she lacked understanding of his reaction, she reassuringly ran her fingers through his hair.

He lifted his face full of anguish. "I love you so much, but I don't know if I have the strength to go through this anymore."

His words caused a severe tightening in her chest. When he began to straighten, she clutched his arms. Panic welled inside at the thought of him leaving. She desperately tried to speak. A harsh hacking cough emitted in conjunction with a tearing sensation in her throat. Then she was gasping for air. The alarms on the machines announced her distress. A female nurse ran into the room.

She spoke into the intercom. "Get Vilanger now!"

Next, she asked the man. "What happened?"

He replied contritely, "She got upset and tried to talk."

If looks could kill, the glare Nurse Shaner shot him would have been lethal. A haze began to close in Elsie's vision.

The nurse administered an injection through the IV tube. "This is a muscle relaxant. It should allow you to breathe easier."

It only took seconds for Elsie to relax enough to realize air was passing into her lungs. Granted, she felt like she was breathing through a pinhole. Dr. Vilanger entered the room at a full run. Nurse Shaner filled the doctor in as he grabbed a scope to peer down Elsie's throat.

The other man stated blame. "It's my fault. I upset her."

"If you do it again, I will have you removed," the doctor muttered sternly, still examining his patient.

"I won't," the culprit stated.

"Okay, dear," the doctor spoke to his patient, "it looks like your forcefulness to speak strained your already weakened vocal cords. In combination with your anxiety, they constricted, making breathing difficult. The muscle relaxant is doing its job. I'll check on you later."

Nurse Shaner followed the doctor from the room. The man paced about the room with lack of certainty. Elsie reached out her hand. He grasped it with desperation as he sat on the edge of the bed. The medication made her muzzy. It didn't take long for her to drift off completely.

In her dreams, she felt a tender kiss on her cheek followed by the words "I will always love you."

CHAPTER TWENTY-NINE

A BRIGHT LIGHT filtered through her eyelids. Opening them, she discovered Nurse Billy Pfeisen opening the curtains wide.

"Good morning," he said cheerily. "We're going to get you out of bed today."

Using the bed controls, she sat up. The nurse kept her steady as she swung her legs over the side.

After checking her reflexes, he ordered, "Push against my hands with your feet."

Apparently satisfied, he helped her into a robe and slippers. "Okay, stand slowly. I'll be right here if you get wobbly."

Her legs shook a bit, but she managed.

"Do you want to try a few steps?" he asked, gently coaxing her.

Taking a normal step was too much for her rubbery legs.

The nurse steadied her. "I'll get the wheelchair."

She pushed him away. Sliding her feet a few inches worked. However, her left leg didn't want to cooperate. She made it a few feet before the nurse had her sit in the wheelchair. He removed all of the leads monitoring her vital signs. Even her IV was disconnected. He tucked her daisy blanket around her lap. They wheeled to the observation patio. The morning was crisply cold but exhilarating. From the edge, she could see small patches of white indicating a recent snow. This niggled at her thoughts. She remembered watching it snow. Now, that was silly. She'd lived in this area most of her life. Of course, she had seen it snow. It was from this same vantage point. If she'd been Dr. Vilanger's patient for a year, it was likely it had snowed during another hospital stay.

The nurse was watching her reaction. "Familiar, but can't place it?"

She nodded emphatically.

"That's a good sign. Just don't force it," he stated, wheeling her inside.

She turned to look up and back at him.

He chuckled. "Yes, that is asking an awful lot for you to not dwell on it."

Instead of returning to the room, they went to physical therapy. Everything worked—her left side sluggishly. However, it took a couple of times to get everything to move the way she wanted. Tomorrow they would begin restoring her strength and coordination.

Nurse Pfeisin retrieved her. "Are you ready for a bath in the tub?"

Washing after this exertion sounded wonderful. Upon rolling her wheelchair into the bathroom, the nurse began filling the tub basin. The nurse spread a towel across the bench.

When he turned to help her into the tub, he stopped. "The gown."

She shook her head no.

"Elsie, I'm a nurse. I've been giving you sponge baths for the last eight days." His puzzlement at her reaction was clearly stated.

She shook her head no again.

The adamant expression told him that no amount of cajoling would sway her.

After considering their options, the nurse suggested, "I'll help you into the tub. Once you're on the bench, I'll leave for you to take off the gown and bathe. If you start having problems, drop the bath gel into the tub. I'll hear the bang. Okay?"

Her head bobbed in agreement.

The bath gel and a washcloth sit on the lip of the basin, ready for use. She ran into a problem with rinsing. The knobs were turned too tightly.

No sooner had she realized it than Billy came to the rescue.

From outside the door, he said loudly, "Cover yourself. I'm coming in."

She quickly concealed her breasts as much as possible by crossing her arms over them. Billy strode into the room to turn on the water. And he stayed to rinse her off. He closed his eyes for her to rinse her chest. With that done, he left her with a towel to dry. Another few minutes, he returned with a button-front nightshirt. After lifting her from the tub, he helped her dress. As they were leaving the room, she caught glimpse of her reflection. Her quiet gasp was audible in the tiny room. As if the stark white bandage encasing her head wasn't sufficiently disconcerting, the raccoon eyes shocked her. The movement of her hand to her face clued Billy in on as to why the noise.

"While you were in the coma, blood clots formed and deposited in your sinus cavities. The easiest way to get to them was through your nose," he continued, pushing her to the bed. "Don't worry. The bruises will eventually go away."

It had been a busy morning. A big yawn formed unexpectedly. With it was a funny squeak as the air pushed through her strained vocal cords. Concealing his grin, Billy assisted her into bed. Breakfast—cream of wheat, milk, apple juice, and hot tea—arrived while he reattached her wires.

"You didn't have any problems with the broth for dinner, so I ordered this. Wait for me to add the milk to the cereal or it will be too thick," he stated as he completed setting the IV machine to deliver her medications properly.

It was a good thing she hadn't put the teabag into the hot water. The cereal also required hot water added to it. Finally, it was a consistency she could swallow without choking. After eating, she napped.

"Hey, sleepyhead." A feminine voice roused her ninety minutes later.

Using the bed controls to sit, Elsie acknowledged her friend with a smile. Once again, she reached for her two questions.

Since the woman was closer to the tray table, she touched them. "Are these what you want?"

Elsie nodded. As the woman picked them up, Elsie pointed to her. The woman read them. Her bright face dimmed as she realized what the questions meant.

However, she quickly recovered to answer cheerily. "Well, I'm Trish. You're very best friend and assistant. We've known each other for eight years. And . . ."

Trish filled in gaps over the next few hours. The topics included how they became friends, trips they'd taken together, her children and granddaughter. When she left late afternoon, Elsie needed another nap. Nurse Shaner came in to check on her. She stayed while Elsie ate her beef barley soup. Dr. Vilanger stopped by to share information from the latest tests and observations on her progress. During consultation with the other specialists, they noticed a pattern. Retracing previous activities or memories aided in opening the neural pathways. This gave them hope for a completely successful recovery—particularly, her memory returning in full. There might be some permanent loss, but not significant people and events. The next days fit a similar pattern, with the physical therapy sessions increasing along with her stamina. It wouldn't be long till she walked fairly normal instead of a shuffle. And if she kept her voice to a whisper, she could converse with everyone.

One evening Elsie felt restless. Sleep was elusive. She could've buzzed for a sedative, but there was a reason for the insomnia. Climbing out of bed, she rummaged in the closet for a bottle of juice. A bag of movies was discovered. Grabbing the top DVD, she put it into the player then curled in the cushioned chair. When the lead actor appeared on screen, the room spun and teetered like a Tilt-A-Whirl for a few minutes. As the movie continued, there was a scene where he stripped to go swimming. Before he removed his clothes, she envisioned every inch of his naked body. And what appeared in her mind matched what revealed on the television, including the full frontal. Maybe she'd seen the movie before. But that didn't explain how her senses could feel the touch of his lips on hers or the smell of him as they held each other. The carnival ride began again. The spinning increased until the room disappeared completely. Memories of him flashed in her head as she groped blindly for the nurse call button.

"Elsie . . . Elsie?" A male voice spoke loudly to her while a hand shook her with force.

She mumbled, "Sean?"

"No. Open your eyes and look at me," the voice demanded.

Dr. Vilanger peering intently into her face filled her view. "What happened?"

Shifting, she realized she was already kind of sitting, or rather slumped, in a chair. Suddenly, all of the whirling images of Sean made sense. She bolted upright in the chair so quickly she whacked Josh with her head.

"Son of a . . .!" he exclaimed, grabbing his nose as he sat on the bed.

"Are you all right?" Nurse Billy asked, looking from one to the other, unsure of whom to help.

Elsie tried to stifle her glee at the ridiculous incident. Josh glared incredulously at her for a few moments. This only made it funnier. The laughter burst out uninhibited. It must've been contagious. The two men joined in her hilarity.

When their joy ended, Dr. Vilanger scrunched his face to check his nose. "How's your head?"

"Don't worry. It wasn't where the incision is," she replied.

The doctor eyed her questioningly. "You know where the incision is because?"

"From the MRI pictures you showed me when you diagnosed the problem," she answered, placing her hand on the bandage over the repaired area. "By the way, when can this itchy thing come off?"

Both the doctor's and the nurse's eyebrows rose expectantly.

"Oh yeah! I remembered stuff!" she stated cheerily with a squeak.

She told them about the movie and what she could recall. A few details were edited.

"Sounds like the last year is there along with bits and pieces from your childhood," Dr. Vilanger said thoughtfully. "Time for a day of tests."

With undeniable sarcasm, she replied, "Yippee!"

"Careful, or I won't remove the bandage." The doctor had no problems keeping her in check.

Billy smothered his chuckle till the doctor exited the room. As she stood to head for the bathroom, she grimaced.

"What?" the nurse asked.

"You try sleeping in that position and see where you get muscle cramps," she remarked, trying to stretch the kinks away.

"When you go to physical therapy, he'll take care of those," Billy said. "I'll be right back with the blood tubes and urine cup."

"Hurry up! I really have to pee," she stated with urgency on her slow shuffle trek from the far side of the room.

By the time Billy returned with everything, she'd just made it to the bathroom. All of the necessary fluids were collected. Dr. Vilanger called to tell them the MRI was scheduled in a half hour. In the meantime, breakfast was delivered. Her stomach rumbled in protest at not being able to eat. While she waited, she phoned Trish.

After sharing with Trish what happened, Elsie made a request. "Sean's flight is in two days. In three hours, please send him a text message with the phone number here at the hospital. And that I miss my 'sodding Scotsman.'"

"Guess we need to start working on the reception." Trish's happiness at Elsie starting to remember things was evident in the lilt of her voice.

Giddiness filled Elsie at the thought of marrying Sean. Billy tapped on his wrist.

"Have to go for an MRI. Thanks for taking care of the message," she said into the phone.

"I'm glad to do it. I'll see you at lunchtime." Trish hung up.

Ten minutes later, Elsie sat on the MRI table. She recognized the nurse who had been there prior to surgery.

Without thought, she asked directly, "May I please see the vial?"

Bright pink infused the young nurse's cheeks as she held it for the patient to read.

"Valium—thank you." And Elsie got comfortable on the metal platform.

Billy concealed his chuckle as he fetched warm blankets for his priority patient.

Chapter Thirty

After the MRI, her head was freed from the heavy bandaging. A gentle washing with baby shampoo helped the itch go away. A soft stretchy cap kept her head from getting cold. This lulled Elsie into a happy nap for the next hour. The squeaky wheels in the hall announced lunch. Her empty stomach compelled her to see what was on the plate under the lid. Macaroni and cheese had her reaching for the fork. Unfortunately, the first bite tasted of not-enough cheese on overdone starchy pasta. As she pushed the table away, Trish entered the room. She dropped her bags onto the chair then hurried to hug her dear friend.

"I am so glad it is you!" Tears of happiness dampened her cheeks. "I sent the text message to Sean from the parking lot. Hopefully, he'll call soon."

"It depends on the satellite relay and what he's doing with his kids," Elsie replied without worry.

Trish went about emptying the second bag.

When Trish placed a warm container on the table next to the hospital tray, she asked, "Any new visitors?"

"Nope." Knowing everything Trish made was delicious, Elsie eyed the lid impatiently, waiting for it to be removed.

"Go ahead," the cook said, putting the other approved groceries into the closet.

Elsie's finger dexterity had greatly improved with physical therapy, but this posed a challenge. If she could turn the container sideways, she could've opened it with ease. The problem was keeping the container flat so the food didn't dump. After a few attempts, she got it open with only a thumb sliding into the mashed potatoes.

Which she promptly stuck in her mouth. "Yum."

Scooping the meat gravy onto the mashed potatoes, she began to eat.

"Is it my taste buds or my memory? This doesn't taste like hamburger gravy," Elsie asked. "Don't get me wrong, it tastes good."

A devious smile formed on Trish's lips. "It's sausage, not hamburger."

"Bangers and mash for the swallowing-challenged," Elsie chirped.

Trish nodded in acknowledgment. While Elsie ate, Trish shared the latest adorable thing her granddaughter had done.

Afterward, a burp accompanied the pop of the lid going back on the empty plastic container. "Excuse me."

The phone on the nightstand rang. Elsie pushed the tray table away in an easy motion to reach for it.

"Hello?" she answered expectantly.

"Elsie m'love, is that you?" Sean's Scottish brogue echoed across the transatlantic call.

"Yes, it's me. Just a little side effect," she replied.

"A side effect! This is the number at the hospital, isn't it?! Fuck! I knew I shouldn't have left!" He exploded.

To rein him in, she blurted. "I had the surgery!"

"What?" His higher pitch and thicker accent were clear indicators of his ire. "The major life-threatening surgery? Without me there?"

"Yeees." She drew out the word for emphasis.

Silence ensued. She chewed on her lip, waiting for his response.

Finally, he spoke. "All went well?"

"Evidently, since we are talking," she said glibly to deflect his anger.

Ignoring her flippant attitude, his voice cracked. "And your memory?"

"Chunks are missing, but I remember you." Her faith in how much he loved her didn't waver. "So much so that I wish you were here."

Another long moment of quiet passed. Prior to hearing him talk again, he sniffed and coughed to clear his crying.

However, he couldn't keep the strong emotions from his voice. "I'll get a seat on the next flight to the colonies."

"It's okay if you wait for your scheduled flight. I just wanted to let you know everything was good," she stated.

"It is more than good!" Everything had sunk in. "I want to see you."

"I'm not going anywhere. Two more days won't change how much I love you and still want to marry you. Enjoy your last days with the kids," she said supportively.

"All right, m'love, I'll call you when my flight lands." The reassurance eased his anxiety. "I love you, Elsie."

They blew kisses across the Atlantic Ocean prior to ending their call.

At hearing the entire conversation, Trish giggled in elation. "I am so glad to hear you are still getting married."

"Why wouldn't I?" Elsie found her friend's remark odd.

"I wasn't sure with all that has happened since surgery," Trish said hesitantly.

Elsie didn't follow. "I don't understand."

Trish moved about the room, straightening things. She stopped to look at Elsie. If Elsie didn't know any better, Trish seemed as confused as Elsie with their current topic.

Trish broke the weird impasse. "I thought maybe you'd be worried about identifying any lingering complications from surgery to make that kind of commitment."

However, her tone lacked its usual confident assertion. Or maybe she was merely voicing concern for Elsie. Satisfied with this explanation, Elsie focused on other topics.

Suddenly, Elsie exclaimed, "Oh my god! Tycho, my flannel nightshirt! Is he behaving?"

"I don't know," Trish replied. "When Sara and I talk, it's about you."

Elsie reached for the telephone. "Do you mind?"

"If you don't, Nurse Cranky Face will be here to see why your heart monitor is showing distress," Trish stated seriously.

After Elsie finished pushing the buttons, she said with excitement, "I remembered the number."

"Wonder what else is behind the curtain?" Trish's sardonic reference to the Wizard of Oz didn't go unnoticed.

Before Elsie could deal with it, Tom answered the other end. "Hello?"

"Hi, Tom. It's Elsie. Is Sara there?" she requested cheerily.

"Hold on." He handed the phone to his wife.

"Hey, Elsie. Is something wrong?" Sara asked.

"I hope not. How's Tycho doing? Is he still guarding my nightshirt? Are he and Sophie getting along, or has he gotten cranky with her?" Elsie pursued what had worried her.

"We had an iffy moment shortly after the snowstorm. Since then, Tom has been going over with me . . ." Sara's voice trailed off as the full impact of what Elsie's call meant.

"Oh my God. Oh my God. Oh my God! You are you!" Sara's tears of relief could be heard in her words.

"I hope that's a good thing," Elsie teased.

"Definitely!" Sara exclaimed with exuberance.

Elsie clarified. "Okay. All of my memories aren't back, but I'll fill you in the next time I see you."

The older woman wasn't going to let her joy be stifled. "We will be there in an hour. Tell Trish to stay. We are going to celebrate!"

When the couple arrived, they had a bottle of champagne.

Nurse Shaner entered to investigate when the cork popped. "Alcoholic beverages are prohibited from the hospital—and most particularly this patient."

Dr. Vilanger intervened as he strode into the room. "It's all right, Nurse Shaner. I approved this."

The nurse headed for the door.

Sara invited her to stay. "Please join us."

The nurse accepted a Dixie cup of the bubbly beverage. A feeling nagged at Elsie that this was premature. To take this joyful moment from all of them would be wrong. For everything over the last twenty days, they deserved this. Besides, any further improvements would be the cherry on top of the sundae.

The next evening no one visited. A couple of movies were on the agenda. The first she selected was *Planetary Motion*. In bed, she worked on a crossword puzzle while it played. A voice she recognized spoke. Looking at the monitor, it was the man who she saw when she came out of the coma. After the day he upset her, he never returned. She figured he'd been an apparition conjured by her imagination. Now her mind avowed differently. Mesmerized, she crawled to the foot of the bed. How did they know each other? Even though her head began to ache, she couldn't stop watching. During the credits, she still had no answers other than the actor's name was Rusty Garnet. Searching for answers, she clicked on Special Features. Included under this menu option was an interview with the director, Rich Taylor. A loud roar of a crowd filled her ears as he appeared on screen. She buzzed for Nurse Shaner. After sharing with her what transpired, the nurse telephoned Dr. Vilanger's pager. He had the evening off, but he called in right away. The nurse relayed the information to him. He ordered a sedative and analgesic. Eventually, she drifted to sleep.

Early morning, she sat up in bed screaming. Nurse Shaner rushed into the room.

With tears streaming down her face, Elsie whispered hoarsely, "Dreams, nightmares."

As Nurse Shaner poured juice over ice for her patient, she said compassionately, "Tell me about them."

As Elsie relayed what she saw, she realized they were recollections—her abusive first husband, her success as an author, her relationship with Rusty, her fall from the horse. The more she shared, the more jumbled they became. Hysteria seized her at processing all of it. The monitors blared in alarm. The doctor had already been paged. Elsie rambled on in a squeaky voice. Nurse Shaner tried to calm her. Not long after the page, Dr. Vilanger entered the room at a quick pace. Clearly, the patient's blathered gibberish initially flustered him. As he examined Elsie, Nurse Shaner condensed what occurred. A few minutes later, a syringe jabbed into her IV. As the medication took full affect, Josh held her hand and talked to her. His muddled words didn't make sense, but his tone soothed her frazzled state.

CHAPTER THIRTY-ONE

IT WAS NOON till Elsie opened her eyes. Glancing around the room slowly didn't prevent all of the new memories colliding at full force. She loved both Rusty and Sean. They both loved her. How did this happen? How could she choose between them? Both men had treated her with care and respect. Even her best friends were divided on who was the best man for her.

"Dear God, please help me choose," she cried aloud.

Ten minutes later, Nurse Billy walked into the room.

"You're awake. How are you?" he asked with concern at seeing her tears. "Are you in pain?"

"No." She reached for the box of tissues.

"Nurse Shaner said you had a rough night. Do you want to talk about it?" he offered.

"Ow!" she yelped as she blew her nose.

"Take it easy," the nurse recommended. "You could burst a blood vessel."

"Too late." Her voice sounded nasal as she held a fresh tissue to her nose.

The first tissue was stained with red. Before the nurse had time to page for the doctor, he walked through the doorway. Dr. Vilanger's already sober expression tensed further at seeing that the tissues at his patient's face were quickly soaking with blood. Nurse Pfeisin pulled two cold packs from one of the drawers of the metal cabinet. The doctor popped one; the nurse, the other to release the chemicals. The first pack went on the back of her neck; the second one, the bridge of her nose. Tilting her back slightly, Dr. Vilanger removed the blood-drenched wad of tissues. The stream had slowed to a trickle.

After peering up her nose with a scope, the doctor remarked, "We need to cauterize."

Along with retrieving the tool for the task, the two medical professionals spoke in low tones. Her racing thoughts blocked any semblance of registering the words. Those same thoughts also had her not particularly caring what they were discussing. Upon their return to her bedside, a needle was stuck into her IV. It didn't take long for the medication to ease her mind.

As her eyes fluttered shut, Dr. Vilanger said, "We're going to stop the bleeding now."

When she opened them again, it was to answer the ringing phone.

She sat while reaching for it. "Hello?"

"Hello, m'love. We're boarding." Sean's Scottish voice floated happily across the transatlantic call.

Rubbing her eyes gently, she said groggily, "Have a safe trip."

He asked, "Did I wake you?"

"Um-hmm," she murmured.

"I'm sorry. Go back to sleep. I'll see you tomorrow morning," he stated with anticipation. "I love you."

"Love you too," she replied with a kiss.

He returned the kiss then disconnected.

Not wanting the recent memories to barrage her, she allowed the drug-induced sleep to overtake again. Instead of the dreamless sleep she'd been enjoying, recollections of the past tormented her. This time she stirred shortly before midnight. An insistent bladder chased her from bed. By the time she finished in the bathroom, Nurse Shaner entered the room. Before either of them could say anything, Elsie's stomach grumbled so loudly it echoed.

The nurse couldn't hide her amusement. "Other than hungry, how are you feeling?"

"Physically, my nose and eyes are tender. Emotionally, I'm a wreck," Elsie stated candidly.

Not knowing how to respond, Nurse Shaner changed topics. "Your assistant stopped by with dinner. Nurse Pfeisin placed it in our refrigerator. I'll heat it then bring it in to you."

"Thank you," Elsie said appreciatively with the realization she hadn't had any food all day.

The smell emanating from the steaming container enticed her hunger. After eating, Elsie tried to organize her thoughts. Her heart was in tatters at choosing between two men who loved her. What was she going to do?

When morning dawned, she hadn't come to any conclusion other than she still couldn't make a choice. To her shock, Trish and Sara arrived together. The tense expression on their faces worried Elsie that they had been arguing. She wondered if Nurse Billy told them about her memories returning. He also appeared red faced and fumbling as he took vitals. After the women removed their coats to settle into a chair on either side of the bed, Billy stood by her feet.

Sara cleared her throat to speak. "Elsie, we have some extremely bad news to tell you."

Trish allowed for a slight pause. "Shortly after takeoff, Sean's plane crashed into the ocean. There are no survivors."

Elsie looked from one to the other in hopes that she'd heard them wrong. They each clasped one of her hands. Suddenly, Billy was by her head, peering intently at her. His mouth moved. All sounds came to her as if she were underwater. The eddy of emotions pulled her under completely.

When she came to a few minutes later, Dr. Vilanger had joined them. "Elsie, can you understand me?"

"Yes," she replied as the bad news replayed in her head.

"Do you understand what Trish and Sara told you?" he asked to gauge her clarity.

Placing her hands on her face, she said tearfully, "Sean's plane went down and . . . he's . . . dead."

"I know this is hard, dear. But tell me how your head feels," he coaxed compassionately.

"Foggy, like this can't be happening." Her answer was filled with angst.

"Any pain? Sharp, dull, pressure?" His questions persisted as he tested her reflexes.

She shook her head. "Nothing anywhere."

"That's good. The recent MRI shows substantial healing. But I'm worried about this stress," the doctor explained to everyone in the room while the nurse administered medication. "We're going to raise your dose of valium to keep you as mellow as possible. And don't even ask about being released for another week."

There was no reason to argue—either that or the medication was already doing its job.

"Ladies, please keep things as light as possible." The doctor gave final orders prior to leaving.

Elsie asked Trish, "Have you spoken to Kaitlyn or Eilish?"

"Eilish called to tell you. She was very upset. Then when I told her you were in the hospital, she handed the phone to her mother." Trish talked. "Kaitlyn understood that you wouldn't be able to attend services and hoped this wouldn't cause a setback in your condition."

"Please find a very nice sympathy card." Elsie gave directions to her assistant. "If we don't have the address, call Rich."

"We have the address," Trish replied calmly, looking across to Sara.

Sara chimed in. "I see your oatmeal is cold. Do you want something from the cafeteria?"

Elsie played with the brown gummy substance with a spoon. "I guess."

Trish quickly volunteered. "I'll go. Be back in a little while."

As soon as they were alone, Sara broached a different topic. "The doctor told us yesterday that your memories have returned."

"Yes." The monosyllabic response sounded flat.

"Your relationship with Rusty?" Sara gently pushed.

Elsie's eyes welled without overflowing. "Yes. How could I do that to him?"

"You couldn't help not remembering." A sympathetic Sara hugged her.

When Trish returned with food, she joined the other two women on the bed. Without saying a word, Trish spooned warm rice pudding to Elsie's mouth. Except for a short period of time when Trish ran for lunch and a card, the two women remained with Elsie through the end of the day. The trio composed a sympathy letter for Sean's family to put inside the card. First thing in the morning, Trish would send it priority mail.

For the next nine days, Sara and Trish rotated daily visits. On the tenth day, Dr. Vilanger released Elsie from the hospital. Stepping across the threshold of her home gave Elsie a sense of relief and fear. She ran her hand across her dormant laptop. The urge to write didn't spark in the slightest. Sara and Tom arrived a few minutes later with a pot of ham and bean soup. After eating lunch together, Tom went outside to run the dogs. The women followed Elsie to the bathroom, where she took a shower.

As they helped her dry off and dress in fresh pajamas, she remarked, "Thank you. It's great to not smell of hospital."

"Sara will get you settled on the sofa. I'll put your clothes in the washer," Trish stated on the way from the room.

Sara grabbed a bed pillow when Elsie began her slow trek to the living room. Elsie situated herself on the sofa that had been prepared for her.

Tom entered via the laundry room. "Are you ready for the dogs yet?"

Sara kissed her husband. "Yes. And don't forget the nightshirt in Tycho's kennel. It can go directly into the trash."

"Gladly," he replied, opening the kitchen door to allow the dog duo into the house.

Sophie and Tycho initially focused on Sara.

She led them into the living room. "Look who's here!"

When they saw Elsie, they banged into each other trying to reach her. They clamored around her in excitement. She hugged them tightly. It only took a few minutes for Sophie to be satisfied with her owner's return. However, Tycho climbed onto the sofa with Elsie to rest his upper body across her lap.

It didn't take long for Tom to pop his head through the kitchen door. "Mission accomplished. Do you need me for anything else?"

"I always need you." His wife smiled sweetly. "But you can go home."

"If there's any heavy lifting, you call." It was his way of reminding them to relax.

Trish and Sara were cleaning up from lunch. Elsie noticed her two friends didn't seem to be breathing a sigh of relief that they were through the worst. Maybe because she couldn't be alone; they weren't ready. She didn't want them running themselves ragged. The next thought brought tears to her eyes. Sean should be here to give them a break. She buried her face in Tycho's fur.

When Sara brought a cranberry juice for her, she asked, "What?"

"Sean" was the only word she had to say.

Hearing his name, Trish joined them. "It will get better."

"How can it?" Elsie cried aloud. "It's my fault!"

"How in heaven's name is it your fault?" Sara countered. "You didn't crash the plane."

"He was on that plane because of me. Otherwise, he'd have stayed in Scotland till his next project." Her words sounded rational, but her tone was full of misplaced guilt.

"Elsie, he loved you and wouldn't be blaming you for any of this." Trish tried a different tactic.

"I prayed for God to help me choose between Sean and Rusty." Between gulps for air, Elsie cried in anguish. "If I hadn't asked, he'd still be alive. I should've never let him in!"

The two women stared helplessly. Her crying refused to abate. Tycho whined in unison with her turmoil. Soon Sophie came to investigate the commotion. After an extended time, Elsie gasped painfully. Body-jerking hiccups replaced sobs. The dogs cocked their heads in confusion about this strange development. Trish rushed into the kitchen to fetch a pill from one of the medication bottles.

"Take this," Trish ordered, handing a valium to Elsie.

Since she wasn't due to take another dose till dinner, Elsie gave Trish a questioning look.

Trish clarified. "Josh explained how much we could increase your dose when necessary."

In a motherly tone, Sara agreed. "This is necessary."

Swallowing the pill took several attempts. It didn't take long to do its job. Aside from easing her diaphragm spasms, it relaxed all of her muscles.

Elsie felt limp. It also dulled her over-fraught feelings. As she sank into the corner of the sofa, Tycho resumed his previous position. His blocky head resting on her chest was a welcome replacement to the emotional heaviness.

Chapter Thirty-Two

Elsie hadn't been home a week when more bad news hit. Red Roget had passed away. From living his middle-aged years in a bottle of one kind or another, his liver suffered irreparable damage. She'd hoped to visit him when her restrictions were removed. Now that wasn't possible. As the weeks passed, this only added to her depression. There were times she coped with her shattered emotions in regard to Sean's death. At other times, she wallowed aimlessly in guilt. Trish became frustrated with not getting Elsie to eat on a regular schedule. Elsie was emaciated. Since she'd been released, she had follow-up appointments scheduled on a two-week cycle.

At her six-week appointment, Dr. Vilanger stated clearly, "The lack of nutrients is retarding the healing process. If you don't show at least a five-pound gain on your next visit in four weeks, you will be hospitalized. And before you think of any arguments, I will admit you to the psychiatric ward for forty-eight-hour evaluation."

One morning the following week, while Trish hung laundry outside to dry, Elsie puttered about her bedroom. She seemed to be searching for something; she just didn't know what. As she wandered around the room, she twisted the ruby ring on her left hand. It didn't belong there anymore. Taking it off, she placed it in her jewelry box with the matching necklace. An odd sense of finality stabbed at her heart with the closing of the lid. In an attempt to face the day with strength, she decided to make an effort with her appearance. After showering, she stepped into the closet to choose something cheery to wear. A dress with a bright flowery print fit the bill. Even though it was August, the summer heat didn't warm her sufficiently. She needed a coordinating sweater. None was warm enough without being itchy. Hardly fashionable, but her zip-up hooded sweatshirt was soft and warm. She realized she'd forgotten slippers. She reentered the closet. For whatever reason, her eyes caught a glimpse of the unmarked box from months ago. Curiosity had her reaching for it.

Trish's voice came back the hall. "Are you awake yet, sleepyhead?"

Elsie answered, "Yes, I'll be right out."

The unopened box was dropped onto the chair prior to her heading for the kitchen.

"Well look at you!" Trish exclaimed. "The sweatshirt is a little tacky."

Elsie defended, "I'm cold, and my sweaters are itchy."

A platter with pancakes and bacon was placed on the table.

"After you eat, we're going to take a walk around the yard," Trish stated tersely while wiping the counter.

Her tone made Elsie ask, "Are you angry with me?"

Her movements paused. "When are you going to start writing?"

"My head is foggy from the medications," Elsie replied. "What difference does it make, anyway? Even with the recent hospital bills, there are more than enough funds to cover everything for at least the next two decades."

"It is ridiculous that I only work three days a week." Trish's voice indicated her frustration. "They are housekeeping duties you could hire someone else to do at a much lower rate. Plus, I really liked being your assistant."

Sitting back in her chair, Elsie thought before answering. "It's not permanent. There are stories spinning in my head. It's just going to take me a while to get into the swing of things."

In a softer tone, Trish added, "As long as I've known you, you've been determined and focused on whatever you do. You've been through a lot, but seeing you lazing around aimlessly worries me."

"Let me make this crystal clear. We've *all* been through a lot—not only me." Realizing the harsh edge to her voice, she eased it. "Consider this a vacation of sorts. A regrouping of spirits, so to speak."

This seemed to satisfy her friend. "Do you want more coffee?"

"Not right now, thanks." The conversation had killed her appetite. "How about we take that walk?"

The other woman placed the uneaten portion into the refrigerator. "Don't forget your hat."

Since Elsie refused to use her cane, Trish didn't bother mentioning it.

Both dogs walked patiently along with the women. Sophie took point to deal with any critter that might cross their path. A few times Elsie stumbled. Tycho quickly positioned himself to prevent her from falling. Walking along the far end of the yard, Elsie swore she heard mooing. But the nearby farms were agricultural, not dairy or beef. The closest dairy farm was the Grimmel farm sixteen miles away. She scanned the countryside, and there weren't any in sight to confirm cattle as the origin of the sound.

When they reached the patio, Trish stated, "I'll get our coffees. You sit on the bench. Maybe the fresh air will clear away those cobwebs."

Elsie obeyed. Tycho stretched across the cement patio at her feet. Sophie trotted behind Trish into the house.

Only Trish reemerged. "Sophie isn't leaving her spot in front of the fan."

Accepting her cup, Elsie remarked, "Can't really blame her with it already ninety and it's not even noon."

"And he'd sooner melt than be away from you." Trish pointed to the big red dog being rubbed by Elsie's right foot. "You know, the whole time I hung wash, he leaned on the door. I had to use the other door to come inside without him."

"You should've seen him yesterday when FedEx delivered royalty statements. Since Jim's on vacation, it was a driver we didn't know. The poor guy was petrified." She sipped at her coffee.

"Royalty statements? Where did you put them so I can enter them into the ledger?" Trish asked expectantly.

Elsie replied quizzically. "Weren't they on the kitchen table?"

"Uh no, or I wouldn't be asking," Trish stated sarcastically.

Both women and the dog stood. The walk around the yard had been good physical therapy. However, now it caused Elsie to be slowed sufficiently. Tycho used an equally halting gait to stay in step with her. Already having checked the kitchen, Trish searched the living room for the envelope. Elsie removed the lid from the trash container to see if she'd inadvertently thrown it away.

Finding the FedEx envelope, she held it up. "Here's the outer envelope, but it's empty."

"What did you do after it arrived?" Trish questioned.

"I opened it to see how much it was, then . . ." Her response stopped midsentence.

"Else?" Concern filled her friend's face.

"I-I don't know." She clutched the counter at the comprehension of lost time.

Trish rushed to fetch her cell phone. "Is Dr. Vilanger available? This is Trish Farland. I'm calling in regard to his patient Elsie Endy."

Regaining her composure, Elsie moved to the sofa.

"All right. As soon as possible please. Thank you." Trish placed the phone in her shirt pocket. "He's with another patient."

Elsie's voice sounded deflated. "I don't understand. I just had an MRI. If there was a problem, it should've shown."

"This could be a normal side effect of the medications. Don't freak out." The words were meant to calm, but Trish's tone quivered with uncertainty.

While they waited for the doctor to call, Trish continued searching the house for the royalty statements. Elsie sat on the sofa, absently rubbing the red dog's head resting in her lap.

After some time, Trish exclaimed from the bedroom. "Found them!"

When she emerged from the hallway carrying the bedding and papers, Elsie asked, "Where were they?"

"I decided to strip your bed since there's a nice breeze for drying everything. I heard paper crinkle as I rolled it all together," Trish responded on her way to the laundry room. "Evidently, you placed it on the bed then forgot about it."

Elsie pushed the dog off her lap to follow.

"Dr. Vilanger called. He believes the memory lapse is due to the combination of medications." Trish continued by adding Tide to the sheets in the filling washing machine. "He wants to stop some of them. I'll redo your pill container. Why don't you check the stuff on the line?"

Most of the items were dry. Instead of hollering for Trish, Elsie carried the basket inside. By the time she entered the house, Trish was working on the computer.

Looking up from the laptop, Trish remarked, "Your pills are reset. And I'm almost done with these entries. Are you ready for reviewing e-mails?"

"Might as well start somewhere." Elsie agreed while reheating her breakfast.

It was time to oblige Trish's earlier request to do real work. Maybe between this and the change in medications, the fog would lift.

At four o'clock, Trish closed her laptop with a happy snap. "We should be able to get through all of them tomorrow."

"But we agreed to a Monday, Wednesday, Friday schedule," Elsie said in befuddlement.

"With the change in meds, Vilanger wants someone to spend the next few days with you." Trish expounded further on the phone conversation with the specialist.

Elsie followed with the obvious question: "Does that include overnights?"

"Only if you feel weird, which means you have to tell us." The meaning of her words was emphasized pointedly.

"Maybe that would be a good idea, anyway," Elsie remarked as they walked to the truck. "Since Josh didn't renew the prescription for sleeping pills, sleep isn't as solid or restful."

"That's why you've been taking till eleven to shower and dress." The realization eased a few lines on Trish's forehead. "I won't show until ten tomorrow. And I can stay overnight, but Friday night I'm babysitting. I'll talk to Sara."

Elsie nodded as her friend climbed into the vehicle. They waved, and then the truck rolled down the driveway. Elsie returned to the house. Tycho stood inside the door, waiting impatiently.

She knelt to his level to grab the fur on his neck and rough it playfully. "You need to chill. You are going to give yourself a coronary."

He licked her face with loyalty. Lying on her side, Sophie lifted her head to identify why the chatter. She flicked her ears in disinterest prior to resting her head on the floor again. This evoked an unexpected yawn from her owner.

"A nap might be the right idea," Elsie said aloud as she tucked herself into the corner of the couch.

Chapter Thirty-Three

When Elsie stirred later, the room was dark. She was hungry. As she rose to check the contents of the refrigerator, the dogs stretched on their way to the door. After letting the dogs outside, she put leftovers in the microwave to heat. Suddenly, there was a commotion of barking and snarling outside. Malamutes rarely bark; howling and whirring were their standard forms of communication. Peering into the darkness from the window, she could see nothing. The dogs were too far away. She opened the door to whistle for them. The pack next door was equally boisterous. This was accompanied by an unfamiliar kind of growl and . . . and roar? Her cell rang.

"Where are your dogs?" Tom demanded.

Something was obviously wrong; she answered quickly. "By the back fence."

"Damn! Stay inside, but watch for them if they run for the door." He didn't wait for her to respond before disconnecting.

She continued to stare through the window, trying to spy either of her beasts. Several gunshots fired. A minute later, Sophie appeared from the darkness. Elsie opened the door for her. From the far end of the yard, Tycho still barked and growled. His sounds were echoed by Deedles next door. The rest of the pack quieted. Elsie whistled for her red dog.

It took a second whistling with a "Tycho! Get your furry butt inside!" for him to jog to the house.

His taut posture was clearly indicative he was still on guard. No sooner had the red dog stepped inside than the phone rang again.

This time it was Sara. "Are they both inside and okay?"

"Yes. What's going on?" Elsie asked shakily from the adrenaline rush.

Tom's voice could be heard in the background. It sounded like he was on his phone too.

When his voice paused, Sara answered Elsie. "Tom swears it was a mountain lion. He's phoning the local game warden for them to investigate."

"Lions and tigers and bears. Oh my!" Elsie quoted to keep her fear from running amuck.

"I can handle our annual black bear. But mountain lions don't make me happy. And if we start seeing tigers, we're moving!" Sara stated emphatically. "Keep the dogs inside for a while. Tom and the guy who owns the farm are going to check the fencing for damage. I'll call back with the all clear."

"Okay. Thanks," Elsie replied prior to hanging up.

It was strange that Sara referred to Slater as "the guy who owns the farm." The dogs pacing redirected her thoughts. It was almost 10:00 p.m. They needed to be fed. After setting their dishes in their assigned spots, she remembered her own food. It felt sufficiently warm when she removed it from the microwave. With a couple of bites of food in her stomach, she took her pills. As usual, only another forkful and her stomach wanted no more. The remnants on the plate were split between the dogs. As she placed the dish in the dishwasher, Sara phoned.

"Everything looks secure. But don't put the dogs outside and forget about them," she suggested.

Elsie countered with amusement. "That goes for both of us."

"Tell me about it! Then again, I'm not really sure I'll sleep much tonight. The sooner they catch it and relocate it, the better." Sara's tone denoted this bothered her far more than the yearly black bear.

Elsie had similar sentiments. "Me too! Give me a call in the morning when the warden arrives."

"Yes. We don't want Tycho giving his group any lip, or he might become their test target for the tranquilizer guns," Sara teased at his recent overprotectiveness. "Will you be all right alone tomorrow?"

"I won't be. Trish will be here. We have a ton of e-mails to review." Elsie shared the latest. "Plus, Josh changed the dosage of my meds. She'll be staying overnight."

"Goodness. Did something show on your tests from last week?" the older woman asked with concern.

"No. I misplaced yesterday's mail," she stated calmly.

After a moment of silence, Sara asked, "Don't you think he's overreacting? I misplace things all the time."

"I was just glad it didn't require a trip to the hospital," Elsie agreed glibly. "Maybe this change will help me eat and gain some weight."

"That would be good. Those backward white jackets with the extra long sleeves aren't very fashionable," Sara teased.

"Tell Tom thank you and we'll talk in the morning." The last thing Elsie wanted was another hospital stay.

"Good night," Sara said to end the call.

Elsie wondered what had brought a mountain lion this close to civilization. Town was less than a mile away. The occasional black bear encounters usually involved two-year-old males in search of a territory. The bears usually steered away from the yards because of the dogs. The coyotes were also kept at bay because of their larger relatives. A mountain lion wouldn't be particularly threatened. It might even consider them individually as prey without the safety of the pack.

She turned on the television to watch the weather forecast. Temperature and humidity would hover at one hundred. Hopefully, that would be enough to keep the dogs from wanting to be outside for any extended period until the cougar could be caught. As she absently flipping channels, *Mountains' Majesty* was playing. It was the perfect night to watch with a nice glass of wine. Two and a half hours later, she let the dogs outside for a quick break. Then the trio went to the bedroom. Snuggling under the covers, she thought about Sean and Rusty. She woke with a start around 2:00 a.m. She glanced around the room; it took a few minutes to distinguish the real world. She turned on the nightstand lamp. Both dogs watched her movements. Falling back to sleep wouldn't happen anytime soon. Initially, nothing on the television looked interesting. In ten minutes, the movie would be replaying. Selecting the appropriate channel, she went to the kitchen for a glass and the bottle of wine. Tycho followed her. Elsie listened carefully to the night sounds prior to allowing him outside. He didn't dawdle. As soon as he'd marked the kennels, he trotted to the door. Returning to the bedroom, he chose to stretch on the tile floor in the bathroom. During the first commercial break, she noticed something she'd forgotten. The errant box sat on the chair next to the dresser. She got up to place it on the bed. It contained pictures and cards. The pictures—Red and Rusty in Montana, her and Rich holding Oscars, her and Rusty with their close friends in Hawaii—were of specific things she hadn't recalled until now. The cards were from Rusty. His written words were beautiful. They were dated across the year prior to her accident. She fell asleep amidst these. The tender memories solidified in her mind.

Sara's voice could be heard. "Else, wake up."

"Mm, what's wrong?" she asked groggily.

"That's what I was going to ask you," Sara stated.

"Why?" Elsie sat.

"It's after ten and you are still in bed," the older woman said.

"I didn't sleep well," Elsie replied, heading for the toilet to empty her bladder. "Where are the dogs?"

"In the yard. The game warden clearly identified we have a mountain lion roaming the area. He has a call in for assistance," Sara explained as Trish entered the room.

"A mountain lion?" the other woman exclaimed.

Elsie stated from the bathroom doorway: "Sara will explain while you make coffee and I shower."

The other two women headed out the hallway. Elsie took a quick shower. Jeans and T-shirt would do. While she was trying to select a sweater, the women brought her coffee.

Before Sara handed it to her, Trish gave her a Macy's bag. "I stopped by the mall on my way home. It's washed so you could wear it today."

Opening the bag revealed a lavender chenille sweater.

"It's lovely. Thank you." She hugged Trish.

Trish returned the embrace but remarked, "Hey, not too close with that or I'll get itchy. I used rubber gloves when I had to touch it last night."

Elsie eagerly slipped her arms into the soft knitted yarn.

"This will help warm you too," Sara said, offering the cup of coffee.

Taking a sip, Elsie welcomed the hot liquid.

When Trish moved to make the bed, she questioned, "What's this?"

As the two other women picked up the pictures, the realization dawned on them. They glanced at each other, then contritely at Elsie.

Sara found her voice first. "When your headaches started last year, we packed away anything that would cause you to dwell on trying to remember."

"The doctors suggested it," Trish added. "We'd forgotten about it, or we'd have given it to you when you started remembering."

Without warning, emotion choked Elsie.

She began to cry. "With as strong as our love was, why couldn't I remember him?"

Sara countered with, "You told us all of the places you went with Sean were places you had been with Rusty. Maybe that was your subconscious' way of trying to trigger your memories. But your strong attraction to Sean created an unintentional roadblock."

Trish continued with her assessment. "Even with as happy as you were with Sean, you felt something was missing. Maybe that something was Rusty."

Trish taking Rusty's side was so astonishing; Elsie's tears stopped. The trio continued placing the items in the box. The lid was stuck to the bottom of the box rather than covering it.

Sara set the box in the center of the dresser. "We'll get you a photo album for these."

"I think I'd like to do a collage. Maybe we can go to Michael's to select a frame and matting?" Elsie requested.

This was the first time she'd mentioned leaving the house. The only time she'd gone anywhere since she'd been released from the hospital was the hospital. She hadn't even ventured across the path to Tom and Sara's home.

"Why don't we go now? The e-mails can wait another day, can't they?" Sara suggested.

Trish readily agreed. "That sounds like a plan."

Elsie wasn't sure. "What about the dogs?"

"I'll put them in their kennels," Sara offered on her way out to handle it.

"I don't even know where my purse is or what's in it." Anxiety about going to the mall with lots of people caused Elsie to balk.

Trish wouldn't allow her to renege. "It's hanging right here on the chair. It has your wallet, keys, tissues, and mints exactly how you left it."

"What about my head?" She stalled.

Trish deftly fended this argument. "Your hair is growing in nicely."

"It's not long enough to hide the scars." It was another avoidance maneuver.

"I'll grab your hat off the rack. Now get your shoes," Trish ordered.

"I haven't taken my pills," Elsie countered.

Trish paused in the kitchen to dump today's doses into a portable pill container and get a cold bottle of water.

Putting them in her bag, she stated evenly, "You can take these on the drive."

Elsie couldn't think of anything else to not go. She had no one to blame except herself. They loaded into the truck. There was a moment of difficulty. But she hoisted her scrawny frame into the passenger seat. Sara and Trish discussed the heat while Elsie swallowed her pills. It was nice to no longer have to take a valium. They always made her feel dopey.

It didn't take long for Elsie to find what she wanted at the craft store. The other two decided they wanted something from Häagen Daz, which was inside the mall at the far end. Along the way, they stopped at numerous stores without purchasing anything, not that they didn't try to convince Elsie to buy a couple of things. If it wasn't soft and warm, she wasn't interested. Several times she stated her desire to go home. The girls thought they were doing her a favor until they saw a movie poster for *Sins of the Fathers*. The main actors were displayed in a family-tree pattern. The picture of Sean, particularly piercing as the pivotal patriarch, practically pounced off the poster. Elsie stopped in her tracks. Grief and guilt gripped her.

In a taut voice, she ground out, "Can we go now?"

Trish made a beeline for the nearest exit to get the truck. Sara slowly walked Elsie to the same doors for Trish to pick them up. In the car, both women tried consoling her. She took a long drink of water then continued in silence. When they arrived at the house, she went directly to her room. Shutting the door firmly was an indication that she did not want to be disturbed. Because she lacked the high levels of valium in her system, the emotional loss forced its release. Sobs racked her frame. Eventually, she took solace in sleep.

Elsie emerged early evening with bloodshot and puffy eyes.

Trish asked cautiously, "How are you feeling?"

"Hungry." Her one-word answer revealed nothing of her emotional status.

"What do you want me to make?" Trish offered solicitously.

Opening the door to the pantry closet, she retrieved a bottle of wine. "Order Chinese."

"What are you doing with that bottle?" Trish questioned as she dialed.

With bold defiance, Elsie stated haughtily, "I'm going to drink it, if you care to join me."

Trish recognized the don't-fuck-with-me expression. In a tactic to avoid Elsie being completely reckless, Trish acquiesced by placing their usual order. Since it would take at least thirty minutes till Trish returned with the food, Elsie placed the wine in the freezer. It would be sufficiently chilled for dinner. She puttered around the house doing ineffectual tasks—check washer, fetch bowls from cabinet, get sweater from closet, peer out front window, check dryer, channel surf—while waiting impatiently. Sophie merely watched her movements, whereas Tycho synchronized with them. When Trish returned, Elsie hastened to the freezer. She'd stumbled across the premiere of a movie Rusty had filmed last year. It was starting on Showtime. Within a few minutes, they were seated in front of the television.

Seeing the main actors' names, Trish asked with concern, "Are you sure you want to watch this?"

"To my masochistic emotional torture," Elsie replied, flippantly holding up her glass.

"You're definitely back to your old self," Trish remarked sardonically.

Ignoring the jab, Elsie forcefully stabbed her chopsticks into the lo mein.

The fiendish character Rusty portrayed was a macabre reflection of his own inner turmoil at that time. With each close-up, it became apparent the heartbreak in his eyes wasn't acted. Till the end of the movie, she yearned for him. Sleep continued the torture with a mishmash of memories. As for the cougar, it didn't make an appearance. Maybe it was merely passing through rather than taking up residency. After Trish left midafternoon, Elsie wrote to purge her swirling emotions. At midnight, she finally set the laptop aside to sleep.

Chapter Thirty-Four

Just prior to dawn, the dogs asked to go outside. Only a few minutes in the yard, they stopped simultaneously. Their ears rotated like radar antennae. This clearly indicated something was afoot. Elsie immediately whistled them into the house. They heeded her beckon without hesitation. Closing the door, she saw her mug from two days ago still sitting on the arm of the Adirondack chair. Without thinking, she stepped outside to walk across the patio to fetch it. As she picked it up, the unmistakable growl of the mountain lion sounded within extremely close proximity. Turning to verify the sound, she spied it on the right stepping over the peak of the roof. Watching it, she cautiously made her way toward the house. It hopped off the roof onto the woodpile. A few feet from the door, Elsie's bum leg tripped her. Tycho went berserk inside the house. He burst through the screen door to get between Elsie and the big cat. Sophie followed. Elsie crawled toward the house. The dogs antagonized the cougar. Sophie initially kept her distance. Tycho got aggressive. Yelling could be heard outside the fence at the other side of the yard. When the big cat took a swipe at Sophie, Tycho attacked. He bit mercilessly into the cat's neck. In desperation, it wrapped its back legs around him. Its sharp nails ripped open the red dog's side, exposing his internal organs; but he refused to relinquish his hold. Elsie made a grab for Sophie's collar, only to miss it. Sophie jumped into the fray. The big cat swatted at her. It connected with the bitch's dewlap, eviscerating it. Within seconds, the gray girl bled out. Gunshots fired. The cougar jerked then dropped to pull Tycho down with it. Three men rushed to the stationary piles of fur. After verifying the cougar was dead, one of the men stepped toward Elsie with purpose.

"Sophie's gone. And Tycho won't survive," Rusty said as he lifted her off the ground.

He quickly deposited her between the dogs. Tycho's soft brown eyes met hers. His breathing labored.

"I'm safe." She spoke softly to her big red dog. "Close your eyes. Go with Sophie. Tribble is waiting for both of you."

Looking at the three men, she pleaded, "Please, I don't want him in pain."

The warden offered, "I have lethal injections in the truck parked at the other house."

Tom suggested, "Can we tranquilize him to give you time to go get one?"

"I guess, but he won't regain consciousness." As the warden responded, he realized that was the point.

Using the tranquilizer pistol instead of the rifle, he fired a dart into Tycho's neck. Elsie kissed the dog's furry face as he fell asleep for the last time. She continued to hold his blocky head in her lap while the game warden fetched the needed item. Sara entered the yard as he exited. Rushing to Tom's side, she burst into tears at the carnage. Rusty remained next to Elsie, but he didn't touch her. Only a few minutes passed till the officer returned. There was no need to search for a vein. The aortic artery had been exposed. He made short work of administering the lethal dose. With Tycho's final breath, Elsie reached for Rusty's arm. He obliged by wrapping it around her upper chest. They didn't need a stethoscope to verify the dog was dead. His blood merely oozed out instead of a pumping stream. Elsie reached to pet Sophie's motionless form for her farewell.

Tom cleared his throat of emotion to speak. "Rusty, take Elsie inside. Check her for injuries. We'll handle this."

When Elsie struggled to stand, Rusty again picked her up to carry her into the house this time. At the door, he yanked the broken pieces away with a vengeance. She could feel his anger by the tension in his muscles. Tears glistened on his cheeks and in his beard. He didn't slow his stride until they reached the bathroom. He set her on the bench in the shower. Her robe and pajamas were saturated with blood. A change of clothes wouldn't be enough.

Rusty stopped assisting after removing her robe. "Stay."

He stepped into the bedroom to bellow along the hallway. "Sara!"

She hurried at his beckon. "Yes?"

"Elsie is covered in blood. I think her knee and hand are skinned," he stated as they entered the bathroom.

"I see what you mean," Sara agreed.

"I'm going to help with . . . outside," he stated with choked tears then left the two women alone.

"When it rains, it pours." Sara spoke softly. "Wait here a minute."

She returned with a large garbage bag. As each piece of stained clothing came off, it went directly into the green plastic bag. With the last piece removed, Elsie turned on the water.

"You okay while I get rid of this?" Sara asked with worry.

"Yes, go ahead," Elsie replied flatly.

The other woman hoisted the bag into her arms to dispose of it. Elsie stood watching the warm water wash away her beloved malamutes. The sweet-smelling shower gel cleansed her skin. Finished in the bathroom, she donned a camisole and flannel pajama pants. Before she had a chance to consider leaving the bedroom, Sara arrived.

"Take this," Sara ordered, dropping a valium into Elsie's hand.

As Elsie accepted the glass of juice, she remarked, "Josh stopped these."

"In this instance, you should take them," the older woman stated.

Elsie swallowed the pill then voluntarily climbed into bed.

Her friend tucked the blanket around her body. "You rest."

As the door closed behind Sara, Elsie sank further under the covers. An empty stomach enabled the medication to work quickly. In her dreams, the dogs snuggled against her for comfort.

It was midafternoon till the medication had run its course. When she reached for her robe, she remembered the incident at dawn. And Sean's didn't hang from the other prong. For whatever reason, he had packed it for the trip to Scotland. Along with Sean, it was lost at the bottom of the

Atlantic Ocean. Tears formed in her eyes. Where was Sara? Elsie limped out the hallway—a trip that took longer than expected due to added issues with her good leg injured from the earlier fall. She heard voices from the yard. Grabbing the lap blanket from the sofa, she wrapped it around her shoulders to step outside. Sara, Tom, and Rusty stood talking. At Elsie's appearance, they curtailed the conversation.

Tom spoke first. "We took their bodies for cremation. The ashes should be ready in a week."

"Thank you," Elsie responded on autopilot.

"I should be going," Rusty said, excusing himself through the side gate.

He climbed into her old jeep then drove toward the open farmland.

"Why is he here?" she asked bluntly.

"He was helping track the mountain lion," Tom stated simply.

"That's not what!" Her temper tantrum ceased at spying the bloodstains on the end of the patio.

The tears ran unchecked.

As she turned to go into the house, she said, "You missed a few spots."

Hearing the heart-wrenching sadness in Elsie's voice, Sara followed. In the kitchen, Elsie banged cupboards searching for the valium. Sara reached by her to open the appropriate cabinet. After taking one, Elsie went to her bedroom. Throwing herself across the bed, she cried some more. Sara gently rubbed her back till the medication took Elsie to a tolerable place.

CHAPTER THIRTY-FIVE

SUNDAY AT 4:00 a.m., Elsie puttered around the house aimlessly while waiting for the coffee to brew. Getting out of bed had been difficult without her constant companions. There was an unexpected knock on the front door. Peering through the window, she saw Rusty.

She opened the door with an uncertain "Good morning."

"G'day, mate," he replied, equally hesitant.

The coffeemaker beeped.

It would be rude not to offer. "Would you like to come in for a cup of coffee?"

"Thanks, I could use one." His muscular form seemed to fill the entire room as he moved inside.

Elsie limped slowly to the kitchen.

In a few strides, he caught her to lift her with one arm for the last few feet. He set her gently down at the table. The brown bag under his other arm dropped on the table in front of her.

"I'll get the coffees." He turned toward the pot. "You look chilly. Open the bag."

It contained her daisy chenille robe. Pulling it from the bag, she dropped the blanket to slip her arms into the soft sleeves. It smelled of a freshly showered Rusty—as if his being there hadn't lumped enough on her emotional turmoil. She had to sit.

Before she could say anything, he said, "After what happened to you yesterday, I thought you might need this."

Regaining some of her senses, she asked, "Why are you here?"

He placed her cup on the table. "I was just going to drop the bag and go. But when I saw the lights on, I wanted to make sure you were all right."

"How is it you were there? I mean, here yesterday?" Elsie's words scrambled like her mind.

"I'd been sitting watch on the next hill when I heard the pack fussing. By the time I reached the fence, Sara called to tell me you weren't answering your phone. The rest you know." At the end, he emptied his cup in one swallow.

"That's not what I mean!" She stood in aggravation only to sit from the head rush.

"I know, but I need to go," he said, dropping a peck on her cheek before he strode through the living room and out the door.

Till she reached the front door to fling it open yelling "Rusty," he was nowhere to be seen.

Slamming the door, she muttered expletives.

She couldn't decide which irked her more: his explicitly not answering her question or kissing her platonically. Anytime she'd seen him over the last year, he'd practically manhandled her to make his intentions clear. Now that she wasn't seeing anyone and remembered him, he wasn't interested. Was it her limp? Everything else was fully functional, or at least as much as she could test without a willing participant. She realized she'd been staring at the front door while these thoughts rumbled through her head. This only added to her anger.

With an aggravated "humph," she stomped back the hall.

After showering and dressing, her ire hadn't lost its fire. She stormed across the path. The dogs running the yard greeted her exuberantly. It took the edge off her cantankerousness. Sara emerged from the house carrying a stack of metal dishes. It was feeding time. At her call, the dogs hastened to the kennels. Elsie wiped away her tears as Sara finished delivering the last pan.

As Sara turned to head into the house, she saw Elsie. "Aaiiee!"

Tom suddenly rushed outside wearing only his fruit of the loom briefs. Embarrassment contoured his face at being seen by anyone other than his wife.

With a polite "Excuse me," he ducked into the house.

The two women made eye contact then simultaneously exploded with laughter. For a few moments, Elsie forgot her grief and exasperation.

When the mirth ended, Sara asked, "Why are you looking all sparkly clean this early in the morning?"

"I have a bone to pick with you!" Elsie's tone didn't sound as harsh as it would've been a few minutes ago.

Sara didn't understand. "What?"

One word from Elsie clarified it. "Rusty."

"Oh." Guilt replaced the confusion. "Come inside."

As Sara opened the door into the house, she hollered, "I'm not alone!"

Tom stood at the griddle making pancakes. He wore a T-shirt and sweat pants. A small tinge of pink highlighted his cheeks at their entrance.

Elsie waited for Sara to pour coffee before forcing the issue. "Talk."

"I really think you should ask Rusty," Sara stated hesitantly.

"I tried to this morning when he stopped in. He avoided answering me!" Elsie halted her rant abruptly.

Even Tom glanced up at the indicator there was more to it than she'd verbalized.

Sara prompted. "And?"

"And he treated me like no one special." With the humbling admission, Elsie slumped onto the sofa.

Tom couldn't help asking the obvious question. "What was he doing at your place so early?"

Elsie played with the cuffs of her sweatshirt. "He was dropping off my daisy robe. I invited him in for coffee. But . . ."

"But?" Sara sat to urge her to continue.

When Elsie didn't answer right away, Tom said, "I'm not listening. I'm just the cook."

In a quieter voice just for Sara to hear, she replied, "He only kissed my cheek. No hug, no taking liberties—it was too platonic."

"And this bothers you?" Sara fought to keep her amusement contained.

"Yes!" Elsie pouted. "Why doesn't he like me anymore?"

"Maybe he's trying to give you a little breathing room with everything that's been going on as of late." Sara tried not to sound morbid. "Recovery, Sean, Red, and now Sophie and Tycho."

The words brought the necessary amount of perspective Elsie lacked. She shrugged and nodded in agreement.

"Breakfast!" the cook announced. "And if you don't eat every bite on your plate, I will never get over you seeing me in my tighty whities."

His teasing remark eased the sadness building at the mention of the most recent loss.

Out of the blue, Elsie exclaimed, "No Double Stuff!"

It took a moment for the couple to connect the dots.

Sara spoke. "We discussed it yesterday afternoon. I called Kay last night to tell her what happened. She offered to arrange getting specimens from Tycho's brother Tabasco."

"Oh my god! I didn't even think about calling Kay." It was Elsie's turn to be contrite. "How'd she take it?"

A chuckle escaped from Tom.

"You were in la-la land. We didn't expect anything from you other than staying in bed all day." Sara shot Tom a dirty look as she explained. "And you know Kay. I had to hold the phone away from my ear while she sobbed. As soon as she stopped crying, she went into make-everyone-happy mode."

"God bless her," Elsie said with a roll of the eyes. "She definitely means well."

The trio dug into their breakfast. They discussed noncontroversial topics till she walked home. The sun shone brightly overhead. For the first time since surgery, the 100-degree temperature permeated her skin to where she broke a sweat. Elsie removed her sweatshirt to soak in the sun. Standing in the yard, she couldn't stop from looking at where the dogs had died. No more splattered bloodstains existed as evidence of those horrible events. The patio gleamed bright white from bleach. Not wanting to be in the heat any longer, she went inside.

From the kitchen, Elsie turned on the television with the remote. While she got a glass of ice water, the Weather Channel reported on severe storms pummeling the Midwest. The same system would hit the East overnight.

She might be spending the night in the basement if the storms didn't lose intensity. Unable to find anything to watch, she put away items in the yard that might blow away. As she approached the back fence, mooing could be heard. Staring toward the farm, she saw cattle roaming the hills. There were horses too. They looked distinctly familiar. She returned to the house for binoculars. Again, she went to the far end of the yard. Focusing on the horses through the binoculars, she saw they were Molly and Hailey. A rider on horseback came into view. It was unmistakably Rusty.

How dare he buy her farm! As Elsie headed for the house, his presence as of late made sense. She considered calling his cell. If he didn't want to answer her questions like this morning, he wouldn't bother talking to her. This needed to be handled face to face. Her driving privileges were still suspended. It was too far to walk. And she knew Sara wouldn't drive her. There had to be a way. Then it came to her. Legally, she couldn't drive on the roads. She could take the truck on the tractor trail since it was private property. No time like the present to discover if she remembered how to drive.

When she put the keys in the ignition, her actions became automatic. The hardest part of the drive was keeping her speed down. If she spun into the field or got stuck, she'd have to call for assistance. With which a lecture would be pending. The path appeared to have been driven on recently—probably the game warden. It had also been rerouted due to the new fencing. It made sense for use between the properties. House front to house front along standard roads would take fifteen minutes. On dry ground, this could easily only be five minutes from yard to yard. The lack of familiarity slowed progress.

Chapter Thirty-Six

ELSIE PARKED BY the farmhouse ready to confront Rusty. A rather large extension had been added to the first floor; a facelift to the exterior had also been done. Nonetheless, she was there on a mission not to view the changes. Getting no answer to her knocking, she went to the barn. This too appeared to have been renovated. He was not there, so she stepped outside to search the hills for him. He soon came toward the barn. Spying his visitor, he rode directly toward her. As he neared, she quickly sidestepped away from the horse's path.

"G'day, mate. What brings you here?" he questioned as he dismounted.

Before she could say anything, the horse swung its hindquarters around, knocking into her. He gave the horse a substantial shove and quickly grabbed for her. The details of the riding accident replayed in her mind. His arms held her firmly while her shaking from the adrenaline surge dissipated.

With his mouth against the scarred side of her head, he asked, "Are you okay?"

"Yeah, you know me and horses." She nodded and shivered. "It didn't help that it instigated a detailed memory of the accident last year."

"I'm sorry. Rowdy is a bit ornery," he stated, shifting to rest his chin on her head.

"That's probably why he was Red's favorite," she replied breathlessly at the feel of his arms tightening around her.

Rowdy pushed his muzzle against Rusty's back.

"Sod off, Elmer's!" After swatting at the beast, his arm returned to its previous position.

"He was trying to irk you, not knock me down," she stated logically.

He rubbed his face stubble with that on her head. His voice cracked with emotion as he said, "I will do whatever I can to prevent you from getting injured."

What could she say? Nothing without getting emotional, so she remained mute.

After a few moments passed, he suggested, "Go into the house while I get him unsaddled."

But it took a major effort for him to relinquish his hold on her. When he finally did release her, he snatched the horse's bridle to drag toward its stall.

She followed a few steps to request with compassion: "Please don't hurt him."

He paused at her pleading tone. She watched him struggle with his anger at the beast. Seeing him gain control over his temper, she finally exited the barn.

At the farmhouse, she discovered the door was unlocked. The interior also underwent a major remodel. Taking a certain amount of liberty, she wandered around to see the changes. It didn't look like anyone lived here. The wall between the living and dining rooms were reduced to two-square columns for one large room. However, it only contained the irons for the fireplace. The hearth restoration included the addition of insulated glass doors for weatherizing and preventing unwanted pests. She hobbled up the staircase to see the master bedroom. Instead, she found two empty rooms. No furniture of any kind adorned them. Even the windows lacked curtains. It wasn't as cool on this floor, almost stuffy. She realized central air conditioning had been added to the house. These rooms must be on a separate control. The bathroom contained modern fixtures in an Old West style. The wood stairs creaked on descent to the main floor. This brought a nostalgic smile to her face. Some things can't be replaced without losing their charm. Running her hand along the banister revealed it had also only been refinished.

Rusty's voice interrupted her wistfulness. "Do you approve?"

"What I've seen is wonderful. I haven't gotten to the kitchen or the addition yet," she replied, her original purpose forgotten.

"Then come with me, mate," he stated, steering her in the direction of the non-addition section of the house.

The wide-open top half of the door exposed the kitchen—a kitchen with first-rate appliances. He pushed open the bottom of the door to enter. The red stone ceramic tiling would hide muddy paw prints. Marble countertops in a coordinating color accentuated the whitewashed cupboards. Crumbs and dried coffee stains littered the counter by the sink. At the far end, an empty nook opened onto a flagstone patio. A table with four chairs would fit nicely there. Another half-door led into a mudroom with washer, dryer, utility sink, raised tub, and second refrigerator. Here Rusty shucked his work boots. At the sink, he removed his shirt to wash away the sweat and dirt. It required every ounce of her self-control to prevent herself from assisting. But she couldn't stop from watching. His movements were unhurried as if he was putting on a show for his private audience. When he finished drying, he tossed the towel onto the washing machine with his shirt.

"Wait." She snatched the towel. "You missed a spot."

As she wiped the water droplets from between his shoulder blades, another set of recollections of the very same thing on numerous occasions flashed in her mind.

"Love?" He turned to ask with concern.

Exhaling the breath she'd been unconsciously holding, she shared, "Evidently, only the big picture memories came back while I was in the hospital. Now detailed memories are popping in without warning. And they are directly related to what I'm doing or seeing at the time."

Taking the towel from her, he guided her from this part of the house. "Any migraines?"

"None thus far, knock on wood," she remarked, tapping on the banister as they passed by it. "Where are we going?"

He replied in a teasing tone: "I need a shirt unless you want pornographic scenes playing in your head."

While opening plain wood double-pocket doors leading into the extension, he continued, "Plus, I thought you wanted the whole tour."

The first division of the room was a study. Red's desk and leather chair were spotlighted by the sun shining through open curtains. A sitting area could easily be created in the vacant area across from it. Midway between, a set of snowflake-motif stained glass pocket doors exposed the master bedroom. The focal point of the room was a king-size bed. The walls and ceiling were painted to look like the winter sky at twilight. The painter deserved to be commended. Rusty fetched a fresh shirt from the walk-in closet.

"Go ahead. Check out the bathroom," he prompted.

A single pocket door with simple blue and yellow glass panels discerned its entrance. Clawfoot tub, corner shower, pedestal sink, daisy-stained glass window, and pale yellow walls all fulfilled her fantasy bathroom. White tiles covered the floor and partway up the walls. On closer inspection, daisies decorated these in a random pattern. The hand towels flanking the sink also had a subtle daisy design.

Elsie turned to exclaim, "My perfect bathroom!"

Rusty leaned easily against the doorframe with his shirt unbuttoned. He grinned with pride.

Straightening, he shooed her from the room. "If you don't mind, I need to use *my* bathroom."

Not wanting to hover, she went to the study. As she gently glided her hand across the soft leather chair, her visits to the ranch were downloaded. She missed the old codger. Cringing at the disarray covering the desk's beauty, she sat to organize the haphazard piles of mail, papers, and file folders. A large envelope had her name scrawled on it. She removed the contents—divorce papers. Only her signature was missing for them to be officially filed.

"What are you read—" He stopped midquestion at recognizing the paperwork in her hands.

She stood to yell at him. "You're divorcing me!"

"You were going to marry McEwan. I couldn't let you become a bigamist," he argued.

"We could've moved to Utah." She shot back with the only thing she could think of.

The pure absurdity of her statement caused him to laugh aloud. Another flash of memories from Hawaii caused her to sit abruptly.

She could hear herself clearly teasing Rusty on their honeymoon in Maui. "Your snoring curled the wallpaper. Did I wear you out that much?"

Her sudden change in demeanor scared him.

He knelt in front of her. "What is it?"

With wide eyes staring at him, she whispered, "We're married."

Sighing with relief, he responded softly, "Yes, mate, we're married."

She placed her hands on his face to trace the worry lines. Turning his head slightly, he gently kissed her fingertips. A tidal wave of emotions flooded her senses. Its ever accelerating eddy threatened to submerge her.

"Elsie?" His voiced sounded panicky as she sunk into darkness.

When Elsie regained consciousness, she glanced around, trying to determine her whereabouts. It was the master bedroom of the farmhouse. Rolling on her side, she struggled to swing her legs over the edge. If only she could find it.

"Finally!" Rusty's arms assisted her to sit as he hollered, "Sara!"

Sara and Tom hurried into the room.

"Thank heavens!" the older woman exclaimed. "How are you feeling? Headache? Dizzy?"

"I have to pee, but this bed is like crossing the tundra," she stated, grappling with the blankets.

Rusty pulled the covers aside to allow her easy exodus. At last, she could stand. The room did a dip.

When he grabbed to steady her, she pushed his hands away. "I'm fine!"

"No, you're not!" resounded in stereo from both Rusty and Sara.

"I called Vilanger. He said if you were out for more than twenty minutes, we should take you to the hospital. It's been eighteen." Sara walked with her into the bathroom. "What happened?"

Elsie slid the door shut for privacy from Rusty's extremely worried hazel eyes. "I think it was too much to process."

"I'm not following." Sara perched on the edge of the tub.

"I remembered the big pieces of my life, but I didn't have the details of specific experiences. They've been coming back as something triggers them." Elsie delayed her explanation to empty her bladder.

Sara filled in what she knew. "Rusty told us about the incident with the horse, touring the house, and the divorce papers. I did think it all rather odd the way you talked about him, but you never mentioned the wedding and you were still wearing the ring from Sean."

After drying her hands on the pretty daisy towel, Elsie held up her left hand to wiggle the ring finger.

"When did you take it off?" Sara asked with surprise.

"Beginning of last week," Elsie stated, not wanting to return to the bedroom.

"Before the box. Wait, there were wedding pictures in the box of you and Rusty from Maui. Why didn't they bring back that you two are married?" Sara put the toilet seat down to sit.

"I don't know. But I was a basket case that night," Elsie replied.

"True. You looked like hell the next morning," Sara remarked, reaching for the door. "Come on. We've been in here long enough. Plus, I need to call Vilanger to tell him you are okay."

When they emerged, Rusty sprang off the bed. "How do you feel?"

"Like an idiot," Elsie admitted. "I just want to go home."

"Since I had planned on coming over today to help with a few things, Sara can drive you home in your truck," Tom directed, moving them to the living room. "If you don't behave yourself, I will remove the battery."

Rusty concealed his amusement by reentering the master suite to close both pairs of pocket doors. Because the large room echoed, Sara went into the kitchen to call the doctor. A few minutes later, the four of them reconvened outside. After both women climbed into the truck, the men kissed their respective wives. Stunned silence filled the cab. It ensued for the entire drive home.

After parking the car in the garage, Sara finally spoke. "Vilanger said you are to take it easy the rest of the day. He agrees it could be too much hitting all at once. But if you so much as start with a headache or get dizzy again between now and your next appointment, our orders are to take you to the emergency room. Is that understood?"

"Yes. Are you angry at me?" Elsie asked apologetically.

"I'm upset that you went off on your own instead of asking for help." Sara's temper was pronounced by slamming the driver's door shut. "I know you are feeling better. And according to the schedule, you should be. But your condition still warrants caution, particularly with the added stress as of late. We're all worried."

She held her hand up to prevent Elsie from talking. "And before you ask, Rusty is too. Unfortunately, you haven't allowed him back into the circle of trust. He has to sit on the sidelines, waiting for you to invite him into your heart again. Tom can't decide if he's daft or going for sainthood."

Sara's rant continued as they walked through the laundry room. "He thrived on helping locate that damn mountain lion. It gave him the opportunity to protect you. Of course, the dogs' heroic deaths overshadowed his effort."

Finally, the lecture ended. Sara embraced Elsie.

In a gentler tone, she stated, "Trish and I are trying very hard to be supportive and not meddle."

"I know. But some motherly instincts can't be squelched." Elsie's smile could be heard in her tired voice. "And I do appreciate it."

"Go take a nap." Sara placed a motherly kiss on Elsie's forehead. "We'll check in on you later."

Elsie took a valium. It would be nice to sleep through the impending storm. She verified the doors were locked prior to going to her bedroom. Even though it wasn't even noon, she changed into her usual bedclothes. As she lay against the pillows, she imagined the beautiful master suite at the farmhouse.

Chapter Thirty-Seven

A LOUD THUNDER clap jolted Elsie awake. Using the remote, she turned on the television. The Weather Channel radar verified the storm was on top of them. A severe thunderstorm warning ran along the bottom of the display. Evidently, there had also been a tornado watch, which was now expired. The cells that had generated the watch had lost their rotational force. The incessant beeping of the warning instigated her to mute the television. The time in the corner of the screen showed it was 8:04 p.m. EST. As she closed her eyes, she listened to the sounds of the storm—strong gusts of wind, nearby and distant thunder, pelting rain. Another familiar rumbling noise not attributable to thunder could also be heard. Elsie went to investigate. She discovered Rusty snoring on the sofa. Since there was no reason to wake him, she headed back to the hallway. She didn't get far when a very loud thudding noise shook the entire house. Whether it was because of her involuntary shriek or the thud, Rusty was by her side in seconds. Both merely stared at each other dazedly. Before either one could say anything, Rusty's cell phone rang.

"'Lo," he answered immediately.

She suspected it was Tom.

Rusty replied to whatever the other end said. "We're safe, but don't know. Haven't had a chance to look yet either. I'll call you right back."

He ordered gruffly, "Stay here while I check things."

First, he went toward her bedroom. After a few minutes, he stepped over her to investigate the rest of the house. He began swearing at reaching the living room. His footfalls took him into the kitchen, and they were followed by the back door opening and closing. It felt like an eternity till he reentered the house.

"Rusty?" she called to him.

"Not now!" he stated curtly as he went into the garage.

Finally, he returned.

"Here's the deal." His tone reflected the seriousness of the situation. "A tree has fallen on the house. The guest bedroom is unsafe. Only a few drips are showing on the kitchen ceiling. Eventually, it will get worse with the amount of rain coming down. We need to get out and turn the power off."

When she didn't move or reply, he spoke further. "Sara and Tom will be here shortly to help empty as much as possible before it gets unsafe. I'm going to get the truck out of the garage. Go into the bedroom to put on pants and a sweatshirt. Okay, mate?"

"Okay," she agreed while he helped her stand.

They went their separate ways. After pulling on sensible clothing, she yanked down the suitcases to pack as much as she could.

Soon Sara joined her with boxes and large garbage bags. "We have the van and the car. Rusty is working on emptying the living room. Tom called 911 to report it. Since no one is trapped and there's no fire or sparking, they'll send someone when they get a break in emergencies."

Elsie said, "How long does Tom think we have till the ceiling is saturated?"

Sara hesitated before answering. "It depends on if the water stays contained to the laundry room and guestroom."

"Not very likely. Plasterboard is porous. It will act like a sponge to soak the ceiling and the walls," Elsie thought aloud. "If the rain doesn't pick up again, we should have a couple hours. And even then, the ceiling will collapse in sections along visible seams."

Sara paused to stare at how calm her friend was. "Did you take a valium earlier?"

"Eight hours ago, or I'd be completely useless," Elsie replied evenly.

"Welcome back!" Sara flung her arms around her dear friend.

This clearly wasn't the time for this. "Sara!"

"Okay, okay." The older woman grinned.

As Elsie packed, Sara moved the bags to the living room for the men to carry outside and load into a vehicle. Within a half hour, the bathroom and bedroom were reduced to furniture. The living room was in the same state. The van and cab of the truck were full. Rusty drove the truck. Elsie rode with Sara in the van. Tom remained behind to empty the kitchen.

Instead of driving across the cutaway between the neighboring houses, they went to the end of the driveway to turn onto the main road. They were going to the farm.

Rusty opened an empty garage bay for Sara to pull into. He parked the truck in front.

"I'm going to put the truck in the barn and get the horse trailer for the furniture." He joined them with a gallon-size Ziploc bag. "Here are your meds. We'll figure the rest as we go."

In control of her faculties, Elsie said, "The furniture can wait until daylight. I don't want anyone getting hurt."

His response tugged at her heart. "Please, let me do this for you."

After kissing him on the cheek, she took the bag. "Be careful."

She'd forgotten how the man smiled at the strangest things. He closed the garage door as he drove the truck toward the barn. Elsie and Sara emptied the van contents into a corner of the big empty room.

"I'm going to head home to check on my dogs. Will you be okay here alone?" Sara asked for assurance.

Elsie knew if she asked to go along, the answer would be no.

Sucking it up, she replied, "Yes. Please check on our husbands."

Again, Sara hugged her with happiness. "That sounded so good!"

Rolling her eyes, Elsie shooed her into the garage. "Go. I'll wait here to close the door after you're out."

As the door closed, Elsie knew she had to do something to keep from worrying. There were no baking supplies so that wasn't an option. She could unpack. The imp inside urged her on. After all, they were married. Even with her clothes hanging with his, the closet had plenty of excess room. There was no dresser in the bedroom. Some of her drawer items could go on shelves in the closet. Her intimates stayed in the suitcase. The stuff from the top of her dresser had no place. She hoped they could save that piece of furniture. It would fit perfectly against the wall directly across from the foot of the bed. Her personal bathroom items filled a convenient shelf in the linen closet. It took a little reorganization and relocation of Rusty's things to a higher shelf. Towels and extra sheets were put in the upstairs bathroom. The flowered file boxes stacked neatly on the floor in the closet. She suspected her laptop had been loaded into the truck. It could be gotten in the morning. Most of her things in the corner had been handled. She glanced at the clock by the bed; it was almost 11. No wonder her leg had begun to drag, between the time and her activities. Rubbing her face in the pillows to get comfortable, she discovered the one Rusty used. Inhaling deeply, she felt safe.

Later, she felt her back press against a firm, warm object. She shifted to see what.

"You're not going anywhere," Rusty mumbled sleepily as he strategically placed his arm and leg across her.

His action was both endearing and infuriating. Torn between relaxing and getting away, she attempted to at least free her legs. From the exertion last night, her muscles cramped.

"Mate, I spent six hours hauling stuff from your house last night. Let me sleep!" he grumbled at her fussing.

"Don't you need to feed the horses?" she asked quietly.

"They are in the field with the cattle." He rubbed his face against the side of her pillow. "The only thing I need is for you to shush."

He ignored her dramatic sigh. Eventually, his low snores lulled her asleep again. Unfortunately, his cell phone rang only a half hour later.

"Krikey!" he muttered gutturally as he rolled from bed.

It took three rings till he located the offending device. No longer trapped, she hobbled into the bathroom. The motif definitely created the intended affect. With sunlight shining through the daisy-stained glass window, an ethereal glow filled the room. It was a delightful way to be woken in such a cheery manner. He entered without knocking while she brushed her teeth.

He stripped off his boxers as he stepped into the shower stall. "The insurance adjuster will be at the house in forty-five minutes."

A few minutes later, he yelled over the water. "Would you hurry up and get in here?"

"What?" She almost choked on the toothpaste.

"It's your house. You need to be there," he stated. "Come on! If he gets there sooner, he might not wait."

By the time she fetched her body gel and stripped, he was rinsing. No sooner did she step in than he stepped out. On his way out, he placed his wet hand on her hip to slide across her buttocks. Instead of a smile, his lips formed a grimace. As she dried from the hurried shower, she noticed the bruising across her side and back. Of course! The mishap experienced with the horse yesterday.

"I'll get the truck. Be outside in five minutes," he hollered as he exited the master bedroom.

Throwing on jeans and a sweatshirt, she made it to the porch in time for the truck's arrival. Last night's saturating rain prevented the use of the shortcut. Leaves and branches littered the regular roads. They rode in silence to allow him to concentrate.

As the house came into view, she gasped. He placed his hand on her arm in reassurance. She hadn't realized how tall that tree was. It covered half the house.

While they waited, she asked, "Did you call the insurance company last night?"

"No. Tom called them first thing this morning to report his damage. Since you have the same agent, he reported yours too," Rusty explained.

Soon another car appeared. The couple climbed from the truck to meet its driver. Several pictures were taken of the exterior prior to stepping inside the house.

"Stay here. There's too much debris," Rusty stated.

She willingly obeyed. However, she did peer through the front door. It was worse than she'd imagined. Pieces of the living room ceiling jutted downward where the seams gave way. Water pooled on the wood floor along with chunks of saturated wallboard. Rusty answered questions as the adjuster inspected the damage. It didn't take long for the two men to exit. They made their way around to the backyard. A few more pictures were taken. Before the adjuster left, Rusty wrote the address to send the results.

"Breakfast?" Rusty assisted Elsie into the truck.

"Okay," she replied, not really feeling hungry.

Five minutes later, they were entering the diner.

While they waited for their orders, she asked, "The house is done for, isn't it?"

He nodded. "Yes, the structural integrity has been compromised."

With that topic more or less moot till the adjuster sent the official results in a day or two, she looked for something else to fill in the silence. "So how is it you are living in the newly renovated farmhouse?"

Before he could answer, their food arrived. The smells enticed her appetite.

To her surprise, he responded to her question while they ate. "Originally, I bought the property as a wedding gift. You always talked about having dairy cows. The property could also be subsidized with free-range Herefords. The addition started shortly before we left for Hawaii and Australia. Interior renovations were completed last summer. Then it sat vacant. Tom and Sara kept an eye on it till I made a decision."

"That's why Tom called last fall about the downed tree." Her tone indicated her insight.

"Yep," he acknowledged.

"But that doesn't explain the cows or Hailey and Molly." She pursued.

Between mouthfuls of food, his narrative continued. "When Red passed away, I received a phone call from his lawyer. In his will, he left us forty head of cattle and four quarter horses. The majority of his ranch was donated as protected open-range land. The house and barn on the base twenty acres was left to his only grandchild. Evidently, Red had known for some time of his impending death. He'd worked with his granddaughter on developing plans to turn it into a spa retreat of sorts. As a trial run, I volunteered you and the girls to be her first guests."

"And that would be when?" she questioned.

He delayed answering as the waitress refilled their cups. "April."

His cell phone interrupted further discussion. He sipped at the fresh coffee while the other end spoke.

"Okay, mate. We're finishing breakfast. We should be home shortly." He stood and slid the phone into his pocket. "That was Tom. He and Sara will be meeting us at home to unload your furniture."

The waitress hurried over with the bill.

Elsie asked, "Could I have a to-go container?"

While Rusty paid the bill at the register, Elsie scraped the uneaten portion of her meal into a small Styrofoam box. She made it to the front of the diner in time for him to hold the door open.

At home, the men removed the furniture from the enclosed horse trailer. Sara wiped it on the porch prior to entry into the house. Elsie made sure everyone had something to drink then prepared a hearty lunch with the food they'd salvaged from her kitchen. During a lull in her duties, she went upstairs to make the bed. The placement of the bed in the room over the kitchen suited her fine.

Soon Sara appeared carrying the drapes. "I washed them this morning."

Elsie exclaimed, "You even got the curtains!"

"I needed to stay busy. And keep an eye on those two," Sara elaborated. "The garage and laundry room ceilings collapsed just after they removed the last piece of living room furniture. Luckily, a fire truck arrived. They shut the power off and turned on their floodlight for us to remove the pieces from your bedroom."

After completing the guest room, Elsie went to the master bedroom to put her intimates into dresser drawers.

Rusty poked his head through the doorway. "Love, how do you want the furniture arranged in the living room?"

"The entertainment center should be put in the front corner with the sofa facing it by the fireplace." She replied then pointed toward the empty space across from the desk. "The two chairs put in here. It can be my workspace."

He disappeared with no comment. She headed to the kitchen to check on the food. When she returned, Sara had begun placing books in the bookcase. Tom worked on the television and accessories. Rusty carried the items in for her sitting room. Elsie tackled where to hang her prints. The sofa was the last piece to come into the house. While Rusty parked the trailer by the barn, she set the kitchen table for the late lunch. Several beers and a filling meal later, the other couple left for home, with Sara in the driver's seat.

Rusty relaxed on the sofa. Meanwhile, Elsie called Trish.

To her relief, the number went directly to voice message. "Hey, Trish, it's Else. It's been an eventful weekend, and need time to catch my breath. I'll fill you in later. Spend the week with your grandbaby and I'll see you next week. Thanks."

Hearing her end the call, Rusty suggested, "Do you think Trish would want to take daily rides? Since I primarily use Rowdy, Molly and Hailey need to be ridden regularly."

She leaned against the back of the sofa.

"She does love riding. Maybe that will make this transition easier for her." As she replied, his comment found another meaning. "Oh, I get it. You are trying to sway her to your side."

"I'll take any advantage I can get." His remark was followed by a huge yawn.

She realized how exhausted he must be.

"In case I haven't said it, thank you very much for everything today, last night, and the few days before." She placed an appreciative kiss on his tired face.

His hand reached to grasp hers. "For you, anything."

Confused by his intimate remark, she went to organize her sitting room. When she emerged an hour later, Rusty's snoring filled the large room. Walking quietly across the wood flooring, she locked the front door. On her return trip, she draped the quilt from her guest bedroom across his torso. Retiring to the master suite, she planned on writing. However, after washing her face, the day caught up with her as well. She stretched across the covers to fall into a deep sleep.

Chapter Thirty-Eight

Erotic dreams of sex with Rusty played in her head. When she woke, the house was eerily quiet. The quilt was folded on the end cushion of the sofa. In the kitchen, she poured a cup of coffee from the freshly brewed pot. After showering, she merely wrapped a towel around her naked body. To her surprise, Rusty stood in front of the television wearing only his boxers.

He turned to acknowledge her. "G'd mornin', mate."

"Good morning. Thanks for making coffee," she replied on her way to the dresser and closet for clothes.

He openly watched her every movement but didn't make any advances. She pulled the closet door partially closed to dress. Throughout the day, they conducted themselves as any married couple—discussing the animals on the farm, sharing gentle kisses, reminiscing about Sophie and Tycho. He invited her to take a walk with him to meet the animals. Hailey and Molly ran to the fence in greeting. The cattle from Red remained distant. The handful of brownish cows made their way across the pasture.

"Red didn't have dairy cows," Elsie remarked.

"I acquired these from the Grimmel farm. We came to a mutually beneficial agreement that included the fourth quarter horse, among other things," he replied, leaning easily on the nearby post. "My mate likes cream in her coffee."

"You do too," she parried.

"But you're the one who needs to gain several pounds in short order," he levied in response.

Unsure if this was a complaint or merely an observation, she scratched each of the cow's wide faces.

Later in the afternoon, he brought her a snack of cookies and milk while she tried to write. Again that night, he snored from the sofa and she dreamed of his lovemaking. In the morning, the same duplicate scenario played. Their day contained similar events as the previous one. And the subsequent days replicated in this manner.

By Friday morning, Elsie chose to confront her mounting sexual frustration. She watched from the kitchen for him to head toward the house from the barn. Then she hurried to the bathroom to begin her shower. As suspected, he entered the tiled room. After a few moments, he exited. With no legitimate reason to linger under the spray, she rinsed. When she appeared in the bedroom, he immediately passed by her for his shower. Had she lost her appeal? Instead of dressing, she put on her robe without tying it shut to reenter the bathroom. He stepped from the stall to discover her holding his towel with her robe slightly agape. Accepting the towel, he began to dry off. She didn't go, merely gazed.

He turned to ask. "Everything okay, love?"

She took a step toward him, her robe opening farther to expose one breast.

"It could be better," she said suggestively, gliding her hand along his muscular chest and down his firm abdomen to stop short of her intention.

For a few moments, she had visual validation of his desire. However, his interest, along with her hope, deflated. He turned away to head into the bedroom. She pulled her robe closed in mortification. Unable to face him, she stood in the same spot, trying desperately to contain the threatening tears. After summoning courage, she stepped into the bedroom. Her emotional distress was obviously displayed.

Now clad in jeans, he hurried to tenderly put his hands on her upper arms. "Mate?"

"You've slept all week on the sofa. Why don't you want me anymore?" Whispering the raw words didn't prevent the tears from flooding down her face.

"Don't want you anymore? Krikey, mate!" His face looked as pained as his voice. "Every night I stand in the doorway, listening to you cry out my name with wanting. It takes every ounce of strength not to make love to you. And if I slept with you in my arms . . . But I can't. You are still too fragile. Not until I'm sure you won't be hurt."

"Fragile?" she exclaimed in exasperation. "Because of my leg?"

"Your leg?" He gazed at her quizzically. "Not at all. It gives me an excuse to assist you."

His follow-up question hit the bull's eye. "Have you used a mirror since coming home from the hospital?"

She allowed him to lead her to the full-length mirror. Sliding the robe from her form, he forced her to view her reflection. It was frightening the way her skin hung from her skeleton. Seeing her shiver, he quickly covered her shame. Wrapping his arms comfortingly around her, he let her cry against his chest. The tears didn't subside. Eventually, he lifted her to place on the bed. Pulling the covers over her, he held her tightly. They lay like that for a long time. The doorbell ringing gave him a reprieve from their shared torture. He grabbed a shirt as he left the bedroom. Climbing out of bed for the second time, she dressed to face the day with more bravado than she felt.

As she entered the kitchen, Rusty discussed dates on a calendar with a man in cap and overalls.

When the man lifted his head, he removed his hat to smile in greeting. "Good morning, Elsie."

It took a second for his sandy hair and boyish smile to connect in her head. "Hi, Keith. I heard you and my husband made a deal on some Guernsey."

"Yep!" He replied with enthusiasm. "Dad is really happy with my decision."

"How are your parents?" she asked with genuine interest.

"Good. Dad still insists on helping, particularly till we get this expansion working smoothly. This winter it will be tough with his arthritis." The young farmer chatted. "You'll have to visit when the new dogs arrive. Jody really wants one to stay at the house rather than working the field. Your experience could make the decision easier."

Not wanting the young man to know her husband had shared nothing with her, she agreed. "Sure thing. Speaking of dogs, I'm sure Rusty told you what happened to mine."

To her own ears, it sounded harsh, bordering on blaming. Only her husband noticed the tone. His lips and jaw tightened in consternation. In the crappy mood she was in, what did he expect—fairy dust and rainbows? She exited through the side door onto the patio before she verbalized her thoughts. While she walked around the enclosed yard, Elsie heard the two men move to the barn. Going into the house, she searched the kitchen for something to eat. Over the last week, they had depleted her groceries. And Rusty only had bread, beer, and coffee in the pantry. A major grocery trip to supply it properly was overdue. Plus, if she was going to avoid a hospital stay, she needed foods to entice her into eating. Finding no paper in the kitchen, she went to the study to fetch some from the desk. In the top drawer, she found pen and paper. She also discovered a scrapbook. In it were pictures of her from the last year. To her shock, Rusty hadn't removed Sean from any of the shots. The man was a masochist. Hearing boots on the wood floor in the living room, she slid the book into the drawer.

"You okay, mate?" Rusty asked as his form filled the doorway.

"Working on a grocery list for Mother Hubbard's Cupboard, otherwise known as our kitchen," she stated flatly to avoid what he was really asking.

"Uh-huh," he muttered. "Um, about Keith's visit."

She prompted when he hesitated. "What about it?"

"He'll be taking care of things here for the two weeks I'm Down Under." He rushed the words. "My flight leaves Sunday."

"Is everything all right with Caleb?" Concern for his brother crossed her mind first.

"No worries. I've had the trip planned for weeks and pushed it several times." He closed the distance between them to sit on the corner of the desk. "It's to tie up a few loose ends with this becoming my permanent residence. I should've told you sooner. It just slipped my mind till Keith arrived."

She stifled her lurking crankiness. If he hadn't said the trip had been planned, she'd be suspicious about his reason for leaving.

Instead, she spoke in a level tone with words of understanding. "A lot has been going on. And we're still getting reacquainted."

His eyes scrutinized her face.

Accepting her felicity, he offered, "Is there anything special you want me to bring back for you?"

"The man I married two years ago." Her answer was both genuine and challenging.

His face registered her full meaning. He stood to get his passport, flight information, and packet of papers from the side drawer. Moving into the bedroom, he went into the closet to retrieve his duffel bag. He only packed two changes of clothing. As he strode through on his way outside, he dropped the bag onto the brocade chair. The paperwork protruded from its side pouch. She ignored the temptation to hide his passport. She telephoned Sara to see when they could go to Sam's and the grocery store. As luck would have it, Sara was free all day. Tom was at the hardware store buying supplies for a project. After the call, Elsie searched for Rusty in the barn. He was at the far end, reconfiguring stalls.

"Rusty?" she called as she neared him.

Her voice muted by his cursing.

She tried again louder. "Rusty?"

"What?" he snapped in anger.

"Sara is picking me up to go for groceries," she stated.

"Do you need money?" he asked, reaching for his wallet.

"No. I'll put it on a card to pay when the bill comes," she answered. "Is there anything particular you want me to make for dinner tonight or tomorrow night?"

"I haven't had your chicken potpie in a while," he admitted sheepishly.

"I'll see what I can do." Her response was noncommittal as she blew him a kiss.

Seeing the burly Aussie send one back lightened the ache eclipsing her heart.

Sara's enthusiasm for the two of them spending the day together fed Elsie's too.

Once they were at the bulk store, Sara couldn't hold back any longer. "How are things going between you and Rusty?"

"We have a few bumps to get over," she replied with a shrug.

"Elsie, the man moved to the other side of the globe for you," Sara remarked with exasperation. "What else does he have to do?"

In a contrite voice, she answered, "The bumps are me. And all that's happened in the last year."

"Oh." Compassion filled Sara's face. "Is there anything the rest of us can do to help?"

"Let's start with putting on those pounds the doctor is insisting upon." Her tone was glib; the sentiment, serious.

Three hours later, they returned to the farm. Both husbands were sitting on the porch, drinking beer and smoking cigars.

Elsie remarked, "Since when does your husband smoke cigars?"

"I'm guessing since your husband offered him a really good one," Sara countered.

"I knew he quit cigarettes. Guess he can justify the occasional cigar," Elsie surmised.

The men emptied the van, and then the other couple drove home across the field. As Elsie busied with spaghetti for dinner, Rusty snuggled up behind her. His lips nuzzled the sensitive spot under her ear. His hands wandered without purpose.

"How many beers have you had?" she questioned his motives.

"No worriesh, mate. Jusht enuf," he slurred noticeably.

She slammed the colander of pasta against the sink. "Are you freakin' kidding me?"

"I can't hurt yew this way," he said with an odd sense of satisfaction.

She supposed that on some level, to him this seemed sensible. It was insulting to have her husband need to be drunk to have sex with her.

Her demeanor changed drastically.

She said sweetly seductive, "Why don't you go lie on the bed? I'll join you as soon as I finish here."

He weaved his way from the kitchen toward the master suite. Elsie didn't rush what she'd been doing. She even placed the pots into the dishwasher. Letting ten minutes or so go by, she tiptoed across the living floor to peer surreptitiously into the bedroom. He lay spread-eagle and naked on the bed, his snoring echoing in the big room. She retraced her steps to the kitchen to eat dinner. It was her night to sleep on the sofa.

CHAPTER THIRTY-NINE

IN THE EARLY morning, she relocated the chicken that cooked all night in the crock pot to a large stew pot on the stove. Concerned he wouldn't wake anytime soon, she dressed to feed the livestock. Since she'd joined him in his afternoon chores earlier in the week, she knew what and how much to feed them. They'd spent the night in the fields. Foregoing the grain portion, she loaded the mass feeder with hay. Initially, the dairy cows came to investigate. Not afraid, she continued filling the contraption while they munched. At hearing the pounding of racing horse hooves, she quickly removed herself to the safety of the barn. The feeder didn't contain a full portion, but it would suffice. Plus, the free-range steers grazed contentedly on the far hill. Not wanting the noodles for the potpie to have hay flavoring, she went into the master bath to shower. On her way by the bed, she saw Rusty hugging her pillow obscenely. If only he would hold her that way.

It was 10 o'clock till he emerged looking a bit green around the gills.

As he stumbled by the sofa, she remarked, "I put hay in the feeder for them."

He stopped his egress. "Thank you. Rowdy behaved?"

"When I heard the horses coming, I didn't stick around," she stated.

Swaying from his compromised equilibrium, he asked, "Did I, um, did we . . . ?

She let her stinging observation fly. "Do you really think I would just climb on top and use you?"

Not responding specifically to her comment, he walked around the sofa to sit with her. "Please promise you will be here when I return."

"What?" Incredulity tinged her tone at both the change in topic and his anxiety. "Why wouldn't I be?"

241

His sad eyes and vulnerable appearance pulled at her heartstrings as he fumbled with words. "We haven't . . . aren't . . ."

She saved him from further embarrassment. "I promise, I will be here."

He leaned against the back of the sofa. She shifted closer to rub his forehead and temples. A sigh of relief relaxed his whole body.

"Do you really have to go?" she asked.

"Yes, mate. I've been putting it off as long as I could," he replied with resignation.

"Why don't you take a hot shower?" she suggested, wanting the alcohol stink reminder of last night removed.

Sitting forward away from her touch, he stated, "I have other chores to do. Plus, it will work the booze out of my system."

As soon as he went outside, she stripped the sheets off the bed. After putting those in the washer, she searched for a spare set. There was none. That went on the list for the next shopping spree. Dinner had to be perfect. Since the pot on the stove needed regular stirring, it enabled her to put the sheets into the dryer when the washer completed its cycles. Only one king-size sheet at a time could be placed in the dryer. Rusty entered the house while she was pulling the top sheet from the dryer.

"Let me help you with that," he offered.

"And then I'd have to rewash it," she rejected.

He smiled sheepishly. "Yeah, I do kind of reek."

"Ya think." She rolled her eyes at him.

Before following her through the house to the bedroom, he tossed his filthy clothes into the nearby basket. The sheet had been smoothed flat when he paraded by on his way into the bathroom. Smothering the urge to smack his bare bottom, she focused on spreading the summer quilt across the bed. Then she went to the kitchen to set the table. Soon enough, Rusty appeared smelling crisply fresh of manly soap.

"Smells great!" he remarked, peering over her shoulder into the pot. "Isn't it kind of early for dinner?"

"I thought you'd be hungry," she stated, not bothering to look at him.

Rubbing his neck, he replied, "Actually, I am starving."

"I'll fill your plate while you go put a shirt on." She bumped him on his way with her hip.

To her pleasant surprise, he rubbed his hand suggestively on her bum before obeying.

A half hour later, he stretched and belched in sated delight. "Absolutely delicious, love."

"We'll have dessert around five," she replied, collecting their empty plates.

He tugged her gently onto his lap. "Dessert too?"

The breakables in her hands put her at a disadvantage.

"I wanted to make sure you had good reason to come back," she remarked coyly.

Eyeing her thoughtfully, he didn't respond immediately. "Hmm. You could either mean your fabulous cooking or that you are trying to fatten up, so to speak."

"Or both," she replied, trying to wiggle off his lap.

He assisted by lifting her. "Sorry, love, I'm a little out of practice."

As he quietly helped her clear the table, she wondered if he meant more with her double entendre. But she'd seen that naked woman in his room at the hotel in California.

He caught her staring at him. "Is something wrong?"

"What? Uh, no," she answered, pushing the uncomfortable thoughts to the recesses of her mind.

After dessert, he selected *Gone with the Wind*. Putting on a cotton nightgown, she snuggled contentedly into him. The last scene she saw was the famed kiss depicted on the movie poster.

At the end of the movie, "Mate? Bed," he stood to steer her sleep-stunned state.

In the bedroom, he helped her under the covers. As slumber renewed, she felt the bed shift and muscular arms pull her close.

This safe cocoon only lasted till 4:00 a.m.

At 4:22, Rusty dropped a kiss on her lips. "I love you, Elsie."

She mumbled a groggy "Love you too" then dozed off again.

Hours later, loneliness infused her. By the time she looked out the kitchen window, Keith's truck was driving away. As she made a mental note to set the alarm for tomorrow morning, the coffeemaker began to brew.

"How does he do that?" she questioned aloud.

She peered into the refrigerator for a breakfast idea. Even though Rusty made a dent in the amount of potpie she'd made, there were plenty of leftovers. It wasn't a meal that froze well. It would spoil prior to his return. She'd be eating it for breakfast, lunch, and dinner for days. Maybe Tom and Sara would take some of it. This morning she saw something better for breakfast. Strawberry shortcake with a big dollop of whipped cream tasted great with a side of coffee. It would be another hour till Rusty's airplane landed at O'Hare. According to the itinerary on the refrigerator, it included a three-hour layover. In Hawaii, it would only be a two-hour wait. She shivered considering all of that confined time. When they'd traveled together to the Southern Hemisphere, he'd scheduled their layovers for days, not hours. It also included a wedding, a honeymoon, and meeting his family—all wrapped into one. Recalling this quickly led to images of the riding accident. Shaking her head to rid these scenes, she fetched her laptop to review e-mails.

An e-mail from Trish indicated she would be at the farm the next morning with fresh muffins. If nothing else, with Rusty gone for the next two weeks, it would give Trish time to adjust to Elsie's new living situation. Since her friend hadn't sent an e-mail detailing why she shouldn't be with Rusty, Elsie feared it would be a face-to-face lecture. Perhaps she could forestall it by getting things ready to keep her busy. Outlines had already been started with notes on needed research. It wouldn't be long till book signing trips would be requested for the two books released in the last four months. These would provide an escape from Rusty if things got untenable. This train of thinking led her to curiosity about his filming schedule. Rummaging through the desk, she didn't find it. Matter of fact, there weren't any such correspondences from Sherry whatsoever. Glancing around, she also realized his Oscars and Golden Globes weren't on display. For the next two hours, she searched the house for them. The only boxes were filled with outdated financial and contractual paperwork. The 10 x

16 food cellar under the kitchen contained wine, beer, bottled water, and an emergency storm kit. She went so far as to carry a chair and flashlight upstairs to view the attic space. When she opened the trapdoor, a built-in ladder pulled down. With apprehension and difficulty, she climbed. As she reached the top rung, she saw a light switch. Lo and behold, the attic space contained insulation. Resting her chin against the rim, she pondered where his mementos could be. Maybe the barn had storage?

When the cows saw her walking toward the structure, they trotted to the fence. A few minutes were spent scratching their broad faces. Refocusing on her mystery, she wandered through the two rooms with tack and milking equipment. The height of the loft prevented her from checking there. Somehow, though, she doubted he'd put anything there other than hay. It would be too easy for other people to access and vermin to infest. Or had he shipped it all to Caleb? But why?

It didn't cross her mind again till the end of the week. In the meantime, she learned how to use the milking equipment. Trish's daily horseback rides certainly improved her disposition in regard to the situation. Not a single negative comment about Rusty came from her lips. And Rusty called at least twice a day. However, the time difference made it difficult for them to actually speak to each other. In response, she'd send a text message letting him know she was alive and well.

CHAPTER FORTY

THURSDAY AFTERNOON, A delivery service called for Rusty and directions. The truck had several cartons. As they finished unloading, Sherry phoned.

"Hi, Elsie. I'm calling to let you know a few of Rusty's things should be delivered next week." She stated her purpose.

"Hi, Sherry. Too late—the truck is leaving now," Elsie replied.

"Damn! I'm sorry. The message I got said it was being loaded onto a plane today," she said in irritation.

Elsie didn't want her thinking it was a problem. "No big deal. It's here now. Was there supposed to be any furniture?"

"None. He donated it all when he sold the condo," Sherry responded unguarded. "So I take it things are progressing with you moving into the farmhouse?"

"Circumstances with a tree falling on my house kind of forced the issue," Elsie shared.

"That's why Harris was working on your insurance," Sherry continued in an easy manner. "Our condolences about the dogs. Rusty was pretty broken up over them when he called to change his flights."

"Hey, while we're on that subject. He only gave me his itinerary for going but not coming back, and I can't find a copy of it. Any chance you can e-mail it to me?" Elsie asked.

"Didn't he tell you? He's chartering a plane home because of livestock restrictions." Sherry's answer was tweaked at Elsie's curiosity.

"Makes sense." However, she kept it hidden. "Trish just got back from her ride, and I need to catch her before she goes. Anything from Harris before we hang up?"

"Nope. He and Rusty were on the phone earlier making arrangements for payment of the final settlement." Sherry closed cheerily. "Tell Trish I said hello. If she needs help with anything at all, give me a call now that I have lots of free time. Talk to you soon."

"I will. Bye." Elsie disconnected absently.

Sherry's parting remark fed Elsie's already growing inquisitiveness. When she went outside to chat with Trish, it repeated obsessively in her head.

Seeing her expression, Trish asked, "What's with the face?"

"I was just on the phone with Sherry. She says hello and if you need help to call her now that she isn't busy." Elsie gave her the abridged version.

"That was nice," Trish replied, switching from boots to sneakers.

The end of the commentary sunk in. "Wait! Not busy? What does that mean?"

"Exactly!" Elsie exclaimed at her friend, seeing it the same way she did.

"We'll discuss this tomorrow. I have to get going, or I'll get to Cassie's late," Trish stated.

"Okay. One quick thing, there are a couple of places I need to go to tomorrow. I'll be ready to leave when you get here." She explained the change in plans.

"Great! I'm glad you're getting out." Trish started the truck and waved as she drove away.

Elsie went into the barn to begin the evening chores till Keith arrived. He found her milking the cows.

"Hey! Looks like you're turning into a decent cowgirl," he teased, leaning casually on the corner of a stall. "If only we could get you on horseback."

"Not happening!" she groused lightly so as to not startle the cow.

Knowing he touched a nerve, he went to handle what she feared. "Since you have this under control, I'll go feed the horses."

She acknowledge with a nod. "Thanks."

When she finished, she placed the hoses in the water-filled washing tub. They could soak for the few minutes it took for her to carry the milk to the house. The morning product had gone home with Sara after she joined

Trish and Elsie for lunch. By the time Elsie returned to the barn, Keith had already hung the clean hoses for drying.

"Thanks, but I could've done that," she remarked.

"Elsie, I'm sorry about the horse riding comment," he apologized.

"No worries. We've known each other for years. There are far worse things you could harass me with." She punched him in the arm.

"So very true!" he teased loudly. "Of course, I'm sworn to secrecy for fear you will share similar things about me with my wife."

The two laughed on the walk to his truck.

After a quick hug, she asked, "Why don't you bring Jody along sometime?"

"Maybe I will just to keep you out of the barn." His jibe preceded his climbing into the truck.

"Very funny," she said sarcastically with a wave.

The delivered items stacked in the living room taunted her. As she ate dinner, the boxes continued beckoning her through the open kitchen door. The debate over whether or not she could open them without her husband getting upset waged in her mind. She busied herself with finalizing her shopping lists and selecting her outfit for the next day. The remainder of the evening was spent watching television in the bedroom. Closing both pairs of pocket doors deterred the lure of the boxes.

Another early morning call from Rusty was missed.

As usual, he left a message lacking any real significance: "If you're bored, feel free to unpack those boxes. Sherry organized and labeled everything. It shouldn't take much effort."

At least he gave her permission to snoop. She planned on doing it alone on Saturday. Friday was a productive day with Trish. Aside from another big load of groceries, Elsie bought throw rugs for strategic places on the floors. The cold under her feet some mornings caused a bout of goose bumps. It also made her anxious for Rusty to return to open the fireplace for use on damp nights. Now that both women were familiar with where everything was stored, it didn't take long for them to put things away. While handling book-related duties, they lost track of time.

Before they knew it, Keith knocked at the door with the evening milk. "Everything is done. See you in the morning."

"Thanks," Elsie replied lamely at his exit.

Shortly thereafter, Trish left Elsie alone with her thoughts. Elsie considered eating dinner but knew it would be futile with her melancholy mood shift—a side effect of the medications. If this emotional state continued, she'd be calling Trish or Sara in tears. This would prompt one of them to spend the night with her. Not allowing this to occur, Elsie tore into Rusty's boxes. As in his voice message, Sherry had orchestrated the packing. Inside each box, a list detailed its contents. The first box of papers could go in the closet with hers. It took till the third carton to find his statues. These she prominently displayed on the bookcase in the study. To her shock, the Oscar Rich Taylor had shared with her was included. This one went on the bookcase on the sitting room side. Another box contained framed pictures of family and friends, which she eagerly hung on the walls in the living room. Coming across an 8 x 10 of their wedding in Maui, she placed it conspicuously on the desk. The box of boyhood memorabilia she left for him to decide. Obviously, he wanted to keep these items or they would have been trashed, not packed. In all of the boxes, no file with upcoming films materialized. Maybe it was listed in paperwork he'd taken along on his trip. But that's what he had Sherry for. None of it made sense to her or Trish when they discussed it at length earlier in the day.

Chapter Forty-One

Finally on Tuesday, the couple connected. However, other than their initial greetings, it didn't go well.

Rusty stated, "I have to stay another week."

Her voice sounded lost. "I'll let Keith know when he stops in tomorrow."

"Is that disappointment I hear?" he teased.

"Yes, but there's something stuck in my head from the night before you left." She started to explain.

When he didn't reply, she continued haltingly. "I have a question for my own peace of mind. I'm not trying to provoke a fight."

"So ask?" His tone changed at her extreme seriousness.

Before she could stop herself, the words spewed forth. "How many women were you with while we were apart?"

There was an extended silence on the other end.

The anger in his words couldn't be missed. "Stop trying to chase me away. Isn't the other side of the world far enough?"

She fretted in frustration. "That's not why I'm asking."

"You're afraid I'm going to be killed on the way back to you just like McEwan." The profoundness of his epiphany resounded across the miles. "It's easier to create an emotional scapegoat than allow yourself to love that way again."

"I, uh, I . . ." His insight about something that hadn't crossed her conscious mind caused her to stammer.

He took advantage at having the upper hand. "You *will* see me in a week. At which time, I *will* answer your question face to face."

Before she could say anything else, the line went dead. It would be another week till she saw him. This gave her plenty of time to consider what he'd said. It bothered her that he'd gotten so angry. She didn't expect things to be this difficult once her memory returned. The relationship with him should've been like putting on her favorite worn jeans and snuggly sweatshirt. It still was in some aspects. Maybe something drastic had happened to change the depth of his feelings for her? Or he was right? Her fear of an intense love for him buried in her heart was the real issue.

Unsettled by both his words and his tirade, Elsie waited till the wee hours of the morning for his regularly scheduled call. It never came. Neither did the evening one. Apparently, he hadn't let go of his anger. The following morning at 6:00 a.m., he finally called while she readied for her doctor's appointment. It provided an emotional respite when she saw he not only called but left a voice message. Granted, the voice message mirrored the banality of the others. What mattered was he no longer sounded irritated. This eased her overall anxiety for the day of tests ahead.

Finally at two o'clock, she sat in Vilanger's office awaiting results. She already knew she'd gained the five pounds required, plus another six.

Reading the numbers the nurse recorded, the doctor grinned in smug satisfaction. "Very nice, keep it going. Your end goal is thirty and to maintain it."

"Test results?" she asked.

"Blood and MRI look good. Finish out your medications with the current dosage. The valium is strictly on a limited-as-needed basis," he stated firmly.

"None of the bottles have refills. Not really an opportunity for abusing any of it." She mocked his stern expression. "What else? Any restrictions lifted?"

"Driving is off-limits for at least six months. Traveling by plane is okay in short spurts. No around-the-world trips or lots of destinations in a short period. As for physical activities, go for it. Your body will tell you what you can't do. If you get tired, rest. If you have too many days in a row, you call. Same rule goes for your leg. I'd tell you to use common sense, but I know that's in direct contradiction with your stubborn streak." For clarification, he reviewed the previous list of limitations. "I think we can switch to a three-month cycle."

Doctor and patient ended the session unprofessionally with a hug. When the doctor reiterated the same information to Sara and Trish, their considerable relief was palpable. The trio celebrated on the way home by having dinner at Red Lobster. Trish dropped Sara at her place, then Elsie at the farm. Due to the lateness of the day, Keith had come and gone. As soon as Elsie entered the farmhouse, she called Rusty's cell phone. She left a non-urgent message for him to call her when he had time. Impatient to share the good news with him, she pressed the number for the ranch phone.

"G'day," Caleb answered.

"Hi, Caleb. It's Elsie. May I please talk to Rusty?" she requested cheerily.

"Sorry, love, he's out. I'd ask if anything was wrong, but you sound great," he said affectionately.

She smiled across the miles to him. "Thanks, I feel great. Just wanted to talk to him, but it's nothing that can't wait."

"'Kay, love. I have to go. One of my neighbors is coming in the lane. I'll let Rusty know you called." In typical Garnet fashion, he hung up without waiting for a response.

Not expecting him to call, she crawled into bed at nine o'clock. The exhausting day caught up with her. Sleep came quickly.

When she awoke seven hours later, her bladder felt like it was going to explode. After using the bathroom, she went to the kitchen for a glass of water and to locate her cell phone. Not finding the phone in her purse, she retraced her actions from last night. She'd called Rusty then changed into pajamas. She pulled the jeans from the hamper, and the phone slipped from the pocket to fall to the floor. As she picked it up, she saw several missed calls from Rusty. She climbed back into bed while listening to his messages. They went from casual to slightly frantic to mad. Before she had a chance to dial him, he called her yet again.

"Good morning," she answered scratchily.

"It's about damn time!" he growled.

Taken aback, she didn't respond.

"Well?" he exclaimed with frustration at her lack of speech.

"Well what?" she asked with growing irritation.

"You asked for me to call you," he stated succinctly.

Exhaling a deep breath to dispel her own aggravation, she explained, "I wanted to share the good news I got at the doctor's yesterday. No more meds. The majority of my restrictions have been lifted. And my next appointment isn't for another three months."

An extended silence ensued. She waited patiently. A bit too patiently, since she began to doze.

"Ahem." His loud throat clearing roused her.

"Did you say something?" she mumbled sleepily.

"Why do you sound sick?" His tone transformed to one of concern.

"Not sick, just sleepy. Yesterday was exhausting. Josh said if I'm tired to sleep. So I'm going to sleep. I love you." She ended with a string of kisses then disconnected.

Another few hours were spent in blissful slumber. This time when she woke, she felt well rested—a vast improvement from previous recovery times. Not wanting to tempt fate, she avoided further calls from her husband. As long as his voice messages remained inconsequential, it should last till he returned home. Plus, she relished having the upper hand. A week of him eating crow and her to add on a few more pounds—both worked in her favor. Hopefully, these were catalysts for him to want to perform his husbandly duties. Perhaps further enticement might be necessary. She opened the dresser drawer with her camisoles. Underneath them was the lavender negligee. As sexy as she felt in it, it would betray both Rusty and Sean's memory. Other than that, the drawer contained nothing enticing. This would require another trip to the mall. When Elsie arranged it with the other two women, they both insisted upon going the next day.

Elsie found what she wanted and a few bonus pieces within the first few stores. The ladies enjoyed lunch prior to returning home. After handwashing the newly purchased delicates, Elsie hung them on the line outside. Trish joined her to report on the conversation she just had with Sherry. Unfortunately, Sherry talked mostly about the trials and tribulations of pregnancy. Trish and Elsie were totally delighted for her. But still, nothing was revealed in regard to Rusty's upcoming projects. Due to frustration,

Trish went for an extended ride. While out, she casually checked the fencing. Elsie handled evening chores. At successful completion, she called Keith to let him know he had the night off.

The Monday before Rusty was due home, a priority mail envelope arrived from Harris. When Elsie opened it, it didn't make sense. It was a copy of a letter from another lawyer stating that since Rusty had paid full financial restitution, there would be no lawsuit. The label on the outside envelope was clearly typed: Ms. Elsie Garnett. The inside envelope had nothing on it. Since she'd already read part of it, she might as well read the whole thing. Till she finished, she pieced together what happened. The dates were the biggest clues. He'd left a set a week prior to the start of filming and never returned. It was the same day Elsie had been notified of surgery. Perhaps his appearance hadn't been a drug-induced delusion.

Trish entered the house from her ride. "What's that?"

"This? Just some legal stuff for Rusty. I opened it by mistake," she replied, placing the envelope at the bottom of his pile of mails on the desk.

"It's taking a long time for Red's estate to close," Trish remarked.

Elsie didn't correct her assistant's misconception.

The following days till Rusty's return, Elsie kept busy with lots of writing. But it was ideas and excerpts rather than the start of a book. Since the publisher wasn't pushing for book signings or another manuscript, Trish was only needed two or three days a week. This worked well with Rusty coming home on Friday.

The day prior to his return, Elsie's thoughts raced. Unable to focus on anything, she cleaned the house and worked in the barn. Again, Keith got the night off. The day exhausted her physically, but her mind began obsessing as soon as she ceased moving. A long hot soak accompanied by several glasses of wine eased this anxiety. It relaxed her so much that she climbed into bed without a nightgown.

CHAPTER FORTY-TWO

SOMETHING DAMP AND fuzzy rubbed against Elsie's face.

She pushed it away. "Tycho, let me sleep."

His ghost was terribly persistent. This time when she put her hand up, she felt a human nose on the furred face.

Rusty pursued to nuzzle her nape. "Missed you, mate."

"You're not due home till tomorrow," she replied in bewilderment.

"A little white lie to surprise you," he responded, trailing kisses along her neck on his way to burying his face in her cleavage.

He pushed the covers away to indulge further. Finding more exposed skin, he continued his exploration. As his hands slid under the blanket along her naked form, a guttural groan rumbled against her chest. The towel at his waist couldn't hide his growing interest. While he tossed the blankets aside, she tugged at the towel. When he moved on top of her, she welcomingly parted her legs. Only a wisp of lace separated them from total sexual intimacy. Fervent kisses, urging hands, moans of pleasure, straining bodies—all declared with undeniable intensity their need for each other. His hand reached for the strip of cloth. As he shifted to remove it, he pulled his right knee up for leverage. A howl of pain followed by a string of curse words resounded. He rolled off her, grabbing at the back of his right thigh.

"Rusty?" Concern replaced the craving for sexual gratification.

"Get my towel!" he hollered in obvious pain.

The requested item lay crumpled next to her. She handed it to him. When he pulled his hand away to replace with the terry cloth, blood pooled in the palm.

"Oh my god! Why are you bleeding?" Her concern quickly evolved to fear.

He muttered under his breath then answered through gritted teeth. "That last maneuver ripped staples out."

"Staples?" she stated. "Roll over."

When he glared at her, she repeated with force. "Roll over!"

He warily obeyed. Removing the towel, she took a closer look. Eight tightly spaced staples demarked a crescent-shaped wound. Two of the staples nearest his buttocks had popped partially out. The skin tore slightly where they'd been attached. In all actuality, it didn't appear that bad. But she could imagine the metal ripping through the skin inflicted serious pain.

"Stay put. I'll be right back," she commanded.

On her haste to the laundry room, she grabbed one of his flannel shirts from the closet. After collecting the dog first aid kit and a clean cloth, she returned to the bedroom.

"You better not have a camera," he grumbled sourly.

"As much as I love your bare ass, this is hardly a Kodak moment," she shot back.

When she rubbed iodine on his leg, he groused, "What are you going to do?"

"Remove the rogue staples and go from there," she answered as she continued her task.

"Is that really a good idea?" he asked.

"Since it looks about a week old, it should hold as long as you restrain your activities," she remarked pointedly while using forceps to steer the bend at the end of the staple out from under his skin. "And you have no reason to doubt my nursing capabilities."

He conceded to her argument. "True. I should've told you, but I didn't want you to fuss."

"Too late now. I'm fussing and fuming." Her retort was emphasized with the tug removing staple number one.

His yowl was intentionally muffled in the pillow.

She didn't wait for him to catch his breath to begin work on the next staple. "You're lucky it was this and not a charley horse that caused coitus interruptus."

This one needed a little help. A tiny snip with cuticle scissors gave enough room for the bent end to come out without injuring him further.

"How many more?" His voice whined in pain.

"That was the last one. Just using a couple of Band-Aids to keep you together," she stated with a pat on his right cheek. "All done."

When she reentered the room from putting her supplies away, he emerged from the bathroom. He'd donned boxers.

Watching him lie gingerly on the bed, she questioned, "Would you please share why you needed those staples?"

"Come lie with me and I'll tell you," he agreed.

She kept enough space between them to watch his face while he spoke. "We were working some new dogs together. A fight broke out. I hopped off my horse to kick them apart. The commotion freaked one of the bulls. He started swinging his horns at them. And, well, he got me."

Reaching the end of his story, he yawned exhaustedly. "No more talking, only sleeping."

She wiggled closer to snuggle into his broad chest. "Is this okay?"

"Mm, preferred," he mumbled thickly.

Chapter Forty-Three

When the alarm blared at 5:00 a.m., Rusty rolled away from Elsie.

"No. Stay with me," she requested groggily.

"Sorry, mate." He kissed her softly on the lips. "I didn't get to spend much time acclimating the newcomers last night."

"Newcomers?" she mumbled. "Oh, that's right. You brought livestock back with you."

"I guess you could say that," he said vaguely on his way to the bathroom.

Snuggling deeper under the covers, she listened as he dressed. Then his footfalls carried him through the house to the kitchen. Twenty minutes later, she still hadn't fallen back to sleep. She climbed from bed for a cup of coffee. The new throw rugs kept her feet from getting cold, but the house was still chilly. As soon as she had the hot beverage, she returned to the master bedroom to dress. Jeans, T-shirt, and redonning Rusty's flannel shirt should keep her warm. She poured coffee into two travel mugs to carry to the barn. Entering the structure, she turned down the corridor that housed the horses. An Australian Cattle Dog rushed forward barking.

Another memory clicked in place. Caleb had asked her to name the new puppy he'd gotten.

"Bonnie? Bonnie Blue!" She knelt to greet the dog.

The barking quieted. The dog approached Elsie with her nose actively sniffing. Suddenly, she did a funny tail-chasing circle with a happy yap and raced to Elsie.

While the two reacquainted, Rusty went near Rowdy. "I was wondering if you two would remember each other."

She stood to hand him one of the cups. "Thought you might want this."

"Thanks, mate! I didn't wait for it to brew." He accepted it gratefully. "Why didn't you go back to sleep?"

"I couldn't without you there to keep me warm." She batted her eyelashes coquettishly to coincide with the flattering remark.

He chuckled. "More like you were eager to meet the newcomers."

"That too!" she chirped. "Bonnie Blue is obviously one."

"Come on. I'll introduce you to the rest," he stated, leading Elsie with one hand and Rowdy with the other.

They headed for the far end of the milking barn. Bonnie Blue stayed at their heels. Occasionally, Rowdy kicked at her; but the dog deftly ducked from harm. As they got near the stalls Rusty had modified before his trip, yips became audible.

"Puppies?" Her eager high-pitched soprano definitively denoted her delight.

"Yep." As soon as the word left his mouth, she freed her hand to hurry to them.

"Don't get too excited. Only two are ours," he warned before she fell in love with all of them.

Peering over the wall, she exclaimed pointlessly, "Puppies!"

By now, he'd reached the stall too. "The red bloke and blue sheila with the spot on her bum are ours. Her name is Opal. The other three sheilas are Keith and Jody's along with Elmo."

"Elmo?" Her face looked aghast at the thought of a dog named after a muppet.

He must've read her mind. "St. Elmo's Fire, not the red furry thing from Sesame Street."

"Don't tell Jody that. She'll take to him better if she believes muppet," Elsie said, still cringing at the idea.

"She'll find out eventually from his registration papers," he remarked, pushing his cap back on his head.

Elsie nodded. "From their differing sizes, they aren't all from the same litter. How many different lines are represented?"

"Bonnie and Elmo have the same dam. Our red and a blue are littermates. As for the others, their papers with five generation pedigrees are on the desk." He kissed her on the cheek. "Go on in to them. Just don't let any sneak out."

Rusty left to continue his chores with Bonnie Blue leading the way. Elsie waited for Rowdy to be a good distance away prior to opening the stall door. The puppies yipped exuberantly at her entry. She dropped to her knees to welcome these foreigners. They climbed on each other in an attempt to be closest to her. The little red male and his sister appeared to be the youngest at nine or ten weeks old. The blue girl with the white spot and the Grimmels' red girl were closer to eight months. The other two blues were somewhere in between. Elsie examined each of them from teeth to tail. By the time she finished, she'd identified one of the blues for Jody's housedog. It not only was more submissive than the others, but it was also incredibly cuddly for a working dog. Elsie wondered if the puppy had been bottle-fed. Bottle-fed pups tended to bond with their people substantially stronger than with other dogs. Following the same premise, herding dogs are normally raised with the livestock they are to herd and protect. And as much as Elsie wanted to take their two new additions into the house, it would hinder their intended purpose. After cleaning their pen of poop piles, she went into the house. She stripped in the laundry room so as to not drag straw through the house.

The spraying hot water felt heavenly after streaking through the chilly house. She really had to ask Rusty to open the fireplace. While spreading lotion on her body, she viewed it in the mirror. Her chest no longer resembled partially deflated balloons. Gentle curves were beginning to replace sharply protruding hip bones. Overall, her muscles had firmed from doing chores in the barn. The next fifteen pounds would give her a butt, finish rounding her hips, and put bounce in her bosom. Rather than appearing sallow and brittle, she glowed with budding health. Even the pronounced dark circles under her eyes had faded substantially. The house phone ringing disturbed her personal perusal.

She hurriedly slipped into a robe on the way to the study. "Hello?"

"Good morning, Elsie." Jody Grimmel's voice chirped across the line. "We're leaving now. Have a pot of coffee on. I made sticky buns fresh this morning."

"Okay. See you soon," Elsie replied.

She realized she had no way to contact Rusty. His cell phone was on the desk directly in front of their wedding picture. Of course, he never took it with him when he stayed on the property. Granted, the barn had a phone, but that wouldn't be useful if he was in the field like now. Mulling this over, she noticed the papers for the dogs. As much as she wanted to read them, she didn't have long till company arrived. After dressing, she took the packet of pedigrees to the kitchen. The coffee in the pot was poured into an insulated carafe. While another pot brewed, she reviewed the papers. The differing lineages made possible for several generations of litters.

Hearing a truck arrive, she headed for the door. Via the window, she saw two trucks—the Grimmels' and the veterinarian's. She sorted through the papers to have the immunization records available on each dog.

Jody came inside. "These can be kept warm in the oven at 225."

Elsie turned the oven on so her guest could place the aluminum foil covered metal pan into it.

Greetings and introductions went around the group prior to entering the barn. The vet accepted the copy of the health records. Keith went into the tack room to fetch Elsie's grooming table. The pups began barking at the sound of voices. Elsie stepped into their enclosure. This ceased their incessant noise. While Keith set up the table, the animal doctor determined what order in which to examine his patients. Elsie handed the pups as requested. Midway through the examinations, Rusty entered the barn with a saddle slung across his shoulders.

Seeing the group huddled around the puppies, he called out, "G'day!"

The Grimmels waved. After dumping his load in the tack room, he joined the party. Keith filled him in on how far they'd gotten and any noteworthy observations from the vet.

The little red guy was the last one before the adult dogs. Rusty stepped out of the barn to whistle. Elsie would need to practice that tune a few times till she got it correct.

The vet's voice pulled her attention to the current puppy. "Looks like those girls were getting rough with you. See here." He pointed to a fresh puncture hole on the pup's left ear. "From the size of it, I'd say the oldest gave the ear piercing some time this morning. He probably tried to nurse from her. Keep an eye on it. And don't let the others lick at it." He talked as he cleaned and stitched it. "Mrs. Garnet, I understand you have lots of experience with malamutes. I can imagine that included a fair share of first aid and stitch removal."

"They do tend to play rough," she replied glibly.

"There are only two stitches here. Give them a week. If he hasn't already scratched them loose, take them out," he recommended.

Taking the puppy from him, she agreed. "Okay."

"Where are the adults?" the vet questioned.

As if on cue, Bonnie Blue raced into the structure. Rusty lifted her onto the table then went in search of Elmo.

With the red dog not in sight, Rusty said to Keith, "He's your dog, mate. Let's see if he comes for you."

Keith whistled like Rusty. Obviously, he'd been coached prior to today.

"Here he comes!" Keith said triumphantly by the time the vet had finished with Bonnie Blue.

Elmo resembled a ball of fire the way he tore into the barn and whipped his body around in a midair circle. Landing, he eyed the group suspiciously.

Rusty commanded, "Elmo, up." And he patted the table.

Elmo hopped onto the table with little effort. His tongue hung out of his mouth as he panted from the high-speed trek across the acres of hilly terrain.

"Elmo?" Jody squeaked with zest. "How adorable!"

She reached to pet him, and he immediately rolled onto his back for her to rub his belly.

This delighted her further. "Are you our 'Tickle Me Elmo'?"

The men contained their groans of disgust. When Rusty made eye contact with Elsie, she had to stifle a giggle. She'd warned him. It didn't help his case any that Elmo turned into a cuddly muppet for Jody. It would ultimately be perfect for Jody to accept these tough working dogs.

Elsie could hear Jody's voice in her head calling a litter of Elmo puppies "muppet babies." And one could only imagine the names Jody would give them. Refocusing on immediate events, Elsie realized Rusty was staring at her with a furrowed brow.

Finished being examined, Elmo and Bonnie Blue zealously zoomed to the fields. The vet and the Grimmels made their way from the barn. Rusty hung back. As Elsie exited the puppy stall, she tripped on something and lost her balance.

He steadied her. "Should I be worried?"

"I'm just lightheaded from not eating," she stated.

"When Elmo was on the table, you zoned like after the accident." His tone and expression indicated his heightened apprehension.

If they didn't have visitors, in all likelihood he'd have hoisted her onto his shoulder.

"It wasn't a seizure. My mind wandered to the inevitable litter of 'muppet babies,'" she explained. "But if I don't eat soon, I will become quite snarky."

"And that would be different than normal how?" he teased in an attempt to alleviate the tension.

"Now, who's being snarky?" she countered.

With no rejoinder, he good-naturedly swatted her butt with his cap to get her moving outside to the others.

Her response was a simple "moo."

At a volume too low for the others to overhear, he said playfully, "Your boobs are filling in with udder beauty."

Reaching the vet and the Grimmels at the trucks prevented any volleying remark.

Elsie offered the vet to join them for coffee and sticky buns. Unfortunately, he had to decline because of two other house calls. Once his truck drove from sight, the two couples went inside. A delicious aroma permeated the kitchen. While the couples ate, they reviewed and signed papers for the four dogs going home with the Grimmels.

Done with a third bun, Rusty pushed away from the table. "We have to transfer the travel crates from my truck to yours."

Keith nodded. Jody and Elsie cleared the table then followed. They carried puppies to the truck. Keith whistled for Elmo. This time it only took one beckon. Bonnie Blue came too. Rusty held her collar.

To get him into the truck, Keith mimicked Rusty's earlier actions. "Elmo, up."

Rusty stated, "When you get home, ride the fence for them to learn their boundaries. And don't worry about the pups. Elmo will keep them in line. Anytime you extend or change the fence line, just do the same thing. It won't take long for the others to be as good as him."

"Thanks, man." Keith shook hands with Rusty. "The butcher called to let us know the meat from that steer will be ready tomorrow."

As they drove away, Jody could be seen chattering excitedly to her husband. Rusty strode into the barn with Bonnie Blue. Elsie trailed after to see why. He released the puppies from the enclosure.

"You up for a walk around the small pasture, mate?" He offered his hand.

"Okay," she eagerly accepted.

"I'll take Opal along when I ride the perimeter this evening. The little guy doesn't go beyond this pasture till that ear is completely healed," he explained. "But no taking him into the house. He needs to work like Elmo."

"I understand," she replied. "What are you going to name him?"

"I will leave that to you, love," he stated with a kiss on her cheek.

Chapter Forty-Four

At noon, Elsie went in search of Rusty. She packed a picnic of three hearty sandwiches and a jug of iced tea. Her old jeep was gone. It wasn't registered for driving on the road, which meant he was on the property. Or he could be at the condemned house. She called Sara. She didn't see him next door or on the adjacent hills. Elsie stood in silence listening for the jeep's noisy pinging. Instead, she heard a chainsaw fairly far away from the house and barn. The top path led directly to the far end of the property in either direction without the impediment of fencing. It was along this dirt road that the chainsawing got louder. In taller weeds to the right, the grass was flattened in two evenly spaced tire-wide lines. She turned the truck to follow it. Not far along, a shallow gulley dipped. There Rusty loaded wood onto a 4 x 6 trailer attached to the jeep. His sweaty T-shirt clung to his torso. With his hat off, she noticed he was in desperate need of a haircut. As she parked next to the jeep, he strode toward her.

He unexpectedly blew his top. "What the fuck do you think you're doing?"

The force of his anger caused her to hesitate getting out of the truck or saying anything.

Poking his head through the open window, he ground through clenched teeth. "I asked you what you think you're doing!"

"Bringing my husband lunch and checking to make sure he's all right." She became defensive as she shoved the food and jug at him. "What the hell is your problem?"

Apparently, her reasoning doused his rage. For a moment, he stood there dumbstruck.

When he finally spoke, it was in a more civilized tone. "I appreciate the gesture. But you are still under a no-driving restriction."

"That would be on the regular roads, not our own property. It's not that I'm incapable. There is a medical timeframe one has to be seizure-free to legally drive." His overreaction wasn't going to be forgiven that quickly. "If you carried your damn cell phone with you, I could've called rather than driving across hill and dale trying to find you."

"I, uh, didn't realize I'd been here that long," he remarked lamely.

He stood there struggling for something to say. The seconds ticked by torturously. He was standing too close for her to drive away.

He finally ended the excruciating silence. "The jeep and trailer are full. If you drive them back, then I can load the truck."

"If that's what you want." Her sarcasm blocked the tears.

He opened the door to assist her. After setting his lunch on the hood of the truck, he removed the blocks from behind the jeep wheels. She adjusted the driver's seat to reach the pedals. Working the clutch with her bum leg was going to be a challenge.

"Just park by the barn," he said, leaning in to kiss her.

She turned her head so his lips landed on her ear.

He tried again to make nice as he took a step backward. "Thank you for bringing lunch."

"Yeah, whatever." In her irritation, she released the clutch with very little finesse.

Thankfully, the jerking of the jeep as it moved forward could be blamed on the heavy load. After returning to the house, she checked on the puppies. They were playing happily in the small pasture. Not wanting to inflict her foul mood on them, she didn't disturb them. She went into the house to type the pedigrees into the computer. This allowed her to mix and match potential breeds with a simple click of a button. While doing this, she researched the breed standard and history. All of this gave her ideas for a name.

Eventually, Rusty returned to the house. Even with the pocket doors closed, she identified his current task—opening the fireplace for use. After a few trips of carrying wood into the house, he slid apart the pocket doors.

Not bothering to say anything, he headed directly for the bathroom. The sound of the shower running brought X-rated images to her mind.

Maybe she should just let go of her anger. After all, it was obvious he regretted losing his temper. This debate waged in her mind till he emerged. As usual, the towel hung precariously across his hips. To pull the material away and feast her eyes . . . She shook her head to dispel those frustrating thoughts.

When she heard him dressing, she hollered to him. "I have a name for the boy."

"I'm listening," he stated.

"Jasper," she said from the leather chair.

Stepping into the room between rooms, he remarked, "Good sturdy name."

His detached demeanor refueled her irritation with him.

She purposefully picked a probable point of contention. "You do realize that spot on Opal's butt is against the breed standard."

"Are you intentionally baiting me?" he questioned suspiciously as he sat on the corner of the desk buttoning his shirt.

"You're the one with the rod. Maybe you should be reeling me in," she sassed.

"Reining you in is more like it." With raised eyebrows, he countered, "What's with the pendulum mood swings today?"

"Pick something—hormones, the X chromosome . . . or maybe I'm just a bitch!" she snapped.

He blinked in shock at her tirade.

Not getting a verbal acknowledgement, she stood to stomp off. Quite unexpectedly, that's as far as she got. Then everything went black.

She regained consciousness with him carrying her.

"Rusty, put me down," she grumbled.

He set her on the edge of the bed with his arm holding her in a sitting position.

Staring intently into her face, he asked a simple question: "When's the last time you ate?"

"The sticky bun this morning," she shrilled peevishly. "Not like I was going to hang around to eat with you after you yelled at me. It killed my appetite."

"I shouldn't have yelled. I knew the driving restriction was because of the seizures." He clarified why he had gotten angry as he walked her to the kitchen. "What I didn't understand is why it was still not allowed if you weren't having them anymore. I thought there was another reason you hadn't shared."

"You thought I was hiding something from you?" she lashed out in an accusatory tone.

Sitting her at the table, he avoided engaging her latest remark. He mixed a glass of chocolate milk for her to drink while he made a sandwich. It didn't take long after she drank the chocolate milk for rational thinking to return.

When he put the sandwich in front of her, she asked quietly, "May I please have more to drink?"

"Another chocolate milk?" he verified.

Having a bite of sandwich in her mouth, she merely nodded.

As he placed the refill by her plate, she briefly touched his hand.

In a hushed apologetic voice, she said, "I'm sorry."

He pulled a chair over to sit next to her. Placing his arm around her shoulders, he kissed the side of her head.

"Well, as you pointed out, it was my fault to begin with." He took responsibility for instigating the situation. "And I should've made sure you ate before I headed off, particularly after you'd gotten dizzy earlier."

His sad tone shared what he wouldn't say aloud.

"Rusty, it really was a case of needing to eat," she stated, peering into his worried eyes. "It's not like before."

"If you say so, mate," he replied unconvincingly as he gave a squeeze to her shoulders.

There wasn't anything she could do to persuade him. At least he hadn't acted to conceal his true feelings. In that aspect, they were making progress. When she emptied the plate, they didn't move. With his arm still around her, they watched through the French doors. Even though he'd spent the majority of the day doing something physical, he hadn't been in need of clearing his head like now.

"Why don't you take Hailey for a ride?" she suggested.

He thought about it a minute. When he turned to speak, he stopped. Whatever it was, he thought better of it.

However, he did take her up on the offer. "I think I will."

While he was gone, she curled on the sofa to watch television. After an hour of finding nothing she wanted to watch, she went outside to the puppies. They barked in excitement at seeing her. She joined them in the pasture. Picking each one up for kisses, she knew Rusty would disapprove. It was only for a day or two, and then they'd be working the field with Bonnie Blue. As she bent to put Jasper on the ground, she saw Rusty and Hailey on the next hill. Moving to lean on the fence, she watched. The three-year-old filly complied with his every command. Red had done a wonderful job training her. Rusty's skill on a horse was equally impressive. If only she had 1/100th of it. Of course, she'd be glad to feel easier around the horses, like she did the other ranch animals. Speaking of cows, the dairy trio was headed to her direction. While she paid attention to them, she didn't hear Rusty ride up. Hailey stuck her face over the fence to greet Elsie too. Elsie cautiously scratched the filly's face.

"Don't worry, mate. She has Molly's soft disposition with people. With the cattle, she's much feistier." His tone relayed his relaxed state.

To prove his statement, the filly gently pressed her velvety nose against Elsie's chest. Rusty chuckled at the wide-eyed look Elsie gave him. Tentatively, she rubbed Hailey's ears. A bit of chill in the wind caused her to shiver.

"Okay, you're getting cold. Give me a few minutes to get her saddled off, and I'll be in to start a fire," he said, tugging on the reins in a manner that made Hailey back away slowly.

As he turned toward the barn, Rusty said sternly, "And stop mollycoddling those puppies."

"Yes, love," Elsie replied obediently with a flutter of her eyelashes.

Exasperation was displayed on his face before he urged Hailey into a trot. A happy feeling formed around Elsie's heart. After a quick kiss to each of the pups, she hurried inside. It didn't take long for the front door to open and close, which was followed by boot steps across the hardwood floor. The timer on the stove beeped. She dumped the cooked tortellini into the colander sitting in the sink. The chicken Alfredo sauce bubbled its readiness. After turning off the burner and giving it a good stir, she headed to the living room. Rusty knelt in front of the fireplace, monitoring its first fire of the season. She silently padded up behind him to place her arms around his neck.

However, this action startled him. "What the!"

He jerked sideways, which caused him to land on his butt. This unexpected motion took her with him. As she landed, his yowl of pain announced her hip met squarely with his groin.

Scrambling off of him, she apologized. "Rusty, I'm so sorry."

With one hand he grasped the juncture between his legs; the other hand, the stapled wound.

Taking a moment to catch his breath, he said sardonically, "So much for tonight's plans."

"What?" she asked in a surprised high soprano.

Groaning while he attempted to stand, he expounded. "I'd rather hoped to finish what we started this morning."

She stood at the same time and inadvertently slammed into him. And they were both on the floor again. This time when she tried to climb off, he grabbed her arms firmly.

"Stop moving, or you are going to permanently maim me," he stated with difficulty through gritted teeth.

She suddenly realized her knee pressed dangerously between his legs. If she tried shifting her weight, she'd inflict far more hurt and possibly irreparable damage. He put his hands on her waist then lifted her high enough for her to move her legs to a safe location. Releasing her, he exhaled with relief.

"Rusty?" she questioned.

"Give me a minute, love," he replied, his voice still strained.

She carefully removed herself. In the kitchen, she put ice in a bag. By the time she returned to her husband, he no longer was lying in front of the fireplace. Suspecting he wanted to check the damage, she went directly for the bedroom. His groans emitted from the bathroom.

"Rusty?" She stepped cautiously into the daisy-decorated room.

He was naked from the waist down facing the mirror. The smeared blood on his thigh prevented her from seeing how severe it was. As for his frontal region, he held it cupped in his hands.

"Would you please get ice and your first aid stuff?" he requested with a grimace.

"Here's the ice." She took a step toward him.

"Just put it on the bed," he growled.

Suggesting a trip to the emergency room would most likely be met with disdain. She deposited the bag then went to fetch the same supplies used earlier. When she returned, he was on the bed. She repeated the same actions from this morning. Another pair of staples had popped. These were at the other end of the crescent.

"How many?" he asked.

"Two, again," she replied.

They didn't speak further. She concentrated on staple removal.

With him freshly Band-Aided together, she suggested, "How about I bring you dinner?"

"I am hungry," he muttered into the pillow.

In the kitchen, she loaded two pasta bowls and grabbed a couple of beers. He was sitting propped against pillows, awaiting the food. Not wanting to jostle him, she sat in the chair she repositioned bedside. They ate in silence for a few minutes until he turned on the television for news and weather. When she set her dinner on the tray only half-eaten, he finished it. He also drank the majority of her beer. She anticipated he would resume such a habit from before her accident. Feeling a chill, she left the room to feed the waning fire. She returned to the bedroom long enough to gather the dishes. Prior to coming inside to build the fire, Rusty had taken care of the horses, but not the dogs. She went outside to feed the three newcomers. The pups were put in the barn for the night. They were both still small enough to be easy prey for an owl. Back in the house, she cleaned the kitchen. Since it was much later, the fire needed refueling. Rusty's snores followed her around the master suite as she readied for bed. She removed the bag of tepid water from his crotch. This roused him in more ways than one, causing him to wince in pain.

"Love, do you mind sleeping on the sofa tonight?" he beseeched with regret.

Dropping a light kiss on his cheek, she tucked the covers around him. "Good night, Rusty."

Grasping her hand, he placed a lingering kiss on the palm. "G'd night, mate."

Chapter Forty-Five

Elsie stretched. Sunlight brightened the living room. Rusty hadn't woken her. He'd be looking for breakfast shortly. She whipped together a French toast and sausage casserole. It would bake for forty minutes. This gave her plenty of time to get through her morning routine. After she stepped from the shower, the phone rang. It was Sara. Did Elsie want to join her shopping? She'd pick her up in fifteen minutes. In ten minutes, Elsie ran into Rusty at the door.

"Your breakfast is in the oven," she said in a rush. "Sara called. We're going shopping."

"Oh … okay," he responded flatly. "I'll probably run to the barber before I pick up the meat at the butcher."

"That would be great. Please don't put it all in the freezer. Leave an assortment in the refrigerator," she requested.

"Yes, love. I'm looking forward to grilling steaks tonight," he offered.

"Yum!" Not hearing Sara's car yet, Elsie asked, "How are your bits and pieces?"

A tinge of red crept into his cheeks. "Tender—I won't be riding a horse today."

"And your leg?" she continued since they had time.

"Seems to be holding," he responded.

The van approached.

"I'll see you later." He leaned in to kiss her lightly on the lips.

As she stepped off the porch, he opened his mouth as if to say something else. But then didn't.

Midafternoon, the women finished shopping. After unlocking the door, Elsie placed the bags containing her purchase on the kitchen table. Then she went to find her husband to let him know she was home. The day had become blustery. On the walk to the barn, the wind tousled her curls about the edges of her face.

"Thar's ma tumbleweed!" he called with a Western twang as he strode toward the fence, with Opal and Jasper nipping at his boots.

Changing her direction, she smiled at the endearment. "Practicing for a Western?"

An odd expression covered his face. He didn't try to conceal it.

Instead, he explained it. "I won't be practicing for any part for a very long time. I'm persona non grata in the industry."

"Why?" she asked, leaning forward against the top rail.

Doing the same on his side, he expounded in a normal tone. "I'm assuming you read the paperwork Harris sent, since your name was on the envelope."

She nodded.

He continued. "I left a movie while under contract and never returned. Even though I paid a large sum of money to prevent a lawsuit, I've been blackballed."

"Why'd you leave the set?" Already suspecting the reason, she wanted to hear it from him.

He answered indirectly. "When I got a message from both Sara and Trish that you were going in for surgery, I had to."

"You really were at the hospital. I thought you were a figment of my imagination." She knocked dried manure off his boot where it rested on the bottom rung.

The red-ticked pup snatched the chunk to speed across the field, with the blue laying chase. It reminded her of Tycho and Sophie.

Her voice unintentionally laced with melancholy, she said, "You stayed till I woke up, but then you disappeared."

"It was like reliving the first accident. I couldn't go through that disappointment again," he stated, taking his cap off to run a hand through his crew cut. "Without you, the only place I could find solace was the ranch."

"And when Sara called to tell you I remembered everything?" She pursued the topic further.

His head shot up to stare into her face. "How did you know?"

"Come now. There's only one other person who wanted me to get all of my memories back as much as her—you." His answers, thus far, fed her confidence. "Well?"

The sound of his callous hand on his freshly trimmed beard rasped enticingly in her ears.

This pleasant distraction filled the extended moment till he found the words. "As elated as I was, there was still McEwan. Then when he, uh, his plane crashed, I didn't know if you'd still want me."

"So you did nothing." Her deduction fell hard between them.

Before he had a chance to defend his actions, or lack thereof, she turned heel to head toward the house. With a grunt of discomfort, he climbed over the rails to follow.

"Love, please stop! Let me explain!" His tone begged as he grabbed her arm firm enough to get her attention.

"Why didn't you just cash in the cattle and horses Red left you in his will?" she ranted, jerking her arm free to storm away.

"Because I was already here making a deal with Grimmel for the dairy cows when Red's lawyer contacted me," he hollered, trailing behind her.

Her steps slowed to a standstill as his response registered.

When he reached her side, he persisted. "I thought if I finished what I'd started when we got married, it would win you back. The cattle and horses from Red felt like a sign I was doing the right thing."

"When on earth did you start believing in signs?" Shock filled her face.

"The night I won the Oscar a certain tumbleweed had predicted," Rusty stated, gently placing his arms around her.

"Oh." Her mouth formed the word silently as she placed her hands on his abdomen.

Of which, he took full advantage. His mouth captured hers in a vigorous kiss. She clutched the sides of his shirt, wanting it to never end. His lips left hers but didn't plunder any other parts of her body.

"I still have quite a few things to do before tonight's storm." His tone sounded borderline distraught.

There was a hitch in his stride as he walked away. His impetuous action must have aggravated his injuries. She felt bad that he was in pain. However, everything else made her heart burst with joy. This encouraged her need to write. After setting the multi-disc CD player, she got comfortable in her chair in the sitting room. As the music filled the house, her fingers clicked away on her computer with rekindled creativity. The world around her disappeared.

Rusty appeared with grilled steak and vegetables. "I don't want to interrupt, but you need to eat."

"Huh?" She gave him a perplexed look. "I only got home a little while ago. Didn't you make yourself lunch?"

"Love, it's almost seven," he clarified.

"Oh, um, okay. Thank you," Elsie mumbled, still a bit befuddled.

He moved to the desk to eat his dinner. With one hand she typed. The other used a fork to stab absently at the cut steak and vegetables. After a while, the emptied plate disappeared and the glass of iced tea refilled.

Paragraph after paragraph filled the scrolling blank screen.

"Mate, the thunder is getting louder." He bent over, sticking his face in her line of vision. "Save. Set your timer and I'll unplug you."

She finished typing the current sentence then selected the necessary options. "Saved. Timer set for an hour. Unplug away."

The plug rested on the floor by the electrical outlet. He exited the room. New CDs were loaded to play at a low volume. The next time she registered his presence, he placed a blanket around her shoulders.

"Don't stay up too late," he said with a kiss on the corner of her mouth.

She turned her head to return the kiss, only to meet air. He'd evidently plugged her in earlier, or the computer would've shut off long before now. This quickly passed from her thoughts as she resumed typing. The story in her mind finally ceased churning. After backing up to a thumb drive, she climbed into bed.

Rusty stirred when she snuggled against him for warmth. "Mm, you're cold. What time is it, mate?"

"A little after three," she replied with a shiver.

"So much for not staying up too late," he mumbled before they both drifted off.

CHAPTER FORTY-SIX

IT WAS 11 o'clock till she roused. A glass of juice with partially melted ice sit on her nightstand. A note was propped against it. She read it while drinking the still cool liquid.

At Grimmels'.
Back by dinner.
XO

There was no rush to do anything. At least the dinner she planned for tonight would be a surprise. Padding out to the kitchen, she put the freshly butchered roast into the slow cooker. On her return to the bedroom, she paused to peer through the side window. Jasper could be seen in the small pasture. A cow nearing the fence caught his attention. He trotted toward the heifer. A limp in his gait concerned Elsie. Rushing into the laundry room, she slipped her feet into worn canvas shoes. Rusty's clean work clothes were folded on the dryer. She pulled one of the crewneck sweatshirts over her camisole. Last night's rain substantially soaked the ground. The mud splashing on her silky pajama pants didn't matter if they had an injured animal. In her hurry, she slid, almost falling. Rusty had mentioned wanting to lay a stone walkway. Now she knew why. As she neared the fence, so did Jasper. Intermittently, he shook his back foot in an attempt to dislodge something. Once inside the pasture, she picked the red dog up to examine him. The mud made this somewhat difficult. However, it felt like there was something hard wedged behind his toes into the front of the center pad. She wasn't going to just yank it out without seeing it clearly. Plus, with all that dirt, it needed to be cleaned to prevent infection.

Depending on what she found, it might require bandaging. Everything in the barn was sized for horses and cattle. It made sense to carry the pup into the house for further tending.

Jasper was too small to climb out of the raised dog tub in the laundry room. Elsie removed her muddy shoes and sweatshirt prior to washing the dog. With the little red dog washed and towel dried, she could examine him much better. A nail or tack was impaled in the pad. After dousing his foot in iodine, she removed the foreign object—a carpet tack. A cotton ball sopping with iodine was stuffed between the pad and toes. She checked his other feet and mouth to ensure there were no more stuck anywhere else. A small wad of gauze with antibiotic ointment replaced the cotton ball. A few rounds with purple veterinarian wrap protected the wound. Jasper remained cooperative throughout the entire the process. If anything, he seemed to enjoy the special attention. In need of a shower, she placed the pup in the crate Rusty originally put in this room for the malamutes. A small bucket of water and an extra large milk bone would keep the puppy temporarily occupied. The waning fire was fueled to fend the dampness from last night's rain.

As soon as she had showered and dressed, she released him from the crate. They walked around the backyard for the puppy to mark a few fence posts. It took a few tries till he got used to the bandage on his foot. They only covered a small portion of the enclosed acre before returning inside. After throwing the wet and muddy items into the washer, she made lunch. The pup followed her with the food into the sitting room. After sharing a couple of nibbles with the young dog, she focused on working. Soon enough, the morning activities tuckered the puppy. He fell asleep on her feet like a pile of puppies.

There was no need to set the timer to remind her of dinner. Two hours later, the pup woke. He hurried his business in the yard to come back inside. She unpacked toys for him to play with in the kitchen while she made a cheesecake. After adding potatoes and carrots to the cooking roast, they moved to the expansive living room. A game of fetch ensued. When the little guy finally wore his batteries down again, they napped on the sofa.

A pungent odor and Jasper's yips disturbed her pleasant dreams. Opening her eyes revealed Rusty clad in only boxers leaning over the back of the sofa.

"Why is he inside?" His tone sounded gruff as he asked. "And his foot bandaged?"

Sitting up, she responded, "He had a carpet tack in his foot. I couldn't leave him outside in the mud with a hole in his foot."

"Which naturally included furniture privileges," Rusty grumbled as the pup in question licked his face submissively.

"I had to give him a bath just to see the tack," she explained

His grousing persisted. "And with that froufrou doggie shampoo you use, you couldn't resist snuggling with him."

"It's just diluted Tide, not froufrou shampoo," she argued with an exaggerated wrinkle of her pert nose. "You might want to consider using some, and maybe I'll snuggle with you instead."

With a grunt, he straightened then strode into the master suite. She grabbed Jasper before he jumped off the sofa to follow. She whispered in the pup's ear on the way to the laundry room. "Do you have a death wish?"

After sending him into the backyard, she made sure dinner was ready to serve. She grabbed a beer on her way to discuss the situation further with her husband. When Rusty emerged from the steamy bathroom with towel knotted at his waist, she offered the small token. He accepted it for a long draft.

Moving toward her, he started to talk. "About Jasper—"

She interrupted to plead her case. "I know I wasn't supposed to bring him into the house. But the supplies in the barn are for livestock, not a dog, especially a puppy. It made sense to work on him where I could easily find everything. And he needs to be in the house to prevent infection. Plus, if not watched, he might eat the bandage, causing a bigger problem."

He placed his hands on her shoulders to say in a normal tone. "I just wanted to say thank you for taking care of him. I agree he's going to have to stay inside overnight."

"So you're not going to give me a hard time?" she asked with uncertainty.

With a cocky grin on his face, Rusty pulled her into an embrace to press against her. "Actually, I've thought about you all day. And giving you a hard time is exactly what I had in mind."

"What about your, um, injuries?" she questioned with concern.

In a voice thick with wanting, he stated, "The pleasure will be worth the pain."

To relay his intentions clearly, he planted a full-open mouth kiss on her lips, which she parted with full reciprocity. Her body molded to his. They both fumbled with her clothing. Eventually, it landed on the floor with his towel. In a few steps, they reached the bed.

"Rusty, please," she panted.

With nothing interrupting them this time, he entered her inviting femininity. The erotically intoxicating building sensations had her arching against him. His strong hands urged her movements since his were limited.

"Oh, Elsie," he groaned as her ardor ensconced him.

They experienced climax with echoing moans of fulfillment.

With his arms squeezing her tightly, he said with satisfaction, "I've missed this."

Still immersed in enjoyment-induced endorphins, she didn't allow his phrasing to burst her happy bubble. They didn't remain in this position long. When his stomach growled for food, it reverberated through her whole body.

Patting his bare butt, she suggested, "Dinner is ready and waiting."

"So there was something fabulous cooking in the kitchen," he remarked, rolling off her and the bed.

As he pulled on pajama bottoms, he remarked, "Come on, love! I'm starving!"

Slipping on panties and one of his flannel shirts, Elsie hurried to catch him. She dished beef stew into the bowls. He opened and poured the wine that had been chilling in the refrigerator.

"Stew and cheesecake. What's the special occasion?" he asked.

Studying his unrevealing expression, she questioned, "Are you acting or being obtuse?"

A wide grin formed on his face as he tugged her onto his lap. "Mate, I am most acutely aware of what today is. And quite glad you remember."

Squirming from his legs to her chair, she chastised, "It's not right to desert your wife all day on your anniversary."

"I couldn't exactly tell Keith no when he called this morning. Last night's storm made quite a mess of his fencing. Elmo was exhausted from locating the cows that had scattered beyond their property," he explained during the meal. "The new pups kept the cows contained once he gathered them together. This allowed us to repair the fence properly."

"They were all accounted for?" she asked.

"Yep. Keith was impressed with the dog's determination." Rusty grinned with pride.

After eating in silence for several mouthfuls, she changed her line of questioning. "Any ideas on where the carpet tack came from?"

"I've been wondering since you said what it was." He chewed thoughtfully for a few moments. "That area didn't get fenced in until I moved in. It was where the construction vehicles would park. There was carpeting pulled from the upstairs bedrooms during renovations. If any fell off the tack strip, they could've easily been buried in the dirt. The heavy rain may have exposed them."

On cue, Jasper yipped at the back door. Elsie realized they'd forgotten about him with their earlier distracting frenzy. Letting him inside, he raced into the kitchen to Rusty. Rusty leaned over to lift the puppy.

"Not at the table!" she yelled.

"Yes, love." He stood to move to the counter. "His bandage is wet."

"Like that's any better. The crate top in the laundry room, please." Her exasperation with him was evident. "There are house rules for dogs."

Her husband obeyed with a sarcastic, "You ignored my rule."

"We went over this a half hour ago," she snapped.

"You're right. Calm down or you'll freak him," he agreed in a relaxed tone.

After taking a deep breath, she stated calmly, "This will be easier since I can use both hands this time."

And it was. In short order, Jasper ran from the room in search of toys.

Rusty remarked receptively, "You really miss having a dog in the house."

"Yes, but I won't have field dogs and a housedog that don't get along. If this is how it has to be, I will get used to it." She didn't want him feeling guilty. "For tonight, I'm going to take advantage of it."

"I suppose one day won't hurt any. Consider it part of your anniversary present." He kissed her cheek while they cleared the table together.

"Part?" she queried.

Before he could answer, Jasper trotted into the kitchen carrying the stuffed pig. He dropped it at Rusty's feet then sat. His tail wagged expectantly.

"He wants you to throw it for him," Elsie explained at noticing his confused look. "I got this. Go play with him in the living room."

Picking up the toy, he led the puppy from the kitchen. Much later, as she closed the dishwasher, the pup passed by her. His tongue hung from the side of his mouth. In the laundry room, he lapped water from the bucket in the open crate. Soon the bucket banged noisily. She filled a cup with water to pour into the bucket.

Rusty stepped into the room too. Then he stepped into his boots and donned his hooded sweatshirt.

Zipping the sweatshirt, he stated, "I have to get kibble from the barn for him. It won't take long. I took care of everything else when I got home."

While she waited for the dog food, she donned her pajama pants that were in the dryer. She looked quite the mismatched waif at Rusty's return. He didn't appear to notice. The portion of food for the puppy in a metal dish used by the malamutes barely covered the bottom. It didn't phase the little dog. He merely stepped into the dish to reach every morsel. Elsie went outside with Jasper for a meandering stroll around the perimeter. Midway she paused to watch the sunset with flares of bright orange from a garnet horizon. Strong arms wrapped around her upper chest to hold her affectionately. Without words, Rusty slid a silver band with a diamond and sapphires onto the ring finger of her left hand. Its mate flashed from the same finger on his left hand. They relished nature's colorful display until the evening lights sparkled above. The little dog chose to herd them back into the house. As they approached the slate patio, the motion-activated light turned on. It was a soft wattage rather than a bright flood light. The top of the fence also lit with low-wattage Christmas string lights to illuminate the entire yard in an ethereal glow. The simple beauty of its functionality made her gasp. A shy smile of pride formed as Rusty watched her. The insistent pup's bark broke the romance. Once they'd gone inside, he quieted.

Chapter Forty-Seven

It was wonderful to fall asleep and wake up in her husband's arms. The alarm wouldn't ring for another fifty minutes. Elsie carefully slipped from bed so as to not wake him. Ideas and dialogues for her current novel darted about in her mind. No point in trying to type them until they fully formulated. She needed to concentrate on something else to allow them to settle into place. After feeding and putting Jasper outside, she made a hardy breakfast for her man.

A plate of sausage and pancakes, cup of coffee, and heated syrup—all loaded the tray she carried into the bedroom. When she turned on the overhead light, Rusty groaned in protest. He rolled over to look at her with only one eye open.

"Come on. You need your strength," she stated sternly.

"It's stamina I need with you, mate," he grumbled, shifting into a sitting position to accept the food.

"Well, if you would have taken care of that sooner and kept up with it," she parried playfully.

"Careful, love, or it will be you across my lap, not this tray," he warned.

She couldn't tell if he was cranky or randy. The alarm announcing 5:00 a.m. interrupted her internal game of seesaw.

He asked gruffly, "Would you please get me two painkillers?"

Aha! Perhaps he'd overdone it yesterday in more ways than one. Keeping these thoughts to herself, she fetched the requested pills from the medicine cabinet.

Half the plate had been emptied in that short span. The television had also been clicked on for the weather.

Clearing the plate and downing the contents of the cup, he stated, "Looks like it's going to rain all afternoon. I better get moving."

She took the tray from him. Barely five minutes later, she snapped the lid onto the travel cup as he entered the kitchen.

Taking it from her, he leaned in for a kiss and a "Thanks, mate" on his way to the barn.

"Hey! Aren't you taking Jasper with you?" she called after him.

"Not until my wife gives him a clean bill of health," he hollered in response.

She rolled her eyes heavenward. "I guess I deserved that."

Closing that door, she opened the one leading to the backyard to let the aforementioned furry creature into the house. The purple bandage hung raggedly from his foot. He'd been chewing on it. When she removed it, it didn't appear as though he'd swallowed any. The pad showed barely a dimple where the tack had been previously impaled. The pup gave no sign of pain or infection when she pressed the area with substantial force. Nonetheless, slopping in mud wouldn't be wise. Another night in the house wouldn't be either. For now, he could stay inside; but this afternoon he would be returned to the barn. In the shower, the next few chapters of her latest book solidified. Impatient to type it into the computer, she dressed in a hurry. Jasper played contentedly with his toys.

Hours later, she didn't register Rusty's entrance. It wasn't till he said a rather loud, "Where's Jasper's bandage?"

"Oh, he doesn't need it," she answered, pulling her eyes from the computer screen to his face. "I wouldn't put him in the pasture today with the rains coming. But he should be okay in the barn."

Rusty picked the pup up to examine the foot himself. Then he checked the other foot.

His brow furrowed. "I know I saw it yesterday when you changed the dressing."

"Dog pads heal extremely quickly. Sort of like our tongues," she explained. "We just need to keep an eye on it should he start favoring it."

"So I can't take him into the field yet," he grumbled as he placed the dog back on the floor. "First, his ear. Now his foot. What's ne—"

"Don't say it!" she shrieked, interrupting his rant. "You know better than to temp fate."

He muttered to himself on his way into the bathroom. Shaking her head in vexation, she took a break. She and Jasper went outside. The heavy-laden clouds signified the rain could start anytime. The stillness in the air added to this sense. A shiver of foreboding chased her back into the house after only a few minutes. The little red dog stayed with her every step. A cup of hot tea dissipated the strange feeling. This allowed her to resume writing. Rusty practiced standard obedience commands with Jasper in the living room. When the pup got tired of this, he came to lie by Elsie. At which point, Rusty carried him to the barn. Upon his return, he brought her a bowl of beef stew. The pocket doors were pulled partially shut to block noise. He ate his lunch and watched international soccer in the living room.

Midafternoon, he knocked loudly on the wood. "We have a thunderstorm warning—unplug. I'm going to put the horses in the barn."

She replied with, "Thanks for letting me know." But he'd already disappeared.

After entering another full chapter, she realized he hadn't returned. Putting the laptop into sleep mode, she went to investigate. The thunder and lighting hadn't amounted to much. However, the rain came down in buckets. She called the barn. Six rings later, there was no answer. This worried her. She ran across the one hundred yards to the barn.

As she closed the big door, she hollered, "Rusty?"

Only Jasper responded with yips. The horses were in their stalls. On her way to the tack room, she heard barking and mooing. The Guernsey entered the barn through the center door. Rusty brought up the rear.

"That's my sheilas!" Rusty praised Bonnie Blue and Opal when they continued herding the cows into their individual enclosures.

Elsie watched him secure each gate. He yanked off his cap to shake the water away. Bonnie Blue and Opal ran over to greet the other person in the room. She knelt to reciprocate.

Finally, Rusty noticed his wife. "Hey, mate!"

"Hey yourself," she replied playfully. "Having fun?"

The big grin already filling his face somehow got wider at her quip.

He whistled. The dogs returned their attention to him.

"Watch the hills." He shooed them back outside to endure the deluge.

With the double doors latched, he said, "Open Jasper's stall. He can work the barn, so to speak."

Jasper swung his body around in a circle at seeing Elsie.

She barely had time to acknowledge the pup and Rusty barked. "Jasper!"

The red dog wavered between obeying his master and basking in his mistress's affection. Elsie reluctantly straightened to enforce Rusty's authority. Jasper rushed to him.

Her husband strode with purpose to the section with the cows. The pup eagerly followed.

Rusty commanded, "Watch."

However, when Elsie joined Rusty on the walk to the end door, Jasper trailed behind the couple.

With a look of annoyance at his wife, Rusty picked up the red dog to carry back to his post.

In a more forceful tone, he repeated, "Watch."

Again, Rusty moved toward the door where Elsie waited. The pup began trotting their direction, but he stopped at the juncture between the horses and the cows. From this spot, he could see them exit the building. Even though it was still raining, Rusty tugged Elsie to the nearby window. Peering into the barn, they spied on Jasper. After scouting the entire structure, he returned to settle in the center of the adjoining aisles to oversee all of his charges. She smiled with glee at the pup's accomplishment. Rusty grasped her hand to head for the house. They entered via the laundry room. Rusty stripped off his sopping clothes first. After hastily drying with a towel, he left her alone. A few minutes later, she followed him with a towel held around her torso. He stood naked in front of the fireplace. She joined him by the restoked and freshly stacked fire.

When she shivered, he placed his arm across her shoulders. "It will take a little while for the room to warm."

Dropping the towel to the floor, she snuggled against his muscular frame. His body reacted immediately. He didn't try to conceal it, nor did he do anything to promote its use. To gauge his mood, she gazed up at his face.

To her surprise, he was looking down at her. "Do you want something, mate?"

Her eyelashes fluttered timidly as her hand stroked his manhood.

A groan of pleasure slipped from his lips prior to locking with hers. Their hands roamed over each other's cool skin. He reached for the quilt draped on the arm of the sofa. He spread the blanket over the floor prior to easing themselves onto it. As they rolled around, their bodies rubbed intimately. They were both ready for final coupling.

Lying on his back, he pulled her with him. "You need to be on top, or those last staples will rip out."

She hesitated. "I don't know if I can."

"No worries, mate. We have all afternoon," he spoke softly.

Her eyes met his, filled with earnestness. And dared she hope, his love for her radiating with verve. She shifted to ease his access. They both sighed with pleasure at the feel of their physical joining.

Caressing her bum, he coaxed her into moving. "Whatever feels good to you. Just being with you works for me."

His moans of enjoyment supported his words as she found her rhythm. This heightened the tantalizing sensations that began to cascade throughout her body. When he experienced final release, it flung her into the same freeing frenzy. After which, she relaxed across his torso.

With a low chuckle, he said, "This went far better than the last time I wanted to do this here."

"Who needs a bear skin rug when I have you?" she teased, running her fingers through his furry chest.

CHAPTER FORTY-EIGHT

THE NEXT MORNING, Bonnie Blue and Opal were whistled into the barn to show Jasper how to herd the cows into the lower pasture. He would spend the day with the Guernsey. Elsie watched from the front porch to not risk interfering with the red puppy's training. Then the blue sheilas trotted toward the steers ahead of Rusty on horseback. To contain Rowdy to a gallop, Rusty had to keep a tight hold on the reins. The sloppy ground would give the feisty stallion a sufficient workout. Elsie giggled thinking of the workout she'd given her stud yesterday afternoon.

An hour later, he completed morning chores. She was on the phone with Trish, planning their schedule.

"We'll play it day by day. There's no reason for you to truck out here every day," Elsie stated.

"If he's not going to be doing films anymore, what on earth will you two do?" Trish asked with sincerity.

Knowing he could hear her easily from the other room, Elsie remarked exuberantly, "Well, we found a perfect way to spend a rainy autumn afternoon."

To discreetly watch Rusty's response, she turned slightly. The brash grin forming on his face made her smile similarly.

Trish laughed heartily over the line. "Okay, but you can't do that all of the time."

"I'm making up for lost time," she replied impishly as Rusty strutted by her in the buff.

"You do sound happier than I've heard in a long time," Trish observed. "Go spend another day with your hunky husband. I'll see you tomorrow. Bye."

Elsie headed for the bedroom.

Rusty paused, stepping into the shower. "What do you say we go shopping for new living room furniture?"

As she stood there with her mouth agape, he spoke further from under the water spray. "It's not that I don't like your sofa. But it has seen better days. And there's nothing else to sit on in the living room."

If they were going into public, she needed to put on a bra—and maybe exchange the sweatshirt for a sweater. The pretty purple chenille sweater over a tank top would be appropriate and comfortable. While Rusty dressed in the bedroom, she used the bathroom mirror for other appearance enhancements. She spritzed her hair to fluff the curls to frame her face softly. A little lipstick highlighted her natural coloring. She caught up with him at the truck.

As he held the passenger door open for her, he remarked, "Don't you look pretty? I should've offered to take you shopping sooner."

Her face grew pink at the compliment. He placed a soft kiss on her warm cheek. Five shops later and lunch at Paneira, their mission had been accomplished. They'd selected a soft leather sofa, two upholstered armchairs, an end table, a coffee table, and a decorative area rug. Some of the pieces would be delivered the end of the week; the other items, the following week.

As Rusty parked, she offered, "I'll take the receipts into the house then handle milking. You deal with the horses."

"Thanks, mate!" he accepted happily.

After she put the papers on the desk, she switched her pretty sweater and top for one of Rusty's T-shirt. In the barn, she prepared the equipment prior to bringing the cows into their stalls. Both Bonnie Blue and Jasper yipped in excitement when Elsie opened the barn door to the lower pasture. Her husband must've whistled in the grand dam to teach the youngster what came next.

"Bring them in!" Elsie hollered and motioned.

It didn't take long for Jasper to mimic Bonnie Blue's actions. Not that the cows needed coercion. They knew the routine too. With the cows properly housed, both herders wanted loving from their master's tenderhearted wife.

She relished the hugs and kisses as much as the dogs did. In doing this, she also checked Jasper's feet. Finally, she got to milking.

Soon enough, Rusty appeared on Hailey. "It's supposed to be a clear night. I'm going to leave them all in the main pasture. Including Jasper, if you're good with it."

"His foot looks healed, and I didn't see any other problems," she replied while hooking the machine to the last cow.

Rusty removed Hailey's saddle and bridle before sending her back outside. He made a clicking sound with his tongue, which was followed by a hand gesture. Bonnie Blue and Jasper took the milked cows to the fields.

He joined her to ask, "What's the holdup, mate?"

"The machine stopped sucking," she groused as she kicked the offending device.

Chuckling, he said, "Let's start at the beginning."

Still unable to squat, he leaned in close. They went through the steps—plugged in, hoses connected, pump primed, and nozzles on cow. This time the tube was filled with white liquid. However, after a few seconds, milk was sprayed everywhere. Rusty reached for the off switch, but not quick enough to prevent a major dousing. The milk dripping from his hair and down his neck and soaking his shirt caused her to laugh. Thinking how similar she looked only added to the humor of the situation.

"Milk baths are supposed to be good for the skin," she kidded while he wiped her grinning face.

His amused expression quickly changed. "Go in the house and get cleaned up. I'll take care of this."

In the shower, she grappled with why he suddenly became testy. After donning clothing, she went to the kitchen to make apple dumplings for tomorrow. Basically, kneading the dough would exorcise her frustration with his transformation in demeanor. She was still preparing these when he entered the laundry room.

He grunted, "That unit is shot. I'll have to order another one."

"Is that why you got mad at me in the barn?" she questioned as he stripped off his sour milk-smelling clothing.

"That's the first time I've heard you laugh unguardedly with me in almost two years. And . . ." He cut his reply short as he headed for a shower.

She quickly filled the last dumplings to place in the refrigerator then chased after him.

Stepping into the bathroom, she hollered over the water spray. "And what?"

Through the opaque shower door he stopped moving for a moment then took a few minutes to rinse.

When he turned the water off, he asked, "Towel, please?"

His sudden modesty only lit her ire. "And what!"

He couldn't look at her as he went by to sit on the bed. "And it made me wish you had wanted to move in here, not be forced to."

"Hells bells! Madame Marna was right. You've become me!" The realization hit her like a bolt of lightning. "Waiting for the other shoe to drop."

"They both dropped. First, the accident. Then McEwan swooping in." His head lowered in defeat.

"Sean did not . . . okay, you're right he swooped in." She conceded part of the point. "Never would I have considered our flirtation as anything. If I remember correctly, you rather liked the fact and even steered me his way at parties."

"I know!" he replied, giving her a sideways glance. "He had a knack for drawing the lighthearted side of you out to play when all you wanted was to hide. I loved seeing your face sparkle with vivacity. Like you did in the barn just now."

It was her turn to be contrite as she sank down next to him. "Don't I sparkle for you that way?"

He sighed. "You do. But it gave me a sick sense of pride that you would never want him the way you wanted me."

Suddenly, a harsh laugh emitted from him. "Guess the joke was on me."

"Rusty!" She grasped his muscular arms. "I love you so much more than I did him."

"But you did love him and are still grieving losing him." Rusty refused to make eye contact with her.

She tried to make him understand. "But not in the way you think. It's like the way I miss Sophie, Tycho, and Red. Not as if I lost you."

When he remained silent, Sean's death, cheating on Rusty, and throwing him aside all came out in a sobbing admission. "What I did was unfair to both of you and cost him his life."

Her guilt-supplied tears softened his harsh judgment of her and himself. His arms wrapped around her.

The way his warm chest rumbled as he spoke soothed her fraying emotions. "But it's all you could give anyone. You needed that time with him. And he needed you to need him. All I could do was wait, a bit impatiently at times. And being with anyone else would never be you. The few times I came close, something in regard to you always interrupted, reminding me not to let go of what was in my heart."

"And you got pushed to the side as if you didn't matter." She hiccupped with regret.

"He wouldn't begrudge you happiness with me any more than I did when you were with him. I know there were times it seemed the opposite." His voice sounded thick with deep emotion. "Krikey, mate, I'm only a man who will always be unashamedly and irrevocably in love with you."

"That's good since I will never love anyone as much as I do you." She snuggled into his chest. "There was always something missing. And I don't mean my memories. But he couldn't reach a part of me because you were already there—in my heart."

AFTERWORD

THE DAY THE Golden Globe nominations were announced, Rich Taylor called with news. *Sins of the Fathers* received several nominations: Picture, Director, Supporting Actress, Actor, and Supporting Actor. He'd already spoken to Eilish. She would be attending the ceremonies for her father's nomination rather than her own. This put Elsie in a difficult position. She'd written Eilish a few times since Sean's death. However, no response ever came. The only conclusion Elsie could come to was that Eilish blamed her.

"Rusty, I can't go. I won't make it uncomfortable for Eilish," she stated while they snuggled on the new sofa in front of the roaring fire.

"I understand, mate. We'll stay home." He shrugged.

Twisting to peer into his face, she urged, "But you have to go. If you don't, they'll think you're snubbing your nomination."

He agreed begrudgingly. "I'll fly out that morning then catch a red eye back."

"You should spend time with the Taylors. I can take care of things here," she argued.

He shifted her onto an unused cushion to stand.

After placing another log on the fire, he stated sternly, "I will go and be gone for no more than twenty-four hours. This is not negotiable, nor am I going to discuss it further."

"Did I miss something that you're getting testy?" she questioned.

He sat back down next to her. "Have you forgotten what happened last year?"

"Still stings?" Her voice was filled with compassion.

His feet fidgeted with emotional discomfort. "I don't want to be the villain."

"Then I guess you'll just need to be charmingly disarming," she teased lightly.

"That might get me into hot water with you," he remarked, pulling her into his arms for a kiss.

Early the morning of the Golden Globes, Elsie gave Rusty a small padded envelope for Eilish. It contained a note and the heart necklace Sean had bought in New York. As Rusty carried his garment and duffel bags to the truck, his expression displayed anguish at going alone.

He whistled for the dogs. The trio arrived while he placed his things into the truck.

After a moment of praise, he held onto Jasper's collar. "Sheilas, fields."

Bonnie Blue and Opal obeyed without hesitation. Jasper tugged to go too.

With the blue girls out of sight, Rusty pointed to Elsie to command the red dog. "Watch!"

"Really?" she asked with uncertain tinged joy.

Releasing the dog's collar to stand and embrace his wife, Rusty conceded. "Really."

"Is it okay if I give him a bath?" She wrinkled her nose with the question.

"Whatever keeps my wife happy and safe till I return home." He gave her another squeeze.

Their parting kiss lingered. When Trish arrived hours later with the daylight, she was greeted by a clean and protective dog. Elsie had already thrown herself into writing to avoid dwelling on the evening event. The dog's barking forced her to investigate.

"Jasper! It's Trish. Now, let her inside," Elsie chastised the red dog with affection.

As Trish entered, she remarked, "You better not let your husband find out you had one of the field hands inside."

"He's the one that brought him in," Elsie explained.

"Really? You must be wearing him down," Trish said with surprise.

Elsie tried to leave the kitchen, but Jasper wouldn't let her. He nipped at her heels to keep redirecting her path back to Trish.

"Jasper, what is your problem?" Elsie questioned with exasperation.

Trish began to laugh. "I've underestimated your husband yet again."

"Clue me in, please," Elsie demanded.

"You haven't eaten, have you?" Trish questioned with seriousness.

"Well, no. I've been writing. But what does that have to . . .?" Enlightenment caught up with Elsie as she answered. Oh."

"Yeah—oh." Trish rightfully harassed her friend. "It's a good thing I stopped for muffins on the way here."

Stretching house rules, Elsie shared a few bites of muffin with Jasper for taking his responsibility so seriously.

Late in the day as the red carpet shows began airing, Sara joined them. Trish made sure they had plenty of food for the festivity. And Jasper ensured no dropped morsels sullied the rug.

The Taylor clan—Rich, Janie, Harry, and Andie—arrived together. Safely cradled in their midst was Eilish. Rusty hovered inconspicuously in their perimeter. At the table, Eilish sat between Janie and Harry; Rusty, between Rich and Andie. Early in the awards, Rusty's demeanor remained subdued. However, after one of the breaks, his charm finally emerged notably by a big grin.

When Eilish stood at the podium for winning her category, she fingered the red ruby heart nervously.

Sara exclaimed, "That's your necklace!"

"But she wasn't wearing it on the red carpet." Trish pointed out it was a recent addition.

Elsie explained, "I sent it along with Rusty to give to her."

"Is that why he's been so down in the dumps?" Trish questioned.

Sara remarked, "I thought he just didn't like being there without you."

"You're both right," Elsie stated.

It was good thing Rusty had relaxed. One doesn't want to look disappointed at winning Best Supporting Actor. However, he did keep his acceptance speech extremely short.

Elsie wondered how many people noticed at the end of the people he thanked that "and my beautiful wife" lacked a name.

During Best Actor, Elsie held her breath for "And the Golden Globe goes to . . ."

It released in a rush of relief at hearing the name "Sean McEwan."

Tears ran down Eilish's face at her father's posthumous victory. So overcome, Harry assisted her to the stage.

Much to Elsie's surprise, Eilish made reference to "his personal attachment and inspiration for this role."

Sara put her arm across Elsie's shoulders. "It doesn't sound like she blames you for her father's death."

Elsie nodded while drying her wet cheeks.

The night rounded out with Rich winning Best Film. Trish cleared their feast prior to going upstairs to the spare bedroom. Elsie readied the sofa for Sara to sleep.

"Even though Rusty was happy at winning, he seemed lost not having you there." Sara shared an observation. "You really should seriously consider joining him for the Oscars."

Guilt filled Elsie as she entered the master suite. And even though she had sent a text to Rusty the moment he won, she called to talk to him. He didn't answer. He probably either didn't feel it vibrate or wouldn't be able to talk with the crowd.

She left a simple message. "Love you, mate."

Shortly before 5:00 a.m., Rusty called from Denver International Airport. "Sorry, mate. My transfer plane is still stuck in Chicago due to snow. They're trying to find us other flights. It may be another couple of hours till I take off."

"No worries," she replied without anxiety. "The girls and I are going gown-shopping. I only have six weeks to find one."

It took a few moments for him to reply.

When he did, his voice was full of emotion. "I'm glad to hear you say that. I asked Trish to call your favorite designers in New York when the Globe nominations were announced."

"Hedging your bets!" she declared.

"No, counting on my wife not wanting to miss such an important moment," he responded sweetly.

"You're right. My husband deserves to have me proudly by his side." Love laced her words.

"Thank you, mate. I love you." Equal adoration filled his voice.

As Elsie put on the final touch—her lipstick—for the Academy Awards, Rusty watched.

"You better keep that handy. I'm going to be kissing it off all night," he teased playfully. "Because you look absolutely beautiful."

Bright pink inflamed her cheeks. "Thank you."

"I see you're wearing the ring from McEwan," he said observantly.

"Please don't be upset," she pleaded with her eyes.

"No worries, mate. It's a special evening," he responded by kissing the palm of each hand. "I'm still represented prominently on your left hand."

"One more thing," he added, handing her a familiar long black velvet box. "Both Trish and Sara approved it to go with your dress."

For a moment, she hesitated opening it. She knew it contained the amethyst-and-sapphire choker he'd given her two years ago. When she did, it took her breath away just like the first time. Unable to speak, she stood on tiptoe to kiss him. With plum lipstick smeared on his lips, he placed the jewels around her neck.

On the red carpet, the Ravine sisters ensnared the couple.

Lana started with, "So this is the 'beautiful wife' you referred to at the Golden Globes."

"Why, I do believe it is author Ms. Elsie Endy who Rusty escorted the last time he won an Oscar. Oh, I'm sorry. I should be saying Mrs. Elsie Garnet," Laura said with saccharine sweetness. "The same lady you and Sean McEwan were fighting over last award season. I guess we see who won. But then again, with the other actor permanently out of the picture—"

"Laura!" While Lana censured her sister for the distasteful commentary, the couple escaped.

"And I'm still the villain," Rusty remarked wryly.

"And I'm a temptress," she replied alike.

"A tempestuous one at that." He dropped a kiss on the side of head.

They gripped each other's hand in consolation as they completed the red carpet gauntlet. It was a pleasant surprise to see Rich's son Harry escorting Eilish. When Eilish spied Elsie, she tugged Harry along behind her.

The young woman embraced Elsie. "I am so sorry for not writing you. I didn't know what to say."

"I thought you blamed me for his death," Elsie admitted with a quiver in her voice.

"Elsie! My father loved you so much. His face would fill with joy anytime he talked to or about you," Eilish stated expressively. "I can't thank you enough for the necklace. I feel he's near when I wear it."

Elsie squeezed the girl's hand with hers, displaying the pendant's coordinating ring. Harry provided the handkerchief Eilish required to dab away the tears.

They all continued into the theater. Again, *Sins of the Fathers* swept the evening.

The clip shown for Rusty's portrayal was the first scene he and Sean worked together. That alone earned him Best Supporting Actor.

His acceptance speech included, "Playing opposite such a skilled actor as Sean McEwan forced me to up my game."

Shortly thereafter, Harry won Adapted Screenplay from Elsie's novel.

Rusty and Harry both returned to their seats in time for the memorandum honoring those who'd passed away. Seeing photographs of Red and Sean appear on the screen in succession was Elsie's undoing. Rusty held her as she cried. Harry comforted Eilish. None of them cared that the camera caught their emotional displays.

For Sean's performance for Best Actor, the academy chose the last scene of the movie. Elsie clutched Rusty's hand for strength.

"And the Oscar goes to . . ." Last year's winning actress paused dramatically. "Sean McEwan for . . ."

Eilish accepted her father's posthumous Oscar for his role as the patriarch in *Sins of the Fathers*. Her speech mirrored similar sentiments as at the Golden Globes.

This time Elsie kept her tears at bay.

Leaning close to her husband, Elsie stated, "I hope I'm around to see Eilish win Best Actress and Andie Best Director and Best Film."

"And I'll be right beside my mate, holding her hand as long as she'll have me." A smile of genuine esteem enhanced the wrinkles at the corners of his eyes.

THE END